Love
IN A TIME OF
Hate

Love in a Time of Hate

MATTHEW LANGDON COST

Encircle Publications
Farmington, Maine, U.S.A.

Paperback ISBN 13: 978-1-64599-234-9
Hardcover ISBN 13: 978-1-64599-235-6
E-book ISBN 13: 978-1-64599-236-3
Kindle ISBN 13: 978-1-64599-237-0

Encircle editor: Cynthia Brackett-Vincent
Cover design by Deirdre Wait
Cover images © Getty Images

Published by:

Encircle Publications
PO Box 187
Farmington, ME 04938

info@encirclepub.com
http://encirclepub.com

Printed in U.S.A.

ACKNOWLEDGMENTS

If you are reading this, I thank you, for without readers, writers would be obsolete.

I am grateful to my mother, Penelope McAlevey, and father, Charles Cost, who have always been my first readers and critics.

Much appreciation to the various friends and relatives who have also read my work and given helpful advice.

I'd like to offer a big hand to my wife, Deborah Harper Cost, and children, Brittany, Pearson, Miranda, and Ryan, who have always had my back.

I'd like to tip my hat to my editor, Michael Sanders, who has worked with me on several novels now, and always makes my writing the best that it can be.

Thank you to Encircle Publishing, and the amazing duo of Cynthia Bracket-Vincent and Eddie Vincent for giving me this opportunity to be published. Also, kudos to Deirdre Wait for the fantastic cover art.

To the Black Lives Matter movement that is fighting to bring about social change, justice, and equality.

ABOUT NEW ORLEANS

New Orleans has been a true melting pot of culture since the explorer Robert Cavelier de La Salle claimed it for the French Crown in 1682. The city itself was founded in 1718 by Jean Baptiste Le Moyne de Bienville in a crescent of land on the Mississippi River, today known as the Vieux Carré, or Old Square, which is now the center of the French Quarter. New Orleans immediately became a hub of commerce for France in the American Colonies, but wars around the world led them to cede the land to Spain in the Treaty of Paris in 1763.

In the midst of Spain's thirty-seven-year rule of New Orleans occurred the Great Fires, which is why so much of the architecture is of Spanish influence. In 1800, Spain was forced to return the land to France, only to have Napoleon sell it to the United States in 1803. Though officially a part of the United States, the citizens of New Orleans refused to relinquish their culture, clinging with tenacity to their mostly French roots, creating a new society of Creoles, American-born offspring of French parents often of mixed racial parentage.

At the beginning of the 19th century, geographically, religiously, and in some sense culturally, New Orleans was an island where African, French, Spanish, Caribbean, Native American, and New American influences collided. Like its famous gumbo, New Orleans was a mix of many ingredients, with, of prime importance, the language, customs, culture, cuisine, and complex social arrangements of France.

A significant example is in the system of *plaçage* recognized right up to the Civil War. These 'left-handed' marriages institutionalized ethnic French men entering into civil unions with women of African, Native American, and mixed-race descent. *Plaçage* utilized contracts and negotiations that settled property on the women and her children, and often gave freedom to them as well. Quadroon Balls allowed these white men to meet women of mixed race, and then a contract was negotiated, and the affair became legal. This developed an entire new caste of people in New Orleans known as the Creoles, often with French culture and black skin, of educated free people of color.

The influx of Caribbean culture with African culture and Catholicism led to the creation of Voodoo. Voodoo is a religion that was begun by slaves in an attempt to understand Catholicism through spirits, or *lwa*, which were more easily understood by the culture and reality they had come from. Voodoo Queens became important power brokers in New Orleans among the Black population, whether freed or enslaved, though many whites visited them for luck, love, or just understanding of life. The most famous of these Voodoo Queens was Marie Laveau, whose legacy is still a part of everyday life in contemporary New Orleans.

The Battle of New Orleans, during the War of 1812, gave African Americans in New Orleans another opportunity to earn their liberty or enhance their already free status. Andrew Jackson, greatly outnumbered, put out a call for Black soldiers to battle the British in 1814. Over six-hundred men answered the call and fought in this rare victory for the newly created United States of America, even if it did occur weeks after the official end of the war.

The years leading up to the Civil War was a time of prosperity for the United States, and nowhere was this more evident than in Louisiana. In the mid-1800s, the highest concentration of wealth lay in the sugar plantations between New Orleans and Baton Rouge. These wealthy plantation owners spent the bulk of their time in their in-town mansions enjoying the food, music, and cultural refinement of the city during this golden age. The *nouveau riche* Americans were rejected by the French and Creoles of New Orleans socially, so they simply settled in their own neighborhoods, creating the dividing line of Canal Street to separate English from French.

As the nation began its path towards war, Louisiana was a

complicated cauldron of enslaved and freed, rich and poor, white, Black, and every shade in between. Half the population was Black, mostly slaves, even though New Orleans itself boasted the largest free-Black population of any state in the South. Civil unions between white men and black women were common under the system of plaçage. Catholicism was mixed with Voodoo. Immense wealth lived side-by-side with great poverty. French culture vied with New American influences, as well as mixing with African, Spanish, and Caribbean elements. The 'normal' rules did not apply to New Orleans, as aristocrats mingled with self-made men, freed men of color, working men, and those *nouveau riche*. In the French Quarter, it was not uncommon for white men to attend church with their black mistresses and mixed-race children.

Louisiana was the sixth state to secede from the Union in January of 1861. The city of New Orleans was in chaos, with the white population rushing to join militia units, and a rumble from the slave population. Mysterious fires ignited around the city every night, supposedly set by the slaves. When shots were fired at Fort Sumter, white volunteers streamed to join the Confederate ranks while the large slave population grew even more unruly, some wanting to join the Union ranks. When Captain Farragut's naval squadron overran the city in April of 1862, they had their chance. Slavery was not officially abolished until the passage of the new state constitution of 1864, but the conquering army welcomed escapees into their encampments, and in many cases, began arming and drilling them for combat. Those that stayed in captivity on the plantations and in the mansions exercised their growing power by refusing to be disciplined, or in many cases, to work. With most of the men off at war, the women, elderly, and children were unable to control this growing unrest.

General Benjamin Butler was given the task of occupying New Orleans, and to this day is a hated figure there for his enforcement of pro-union provisions, as well as his corrupt ways. He had a man hung for taking down a United States flag, had people imprisoned for minor offenses against the Union. Most infamously, his Order Number 28 of May 15, 1862, issued after many provocations and displays of contempt by women in New Orleans, stated that any woman who insulted or showed contempt for any soldier of the United States would be regarded as a 'woman of the town plying her avocation', and treated accordingly. This garnered him the nickname 'Beast Butler' and fed the simmering hatred between the southern white plantation society and the interlopers from the North.

Three regiments of Black troops were formed first as part of the Louisiana Native Guard, and then later as the 1st, 2nd, and 3rd Corps d'Afrique. These regiments were unique in that their line officers were men of color, such as Pinckney Pinchback, who I've borrowed as a character (as well as Henry Warmoth). Pinchback is known as the first Black governor in the United States of America, elected in 1872–1873. This formal recognition of freed slaves as armed and trained U.S. soldiers further fueled the unrest between the white plantation society and their former slaves, but it also created discord between the freed men of color who had earned their freedom before the war and who saw their favored status being diminished by the end of slavery.

When the war ended in April of 1865, Southern white men returned to their homes to find their lives forever changed. In many cases, their plantations had been stripped from them due to their involvement in treasonous actions against the Union. Their former slaves were now free, and with that, insolent. Black former soldiers walked the streets with a swagger, having participated in the epic battles that enshrined the freedom Lincoln had merely declared. The former political leaders were denied office due to their involvement in the fight to secede, and there was a movement towards Black suffrage. This huge shift in the electoral population led to men of color being elected to make the laws, as well as northerners—called carpetbaggers—who had sensed the great opportunity presented by this chaotic place and time.

The halcyon days of antebellum New Orleans were gone forever. The new normal became poverty, racial tension, and chaotic government characterized by frequent power grabs, backroom iniquities and conspiracies, and even armed clashes between parties. The federal army remained in place to keep the peace, while the former plantation society seethed in private, eventually giving birth to secret societies such as the Ku Klux Klan and the Knights of the White Camellia. The ultra-partisan newspapers of the era took sides and promoted either Black hatred or Black rights. Armed gangs roamed the streets, both Black and white. The situation was rife for the acquisition of power. The carpetbaggers streamed in from the North to lay their claim, but so did former freed men of color, as well as the returning plantation elites. This is the New Orleans that my historical takes place in, beginning in the summer of 1866, as Black suffrage is being considered…

PART I: VOODOO

July 30, 1866–August 10, 1866

CHAPTER 1

July 30, 1866

Emmett Collins watched in helpless trepidation as the mobs below threatened to erupt into violence over the precise actions he was participating in at this very moment. It reminded him of that hushed lull seconds before the rebel yell had echoed across the way and Confederate soldiers had come spilling out in a frantic charge. Perhaps New Orleans was not yet ready for Black suffrage, he thought with mounting apprehension. What would General Chamberlain do in this situation? He'd probably stride out into the melee and sternly talk sense into the horde, but that wasn't in the bailiwick of an eighteen-year-old from rural Maine washed up on the shores of New Orleans after four years of war. He'd been in the South for almost a year now, but still didn't understand the politics or the culture of the people. He felt like he'd gone to a foreign country without knowing the language.

The Special Convention at the Mechanic's Institute on Black suffrage had immediately experienced complications when its members fell short of a quorum due to threats of violence and intimidation from Conservative Democrats. The sergeant-at-arms had fought his way out to the street through the mass of white protestors in front of the building to go in search of the necessary representatives. It was then that a rising crescendo surging down Burgundy Street signaled the arrival of the Black former Union soldiers come to support the convention. The thirty-eight appointees in attendance, predominantly white, almost entirely from the north of Louisiana, crowded to the windows overlooking Dryades Street, while the gallery of over a hundred, mostly Black, audience members remained seated.

As the cavalcade of approximately 200 Blacks reached the end of Burgundy, there was the slightest pause as they regarded the waiting crowd across the wide Canal Street. This thoroughfare had originally been designed with a waterway running down the center, a notion still unrealized, and had instead become the unofficial dividing line between two territories, one home to white supremacy, the other to Black equality. With an intake of breath, the marchers squared their shoulders and began to traverse this no-man's-land, many wearing the blue uniforms they'd earned fighting for freedom and unity. Shoulder to shoulder, these former slaves and soldiers marched across the street to show their resolve in gaining the liberty and equality they perceived to be their due. *Why couldn't they have just stayed home?*, Emmett wondered, asking under his breath. What good would they accomplish arriving en masse and in uniform at the most delicate moment of this convention, the seating of those whose purpose was gaining the right to vote for Black men?

The milling crowd parted way in front of them, yelling curses, "Ya fuckin' darkies, git off our street, and take them northern lickfingers with ya!" Grizzled white men sporting the threadbare uniform of the Confederate soldier grasped recently emptied liquor bottles by the neck and waved those ugly weapons as if sabers. The occasional man waved a pistol or gestured with a rifle, but for the most part they were unarmed, which was a good sign, for the Federal troops were stationed three miles away in the Jackson Barracks. Life in the army had been so much easier, Emmett mused, his nose a scant inch from the glass window. You followed orders. That was it. How was he supposed to diffuse the situation below? There was nobody to go to and ask, not his father, long passed, not the man who had become his mentor, General Chamberlain, now more than a thousand miles away in Maine recovering from terrible war wounds. Since arriving in New Orleans, Emmett had made few if any friends.

As the Black former soldiers crossed the street, taunts, curses, and spitting became shoving, punching, and kicking. A bottle flew through the air, catching one man in the temple, his knees buckling, but a steadying hand on either side kept him on his feet. A group of white-sleeved men hurled a volley of bricks, the projectiles sweeping marchers off their feet like bowling pins. Those left upright in the vicinity picked up the bricks and threw them back, and then it was a whirling mayhem as men struck each other with sticks, rocks, canes, and fists.

As Emmett watched in horror, a white woman slashed a man in the face with a razor, the blood arcing through the air as if in slow motion, while a crowd of four men kicked an inert figure lying on the ground. Several Black soldiers pinned a man in a worn suit against a forlorn carriage, normally pulled by a mule as public transportation, but deserted on this day of horror. As two of the soldiers held the man, a third picked up a brick from the ground and began to smash his face, his nose quickly flattening into a gooey pulp, until he slid to the ground as if his bones had turned to liquid.

A shot rang out—from where, it was impossible to tell—and then the fire department alarm began to sound, the gongs pealing through the vicious battle below. On cue, the police department descended into the donnybrook, and Emmett realized that the best-case scenario was for everybody to be arrested.

So it was with dismay that he watched the newly organized city police begin to shoot the Black former soldiers, slaughtering them like hogs in a pen. As the white crowd would beat a Black man to the ground, they'd call for the law enforcement officials to come finish the job. "We got one here, come kill this ungrateful Sambo, teach him a damn lesson."

Black men would occasionally fight their way clear of the massacre, stumbling back down Burgundy, across to Dauphine and Rampart Streets, small gangs of white men in pursuit. Men walked around kicking those who had fallen to appraise whether they were alive, any movement the excuse for a bullet at close range.

As the police captains began to reorganize into companies after the initial assault, Emmett realized that they were pointing at the Mechanics Institute where he, the delegates to the convention, and a group of Black onlookers now awaited their fate tensely. *Where were Major General Baird and the Federal troops?* Emmett wondered in frustration. "Barricade the doors!" he yelled over his shoulder, giving voice to what they all feared. Tables, desks, chairs, anything that could be moved was shoved in front of the doors, blocking access to the growing white mob outside, this canaille led by the police and fire departments, sanctioned by the mayor, all puppets of the opposition political party.

Voices could be heard now at the door, yelling for them to come out and surrender. The Reverend Horton, who not so long ago had given the invocation to bless their meeting on Black suffrage, went to the entrance with a piece of white cloth wrapped around a stick, cracking the door ajar and cautiously poking the peace offering through the opening. A salvo of bullets answered him, his body twitching with each impact, taking one, two, three steps back before falling to the floor.

A delegate rushed to the window, pulling the heavy frame open, climbing into the aperture on his knees, before rising to a crouch and thrusting himself out into space. It was a distance of twenty feet to the ground, and he came to his feet with a limp, no match for the crowd that descended upon him, pummeling him back to the earth. Other men followed in a desperate attempt at flight, some gunned down before even jumping, others set upon once they had, with an occasional escapee darting away with men, women, and even young boys in hot pursuit.

The front doors were breached, shoved wide, angry men clambering over the pile of furniture while others pushed it aside. Dr. Dostie, who'd lectured so eloquently in favor of Black suffrage, rose to his feet and ran for the windows before bullets mowed him to the ground, where he lay gasping in agony. A deputized policeman, recognizable by his white kerchief, ran him through with his sword, pinning him squirming and screaming to the ground, before withdrawing the blade and repeating the action.

Former Governor Michael Hahn was plucked from the floor, men punching and kicking him, screaming all the while, "Kill that darkie lover!"

Emmett wished that he'd brought his pistol with him, a cherished gift from General Chamberlain. With his own self-preservation in doubt, he moved to the rear door, behind the podium where there was an antechamber, with small windows nailed shut. He took a chair and smashed through one, climbing into the opening and jumping to the ground below.

He lessened the shock by softening his knees and rolling with the impact, coming quickly to his feet. A pack of boys who'd been hiding furtively around the corner from the excitement of the brawl came at him with sticks. So far, they were the only ones to spot Emmett's escape. He judged them to be the same age as he'd been when he joined the Union Army, fourteen, his first engagement being the carnage of Antietam, and thus he knew better than to underestimate these lads.

They circled him, wary to be the first to strike, hoping that some of the older men would appear around the corner, an eventuality that Emmett knew must be only seconds away. With no time to spare, he stepped towards the largest of them, blocking the stick with his forearm, and drove his fist into the boy's stomach. Emmett took the moment of frozen shock to run down the alley behind the Mechanics Institute, the remaining boys indecisive on whether to chase him or tend to their friend who lay doubled over snorting in a desperate attempt to get oxygen into his lungs.

"There's one over there. He just whacked Tommy." Emmett heard the high-pitched voice, presumably leading others in his direction, and then felt a jolt in the meaty section of his arm just below the shoulder, followed by the stinging retort of a gunshot. He stumbled, the impact dropping him to his knees. Risking a look over his shoulder, Emmett saw a man drawing a bead, carefully lining the pistol up like a duelist. Without a second thought, he dropped flat and rolled, the bullet kicking brick dust and particles into his face, but then he managed to crawl around a corner and out of sight.

He had to get back to the *Vieux Carré*, the old square of New Orleans where he had a room, or perhaps find sanctuary in Saint Louis Cathedral. He knew one thing for sure—that he wouldn't survive on the streets for long. He chose Carondelet Street to cross over the wide expanse of the neutral ground that was Canal Street, but in doing so, attracted the attention of another group of men who immediately gave chase. If he were more suave, he probably could've slowed to a walk and blended in with the crowd, but as it was, he was bleeding, out of breath, and practically hysterical.

He gained a few feet of space by darting down Bienville, but at the corner of Chartres two men stood blocking the way. Emmett plowed into them, righting himself quickly, but it was all the time needed for the others to catch up. A horde of men plowed into Emmett, hurling him to the ground under their weight. He thrust his thumb into an eye, bit the neck of another, and jerked his fist into the groin of a third, fighting for his life much like on the ridge of Little Round Top at Gettysburg during the Great War.

A man stuck a thin tapered blade into his thigh, but lost hold of it as Emmett twisted away. With a bellow of pain, he found the haft and pulled it free, slashing the chest of a heavy-set and foul-smelling man, and then, without pause, he sliced an unshaven face splattered with chewing tobacco. Emmett fought his way to his feet, his attackers backing away, wary of the dagger in his hand.

He saw the recognition in their eyes that he wasn't some overweight, middle-aged politician, but a seasoned fighter and adversary. When he turned to go, they didn't pursue him, but chose to lick their wounds and look for easier prey.

There was no time to tend to either wound, both of which were in need of binding, for he knew he must get off the street. A band of men blocked his way to the *Vieux Carré*, and he changed directions, heading north, thinking that perhaps he could find refuge in the swamps outside the confines of the city, but when he reached the top of St. Ann Street, he was stymied by roving bands of raucous men, many who appeared to be armed, patrolling Rampart Street looking for survivors endeavoring to return home to the Black neighborhood of Treme just across the way.

By this time, Emmett was feeling weak and lightheaded, and was afraid that he'd pass out on the street and be killed like a dog. It never crossed his mind to blend in, to clean himself up, or to do anything but run and hide. He yanked on a locked gate before pulling himself up and over the tall fence, falling to the other side in a heap. He was in a large yard fronting a raised porch attached to an elongated house. A pomegranate tree gave shade over the covered gallery, and along the side were fig and banana trees as high as the roof. There was a sweet smell, and Emmett saw bare honeysuckle vines climbing the house, past their bloom, yet their pungent aroma placidly perfumed the air. Through the haze of pain and flickering consciousness, he realized he was in a place of quiet beauty. What a paradise—and on such a bleak day, he mused, before darkness descended, and he slumped to the ground.

The young girl sat silently in her chair, staring at the wiry man on the bed. Earlier that day, one of Marie Laveau's many informants had come with news of the day's events at the Mechanic's Institute, and there had been the red-haired, battered and bloody man, lying as if dead. They had carried him into the house, and Marie Laveau bandaged his wounds and left the girl to watch over him. She'd been studying his face for the good part of an hour so far. His nose had a crook to it, like it'd been broken. His cheekbones were craggy, dropping to a firm jaw. There was just a hint of hair on his chin and upper lip. He wasn't much older than her fourteen years, yet there was a worn look to his rugged features that suggested he'd seen a great deal in his young life.

Of course, she had also seen quite a bit in her years on this earth. Her mother, Esther Lescaut, had named her only child Manon. Not Marie, as was the common French, but simply Manon for her favorite character, the famous Manon Lescaut of the 18th century romance about a love affair between a poor Black woman and a noble French man, a story she felt mimicked her own in that her father had been a wealthy French plantation owner, officially married to a proper lady but in love with her mother. They'd met at a Quadroon Ball, which was a fancy name for a dance where a wealthy white man might meet women of mixed race and, and if a match was made, negotiate a contract to make her his official mistress. Women trading sex for money—a transaction only the most deluded thought had anything to do with love in such circumstances—was a tale as old as time. He'd given them a house to live in, made sure his daughter was educated by tutors, provided them with the finest of clothes, and ensured they never felt the pangs of hunger. He had spent more days and nights with them than with his own wife on the plantation up the Mississippi. Manon's grandmother had entered into a similar arrangement in Haiti, fleeing with her own French plantation owner when the revolution had erupted there in the late 18th century. Thus, Manon grew up speaking French, with her English nearly as good.

Then the War of Northern Aggression had come, and her father had formed a militia group, was named its colonel, and off to war he'd gone. At first, things had gone along as before, minus the visits, but then word came that her father had been killed at a place called Manassas. His widow had evicted them, and with little choice, her mother had taken to selling her body to feed her daughter. Three years ago, she'd been found, her body naked, lifeless, and badly beaten, thrown like so much trash in a ditch on the outskirts of New Orleans. Marie Laveau had taken Manon into her home, as she had so many other suffering souls. There were no more private tutors, but Manon attended the local school, and was no longer hungry.

Emmett woke in a small room lying on a cotton-filled mattress in a simple walnut bed frame. There was a rocking chair in the corner and no windows in the room. Several candles flickered upon an armoire crafted from cypress wood, scattered on shelves among statues of saints, and mixed in with gold bells, gourd rattles, mirrors, and various other objects jumbled together.

Next to him on a small table there was a pitcher of water and a glass. Suddenly conscious of his tremendous thirst, he struggled to a sitting position. With shaky hands he slopped a bit of water into the glass and pressed it to his parched lips. He became aware of a throbbing in his bandaged right arm, inciting a host of memories, causing him to reach down and feel a similar dressing on his thigh. A simple cotton nightshirt that spread from his neck to toes covered his body. His fingers touched a small chamois bag attached to a string around his neck, but before he could investigate further, a shadow glided through the open doorway.

"You are awake." A young girl stood in the doorway wearing a blue dress with a full skirt and a patchwork madras cotton *tignon* wrapped around her head.

"Who are you?" Emmett croaked, somehow surprised at the appearance of another in his room. He was well aware of the rich blackness of her skin.

The girl flashed a smile and sashayed over to his side. "I am Manny." A boy at school had given her this nickname, and it had stuck. She laid the back of her hand across his forehead and held it there for a moment. "Very good. Your *fièvre* is gone."

"Where am I?"

"You are in the home of Madame Marie Laveau."

"The Voodoo Queen?" Emmett blurted out, his voice cracking. He'd been in New Orleans long enough to hear the tales of this woman who carried the power of life and death in her fingertips. She prayed to the Serpent King, danced with Satan, and cast spells upon her enemies and for monetary reward. He realized he was still touching the chamois bag around his neck and involuntarily clenched down upon it. He considered tearing it from his neck but was afraid to do so at the same time. "What curse have you placed upon me?" he demanded hotly.

The tenderness disappeared and Manny stepped back from the bedside with a trace of unease. "No curse, *monsieur*. It is *gris-gris*. Madame Laveau has mixed St. John's wort and other ingredients for your protection."

"My protection?"

"We found you in the front yard half-dead. It would seem that you have enemies."

"I'm sorry... what did you say your name was?"

"I am Manon Lescaut, but everybody calls me Manny." Her eyes were still narrowed and she remained out of arms' reach. "And who are you? You have been here three days and yet we know not your name." She carried a quiet confidence not often seen in a young girl.

"Emmett Collins." And then the words sunk in. Three days.

"And why do we find you, Emmett Collins, lying in our courtyard carrying on with Baron Samedi?" She stepped back to his side, her hazel eyes again friendly, and began to remove the bandage from his arm.

"Baron who?"

The corners of Manny's mouth turned up just slightly, but she patiently explained, "Baron Samedi. The *lwa*… spirit lord… of the dead. The two of you seemed *très amis*, almost as if you had known each other and been friends for quite some time."

Emmett shook his head in confusion, a movement that sent arrows of pain slicing through his brain. "I was at the Mechanic's Institute and a riot broke out." Emmett bit his lip in recollection. "I jumped from a window, was attacked, shot, chased, stabbed, and finally ended up climbing over a fence." He shrugged his shoulders, causing more pain, and a glance of disapproval from Manny as she unwrapped the last of the dressing from his arm. The bullet had gone in his triceps and out his bicep, missing the bone, but coupled with the knife wound, had caused a substantial loss of blood.

"You are lucky," Manny said. "Madame Laveau is a trained nurse. The hospitals all call her in when Bronze John pays a visit." Noticing his again perplexed countenance, she giggled, and Emmett realized that she was barely into her teens. "Bronze John is what we all call the yellow fever." She put some clean gauze on the tender and puffy puncture and began to rewrap his arm.

"Thank you for taking me in and healing me up." Emmett did not add, *and hiding me*, but he knew that was part of it. The mobs patrolling the street would've finished the job if they'd found him.

"The white men were certainly in a murderous rage. Madame Laveau has not let us out of the house since. What was it all about?"

Emmett wished he knew. After several minutes of speculation, he wobbled his head in frustration, and muttered, "I don't have any idea," before drifting off to sleep.

Manny stood for a moment staring at this Yankee, her bowed upper lip pressed down upon her plush lower lip as she contemplated this young man who'd seemingly dropped from the sky. She wished to see his stormy blue eyes and find out more about him, but she knew he needed sleep, healer of all ills, to recover. She finally sighed, and blew out most of the candles, pausing at the altar to send a thank you via Papa Legba for this gift of life, asking this intermediary *lwa* to share her gratitude with Baron Samedi.

When Emmett woke again, all but one candle had been put out. On the table next to him were his clothes, neatly folded, the holes sewn up and most of the bloodstains gone. He hoisted his legs over the edge of the bed and pushed himself to a sitting position, the blood whistling in his head like a steamboat on the river. He had a need to piss, but could spy a chamber pot nowhere in the room.

After a bit, he reached for his pants, pulling first one and then the other leg through, before standing and putting on the collared shirt. He saw his waistcoat and jacket hanging on the front of the armoire, but didn't bother with them or his shoes. He figured he'd just step outside and do his business, but finding the door in the dark was more onerous than he would have thought, a task complicated by his stiff joints, light head, and wounded leg.

After an agonizing time of fumbling about, in which he was certain he'd woken the entire household, he found the low handle to the door that spilled him out onto the covered porch. After carefully navigating the few steps down, he shielded himself behind a fig tree, and with a grunt of relief began to urinate.

It was only once his discomfort was alleviated, and the emergence of the moon in a crack of the celestial overlay, that Emmett became aware of a scurry of activity in the front yard. He crept closer, realized the rustling was that of seven or eight figures, and then heard the unmistakable cry of a baby. Another breach in the night clouds illuminated Indian women, gathering baskets, several with babies to their breasts, and then they slid away through the gate, leaving the lawn empty as if they'd never been there.

Emmett returned to his room and sat down in a rocking chair in the corner and reflected on the strange turn of events that had led him to this mysterious home. The girl was more cultured and refined than the Black people he'd been dealing with in the rural parishes in his current job working for the Freedmen Bureau. For the most part, he had a hard time understanding their thick dialect and seeing past their tattered clothes and dirty faces. Manny? She was different than these recently freed people of color, even down to the lighter shade of her skin.

The faintest lifting of the darkness announced the arrival of dawn, followed by a knock at his open doorway, and a woman sweeping into the room holding a candle. Her bearing was regal, her skin and features belonging to what Emmett had come to know as Creole, a mix of French, African, and Indian. The *tignon*, the cloth holding back her dark hair, was folded and tucked into itself, sitting upon her head in such a way that there were seven points to it.

She regarded him silently for a long minute, her eyes piercing the murkiness of the morning to look into his own blue eyes deeply, and to slide into his essence with a simplicity borne of understanding as if she were reading his soul. "Good morning, Emmett Collins," she finally said in punctuated English. "You look better."

"Thank you," he replied, struggling to his feet. A recognition that encompassed not only her comment, but also, all that she'd done for him. "You must be Madame Laveau."

She tilted her long neck in acknowledgment. "You are not from New Orleans, Emmett Collins."

"No," he conceded. "I spent my childhood in Maine."

"Sit," she commanded, gesturing him back down into the rocker, as she herself settled onto the side of the bed. "We have been through times where many have *grandi plus vite qu'il ne le fallait*. What hard times presents a man to me in the frame of a boy?"

Emmett wasn't insulted by the nod to his youth, but rather was inclined to share whatever she cared to hear.

"What do you want to know? My mother died of consumption, and then my father was killed in the war at Malvern Hill when I was fourteen. I joined the Union as an aide to then Lieutenant Colonel Joshua Chamberlain, in the late summer of '62. When the war ended, I went back to his home in Brunswick, Maine, to figure out my next step. He'd become my mentor, almost a father to me, and when Generals Ulysses S. Grant and O. O. Howard visited Chamberlain while attending the Bowdoin College commencement last summer, my path was chosen."

Emmett, his reticence evaporating, found himself pouring out his story to this woman, wanting to tell her everything. His mind flashed back to that beautiful day last August in Maine, and how General Chamberlain had introduced him to these two legends who had been given the task of reconstructing the South. "They appointed me as a special agent to the New Orleans branch of the Freedman Bureau, reporting directly to General Howard. I arrived almost a year ago aboard a steamer and have been here ever since."

"And what is it that you do as a 'special agent'?"

"My most important job is to create schools for recently freed slaves. I left school early to work in the brickyards, and if it hadn't been for General Chamberlain tutoring me..." He left unsaid what might have been before continuing, "So I understand the importance of learning to read and write, I guess."

Marie Laveau touched her fingers to the bare skin of her upper chest left exposed from the flowing dress of silk she wore, an ensemble of multi-shades of bluish-green. "Education is the key to everything," she said. "And how is your work going?"

Emmett shook his head in frustration. "Not well. Not well at all, unfortunately for them."

"What difficulties obstruct you?"

"Everything?" he suggested. Emmett took a drink from the glass on the table next to him. "The fact that almost all the Southern white people are intolerant of the recently freed slaves creates problems. Teachers and students are threatened. We've had Black schools burned down. But of course, the largest problem is money."

Madame Laveau nodded sagely. "Money is always a curse."

Emmett wasn't sure that he agreed that money was a curse, but he chose to not pursue that particular thought. "I have considered returning home to Maine."

"But you will not," she replied simply. "I understand that you have doubts, but that is a far different matter than hanging up one's fiddle."

"It's just that... I don't understand the hatred. Towards the end of the war, I began to wonder what it was all about. We'd line up opposite each other and try to kill any way we could. I murdered people I never even knew. Men who had children at home." Emmett thought of the blood-spattered letter he'd received from his own father, written right before his death, with a postscript on the bottom informing him that

that father had been slain, making Emmett an orphan. "What was the point?"

"I believe you know the answer to your own question," Marie Laveau replied.

"I thought so until just the other day." When he'd arrived in New Orleans and seen the recently freed Blacks walking the streets, he thought he had his answer. The war had been fought to emancipate these millions held in bondage like animals, and now it was up to him, Emmett Collins, to help them take their place in society. "I figured the war was over, but it's not. I've been in a lot of battles, Madame Laveau, but I've never seen the hatred like what happened at the Mechanic's Institute the other day."

"So, you would go away and pretend that it never came to pass?" she asked seriously. "You would go back to New England and sweep the memories of New Orleans from your mind like crumbs from your lap?"

"It's not like that," Emmett entreated in a hollow tone, a voice that rang falsely even in his own ears. "I just think I'm making things worse."

"You think fighting to get Black people an education is a bad thing?" Madame Laveau retorted in a steely voice that startled Emmett and made him raise his eyes. He was immediately trapped within her fierceness like the Africans during their many years of slavery, unable to escape, dissent, or even opine without fear of punishment.

When it became apparent that Emmett was supposed to reply, he cleared his throat and stammered through several unintelligible beginnings before finally muttering lamely, "It's just that everything I do ends up with someone getting hurt. Just last week they burned a school that I helped build, the following day a teacher was beaten by hooligans and intimidated into leaving the state, and now this bloodbath. The more I do, the more people die or are hurt. And always by people who look like me."

The savagery of Madame Laveau's face melted away into the gentle lines of compassion. "People always die, Emmett Collins. You cannot let that keep you from doing what is right."

"But what's it all for? It can't just keep on like this, this city, this place will explode!"

Madame Laveau stood up in one simple flowing motion. "I have some guests coming in a moment, so I must leave now. I will have Manny bring you some breakfast, and then show you the way out. If you still desire an answer to your question, come back here next Friday night."

A protest formed on Emmett's lips, but she was already gone, and in her place was the girl from the night before. "I have brought you *pain perdu*, or what you English call French toast," she said, proffering a plate of bread battered in beaten egg and milk with powdered sugar and jam on top. Emmett realized that he was ravenous, finally having cast the fever from his body. He greedily took the plate, and then caught himself. "Please join me?"

"There is a table and a chair that I will bring. Madame Laveau is having breakfast in the kitchen with guests. I will be right back."

Emmett placed the plate upon the bed and followed her. In the kitchen, Marie Laveau was seated at the table with several men. Emmett leaned to pick up the small table that Manny indicated, and as he stood, his eyes fell upon the face of Police Chief Thomas Adams. Emmett realized he was frozen in place gawking at the man, and hurried out of the room. "What's he doing here?" he hissed at the girl once they were back in the room he'd slept in, keeping his voice low, for there were no doors nor hallways in this home, and the kitchen was the adjacent room.

"Who?" Manny's voluminous eyes stretched even larger.

"Chief Adams."

"Oh, *Monsieur* Adams. He is such a sweet man. He comes for breakfast every Friday morning."

Emmett bit his tongue on a hasty snarl, checking his ire before he replied. "You asked me last night what happened at the Mechanic's Institute. A group of us were meeting to create a plan to allow Black men to vote in elections," he began, relating the events that had unfolded with such violence and carnage, how the police had entered the fray, killing every Black man they could, whether they were fighting, running away, or lying injured upon the ground. "And there's no doubt," he finished, the words coming hot and fast, "that the police did this either on the orders, or at least with the complete knowledge, of that very nice man, Chief Adams."

Manny's eyes glistened slightly, but she sat down and motioned Emmett to do the same, her actions deliberate as she processed this information. "Madame Laveau always has a reason for everything, but it is not always for you or me to know."

"I'm sorry. It's just that they almost killed me..."

She reached out and put her hand lightly on his arm, and he took several deep breaths. "Let's eat and talk of other things," she said softly.

It was then that Emmett noticed there was only one plate and one chair. "You aren't eating with me?"

"No."

"Will you at least join me?" It took several minutes of cajoling, but Emmett convinced her to go retrieve another chair and sit with him.

Manny set the chair down, her hand resting on the back of the mahogany, the crescent top beautifully crafted, a leather seat stretched tight for comfort within the frame. "If I join you, will you describe your home up north?"

Emmett told her about the rolling hills, the ocean, and the wildlife, but she was most fascinated by his description of snow. He discovered that she was an orphan, same as him, taken in by Madame Laveau, as many others had been. The Indians he'd seen earlier often slept in the front yard so that they could be at the market with their wares at first light, and in exchange they left vegetables and herbs. Many others drifted in and out of this house, including Marie Laveau's two adult daughters and families, other more distant relatives, and just about anybody who needed a helping hand.

After an hour, Emmett rose, knowing it was time to return to his own world and leave this small oasis in New Orleans behind. "Goodbye, Manny."

"*Jusqu'à ce qu'on se revoie,* Emmett Collins," Manny murmured in reply. "Until we meet again."

CHAPTER 2

AUGUST 3, 1866

After Emmett left, Manny went to school for the first time that week, Madame Laveau having a gentlemen friend escort her there and back in his buckboard. She had a host of chores to do after getting home, and thus, it wasn't until after dark that she found the opportunity to speak with Madame Laveau. She found her by the altar, tucking a few coins into her purse, having just prepared a love potion for a young Black woman trying to gain the attention of a clerk in the haberdashery that the woman's father owned. She had mixed the ingredients into a small bottle that had once held medicine, corked it, and told the lass to put a few drops into the herbs in the *gris-gris* bag around her neck twice a day.

"What troubles you, child?" Madame Laveau asked, seeing Manny's unhappy face.

"That boy," she knew he was a man, but to her, he just seemed to be a boy, "he said that a whole bunch of Black folks got hurt the other day just because they want to be able to vote."

"That is what some people are saying."

"Is it true?"

"Did you talk about it at school today?"

"Mr. Johnson is overwhelmed with all the recent slaves flowing into the school," Manny replied.

Madame Laveau frowned. "Certainly, none of them are at your level."

"The lower levels are packed so tight they have been squeezing some of the older students in with my class, even though they can't keep up."

"I have a book by Frederick Douglass. It might help you to understand," Madame Laveau said.

"I have read the narrative of his life."

"This is his second book, called *My Bondage and My Freedom*." Madame Laveau began to put away the various herbs scattered across the altar, tucking the small containers onto various parts of the shelf behind her.

"That boy said that it was the police doing most of the killing, and that *Monsieur* Adams most likely knew what was happening."

"I do not know if that is true or not," she said slowly. "But if the police were doing the killing, I am sure that the chief most likely ordered them to do it."

"He seems like such a nice man," Manny said.

"*Un homme n'a pas qu'un seul visage,* Manon. A man has many faces, and there is no such thing as a man all good or all bad. I imagine we see his *zanmitay* side because he likes us. If we were something else, we might see a less-friendly version of Chief Adams."

"Why does the Chief like us, but not those other Black folks?"

"We are a bit more sophisticated than most of those so recently freed," Madame Laveau replied. "And we do not go around raising a ruckus like those folks that were at the Mechanic's Institute, but instead help the Chief, even in some small way. We create a safe place for those who have no other—and keep them off the streets. You want to create change, real change—then you must be sly. The white people all got the upper hand, and it does no good bashing one's head against the clubs they hold."

"Do you suppose that women will ever get the chance to vote?"

Before Madame Laveau could reply, there was a horrible banging at the front door. This was not an unusual occurrence at the Laveau household, as many desperate people, often with too much drink in them, showed up at all times of the day and night needing a remedy for one thing or another. With the recent unrest in the city, though, Madame Laveau told Manny to stand back, even though there was nobody in New Orleans foolish enough to bring violence into the home of the Voodoo Queen.

The woman at the door was of moderate height, but had a thick frame supporting a bosom that threatened to burst from her too-small bodice as she raised her hand to pound on the door again.

"Hello, Lulu." Madame Laveau reached out calming hands to soothe the obvious agitation of this powerful Black woman.

"I'm sorry to bother you," Lulu gasped. "'Specially at home, Madame, but Victoria got done up, but good."

"Is she with you?"

"Sure enough. She out in the wagon with Harold."

"Was it…?" Madame Laveau left the name unsaid.

"It sure enough was him."

New Orleans Crescent Fox

======================================

The Fox is Published Daily (Sunday Excepted)
By S. H. Hannity
Terms: Daily $16, Weekly $5; Per Year

======================================

Tuesday Morning July 31, 1866

======================================

Official Journal of the State of Louisiana

Negro Uprising—

Yesterday an armed group of Negroes threatened the peace and tranquility of the streets of New Orleans. A mob of 500 demonstrated outside of the Mechanic's Institute to support the illegal convention of usurpers trying to replace the duly elected officials with their own. All of these men were armed with clubs, bricks, rocks, and often time pistols.

When a local prominent businessman was knocked to the ground by this lawless mob, Mr. Crevon, aid to the Chief of Police, fearlessly went into their midst and arrested the culprits under great duress to himself.

As they approached the convention, northern whites and Negroes alike encouraged the mob to kill all the southern gentlemen that stood against them. Alerted by Mr. Crevon, the police arrived on the scene and were promptly attacked by the darkies.

Many police were injured in the resulting riot, while some twenty or thirty Negroes were killed. Dr. Dostie, who incited the riot, has been mortally wounded. Mr. Michael Hahn was somewhat injured but very slightly.

Federal soldiers arrived on the scene after about two hours, but the police had already restored peace. It is pleasant to record that in all the unhappy circumstances of yesterday, the white soldiers and the white citizens sympathized with each other heartily.

Emmett set the newspaper down in disgust. He'd finally torn himself away from his landlady, Mrs. Marchant, who'd thought him dead, and was now browsing through the newspapers from the past few days. *The New Orleans Tribune* was the only publication that didn't blame the Blacks for the 'incident.' This was probably due to the fact that this bilingual daily paper, the first of its kind in the United States, was published by a Black editor.

After sitting silently at his desk, a design of William McCracken, a furniture craftsman with a shop just downstairs, Emmett picked up an Esterbrook nib and attached it to the rosewood handle, both recently arrived birthday gifts from Joshua Chamberlain, and began to write his report to General Howard.

Major General O. O. Howard,

I am sorry to only now be submitting this correspondence to you, my delay having been a result of being injured during the massacre that occurred at the Mechanic's Institute on July 30th. Please make no mistake about the events, for they were quite simply butchery, notwithstanding what the newspapers and public officials are declaring. I was present at the convention in which the idea of black suffrage was to be discussed, when white protestors attacked black supporters, and then armed and reinforced by the police, proceeded to murder hundreds of black men, as well as white men who promoted their cause.

Meanwhile, the Federal Troops at Jackson Barracks were nowhere to be seen. General Baird had been notified of the rising tension created by the convention, but claims to have gotten the times wrong, or perhaps had no firm orders to maintain peace. The situation here is bleak. Violent repression of freedmen lurks on every street corner, schools are being burnt to the ground, teachers intimidated, and there is no land to parcel out due to President Johnson's pardon of all former Confederate officers.

Please advise me of how you would like to proceed,

Your Agent in New Orleans,
Emmett Collins

It was several days later, on Wednesday night, that Emmett ventured out for the first time. He was attending a fundraising event hosted by Campbell MacLeod, a very successful businessman with political and social ambitions, at his home on Magazine Street. Emmett paused to catch his breath in front of the mansion, the shortage of oxygen due to his injuries as well as the magnificence of the estate. Fronting the white mansion were curved stairs on either side of a wide, covered veranda, the roof held up by four pillars as thick around as his arms could reach. The house itself stretched massively in all directions, filling the entire block with its shining presence, far different than the surrounding Spanish-style structures. A butler welcomed him at the door, leading him down the long hall to the interior courtyard.

As he stepped back outside, the sound of a band playing *habanera* music—a rich mix of French, Cuban, and African influences—wafted across to caress his ears. There were thirty or forty people mingling among tables placed here and there, a space for dancing, and a bar that ran across the rear of the expanse in front of the servant's quarters. Emmett thanked the butler and stepped sideways to blend in with a bush taller than his head as he attempted to acclimate to a scene that held no comfort for him. He wasn't much of a drinker, hadn't the slightest clue how to dance, and didn't even know the proper fork to use at a manse as fancy as this. Yet, the money being raised was to fund a teacher's salary in a Black school Emmett was planning on opening soon, so he figured he had to attend.

"Emmett, my *loon*, even hiding here in the shadows I can tell *ye* been rowed up Salt River." Campbell MacLeod laid his hand on Emmett's shoulder, gently, as if the boy might break. "Here, take this drink, *ye* looks like *ye* need it more than me."

Emmett found himself holding a glass with brown liquor that he suspected was whiskey. He took a small sip, remembering his first taste of alcohol during the war in which he'd taken a gigantic slug and thought the liquor might burn his throat clear through. This firewater slid smoothly down his gullet, leaving just a tickle of flavor. "Thank you, Mr. MacLeod," he said, holding the glass up to one of the lanterns strung overhead.

"*Ye* must call me Campbell or else *ye* make me feel old." He wiped his balding head with a handkerchief, the humidity and heat of the August night sweltering. He then carefully smoothed over the unruly reddish hair still cropped to each side of his balding pate, before nodding at the glass and continuing, "It's a Talisker scotch from the Isle of Skye, the closest distillery to my home in Scotland. My pa would break out a bottle for special occasions, no more than a nip at a time. Since I've made my fortune here in New Orleans, I buy it by the barrel and make sure to always have a ready supply available."

"It's less bad than other types of alcohol I've tasted," Emmett admitted, meaning his words as a compliment.

MacLeod chuckled, his hand squeezing Emmett's shoulder. "Does your face confirm the rumors that *ye* were caught up in that *rammy* at the Mechanic's Institute?"

One eye was still puffy from a particularly vicious blow, and his right cheek was scraped raw from the rough cobbles. "I reckon I was there, sure enough," Emmett replied, hoping the man didn't press his arm where he'd been shot.

"Terrible business." MacLeod shook his head "I'm hugely pleased that *ye* suffered only bumps and bruises. It'd seem that several others laid down their knife and fork that day."

"I fought in the Great War, Campbell," Emmett replied, murmuring the man's given name, "and I've never seen anything like what happened there. More than 'several' men were murdered in front of my own eyes."

"People down south here are terrified of giving the Blacks too much power, for fear they might take over, or worse yet, rise up and kill all of a paler hue. *Ye* got yourself right in the middle of a huge mess. I surely don't envy your task, but will certainly aid in whatever way I can, short of having my countenance rearranged as yours has been so kindly." Campbell guffawed again, taking the opportunity at a break in the music to holler out, "Play 'Dixie Land.'" The musicians obliged, for after all, it was he paying their wages, and the music and words of the song of the South began to float through the air.

I wish I was in the land of cotton,
Old times there are not forgotten.
Look away! Look away! Look away,
Dixie's Land

In Dixie's Land, where I was born in,
Early on one frosty morning...

Emmett tensed up, his heart suddenly racing and his senses on alert, for the associations called up by the familiar music were savage and raw, the lead-up to so many bloody battles too near in memory. He could picture the grey backs picking their way through the woods or marching on just the other side of a rise. Then the memory of Gravelly Run sprang to mind, "Dixie's Land" playing right before the Rebs charged, and Emmett following General Chamberlain into the fray on horseback.

The thought of Midnight, his horse at the time, calmed him, and he sipped his whiskey. That was one good thing to come out of those awful years, a burgeoning love of horseflesh and riding. He'd barely mounted a horse before the war, but over the course of those few years, he'd found himself becoming most comfortable in the saddle. Perhaps it was the vantage point looking down on the enemy, or the power of the mount below him, or just the bond between man and beast during long hours of patrol in all kinds of country and weather.

Shrugging off the hard memories, Emmett turned to his benefactor as the music played on in the summer air. "You've been most helpful in every way. This is an impressive event you've put together, and the Freedmen's Bureau thanks you."

"From what I've seen of the contributions, *ye* might be able to fund two teachers for a year."

"I'm sure that the band has no small part in people opening their pockets. I've never heard anything like them." There was a fiddle, a banjo, an accordion, two horns, and a piano player.

"Can *ye* keep a secret?" Campbell asked with the excitement of a child. Without waiting for assent, he continued, "The piano player is Louis Gottschalk."

Emmett stared blankly back. "Who?"

"*Ye Jimmies* from the land of steady habits need to work a little less and enjoy life a little more. I guess I can forgive *ye* as *ye* spent your few adult years in the army shooting Southerners, but you've been here for a year now, so *ye* better broaden your horizons a tad. Alas, I can't say I knew much at all when I was your age."

"Is he famous?"

MacLeod grunted in exasperation. "He's a musical prodigy from New Orleans born to a Jew pa and his Creole mulatto mistress. The tune he's playing now, 'Bamboula: Danse des nègres,' he composed during a delirium of typhoid fever in the French town of Clermont-sur-l'Oise in the summer of 1848." Campbell glowed as he spoke, almost as if the achievement were his own.

"He sure does make nice sounds," Emmett agreed, trying to brook over his ignorance. "But why's it a secret?"

MacLeod looked left and right to make sure nobody was eavesdropping before telling the story in a low whisper. "It seems that Louis was caught sleeping with a very young student last year in San Francisco, and the girl's pa was outraged that some quadroon molested his little girl. Louis got out of town just ahead of the lynch mob and has been hiding out in Rio de Janeiro. I heard he was in town paying a visit to his family, and with a bit of persuasion, a great deal of money, and the promise to keep hush about his presence, I was able to convince him to play."

A servant approached with another glass of Talisker for Campbell. "I guess I shouldn't be telling *ye* of all people, seeing as *ye* work for the Federal Army."

"I don't believe my duties involve arresting men for, let's say, affairs of the heart—or some other body part—but if it did, it'd certainly be a full-time occupation here in New Orleans."

"A white man engaging in amorous congress with a Black woman is a far different tune than a man of color fornicating with a white girl," Campbell replied icily. He saw Emmett's expression harden at the harsh words and softened the rebuke by adding with a manly chuckle, "but what do men from Scotland and Maine know about any of this?"

"When did you come to America, anyway?" Emmett asked.

"Actually, I was born right here in New Orleans. My ma was pregnant with me on the boat. She died giving birth to me, and my pa packed me up and went back to Scotland. As soon as I was old enough, I came back."

A tall man in possession of an exceedingly bushy mustache in a time and place when impressive facial hair was more than common approached with a firm stride and slapped MacLeod on the back. "This is quite a shindig you've got going here, Campbell. The band is brilliant, and the women are delightfully captivating. How you got so many of the New Orleans nobs to return from their lake homes is beyond me."

"I guess free food, whiskey, and music beat summer heat, poor drains, and yellow fever in the poker game of life." MacLeod chuckled.

"I don't think anybody is getting out of this for free," the man replied, adjusting his white bow tie. "But it can become rather dull out to Lake Pontchartrain."

"Henry Clay Warmoth, I'd like *ye* to meet Emmett Collins of the Freedman Bureau." As the two shook hands, Campbell continued, "Henry was elected a territorial representative last autumn. Unfortunately, the ballot was deemed invalid due to the acceptance of Black votes."

"Oh, I've followed Mr. Warmoth's career with interest for some time, but this is the first opportunity I've had to meet him." Emmett noted the youthful skin and thick, perfectly combed hair parted down the middle, and realized that the man must still be in his mid-twenties. "The radical republicans are well-served with you, sir, at their head."

Warmoth laughed, his whiskers bouncing up and down with a life of their own. "If you listen to Roudanez and the *Tribune*, we're merely the Compromise Party, and they are the Pure Radical Party. It's one thing to have Black suffrage, but another thing entirely to let the government be overrun by Blacks. I'm not opposed to a few of those educated Creoles holding positions in the bureaucracy. But—mark my words—if too many of them get elected, the whites will fight back, and there'll be blood in the streets."

"There already is blood in the streets," Emmett commented dryly.

"Speaking of blood in the street, if it isn't Frederick Nash Ogden." Warmoth was suddenly tight in voice and body.

A man stuffed into black tails with red cheeks matching his hair had approached with the walk of somebody stomping snakes. "Mr. Warmoth," he replied as if spitting tobacco juice, before turning back to the host. "Campbell, I just wanted to make my apologies, but I've business to attend to and must leave."

"How *is* the cotton baling business?" Warmoth pressed forward, insinuating something for sure.

"It'd be better if we didn't have people from away coming down and nosing into our business," Ogden growled. "Sorry to have to leave before the food is served, but I do have pressing obligations."

"I'll see *ye* to the door," MacLeod said, and the two men walked away.

"I beg your pardon for my behavior." Warmoth broke the silence, speaking in a clipped tone. "Men in Louisiana seem to think that their birthright makes whatever they do to be the moral and correct solution, while everybody else is just some interloper."

"You aren't from around here?" Emmett asked, feeling as if he must say something.

"I came towards the end of the war. I was born and raised in Illinois, the home state of our dear departed president. My pa was a Justice of the Peace in our small town. That's where I got my love of the law, reading all of his books and haunting the courthouse benches."

"My education came by the campfire between battles." Emmett thought back nostalgically about those years that'd been the worst and best times of his young life. "General Chamberlain would give me nightly assignments. He said the country had enough imbeciles in it, and I shouldn't add to the growing number."

Warmoth laughed at that, twirling one end of his mustache with his pinkie. "I knew of the man. I believe we both entered the war as Lieutenant Colonels of our regiments, but he perhaps had more success than I did. He most certainly made his name at Little Round Top. Were you there?"

"I was. It was certainly a battle I will never forget," Emmett replied. "And likewise, you must've been at Vicksburg?"

"I was wounded and missed the victory. Soon after, I was transferred down here and became a provost judge of New Orleans." Warmoth realized that Emmett was no longer paying attention to him, but rather was gawking at a cluster of women by the entrance to the courtyard from the house. "Although my life story is a fascinating subject, I believe I've lost your attention."

"What?" Emmett murmured, almost gasping. "Who is that?" he asked with deeper feeling, nodding towards the ladies.

"Which one?" Warmoth scanned the crowd for the person in question.

Emmett looked at him in disbelief, as there could be no question as to which delicate flower had drawn his interest. "The woman in the sheer black dress with purple lace stripes." He nodded his chin towards the golden-haired lady in a frilly dress with sleeves trimmed in silk piping, and a thin-cut waistline with a bustle in the back.

"Ah, you've caught sight of the widow de Villiers. Quite the vision of beauty, is she not?"

"The... widow?"

"It was no more than two years ago that F. C. de Villiers went up to Washington, D.C., to appeal for the release of his son who'd been arrested for being a spy. He was unsuccessful, and they hung the lad. But when F. C. returned, he did so with a new bride, the ravishing Susanna de Villiers." The obviously often-repeated story rolled off Warmoth's tongue, the man relishing the suggestion of something salacious in the circumstances of the courting. "A few months back the yellow fever got him, and thanks to an update to his will, his bride of just over a year inherited one of the largest plantations in all of Louisiana."

"She is quite striking," Emmett agreed lamely, his mind elsewhere—for he knew this elegant lady from quite another life, another city.

"Perhaps I could introduce you?" Warmoth welcomed the opportunity to bask in the seductive allure cast by this bewitching gentlewoman.

"No!" Emmett exclaimed too loudly. "Perhaps later."

Later came as they were seated for the dinner party. Emmett found himself seated at the table of distinction with Campbell MacLeod and two others. There were ten small tables in the courtyard, cotton tablecloths covering each, the lanterns swaying above in the gentle breeze that'd brought them outside on this night, a welcome relief from the oppressive heat.

"Emmett Collins, this is my wife Izora."

Emmett leaned forward to give a small bow and she held out her hand, a move that surprised him, and he awkwardly planted a kiss upon her plump fingers. "The pleasure is mine," he said, straightening.

"And this is Mrs. Susannah de Villiers."

"Mrs. de Villiers, it is a delight to meet you."

"And you, Mr. Collins." Her eyes weren't screaming fear, for there wasn't much that could distress this young lady who'd already seen her share of horror in life. But they were most certainly leery. "Campbell was telling me that you are trying to educate our Southern Blacks?"

"I'm attempting to build schools for the recently freed slaves, as well as negotiate jobs, and when possible, find land for them," Emmett elaborated. A bowl of gumbo was placed in front of him, the earthy filé herbs drifting lazily up from the mixture of meats and the Holy Trinity of creole cooking: onions, celery, and green peppers, all served over rice.

"The cooks have added alligator to the shrimp, sausage, and chicken," Campbell told them loudly to be heard over the piano and accordion playing right next to their table. He then leaned over and whispered to Emmett, "Izora is angry with me for serving a traditional Louisiana meal. She prefers a fancier French menu."

Emmett tipped a spoonful into his mouth and nodded his head. "Mmm, that sure is some good." At first, he'd been skeptical of the food in Louisiana, but over the past year had come to love and appreciate the many flavors and tastes, so different than the bland New England fare he'd grown up with. He turned to Susannah on his right, shielding Campbell with his body, and whispered, "I didn't think I'd ever see you again."

"*Ahhm* as plumb shocked as you."

"What happened to you?" She'd disappeared from his life a few years earlier, and appeared to have picked up a Southern accent in that time.

"*Ahh* was so confused and in such a bad place, and then *ahh* met François and he offered to take me away and marry me, no questions asked. *Ahh* knew that *ahh'd* ruin your life if *ahh* stayed, and he was so sweet," Susannah replied softly, her words running together in her haste to explain herself.

Campbell waved to a server, a dark-skinned man dressed in a black jacket and white shirt. "Emmett, *ye* must try this Italian wine I imported. Ever since the French vineyards ran into their difficulties, I've been drinking this guinea juice, and I have to say it's quite tasty, even if it's not good Scotch liquor."

Emmett obligingly let his glass be filled, and swished the red grape juice around in his mouth. He wasn't much inclined to drink wine, but nonetheless, nodded his head appreciatively, hoping he wasn't getting two or three sheets to the wind.

Izora MacLeod leaned across the table, her abundant breasts

jutting precariously out of their tight bondage. Elaborately coiffed graying hair framing a round face which sat delicately upon broad shoulders and a short frame. "Emmett, Campbell tells me that you've been involved with the relocation of the darkies on the Destrehan Plantation. When will they all be gone?"

Emmett sat forward to reply, trying his best to avoid eye contact with her bosom. "We've moved most of the capable workers to other locations," he said, "but have had some trouble with placement of the elderly, the sick, and the orphans." Recently, President Johnson had pardoned Pierre Rost, forcing the Freedmen Bureau to relocate the thousand-plus people living and working on his plantation. Originally, many former plantation owners had been stripped of their lands, and Louisiana had experimented with giving ownership to the recently freedmen, but this had been undone with one stroke of President Johnson's pen.

"Can't they just move in with family?" Mrs. MacLeod tipped her wine glass to her mouth and let a steady flow stream into her mouth. "I know that Louise and Pierre are anxious to move back into their home."

"We're finishing up many of the details and will have everybody out by the end of the year," Emmett replied, biting back a sarcastic reply on the impossibility of sending orphans to live with their families.

The conversation was interrupted by the next course, a steaming dish of jambalaya—ham, sausage, rice, and tomatoes mixed with spices. These seasonings were probably bought down at the market, possibly even from the same Indian women Emmett had seen a few days prior at the Laveau residence.

Campbell eyed Emmett taking a bite over the rim of his wine glass. "Quite a kick to it," he said, laughing as Emmett reached hurriedly for a water glass.

"I can't say I've adapted to the spice of New Orleans cooking, but it certainly has more flavor than the biscuits we existed on during the war," Emmett replied with a grin. "Do you think I might stop by in the morning to pick up the contributions you've collected?"

"I'll bring them by your office early next week." Campbell stuffed a heaping forkful of the meat and rice with the jalapeno and cayenne, swallowing it down after barely chewing. "I've actually got to go to my lake house after this dinner party for a few days, but I should be back by Sunday for church."

Emmett briefly wondered what could be forcing MacLeod to travel out to the lake at midnight, but then Susannah asked him if he cared to dance, interrupting his thoughts. He agreed, even in the knowledge that his feet had never previously proved capable of following the rhythm of music, but it was the only option to converse with her in private. Louis Gottschalk's fingers were dancing over the black and white keys of the piano in his Caribbean-inspired syncopated style infused with the local Black music of New Orleans, a beat that Emmett stumbled to keep up with as they bounced around the makeshift dance floor.

"To think that we found each other in such a distant place," he whispered into her ear.

"It was quite a shock to see you. *Ahh* know that Campbell was raising money for helping Black folks out, but I never imagined..." She left the rest unsaid, before continuing, "*Ahhm* glad you didn't die in that dreadful war, but *ahh* thought for sure you'd have gone home to Maine by now, not ended up here in New Orleans of all places!" Susannah was maneuvering cleverly to avoid injured feet, a woman used to covering a partner's inadequacy on the dance floor. "What else don't *ahh* know about you? Have you found yourself a Mrs. Collins?"

"No," Emmett admitted. "I've been awful busy."

"That's too bad," Susannah said lightly, not overtly too distraught over his unmarried status.

Emmett told her how he had come to be offered his current place by Generals Howard and Grant, the two men responsible for the integration of the freedmen into society. Susannah, in turn, filled him in on how hard she had attempted to assimilate to the Southern culture, though she was still treated like a pariah by the other aristocratic women, who all seemed to know she wasn't of noble birth as they imagined they were. The topic of Marie Laveau had come up, and Susannah filled him in on all of the gossip about this mysterious woman.

After an hour of dancing, Susannah finally said, "*Ahh* should be getting home. It's not appropriate for a recent widow to be out so late."

"I'd see you home if you'll allow it?"

"My calèche is outside. I'd like that."

They made the proper goodbyes and went out to her enclosed carriage, with its small front wheels and oversized rear wheels, pulled by just a single horse. Her driver was a Black man in a tuxedo with a high hat and a short whip in his hand. Once they were settled, the driver slapped the reins. The carriage slipped through the dark city, and they had their first real privacy of the night.

"I thought you must have died," he said.

"*Ahh* did what was best for both of us." Her blue eyes still burned with that defiance of convention that he remembered so well.

"A goodbye would've been appreciated," Emmett responded dryly, fighting back fiercer, angrier words.

"You were a boy with your entire life ahead of you, and *ahh* was a fallen woman. What *ahh* did was for you as much as me." Susannah had run away from home as a young woman with her sweetheart and married him against the families' will. The war took him soon after, and, afraid to return home, she'd ended up plying her wares in a brothel.

"I loved you," Emmett said simply. During a leave from battle, two years earlier, Emmett had spent one glorious week in Washington, D.C., at the Willard Hotel with Susannah, a time in which he lost his virginity and fell in love with this soiled dove. And then she disappeared from his life without a trace.

"*Ahh* think about you every day," Susannah replied.

"I wrote you every day, but never heard back. When I mustered out of the service, I spent weeks looking for you, but you'd melted away like you never existed."

"You were barely sixteen years of age and *ahh* was… well, what I was," she reiterated. "*Ahh* had ruined my own life, was estranged from my family, and didn't want to be part of destroying any more lives." A lock of hair fell across her eyes, the signature curls that he loved so much, now pinned upon her head with flowers, while her milky-white skin glowed softly in the low light, the dimple on her left cheek creating an aura of innocence.

"So, you fell in love and married another man?"

"François was a gentleman. He visited with me while trying to win a pardon for his only son, who was on trial for treason. His wife had died years earlier, and all he cared about in the entire world was his boy, and when they hung him…"

"And he was rich," Emmett added bitterly.

"He offered to take me away from my life," Susannah agreed. "Was that so bad?"

"Did you love him?"

"*Ahhm* not sure what love is anymore. But he adored me and treated me like a princess."

"So you gave him your body in return?" Emmett wished he could take the words back as soon as they were said.

"It was better than several different men every night," she said quietly.

Emmett found his anger dissolving in the intoxicating blend of sensuality that comprised Susannah. "I'm happy that you no longer have to… that you gained your release from the madam."

"So am *ahh*. And now look at me." Her eyes fell, settling on the intricately-layered dress made of the finest fabrics, the embroidered patterns, and the dainty white gloves she wore.

"I was told you're the owner of one of the largest plantations in all of Louisiana."

"It's forty miles upriver, but *ahh* spend most of my time in New Orleans, although *ahhm* usually in my lake cottage during the summer months."

"You certainly have changed," Emmett said. "Not the least of which is how quick you picked up that Southern accent."

Susannah laughed gaily. "*Ahh* thought it best to fit in with all the other Southern belles." A look of sadness flitted across her face, but she banished it with a shrug of her shoulders. "As you have changed. *Ahh* last knew you as a young lad trying to wend his way through a war, and now discover a confident man rubbing elbows with the elite of New Orleans."

"I guess I know who I am," Emmett agreed.

"Enough that you weren't too embarrassed to dance, even though your legs appear to be two separate lengths," she said with a deadpan expression as the carriage pulled up in front of her imposing house.

He flushed, but then laughed, as did she.

They descended and went to sit in an open, airy veranda. He was tempted to take her hand but resisted, and they sat in easy silence for several minutes. "Have you heard of Marie Laveau?" he asked.

"The Voodoo Queen? Of course, but why do you ask?"

"I met her the other day, and she proved to be a most intriguing lady. What do you know of her?" Emmett avoided telling the circumstances of their meeting.

"Only that she is a witch who casts spells and participates in human sacrifices," Susannah said in a hushed voice. "Oh, let's not talk about that awful woman."

They returned to their silence, this time not quite so comfortable, until, finally, he rose, and Susannah came to her feet slowly, telling him to take her carriage back to his digs, even though it wasn't far from where Emmett lived on the *Vieux Carré.* He assented, climbing back into the rear seat though he would've felt more comfortable up on the seat with the Black driver.

CHAPTER 3

AUGUST 4, 1866

Lizzie was exhausted, the kind of tired that made you feel like you had molasses for blood and cotton bales for eyelids, but nonetheless, she needed a bit of fresh air. She came out onto Basin Street where there was just a bit of breeze coming off the river, cooling her heated body like a damp rag, washing away the sweat, both hers and that of the men who'd used her this long night.

The brothel was just barely into Treme—the Black section of New Orleans—close enough to the dividing line of Rampart Street so that white men felt as comfortable frequenting the establishment as Black men, the only prerequisite being cash. This evening, she'd serviced six separate men. Two had been nice enough, lonely-eyed fellows looking for tenderness, the touch of a woman, and of course, sexual release. A wiry Black man had methodically gone about his business without once looking at her. There was a gentleman in a tuxedo who had just come from some fancy function, and another who was very nervous the entire time, as if his wife was going to barge in at any moment. The worst was the cracker from the country, the man who made his money driving a wagon for a sugar plantation, and his moniker from the whip he constantly cracked to keep the team moving. He was a hulking brute, and his smell had been nauseating. He was also drunker than the others, and had taken longer to finish, as she tried not to gag or suffocate under his mounds of flesh.

She walked further into Treme, breathing deeply. This was her favorite part of the day, just a couple hours until sunrise, not yet dreading the next line-up of men, nor yet trying to sleep through the stifling humidity while swatting away cockroaches. It was now that she could almost imagine her freedom. The man who would whisk her away and marry her was her favorite daydream, but she also entertained the notion of saving enough money to leave the business behind and get a job as a shop girl.

Lizzie heard the clip-clop of a horse coming down the street behind her, and the rattle of wooden wheels. She assumed it was an early morning delivery, perhaps to the pub around the corner that served breakfast with the sunrise, and was surprised when she heard a man's voice saying "whoa," and a carriage pulling up next to her. A Black man sat in the driver's seat wearing a black tuxedo. He held the reins with one hand, and tipped his tall hat with the other.

"S'cuse me, ma'am, but I was wondering if you might be looking to make some money?"

Lizzie eyed the man. Was he asking for himself or somebody in the enclosed carriage? Lulu would be angry as all get out if she found out, for it was strictly forbidden to ply her wares outside of the brothel. Plus, she was dead-tired. "I'm afraid not," she replied. "Miss Lulu wouldn't like that at all."

The man's teeth gleamed from the shine of the moon. "I'd give you ten dollars now, and ten more after."

"Twenty-dollars?" That was more than four times her going rate, and she only got to keep a tiny part of that.

"My boss is very discreet. He don't want anybody knowing any more than you do," the driver persisted.

"Where at?" The tiredness was gone from her body and eyes. Twenty dollars would go a long way towards leaving the business. That would about double her stake.

"His lake house. Won't take us no more than a half hour to get there, an hour there, and I'll bring you back when you're done."

Lizzie looked up at the moon as if to judge the time. She should be able to be back before it got too light, and hopefully sneak in before Madame Lulu spotted her. The Black driver held out a crisp ten-dollar note, but when she went to take it, he pulled it back slightly.

"Only thing is, I got to blindfold you. My boss, he don't want you knowin' where he lives."

"You're not covering my eyes and taking me some place strange," she retorted.

The driver shrugged, and made to put the money away. Lizzie could size a man up in a split second, and could read the many tells people sent when playing poker, but she had never been much at bluffing. Twenty dollars was twenty dollars.

Not only is it difficult to see when you are blindfolded, it is also awful hard to judge time. The minutes seemed to stretch endlessly as the carriage rumbled over the rutted road, but Lizzie would guess that it was probably about what the man had said, a half-hour until they stopped, and he led her carefully from the carriage. There were just four steps to go up, and then the creaking of a door, before she finally found herself seated at a table and was allowed to remove the handkerchief.

There were two rooms separated by double French doors that were now opened wide. She sat at a table with eight chairs and a bottle of red wine. There were two lace place mats and two empty glasses. A candle flickered on the table, its meager light bolstered by several oil lamps on the walls. The doors led to a sitting room with several armchairs, small tables, and ornate artwork. A piano was in one corner, with blue-patterned curtains drawn tight across the windows.

A door opened, and a white man with reddish hair came in. He was carrying a tray that he placed down on the table before sitting catty-corner to her. There was a lit cigar clenched between his teeth. He poured wine into two glasses, and then sat back and looked her up and down while he puffed on his cigar. She knew her body well, and stretched out to give him a better view. Her legs were slender and long, disappearing into a thin waist. Her breasts were ample, if not large.

He nodded at the tray. "Canapé. These have cheese, these are just butter, and these have foie gras pâté." When her eyes revealed her confusion, he added, "It is duck liver." He laughed as she now wrinkled up her nose. "What is your name?"

"Lizzie, sir."

"Call me Simon," he said.

She knew when a man lied about his name, but was this any surprise after the blindfold?

He held up a glass and motioned for her to do the same. "Thanks for coming," he said, clinking her glass and tipping his own to take a careful sip of the wine. He waited for her to drink, and then continued, "Please have some of the canapé."

Lizzie was starving, so she was glad he offered this up, but she wasn't going to be eating the duck liver. She tried the French bread with butter, and it melted in her mouth. She swallowed another mouthful of wine, thinking she was sure glad she'd agreed to come, and that she'd chosen to go for a walk in the first place. Twenty dollars!

"Tell me about yourself, Lizzie." The man stared at her from eyes pinched behind ruddy cheeks, his hair sticking out in tufts from the sides of his head.

"What do you want to know?" she asked, easing another piece of bread from the platter, this time with a sliver of cheese atop.

"Let's start with your age."

"Nineteen," she lied. In fact, she'd just turned sixteen last week, even though she was the only one in the world who knew this.

"Born in New Orleans?"

"No, sir… I mean, Simon," she replied. "I grew up on a plantation just up the river. When that General Butler came into New Orleans, my mother took me to their camp, hoping for what I don't know, I think to work as a maid or washerwoman. But she caught the fever and died." She looked down at her hands.

"That must have been tough," he said, leaning forward and placing his hand on her knee.

Lizzie finished her wine and put her hand down over his. "You sure seem to be an important man." She'd been around long enough to know that most men didn't really want to talk about her, while talking about themselves—their business, their money, their horses—never seemed to become dull to them.

"I've done okay for myself." He puffed up as he spoke the words. "Even though those goddamned Northerners freed all my slaves." He went on to tell her about his possessions, which, even if only half true, indeed made him an important man. As he spoke, he moved his hand up her short dress until his fingers were kneading just below her womanhood.

Lizzie tried to not flinch from his thick thumb and fingers massaging her flesh, wondering if they were going to do the thing right here in the dining room, perhaps on the table or the floor? Or would he move them to the bedroom? She turned towards him, widening her legs invitingly, and reached out to rub his arm that was rubbing her. He pulled his hand back, and undid his belt and pants so that the material yawed open. He grabbed her hand and guided it inside, pulling her forward on her chair. Her fingers found his thing, tiny and soft in her hand, and she began to stroke it, rolling it between her fingers. He leaned back, breathing heavily, sweat beading on his forehead, but his member refused to grow.

After about ten minutes, she began to worry that she might not get her money after all, and she moved to her knees, using every means she knew how to bring life to his little fellow. He slid his hand down the front of her dress and grasped her nipple between thumb and forefinger, squeezing roughly, and she gasped slightly, and for the first time felt a quiver in the flaccid organ, so said nothing as he manhandled her breasts, but then the pain became too much, and she pulled back, and when she did, he slapped her full across the face, knocking her flat. As he stood over her, she noticed he'd become almost fully erect, and then he twisted her onto her stomach, cursing in more filthy language than she'd ever heard any sailor use.

Outside, the driver sat in his seat atop the carriage smoking a cigarette. He knew enough to not go inside until he was called, but to be ready once he was. Once the boss was done with the girl, he usually wanted her out of the premises as quickly as possible. The screams were worse this time, and he clenched his teeth in sympathy as the girl wailed away. Suddenly, she fell quiet. He raised his head expectantly. He had already put a bucket of clean water and sponge in the carriage with a towel so she could clean herself up on the ride home. They were always so filthy with blood after that he threw them away. Usually the boss yelled for him when he was ready, but this time the door was flung wide with a bang. The boss stood there with a wild look in his eyes, his hair tousled and clothes rumpled. There was a scratch across his cheek, but not deep enough to be the source for the blood streaking his face.

"She's ready to go," the boss said gruffly. "But you'd best get one of those burlap cotton sacks out of the shed, and then come collect her in the dining room."

He did as he was told, wondering what the bag could possibly be for. All sorts of horrible possibilities floated through his brain, but none as bad as what he found in the dining room. As far as the driver could tell, women fell into two categories after being beaten and raped. There were those that would be sobbing as he led them back outside and would cry all the way home, and then there were the tight-lipped ones surviving on anger and hate.

This time it was different. The girl was lying naked and contorted on the floor, one arm twisted at an impossible angle, her nose smashed flat with pieces of teeth speckling her cheeks, embedded in the crusted blood. There were angry red circles on her back, her neck, her legs, and with revulsion he realized they were burn marks from the boss' cigar.

He gagged, covering his mouth with his hand and half-choking, bending over as if he'd been kicked in the stomach. He knew the boss liked to smack the girls around a bit, and while it disgusted him, he'd had little choice but to keep his mouth shut. A voice inside his head told him to just turn around and leave, but where would he go? The boss would find him. The boss knew where to find his mother. The boss was a rich and powerful man, and he was a poor Black man, who only four years earlier had been a field hand on a plantation.

He stuffed her into the burlap bag and threw in the bloody and torn cotton dress he found under the table, and then went to the shed for a second grain bag to put over the top of her and rope for tying the bags together in the middle. He slung the awkward bundle over his shoulder and took it outside to the waiting carriage. He could take the body to the police, and tell them what had happened, but the boss was the boss. He knew it would be he who was blamed for the horrific murder—for the girl was just plain dead, gawping eyes and all. Men like the boss never got into trouble. It was always men like him, a carriage driver, who took the blame and paid the penalty. He knew he couldn't dump the girl too close by and that he also needed to clean up the dining room before the sun was too high. He dropped her in the bayou halfway between the lake and the brothel, pushing the bag down with a stick.

What he did not know was that a group of boys came there to fish most afternoons, and that the very next day they would reel the bag in, cutting it open with excitement at their find, their faces freezing at the image this gruesome murder imprinted upon their souls, an image that would appear in random nightmares for the rest of their lives.

CHAPTER 4

AUGUST 10, 1866

Just two nights after his surprising discovery that Susannah was alive and in New Orleans, Emmett took a moment to enjoy the magnificence of the St. Louis Cathedral on his way home. Three spires soared into the sky, the center one significantly taller, dwarfing the two immense buildings on either side of the house of God. The sheer majesty of the edifice caused him to wonder about the truth of a higher spiritual being. He'd never admit to anybody that he had serious doubts as to a Grand Creator who ruled over the world like a sovereign king. He'd lost his belief in that benevolent being during the war, but hadn't entirely lost his faith. Every Sunday morning, he entered the doors to this St. Louis Cathedral and sat through the homily with everybody else, all the while keeping silent in regard to his qualms about the existence of God. He felt guilty taking communion, singing the hymns, and praying on his knees with the parish, but he truly hoped to regain a sliver of faith.

As he paused on the corner of Chartres and St. Ann Street, the sun was descending at an angle behind the steeple, casting a supernatural radiance upon the building and the *Vieux Carré*. In the presence of such beauty, it was somehow easier to believe in the Almighty than when he sat in a pew listening to the priests pontificate. The God they spoke of had been nowhere near the battlefields that had defined Emmett's youth, certainly not at Antietam where the lucky ones of the twenty thousand casualties in that single, blood-soaked day were those who had died quickly, as opposed to the injured whose screams of pain, entreaties, and desperate cries for water filled the air of that vast, uncaring battlefield.

What kind of Absolute Being would've orphaned him, Emmett Collins, thrust him into the slaughter that was the Great War, and freed the slaves only for them to be hopelessly mistreated? How could one believe in God after the past year? One year out from the most devastating war in history, and the punishment continued. When Emmett had arrived in Louisiana, there were over a hundred thousand freedmen who didn't even own clothes. Turned loose with less than the shirts on their backs, these people had flooded into New Orleans looking for relief. As if this social upheaval wasn't difficult enough, the spring had brought flooding as the neglected levees burst and invited the Mississippi River into the fields, ruining the cotton, sugarcane, and other crops. And now there were rumors of yellow fever sweeping through the streets, coming in from distant plantations already ravaged by the fast-moving and deadly disease.

The day before, Emmett had borrowed a horse from the Jackson Barracks, where General Baird, head of Louisiana's Freedmen Bureau, was stationed with Federal troops, and rode the twenty miles to the Ross Colony. It had taken him four hours to get there, and, far from a trial, he had wished it had been longer, for time in the saddle was time in contentment. He dreamed of the day he could buy his own horse—and not some beaten down nag but a true pedigree—maybe a Tennessee walker, so many of which he'd seen during the war, or a pair of matched Morgans like Chamberlain used to have back in Maine. Then, when the day was done, he could ride into the night and wash away all the difficulties that endlessly piled up in the fraught process of integrating the former slaves into their new lives as freedmen responsible for supporting themselves and their families.

This morning, he had awoken before dawn, overseeing the loading and transportation of eighty-three elderly, orphaned, and sick people to the Marine hospital in New Orleans. The Freedmen Bureau had taken over several wings of the facility, one to be the Dependents Home for care of the elderly, a ward for the sick, and a space for an orphanage under the care of the matron, Mrs. Mortié. He'd plodded alongside this rolling parade of misfortune for the ten-hour journey, dropped his horse back at the barracks and was just now arriving home from an exhausting expedition.

As Emmett turned to climb the steps to the covered terrace leading to the Marchant's apartment, his eyes were drawn to the girl, Manny, from Madame Laveau's house. Emmett fingered the *gris-gris* bag that hung from a string around his neck, unsure as to how much protection from his enemies it offered, but more worried to remove it than keep it. It certainly provided as much protection as God, that was for sure. The girl stood straight as an oak, he noticed, even though she appeared at ease, her chin high and eyes direct as she watched him approach.

His invitation to return to the Voodoo Queen's home had been on his mind all week. He'd flip-flopped back and forth, but the events of this exhausting day after his recent injuries, and the hope of running into Susannah had cemented in his mind the decision that he would not be visiting this mysterious home on this evening, or any other for that matter.

"Mr. Collins, I have been sent to fetch you."

"I wasn't aware that I was an item to fetch." Emmett stopped in front of the slender girl, estimating that, at just over five feet tall and rangy as a filly, she couldn't weigh more than eighty-five pounds.

"Madame Laveau feared that you might choose to not heed her invitation," Manny replied with a shrug. "So here I am."

Emmett eyed her carefully. While he was most certainly intrigued by the idea of visiting this Marie Laveau and hearing what she had to say, he was frightened at the same time. The night he'd seen Susannah home, he'd asked what she knew about Marie Laveau. It seemed that the Voodoo Queen was a heavy topic of gossip in the upper circles of New Orleans society, for there were tales of her conjuring storms, turning people into animals, sacrificing babies, and other, equally horrific yarns.

Just the thought of Susannah, of course, brought forth a salacious vision of this bewitching woman he'd given up for dead, but who'd been suddenly thrust back into his life. The past few days Emmett had played over every moment of the dinner party countless times, the tinkling laugh, the mischievous eyes, the curls that escaped the pins meant to hold them, and…

"Mr. Collins?"

Emmett came back to the present and to the girl who stood awaiting his answer. "Please call me Emmett. I'm not old enough to be a mister yet." A cook today at the Ross Home Colony had contradicted Susannah's anecdotes about Marie Laveau. This withered Black woman with laughter crinkles in the corner of her eyes had told him that Laveau was a loving, benevolent, and spiritual priestess. She shared advice, charms, potions, and even money to protect people, to help them find love, or to bring their husbands back. He sighed, and gave in to the pressure. "I need to wash up."

"I will wait here for you."

"You don't have to do that. I've agreed to come, and it's right up the street. I'm sure that I can find my way."

Manny shuffled her feet, her eyes dropping to the ground. "We will not be going to my home," she mumbled.

"Where might we be going?" he asked in exasperation.

"Milneburg, or close by, anyway." This was not the final destination, but they'd certainly go through the Lake Pontchartrain town before reaching their destination.

"I've had a long day and been in the saddle for most of it," he replied, his mind in a quandary. On the one hand, he'd felt a momentary relief to be pushed into visiting with Madame Laveau, who seemed to possess a knowledge of many things—and a peace that he truly wanted to find. Then again, Milneburg would take at least an hour to reach. "I'm sorry, but tonight would indeed be a trial for me after the day I've had." He made as if to go.

"You must come, Emmett Collins," Manny beseeched him, her wide eyes filled with worry. "Madame Laveau has been preparing for you all week."

"Preparing?" Emmett asked, his fingers again reaching for the *gris-gris* amulet hanging from his neck. "In what way?"

"To answer your question, of course. She has been mixing potions and lighting candles and conferring with the *lwa*."

"My question?" But Emmett knew his question. It was something that he'd toiled with all week, and the best possible answer had presented itself in the form of Susannah Shaw, or de Villiers, as she called herself now. He now believed that all the trials and tribulations and hard work were made worth it by love.

"What is it all for, you silly." Manny smiled, her teeth gleaming like ivory, followed by a snicker that suggested he well knew what the question was. "I am most interested in hearing the answer myself."

"I haven't eaten anything since this morning," he said weakly.

Manny held up a satchel. "I have brought you dinner. You may eat on the train."

Emmett sighed and turned back the way he'd just come from. "Not much sense washing up if we're going to be riding Smoky Mary." The train engine that ran between the neighborhood of Faubourg Marigny and Lake Pontchartrain in Milneburg was well known for covering its passengers with a layer of soot in the course of the five-mile ride. Ten minutes later they were on the train, and Emmett was eating the fried oyster sandwich on French bread that Manny had brought for him.

Milneburg was a twisting maze of boardwalks built over the shallows of the lake. The original buildings had been fishing camps, but since the booming brick industry and arrival of the railroads some thirty-five years earlier, saloons, stores, and hotels had sprung up. Ships were able to access Lake Pontchartrain from the Gulf, and unload their cargo directly onto Smoky Mary, which then toted the goods into New Orleans.

"Where to now?" Emmett's mood had improved since eating, and he was excited to visit this lakefront community he'd not yet seen during his time here. It was known as a summer party destination, a place where the color line was blurred, and money was more respected than family lineage.

"Follow me." Manny led them off, wending her way back to shore and along the road west to Spanish Fort, where the Lake Pontchartrain Hotel rose majestically from the mouth of Bayou St. John.

Emmett fingered the walnut handle of his Colt Army Model pistol, the worn wood comforting to his hand. He was glad that he had the weapon holstered at his side, as there were clustered groups of men already drunk as the sun slowly sunk to the horizon in the sky. "Is Madame Laveau here at the hotel?"

The Lake Pontchartrain Hotel was a group of buildings that included several saloons, a livery stable, restaurants, and rooms for rent. A footbridge crossed over the Bayou to a pleasure garden for outdoor strolls and clandestine meetings of lovers—and goings-on of a more nefarious nature as well.

"In a way, yes, I guess you could say that she is," Manny replied mysteriously, pushing open the door of the saloon and stepping in without hesitation. A cacophony of noise burst from within. There was a group of men, and possibly one woman, playing a variety of horns in an upbeat rhythm chasing itself this way and that, while a man with a drum kept the beat loosely united.

Emmett stepped in, his eyes sweeping the interior. There was a bar running the length of the back of the establishment, the band playing in the front, in between scattered tables of boisterous men of various colors, a slew of whores mingled amongst them. All of the furniture was made from swamp wood, mostly cypress and pine, and a badly cracked mirror distorted images behind the burly bartender.

"Madame Laveau is *here*?" he asked incredulously. "This is where we are to meet?"

"Madame Laveau's daughter is here, who is also named Marie, and we are to collect her for *la cérémonie* tonight. There she is." Manny nodded her head towards the gaming tables in the corner opposite the musicians.

Sitting at the faro table, playing the two-card game known to the locals as "bucking the tiger," was a thickset man, his mustache hanging on either side of his mouth. He wore a holstered gun on each hip, and his manner suggested he knew how to use them. On his lap was a Creole woman approaching middle age, but with the unmistakable regal features of her mother. She had a few more curves, and there was just a bit of puffiness to her eyes, but she was the spitting image of Marie Laveau.

"*Laissez les bons temps rouler*!" yelled a wiry Frenchman at the roulette table, metaphorically and literally calling for the good times to roll.

"Manny, what brings you here?" the younger Laveau asked in a lazy voice, attempting to rise from the lap of the German, but he pulled her back with one arm while placing a bet with his free hand.

"There is a *fête* on the Bayou tonight. Your mother hopes that you will come."

"Of course. I'd heard that it was happening. And who is this *peart* lad?" she asked, nodding her head at Emmett. Across the room a scuffle broke out as a whore slapped the face of a man grabbing at her, while at the poker table voices were raised as a large pot exchanged hands.

"You be careful out there," the walrus-mustache said with a German accent. "I know you heard full-well about that young woman they found stuffed into a bag in the bayou yesterday morning."

"What's that?" Emmett had been out of town all day and hadn't gotten a chance to read the newspaper or hear the gossip yet.

"This is Emmett Collins. He is a Yankee from Maine," Manon said.

The German eyed him carefully, noting the dusty clothing and worn pistol on his belt. "A couple of boys drug out a cotton sack and found her stuffed into it. She was beat to hell, naked, tortured, and prob'ly raped."

"There is an evilness in some men," Marie the younger said, shaking her head.

"I'll have to catch up on the news tomorrow, I guess," Emmett said grimly.

"Won't be in the papers," the German said.

"Why's that?"

"I told you she was Black didn't I?"

Emmett didn't know how to respond to that, so he kept his mouth shut.

"We should be going," Manon said.

The younger Laveau nodded, her face trying to hide a grin. "You ever been to a Voodoo *fête,* Emmett Collins?"

"A Voodoo ritual?" Emmett stared dumbly at her. "I was just meeting up with Madame… your mother… as she told me to come…"

The German was still laughing as Emmett left the saloon with the two Creole women, one no more than a child, but seemingly fearless walking into a saloon filled with questionable characters of all stripes like this one.

They went down a narrow path to the bayou, the slow moving, often swampy, body of water that stretched from the lake back to New Orleans proper. Sitting in a rowboat was a shadowed figure. Emmett's steps faltered as his anxiety at the coming event mounted. What did he really know about these people? Or about Voodoo *fêtes*?

Fighting his irrational fears, Emmett untied the line and clambered in behind the two women, and the wiry operator stretched his back, rowing them into the swamp. Emmett supposed that, if he could charge into a mess of Confederates with an empty rifle, he could sure enough get in a rowboat and go into a swamp. He could hear alligators sliding through the brackish water around them, and once, when the moon broke through the clouds, he saw snakes following the wake of the skiff as if intent on catching and boarding the vessel.

"They come for the *fête*," Maria the younger said, noting his eyes on the trailing serpents.

"I wouldn't be surprised." Emmett muttered.

Manny smiled reassuringly at him. "*Li Grand Zombi* is a serpent who created heaven, earth, and all of its animals. He lives in the ocean between the two worlds of the spirits and the humans, going back and forth, and thus will hopefully attend our ceremony this evening."

"Oh? That makes me feel much better," he replied sarcastically.

They rounded a bend in the bayou, the vessel guided carefully into a crevice in the bank, displacing an alligator as they approached. Manny hopped spryly out, and Marie the younger followed more carefully. Emmett hesitated to follow the two women into the darkness, for the sun had settled out of sight, leaving only streaks of faint light through the dense foliage of the swamp. He chose Manny, believing that this innocent young girl would not knowingly bring him to his death.

"Wait for me," he croaked, his foot stepping into the brackish shallows before he scrambled to dry ground, fighting a fear that a snake would get into his boot and perhaps up his pants, a fate worse than an alligator chewing on his leg. It wasn't far to go, as just fifty feet into the umbrage they emerged into a clearing. The moon was bathing the white-clothed figure of Marie Laveau the elder with an arrow of light as she stood by a pyre of wood.

As Emmett stumbled to a stop, jostling into darker figures around him, Madame Laveau suddenly banged a club three times on the ground while chanting in English, "In the name of the Father, and of the Son, and of the Holy Spirit." The throng Emmett now found himself immersed within replied in kind. Raising her palms heavenward, she continued, "faith, hope, and charity." There were probably at least fifty people crowded together who repeated the phrase of the three virtues in the Voodoo religion. Madame Laveau then bellowed out prayers of the Catholic Church, waiting for the dark mass to holler back the refrain.

Our Father who art in heaven,
Hallowed be thy name;
Thy kingdom come Thy will be done
On earth as it is in heaven.
Give us this day our daily bread;
And forgive us our trespasses
As we forgive those who trespass against us;
And lead us not into temptation
But deliver us from evil.

The Voodoo Queen then traced a cross in the dirt, touched the ground three times and made the sign of the cross before spilling water three times on the ground and uttering the words, "*nous honorons nos ancêtres.*"

"She says we honor our ancestors," Manny whispered in Emmett's ear. Manny continued to interpret as the congregation repeated Marie Laveau's prayers. "*Papa Legba ouvre baye pou mwen*, Papa Legba, open the gate for me, *Papa Legba ouvre baye pou mwen*, Papa Legba, open the gate for me, *Ouvre baye pou mwen*, *Papa*, Open the gate for me, Papa, *Pou mwen passe, Le'm tounnen map remesi lwa yo*! For me to pass, when I return I will thank the *lwa*!"

Marie the elder held out a torch to be lit by her daughter, who'd worked her way to the front of the multitude. The rag soaked in whale oil attached to a long stick ignited with a whoosh. As she walked toward the pyre, Emmett leaned over to whisper a question in Manny's ear. "Who is this *Papa Legba*?"

"He is the old man at the crossroads between the *lwa*, or the spirits, and us humans." Manny leaned into Emmett's body, her lips tickling his ear slightly. He liked the comfort of her body touching his, and allowed himself to enjoy the sensation. "To speak with the *lwa*, we must first ask his permission. Look, Madame Laveau is offering him rum now, which is his favorite drink, to get in his good graces." She pointed to the Voodoo Queen, who'd lit the stack of wood also soaked in whale oil, and was now spitting mouthfuls of rum onto the blaze.

A cheer went up and the drums began to beat in a rich-deep timbre, the people swaying in cadence with the rhythm. Emmett found himself lurching side-to-side, unable to stand still, yet out of sync with the men and women around him. With the light from the fire, he now realized there were several white women in the crowd, their sinuous movements fitting in much better than his clunky efforts, his pale skin and burnt red hair setting him apart as well. Manny moved so she was facing him, and gripped his hands with her long fingers, saying, "*Danse avec moi.*"

Her fingers sent shivers up and down his spine, and the drumbeat burrowed into his body through earth and air, the tremors rustling through the ground and entering his feet before flowing into his legs, shimmering upwards into his arms and chest, before touching his mind. Marie the elder danced with an enormous snake wrapped around her torso and arms, the serpent's head poised above the Voodoo Queen's own, its eyes piercing the night like beacons. What had Manny said? *Li Grand Zombie* appears in the form of a serpent that connects earth with the *lwa.*

A woman whose skin was black as night began to gyrate faster and faster, arms flailing this way and that way, causing the drumming to come to an abrupt stop. Her eyes rolled back into her skull, leaving white shining orbs, while a trail of spittle worked its way over her lip and down her husky chin, before stretching down into the wide cleavage between her breasts.

Even the night birds and insects paused to hear better, as suddenly a male voice issued forth from the cavity between her motionless lips. "I will aid in your quest for revenge. If you present me with a bucket of pecans before sundown tomorrow, your husband will no longer draw breath." The voice slid up and down in a cunning manner, wheedling to and fro. "Once that happens, I will expect a bottle of good rum and a scimitar as payment for my service." The woman slumped to the ground unconscious, as many hands hoisted her back up, patting her cheeks and forehead with a rum-soaked cloth.

"What in tarnation?" Emmett stood stock still even though the drumming had resumed, his mind grappling with the bizarre scene while his eyes turned to Manny for an explanation.

"She had a visit from Iron Joe," Manny said with a dark countenance.

"Visit? You mean like a vision?"

"Something like that. She must have sent a prayer to the warrior *lwa,* Joe Féraille, who is a soldier and blacksmith, which is where the name Iron Joe comes from. He is a wily and shrewd enemy, as you most certainly could tell from his voice. He entered her body to negotiate what sounds like the murder of her husband."

"Murder? Should we do something about this? Report it to the police?"

She squeezed his hand. "Don't worry, Emmett Collins. I attended my first *fête* just three years ago, and I can assure you that it is no more bizarre than your Roman Catholicism." Manny laughed, her eyes mocking him. "Besides, what are you going to do, go to Chief Adams and tell him that you were at a Voodoo *fête*, saw a *lwa* possess a woman, and negotiate the murder of her husband?"

Emmett shook his head in annoyance. "I reckon not, but should someone tell her husband?"

"It's best to not get involved in the concerns of the *lwas*. I would guess that his transgression is more than a trifling matter. Did you notice her swollen face?" Manny searched Emmett's eyes for her answer, before continuing; "Iron Joe does not take kindly to interference in his business. Unless you want to find yourself at the wrong end of his cutlass, I suggest you mind your own, which hopefully will not be long in being revealed."

Emmett stared at her in horror, all of a sudden realizing that his summons to this ritual was Marie Laveau introducing him to the world of the dead. He looked off into the darkness, wondering if the rowboat was still tied to a tree or if the man had continued about his business. How far from Spanish Fort was he? How far the other way to New Orleans? Then he remembered something General Chamberlain had said to him as they lay huddled behind mounds of dead men in a hollow on the slopes of Fredericksburg. Emmett had revolted against using dead men as a shield, and Chamberlain had said dryly, "Dead men can't hurt you nearly as much as the live ones, Emmett."

He felt a hand on his chest and another at his elbow, and was not sure whether they were comforting or trapping him. He looked down into the innocent eyes, the playful smile almost daring him, and couldn't help but smile himself, for he trusted this girl he'd just met, enough to let her drag him into the swamp at night. "I suppose I'm in no position to disobey Iron Joe," he said lightly.

"Three years ago, they found my mother in the bayou much like the young woman they found yesterday. Madame Laveau took me in and helped heal my soul. I have never had a visit from a *lwa*, but her *gris-gris*, love, wisdom, and steady hand have brought me back to the world of the living." She did not add that Madame Laveau had told her she had a special purpose laid out for her, that she could not turn her back on that because it was of the utmost importance. It was this that had finally put her feet back underneath her, and she had tucked the sadness and anger away into a tiny portion of her head and heart.

Manny took his elbow and began to rock back and forth in time with the vibrations filling the glade. "The visit was good news. *Papa Legba* has opened the portal to the heavens. Perhaps you will find your answer tonight."

Emmett was suddenly aware of the beautiful bodies on all sides, bodies of every shade of skin, but now was stunned to realize that the scanty clothes had all but disappeared, with several woman bare from the waist up, their breasts jiggling and bouncing in time with the drums in a sexual frenzy that was more lascivious than anything he'd ever seen. It was an orgy of the senses hidden away in the swamp, the beating drums coursing in his veins, the snake twisting and writhing wrapped around the Voodoo Queen, bodies gyrating around and against him, flesh against flesh, breasts, bellies, butts, all swinging and shaking in a crescendo so powerful that Emmett felt he would burst as he was inflated with fear, desire, happiness, sadness, anger, and an overwhelming lust for life. And then everything stopped.

All eyes turned to Marie Laveau the elder, the snake coiled and hissing around her, as she held her arms high in prayer. "Mister Daniel Blanc, warrior against the wicked, you who are sovereign over all the angels, you who cast Satan from the heavens and loathe injustice more than all others, we have one with us that fails to understand why we must fight against injustice in our world." Into the silence that followed came the rush of wings above, a splashing in the Bayou beyond, a quivering in the earth below, and a pulsation all around.

"Emmett Collins." Manny stood slackly in front of him, speaking in a deep baritone, her head crooked at an odd angle. Her pupils had shrunk to tiny pinpoints surrounded by a milky-white swirling sea. "You have come to New Orleans to assist and guide my Black brothers and sisters in their struggle to overcome pain and suffering. Let me do the same for you." Manny's hazel pupils began to expand, and then became transparent and invited Emmett inside.

Emmett found himself walking purposefully forward through the darkness, a hand guiding him at his elbow. At one point a serpentine figure with wings breathing fire flew past, for some reason failing to spark fear or even unease in Emmett as they continued on, finally stopping, light and noise beginning to seep in around the edges. A Black man stood at the top of massive steps, his hair cropped close to his head, a neatly trimmed mustache adorning his upper lip. As Emmett watched, the man began to speak, his words booming into space.

"I am happy to join with you today in what will go down in history as the greatest demonstration for freedom in the history of our nation.

"Five score years ago, a great American, in whose symbolic shadow we stand today, signed the Emancipation Proclamation. This momentous decree came as a great beacon light of hope to millions of Black slaves who had been seared in the flames of withering injustice. It came as a joyous daybreak to end the long night of their captivity.

"But one hundred years later, Black people still are not free."

Emmett was aware of murmurs of assent around him, and with effort, tore his eyes from the charismatic figure at the podium and looked around. Manny was on one side of him, her attention fixed upon the man speaking, her eyes wide in wonder. On his other side was the man who guided him here, who was it? Mister Daniel Blanc. He was a Black man with kinky hair combed out bush-like around his head, slightly unshaven, with black eyes exuding an inner light as he listened, seemingly oblivious of the crowd around him.

Emmett guessed that everybody in the entire world was here, crammed into a long rectangular space, which he surmised might be the mall in Washington, D.C. (How had he gotten here?) At his back in the distance was what appeared to be the Washington Monument rising proudly into the air, but the stone construction was much taller than he remembered. The majority of people were Black, but there were white men and women mixed in.

"I have a dream that my four little children will one day live in a nation where they will not be judged by the color of their skin but by the content of their character. I have a dream today." Cheers erupted from the crowd.

Behind the man speaking was a gleaming white building with twelve massive columns across the front, and recessed within was the unmistakable figure of Abraham Lincoln, but in godlike proportions, his seated figure as tall as a house, illuminated as if by an inner light, and his wise eyes staring out at the crowd.

Emmett felt Manny slide her hand into his and he gave it a squeeze, soaking in the essence of love pouring from the man speaking into all of their souls and filling the air all around.

"And when this happens, and when we allow freedom to ring, when we let it ring from every village and every hamlet, from every state and every city, we will be able to speed up that day when all of God's children, black men and white men, Jews and Gentiles, Protestants and Catholics, will be able to join hands and sing in the words of the old Black spiritual: 'Free at last! Free at last! Thank God Almighty, we are free at last!'"

The uproar was deafening. Emmett felt the love of all mankind rising in his breast, and realized he was cheering wildly, and then arms were pulling at Emmett, jerking him to his feet, brushing off his face dusty where he'd fallen in the dirt. He looked around at the black faces regarding him in disbelief, kindly helping him back up but shocked that Mister Daniel Blanc had entered the body of this white person, and a man no less, but with respect, for it was a great honor to be chosen by the *lwa*. And then the drums began to beat, filling the clearing in the swamp, and the dancing resumed.

Emmett stumbled his way to the edge of the clearing, finding a seat on the branch of a live oak tree, this particular limb twisting its way to the ground before rising back into the air. His mind was baffled at what he'd just experienced. He sensed another presence, and then felt the warmth of another living being next to him, and Manny grasped his hand and put her head on his shoulder.

"Are you okay?" she asked.

"What just happened?" he asked.

"Mister Daniel Blanc showed us a vision," she said simply. "Which was far different than the normal visit, in which he inhabits the body of the person."

"And he is a Voodoo… spirit?"

"Yes," she concurred.

"Why?"

The question could pertain to many things, but Manny sensed it meant 'why' did this *lwa* take them on a journey to view this speech. "I don't know." She squeezed his hand. "But the words that man spoke are still ringing in my soul."

"He sure did make a lot of sense," Emmett admitted. "How long were we gone?"

"There is no such thing as linear time in Voodoo. Most likely we were only gone a few seconds before we fell to the ground."

"Was it real?"

"I don't know," Manny said. "But I never thought I'd see a Black man in front of a crowd so large giving a speech about being free at last. I hope it is real."

PART II: POLITICS

MARCH 7, 1868–NOVEMBER 2, 1868

CHAPTER 5

March 5, 1868

Manny Lescaut fiddled with the single sheet of paper in front of her. Her teacher at the Normal School had given her an assignment to write a paper on Black suffrage, probably due to the fact that it was all she could talk about, and he was tired of her pestering him with questions. She had thought she was in trouble when he asked her to stay after class, seeing as he had such a serious expression on his face, but it turned out he was so impressed with her paper that he wondered if she would share it with some other Black women from St. Augustine's, the local church.

It seemed this group of women got together every Thursday afternoon for tea, and discussed various social issues involving equality. They were educated and well-to-do women of color who hoped to improve Black lives in New Orleans. He said that their topics included suffrage, even if it was mostly for Black men, and not for women of any color. They also held discourses on schools that mixed Blacks and whites, Blacks having only the rearmost seats on the streetcars, job opportunities, and a whole host of other things.

Her natural instinct had been to refuse the invitation, for she was terrified to get up and speak in front of a bunch of women about her thoughts. The more she had become involved in this project, however, the angrier she had become. She had been too young to understand or do anything about those awful years of slavery, but now that the war had put an end to that evil institution, and her being sixteen years old, she could not but help be horrified at how Black people were often treated. And the further she thought on it, a further indignity came from her sex. Why, she wondered, were women not the equal of men?

She had spent the past month talking it out with Madame Laveau, who she well knew was one of the more powerful people in New Orleans, woman or man. In the eyes of God, all of His children were equal, so it should be the same in society. Her teacher, perhaps on the basis of her essay, had recommended her to a seminary college all the way up in Massachusetts, and she had recently heard she was accepted. It seemed that many more Northerners thought as she did in regards to women's rights, so she figured that she might go there, to New England, to further her education, her dream being to become a teacher fit to teach others what she was so desperate to learn.

Her reverie was interrupted by the hostess of the event, Mrs. Roudanez, introducing her to the group as Marie Laveau's goddaughter and a rising young mind in the Black political movement. Manny thought this was a bit of a stretch, as she had only just got her toes wet so far, but she vowed to make it a fact. She stood up, holding the paper in front of her like a shield, her fingers shaking only a little bit. There were about fifteen women crowded into the living room, all their eyes on her. She noticed the wife of that man Pinckney Pinchback, her name being Nina, and wondered if she was as drawn to politics, as was her husband, or if that was banned in their household? Did equality pertain to only color of skin and not gender? She cleared her throat, and began to speak, "The greatest obstacle to overcoming bias in our world," she began in a strong voice, "is the achievement of education. Education is the tool that makes us all equal, whether we are Black, white, Indian, woman, or man…"

A lot had changed over the past couple of years, Emmett thought, tapping his cigar ash on the floor. He'd gone from knowing almost nobody in New Orleans to where he was now, conversing with Henry Clay Warmoth and Pinckney Benton Stewart Pinchback, two of the most powerful political forces in the entire state. His friendship with

Warmoth had blossomed after meeting him at MacLeod's fundraiser a few years back, and through him, he'd become close to Pinchback, who was arguably the most influential Black man in the entire South.

"With the Black vote you're a shoo-in for governor," Emmett said, tilting the cigar in his hand first to Pinchback, and then to Warmoth.

Henry Clay Warmoth was the perfect image of a well-groomed gent, his hair immaculately styled and parted in the center, unlike Emmett's disheveled locks tousled this way and that and much too long. Warmoth drew on his own stogie, taking his time before answering. "That might get me elected. But to get anything *accomplished* we need to curry more of the white Southern vote." At just twenty-five years of age, he'd become one of the true power brokers in New Orleans.

"I don't see that happening," Emmett replied, remembering the incident just two years earlier right here at the Mechanic's Institute when he'd almost been beaten to death and so many other righteous ones slaughtered.

"I have to say, this constitution concerns me." Warmoth tapped ashes absently on the floor.

"You've just spearheaded the most forward-minded constitution in the entire South, and probably all of the United States." Emmett's eyes were drawn like a magnet to the window he'd smashed and slipped through before plummeting to earth, then making his escape through the streets of New Orleans. "Why are you so worried?"

"The problem with the document," Pinckney Pinchback replied, "is that it's too much too fast."

Emmett shook his head in frustration, for he knew where this was going. "How can you, of all people, claim that this piece of paper that will soon be the law of Louisiana, that this document that extends equal rights and privileges to all men, irrespective of color or race, that it goes too far?"

"You asking me that because I'm colored?" Pinchback asked sardonically. At first glance, nobody would guess that this refined gentleman with his straight hair combed to the side and Germanic features was the son of a mulatto mother. "I'll give you a pass on questioning my desire to be treated no different than any white man out there." He stared at Emmett with his slightly slanted black eyes. "You being nothing more than a carpetbagger."

Warmoth snorted. "Careful there, Pinch, you know what they say about people who live in glass houses."

"I lived in Mississippi until my daddy died when I was eleven," Pinchback retorted, "so that makes me a bit more Southern than you, born and raised in Illinois as I recall. That's just about as far north as Maine." When Pinchback's white father had died, his mother had taken him and his brother and three sisters and fled to Ohio, afraid that the man's wife would now take the opportunity to re-enslave them. "And besides, I began working on steamboats going back and forth to N'Orleans from Cincinnati. Hell, I practically grew up here."

"I didn't come here to take advantage of anybody, and I ain't no carpetbagger," Emmett protested emphatically. He detested being identified as such—just another slick Northerner who had packed his sparse belongings in a small bag and come south to get rich in the aftermath of the Civil War.

Warmoth laughed again. "I believe that that just may be true, Emmett Collins, and if it is, you are indeed a rare breed in a land where corruption is the fashion."

"An honest and moral man." Pinchback nodded. "Not too many of them around these here parts."

"You're an honorable man, Pinch," Emmett said.

Now it was Pinchback's turn to laugh, a dry chuckle that never quite reached his eyes. "When I was your age, I was cheating men at cards every chance I got, taking all they had on the riverboats. And I have scars all over my body that were given to me by men who dispute that statement."

"And now you're one of the most influential politicians in all of Louisiana."

"Politics is a lot like gambling," Pinchback replied, shrugging. "You bet when you hold the cards, bluff when you have to, and cheat when you can get away with it."

"I would trust you with my life," Emmett said quietly. "But maybe not cards." All three of them laughed.

"As you both know, I'm an admirer of the Prussian statesman, Otto von Bismarck, who espoused that blood and iron is necessary to resolve the greatest issues of unification, or in this case, ending the system of enslavement, but this is followed by diplomacy," Pinchback said.

Emmett took a slug of the whiskey in his glass, enjoying the biting liquid even if it wasn't as smooth and pleasant as the scotch that Campbell MacLeod shared with him during their weekly get-togethers.

"Men born and raised here might be able to accept the end of slavery, and they might even be okay with some of us Black folks establishing our families and businesses." Pinchback lived in a fairly elegant two-story house on Derbigny Street, a bit less than a mile straight out of town on Canal Street from where they were now. "But they are most certainly not going to accept coloreds as social equals in school or church or—God forbid!—the courthouse or voting booth, and that is *exactly* what our constitution has gone and done."

"But it will allow the fine state of Louisiana to be readmitted into the Union." Warmoth raised his glass. "A toast to statehood." The three men drank. "And a toast to ol' Pinch here for turning down the nomination of governor."

"If I wanted to get strung up from the nearest cottonwood, I might as well run for President of the United States," Pinchback replied, raising his glass. "As it was, I was down by Lafayette Square earlier today on some business, and that fellow Ogden and a bunch of his cronies were eyeballing me like they wanted to eat me for lunch."

"That one is a true bastard," Warmoth agreed.

Emmett thought the man had seemed nice enough the few times he'd met him, but knew as well that what looked like calm water often hid turbulent currents below. "Why do you say that?"

Warmoth and Pinchback exchanged glances, before Pinchback took the reins. "Henry and I both fought down here in the deep South while you were whiling your time away up in Virginia," he said, and then paused to throw back some whiskey, his brow furrowed as he formed his thoughts. "It was in the last year of the war that Ogden formed a cavalry unit that roamed the countryside in a guerrilla fashion. They'd occasionally raid the Union Army, but mostly they spent their time killing any Black people they came across. He was riding with General Nathan Forrest then. And when they were defeated at Selma in April of 1865, a group of them escaped and made a run back this way."

"No one ever proved it was them," Warmoth cautioned.

"But I know damn well it was," Pinchback replied. "I'd spent the last year of the war up North, but in '65 was back in Selma, and then came across to N'Orleans following the same path that Ogden and his men did. The locals knew who did it, alright, even if it was never proven."

"What?" Emmett asked. "What was never proved?"

"About fifty miles southwest of Selma, in the direction they fled, Union troops pursuing them found about forty Black men, women, and children swinging from nooses in a copse of cottonwoods. Every branch that would hold a body had been used. They must have put some thought into it, because the larger limbs were used for the men, and the smaller were used for the children. There was one little boy no more than two years old."

"They'd been living there, foraging off the land, had some crops planted," Warmoth interjected. "Looked like they'd been there for a couple of years, off in the middle of nowhere, just trying their best to not be noticed and to survive until the war was over."

"And I damn well know that the man helming the Crescent City Democratic Club either ordered, or at the very least, had a hand in stringing them up," Pinchback said.

Emmett had seen his share of atrocities during the war; even lynching's and the hanging of deserters, but the image of forty bodies swinging in the breeze made him shake his head, trying to erase the grim picture his mind had conjured. "I guess it's up to the two of you to make sure he doesn't gain too much political power," he finally said into the silence, rising to his feet and finishing his glass all in one fluid motion. "Gentlemen, I must leave as I have a dinner date."

"Ahh, the exquisite Susannah de Villiers." Warmoth was able to admit to himself that he was quite jealous of Emmett for his relationship with this charming and gorgeous woman. "Make sure you tell her that I pine for her."

"I've already been sure to fill her in on your philandering ways, so don't bother drooling in her direction," Emmett replied half in truth and half in jest.

"It has come to my attention that many women actually like men who don't try to hide behind a wall of false propriety." Warmoth grinned wolfishly.

"Hmmm." Emmett looked fleetingly into Warmoth's eyes, wondering if the man knew something about Susannah's past. Then he grinned. "Perhaps that's why I've also told her," he added, "that you're suffering from the great pox." With that, Emmett bid farewell to these two men he'd come to call his close friends over the past year.

As Emmett walked, he thought of the past twenty months in which Susannah had come back into his orbit, radiating an aura of comfort and desire tangled into one delightfully messy ball of yarn. His mind and body had been consumed with her since he'd escorted her to her lavish mansion after MacLeod's fundraiser. Her smell, the touch of her arm against his, and the crinkle in her eyes had obsessed his waking moments, while his dreams had led him back to the glorious week spent in her company several summers ago, and with shameless pleasure, his sleeping mind would recreate their bedroom escapades. He'd wake embarrassed at the sticky goo coating his private parts, or worse, the throbbing that he'd have to attend to before rising from his bed.

Emmett was brought back to the present by the shouted warning of a teamster rushing his wagon down Conti Street. He stepped back from the crossing before continuing on to his dinner with Susannah. They were meeting at Antoine's Restaurant, recently moved to its new location on St. Louis Street. He'd no sooner arrived when the fancy calèche owned by the woman he loved arrived as well. He beat the Black manservant to her door, his breath catching in his throat as it always did when he saw this ravishing woman of his dreams. He took her gloved hand to help her step down, his skin flushing at the contact.

Their relationship had developed in an unconventional fashion, Emmett reflected not for the first time, having started with a week of blissful sexual adventures some four years earlier, before she disappeared, running off to marry a rich man who had subsequently left her a widow. Since rediscovering her at the dinner event hosted by Campbell MacLeod less than two years earlier, Emmett had courted her properly, wondering all the while at the social etiquette of keeping company with a widow. Thus, he was immediately aware that her green dress had no markings of black, the first time as far as he knew, that she had thrown off the color of mourning. Perhaps, soon, he would have the opportunity to once again enjoy the pleasures of the flesh with her that he had years earlier.

"You are enchanting as always, my dear." Emmett fumbled over the words, wanting to flatter but not offend, be familiar but not too, and, as usual, feeling utterly his lack of mental faculties to accomplish either task.

"Thank you, Mr. Collins." Susannah fluttered a fan in front of her face, flirtatiously, as it was a cool March evening. "You cut a fine figure yourself." Which was not quite the truth, she admitted inwardly, for he was as rumpled and tousled as ever, his tie askew under the scrunched waistcoat, his jacket unbuttoned and flapped open, and his red hair jutting out in various angles from underneath his bowler.

The host saw them to a table, fawning over Susannah, obviously knowing of her stature and wealth, while casting surreptitious glances at Emmett. "I will have your server over promptly," he promised, backing from the table carefully. "Can the house send you some chilled Vouvray?"

"That would be kind." Susannah drawled, nodding in agreement. After he had left, she turned to Emmett. "*Ahh* heard that your convention has adopted the new constitution for Louisiana," Susannah said demurely. "So *ahh* guess that congratulations are in order." She took the glass of wine from the proffered hand of the waiter, who'd appeared magically at her side as she spoke. Tipping the contents toward Emmett, she took a tiny sip.

Emmett accepted a delicate, thin-stemmed glass, raised it slightly, nodded, and took a longer pull on the fruity white wine. "Well, it certainly wasn't my convention, but it is a glorious document," he replied absently, once the waiter had moved away. He was busy speculating whether an appropriate length of time had passed to ask

Susannah to marry him, for he felt that was the next stage. How he looked forward to again tasting the nectar of her flesh.

"Does it have the provisions for social equality of the darkies that you worked so hard to have included?" she probed with keen eyes.

Emmett winced at her use of the word 'darkies,' but rationalized that her childhood in the South and current position as plantation owner influenced her speech. "It's quite clearly spelled out that people shouldn't be discriminated against in any way due to their race."

"That's wonderful," she said faintly, scanning the entrée choices.

The menu, in French, presented an embarrassing and awkward situation for Emmett, but Susannah gracefully ordered for both of them, the waiter's eyes reflecting disdain for the peasant-like Emmett Collins. He doubted she knew French, but must have eaten here enough times to know what to order. The delicious *bisque d'ecrevisse à la cardinale* more than erased any snub, as the thick crayfish soup—at once rich, velvety, and delicate—delighting his taste buds would've expunged far greater humiliation. By the time he got to the *oyster bordelaise*, he'd quite gotten over his sense of inadequacy.

It was only when he had sopped up the last of the oyster's tasty sauce that Emmett was able to converse in anything but the most basic of replies. Susannah, he noticed, had also cleaned her plate, her appetite belying her slim waist and fine figure. "You went to the National last night to see that young girl play the piano, didn't you?" he asked. "What was her name? Philly or some such thing?"

Susannah laughed at him, a bubbly giggle she'd contained until then as he had attacked the food placed before him. "Senorita Josefina Filomeno was enticing on the piano, but it was her violin performance that was truly exquisite. *Ahh* had tears running down my cheeks. She has such musical taste and delicate expression that her violin virtually sings."

"What sort of name is that, anyways? Filomeno?"

"Chilean. Quite a prodigy, really, at fifteen years of age."

Emmett had heard some local Cajuns playing violins, and vastly enjoyed the wild music that spewed forth from them, but he was fairly certain that he would've fallen asleep after just a few minutes of listening to some girl from Chile playing with 'delicate expression.'

He nodded and continued to feign interest. "What pieces did she play?"

"Oh, she started off with Thalberg's 'Grande Fantaisie de Moise,' and then moved on to Gottschalk's 'Concert de Weber,' and then Liszt's..." Either she'd memorized the program or had been rigorously working at learning her classical music.

Emmett briefly caught the name of Gottschalk, the man he'd seen playing the piano at MacLeod's dinner party, but then the foreign names and titles blurred as more carnal thoughts invaded his mind. If he married Susannah, he'd for the second time experience the wonders of her flesh, a thought his mind returned to, and not just in his dreams. Three times since arriving in New Orleans he'd been tempted into the brothels that crisscrossed the city in a thick patchwork design, but had never felt the pleasure he'd hoped for. The experiences had alleviated stress, even brought him comfort and enjoyment, but lacked some essential ingredient. And he was fairly certain that that missing something could be found in the woman sitting across from him right now. In the back of his mind, he did wonder from time to time about the ease with which she'd picked up a Southern accent, and the comfort she felt in a fancy French restaurant. And the Susannah he remembered from so long ago, had she ever back then showed enmity towards the colored? Or had the war and its tumultuous events blurred his memories, leaving only the happy times, the awakening of his teenage body to the delights of the bedroom. Who was the real Susannah Shaw de Villiers?

An oyster hit him in the face, and Emmett was jolted out of his reverie, his face flushing at his fantasies, but was pleasantly surprised to look up into the mischievous face of the Susannah he'd known years earlier. "Sorry."

"An oyster for your thoughts?" Susannah giggled, as Emmett carefully retrieved the fried morsel from his lap, and placed it on his previously empty plate.

"I was thinking about you," he replied honestly.

"Good thoughts *ahh* hope?" she asked with a coquettish aura.

"You, Mrs. de Villiers, are most certainly a huckleberry above a persimmon."

"*Ahh* will trust that is a good thing." She set her folded napkin back upon the table and stood. "*Ahh* was suggesting that we should be going if we want to walk to the theater."

"If it's not too chilly for you, I'd be willing." Emmett flinched inwardly as Susannah signed the bill, putting it on her monthly account, something he would never be able to afford to do on his salary.

"Fresh air sounds splendid. Soon it will be too oppressive to go outside at all."

Susannah instructed the carriage to pick them up later at the St. Charles Theater, Emmett offered his arm, and they strolled down St. Louis and took a right on Royal Street. They meandered along looking in the windows of the expensive shops that lined this street, each lost within their own thoughts, the flickering oil lamps casting shadows this way and that.

"They want to take it all away from me," Susannah burst out. She'd stopped to eye an ornate mirror and stood with her back to Emmett.

"Who wants to take what from you?" he asked.

Susannah began to cry, and Emmett wrapped his arms around her, the loose embrace sending tingles throughout his body even as he tried to deaden that reaction. They stood that way for a minute, and, as her sobs began to lessen, they were roughly bumped from behind. Emmett stumbled and Susannah was smashed against the window, cracking the glass in a long sliver.

"Sorry about that, mate." A Black man teetered behind them, his voice slurred with alcohol. From the looks of him, he'd come in on one of the ocean-going ships harbored in Lake Pontchartrain that delivered its goods and seamen via the train, Smoky Mary, to New Orleans. The sailors, he knew, generally squandered their pay packet on various vices as quickly as possible before heading back out to their next port. "I didn't mean to shove into ya and your hussy."

Susannah stepped at him and slapped him hard across the face. "You shut your darkie mouth."

Two other sailors kept him from falling as he tottered backwards, his legs made unsteady by booze and by solid ground. "I meant no dis-re-spect, ma'am. I jus' seen the two of yas tied up together like that and figured ya for a strumpet."

"Are you going to let him disrespect me like that?" Susannah turned on Emmett with blazing eyes. "Do something."

Before Emmett could react, a group of men appeared out of nowhere sweeping in like a rainsquall and lit into the Black shipmates. The sailors were a hardy lot even in their inebriated state, but they were no match for the nine or ten men that jumped them. In a matter of seconds, they were pinned facedown.

Campbell MacLeod stood next to Emmett, the wide grin of the victor on his face. "Why don't *ye* take those darkies down to the police station and let them sleep off their *rat-arsed* behavior," he ordered the men in the street. He turned to Susannah with concern in his voice, asking, "Are *ye* hurt, Mrs. de Villiers?"

"*Ahh* have never been more offended in my life," she spat out, her tiny nose quivering in rage. "But *ahhm* not injured."

"I'm sorry that *ye* were exposed to such cheeky behavior, but the streets of New Orleans are filled with such trash. The time is coming to clean the filth and restore our wonderful city to its previous grandeur."

"*Ahhm* much obliged that you came along." The fan was back in her hand, fluttering her ire away.

Emmett was aware for the first time that he'd done nothing but stand there while her honor was insulted. "I was just about to handle it," he offered somewhat lamely, "but thanks for the help. Where'd you come from?"

MacLeod waved his hand dismissively. "We were just coming from a meeting around the corner and saw the whole thing. To tell you the truth, the boys had them down before I even knew it was *ye*."

"*Ahh* hope they educate them on the proper way to treat a lady before taking them to the station," Susannah said.

"They didn't intend to offend, Susannah. Sometimes drink interferes with common sense." Emmett felt himself in the role of defender, but the seaman had tried to apologize after all, hadn't he?

This produced an awkward silence, finally broken by MacLeod asking, "Where is it that *ye* two are coming from or going to?"

"We just had dinner at Antoine's," Susannah said.

"And are on our way to the St. Charles Theater for Hamlet," Emmett added.

"Ah, a mighty fine production." MacLeod nodded his head with lips pursed. "To be or not to be, that is what *ye* must decide, Emmett Collins."

"Sorry?" Emmett asked after a pause.

"Not to worry," MacLeod said mysteriously. "Perhaps we can discuss it and a few other matters over a drink later? Stop by once *ye* see Mrs. de Villiers home."

The St. Charles Theater was wedged between a music hall and a saloon, the large block letters on the building proclaiming its place. Slender columns rose to a veranda on the second floor. The imposing structure, while not as impressive as the original theater, which had burned to the ground some twenty-five years earlier, was magnificent nonetheless.

The play was equally grand, spellbinding to Emmett, for the rich language of Shakespeare's words flowing over him like balm took him back to times with Chamberlain, who had insisted the Bard be a pillar of his education.

When Hamlet struggled with the question, 'to be or not to be,' Emmett realized what MacLeod had been referring to, and it was right on the mark. But the line that truly resonated in Emmett's heart was when Polonius was sharing his wisdom with his son before the young man left for Paris, telling him, 'This above all: to *thine* own self be true, and it must follow, as the night the day, thou canst not then be false to any man.' Emmett found himself studying Susannah's face as she watched raptly, with these two important thoughts swirling in his head.

Susannah insisted on her coach dropping Emmett off at MacLeod's mansion on Magazine Street after they had left the theater. Silence fell over them for the short ride, the earlier incident heavy in the air between them, or perhaps it was just that they were both in a state of reflection, pondering the substance of the Shakespeare production. Either way, Emmett was happy to escape the confines of the calèche, bidding Susannah farewell with a chaste peck on the cheek. He climbed the crescent staircase, raising the doorknocker of fine silver with a sun in resplendent grandiosity, with words that Emmett discerned to be Latin, but did not understand. The door opened while he was still studying the ornate detail.

"Master MacLeod is expecting you. This way please." A butler gestured for him to follow.

Emmett was escorted to the majestic study, somehow finding a smooth scotch in his hand, biding his time by examining the titles of the walls of books that rose from floor to ceiling. He didn't have to wait long, as MacLeod appeared through a side door.

"Did *ye* enjoy Hamlet?"

"The... words... were hard to understand," Emmett admitted with a shrug of his shoulders. "But what I got was pretty darn good."

"A sad story of how fighting within a family can ruin a kingdom."

"The desire for power can be overwhelming for some people," Emmett concurred, his thoughts turning to the Great War that had been fought so recently, and the battle for integrating the freedmen into society that still raged.

"It is hard to rule through murder and force," MacLeod said gravely.

Emmett had an inkling that this conversation was about more than just Hamlet. "I suppose that everybody must do what they feel is just."

"To be or not to be. But enough of such talk. How is the *bonnie* Mrs. de Villiers after the unfortunate incident earlier?"

"Only her pride was hurt, but she's a tough woman. I'm sure she'll be fine." Emmett's mind couldn't but help return to the knowledge that she'd been a prostitute, years earlier, and that her gentility had been far greater violated than the loose terms spoken from a drunken Black man.

"She sure is something," MacLeod agreed.

"Can I ask," Emmett said, turning the subject away from Susannah, "what the Latin inscription on your doorknocker means?"

"*I birn quil I se.* I burn but am not consumed. It is the motto of Clan MacLeod, who ruled the Western Islands of Scotland for many generations, but much like Hamlet, whose downfall came from family infighting."

"That seems to be a common problem. Let's hope that North and South will be able to repair their difficulties, as well as black and white."

"Sometimes every family needs some time apart before they can see their way to mending differences."

"What did you want to see me about?" It was getting quite late, and Emmett did not much feel like playing the hidden meaning game. A certain segment of the New Orleans population stayed up to all hours of the night, but he suspected they did not rise with the dawn as he did.

"Please, have a seat." MacLeod gestured to a pair of walnut chairs, an intricate flower pattern stitched onto the padded seat. "Well, as *ye* know, I'm opposed to the liberal nature of the constitution that was adopted earlier today. I fear that it will lead to unrest amongst the whites and the darkies, but I'm willing to concede that nothing can be done about that now." MacLeod set his drink on the small circular table between the two chairs. "But let us move forward. Elections will be next month. I wanted to let *ye* know that I plan on supporting Henry Clay Warmoth for Governor." He knew that Emmett had become quite close with this carpetbagger from Illinois.

"I'm sure Henry will be glad to have your support," Emmett replied carefully, having learned over the past year the intricacies of politics.

"I was wondering if *ye* had ever thought of running for local office?"

"Me?" Emmett asked with surprise.

"*Ye* have become a respected man in New Orleans," MacLeod replied. "It would be good to have a man I can trust in the Congress. Of course, *ye* don't need to give an answer right now, but think it over. If *ye* decide to give it a go, I would back *ye*."

Emmett sat stunned for a few moments. The thought of being a politician had never crossed his mind, even though he rubbed elbows regularly with some of the most powerful men in New Orleans. "There is another man running for state senate from the Second Ward who might merit your support as well. Pinckney Pinchback proved himself very astute during the convention."

"The darkie from Ohio?" MacLeod cut him off before he could say more. "I heard he made all his money cheating men at the gaming tables. I can't support somebody like that. Now, I.E. Jewell comes from a fine New Orleans family and will be a much better senator, I do believe."

After Emmett left, MacLeod absently swirled the brown liquor in his glass as he mulled over the importance of the young New Englander. He liked the boy, seeing a bit of himself at that age, full of ideals and ready to take on the world. It would be a shame to lose him. With that thought, he finished the scotch and went to the door. He thought he might send his driver on an errand.

"Who goes there?" A voice rang out, the sentry's body concealed by the thicket and the dark night sky.

"A son of your race," the man replied, pulling his gelding up.

"What does he wish?"

"Peace, order, and the observance of the laws of God."

"And how will this be achieved?"

"The cause of our race must be triumphant. We must be united as are the flowers that grow on the same stem." The man had been brought into the Knights of the White Camellia earlier this year by its founder, Alcibiades DeBlanc, and had since started a council in New Orleans.

"You may pass. They're waiting for you at the hanging tree."

A fire had been started, illuminating the macabre scene in the small glen surrounding the twisted tree, gnarled branches reaching in every direction. One branch stretched forth about twenty feet above and parallel to the ground before descending to earth. Underneath this sat three horses, and astride each horse was a Black sailor with a rope around his neck. About a hundred men in robes stood in a semi-circle in front of them, some with masks, while others had not bothered. The moonlight glinted off the white robes like white caps on the ocean on a windy day.

"You darkies have been accused of assaulting a lady of New Orleans, and then showering her with insults and profanity." The second-in-command of the Knights of the White Camellia who stood facing the three men proclaimed.

"I didn't do nothin'," one sailor spoke up. As his hands were tied behind his back, he jerked his head sideways to indicate the man to his left, the heavy noose restricting his motion. "It was him that did the offendin'."

"You're right. Billy, why don't you give his mount a little start." A man stepped behind and slapped the middle horse, and the sailor who'd called Susannah de Villiers a strumpet was dangling in the air.

It wasn't enough of a drop to break his neck, so the death was slow. He tried to reach the ground with legs too short for the task, kicking and contorting his body in a mighty, but doomed, effort. He tried to yell, to scream, to curse, but by this time the rope had tightened too firmly around his throat, and only wet, gurgling noises escaped. The pressure caused blood vessels to begin bursting in his face, red blotches erupting across his black skin. It took about six minutes before the last twitches subsided. Throughout, the Knights of the White Camellia remained silent and impassive.

"You gonna' let us go?" the sailor on the right asked.

"We've been tasked with cleaning the filth from the streets of the South," the second-in-command spoke loudly for all to hear. "It is our duty to ensure that the superiority of the Caucasian race remains pure, like the snow-white camellia flower. It's not our intention to resort to violence, but we must do what is necessary. We must defend against the miscegenation of the two races, and the ensuing amalgamation, and the production of a degenerate and bastard offspring that will soon fill our streets with a degraded and ignoble population. We must stand up for the purity of white blood."

"We was just walkin' down the street," the sailor on the left said, tears streaming down his face.

"That might be true, but you darkies have seen my face now." He nodded at Billy, who slapped first one, and then the other horse on the rump, sending them careening into the woods to be rounded up later, while the two Black sailors who had gotten drunk in the wrong city danced grotesquely at the end of their ropes.

CHAPTER 6

APRIL 24, 1868

Susannah de Villiers stood naked in front of the mirror at her lake cottage. She'd just taken a bath, and was now examining her body. Her legs rose from the floor much like the white-faced ibis she'd seen in the bayou yesterday, toothpicks emerging from the water to support the body, a trait that men seemed to find attractive, or so she'd been told countless times in Mary Hall's brothel in Washington, D.C. Her knees were a bit knobby, more wrinkled than she cared for, but that was a minor flaw easy to overlook. With a critical eye, Susannah turned sideways and viewed her thin rear-end and stomach, running her hands up her sides to cup one breast in each palm. *Have they begun to sag?* She wondered.

At twenty-four years old and twice widowed, with a stint as a reluctant prostitute in between husbands, perhaps life rather than age was the reason for the slight pendent nature of her bosom. Her neck swooped long and elegantly up to a pretty face, even if it was slightly too narrow. A thin upturned-nose was set between defined cheeks, which encased full lips that were her pride and joy. Blonde ringlets cascaded down her forehead and covered her ears, one of the few times of the day that it wasn't pulled demurely back, even though it had the habit of escaping here and there from the confines of austerity.

Although caviling of a thousand tiny perceived flaws, Susannah still saw no reason why Emmett hadn't proposed to her yet. She knew she was beautiful. Men had told her that all her life, and while she'd taken to coyly dismissing such compliments, innately she knew that it was true. Perhaps the reason Emmett was dragging his feet in asking for her hand was his knowledge of her past? Was it because she'd been a whore? Emmett had loved her when she was a poor prostitute in Washington, D.C., so it would certainly seem that her past was not the reason for his reticence. She had put off what minor amorous advances he'd made, hoping this would spur him into proposing. But as of yet, he'd made no such overture.

If she were to lose her inheritance, she'd need to find a husband, and quickly. She would never return to prostitution, and really, how else could a single woman in New Orleans survive? In the throes of his lust for the younger Susannah, Francois had written a will leaving her the majority of his assets. This bequeathal had been challenged by his two daughters' lawyers and was set to be adjudicated shortly. Her own attorneys had promised that the suit held no merit, but there was hollowness to their voices, and emptiness in their eyes belying another truth, this as they collected their hefty fees. Common gossip had it that the judge, scion of an old New Orleans family, was seemingly predisposed to rule against this interloper from away. She was hoping that Campbell MacLeod might put in a good word with the man, as they traveled in many of the same circles. Today, however, would not be a good day to make this request, for it was the funeral of the poor man's wife that she was preparing to attend.

Emmett arrived two hours later in a rented hansom cab. The two-wheeled cabriolet was a rakish carriage in which the driver sat behind the enclosed coach and drove the two-horse team from there. Emmett had met the driver attending one of the adult education programs he'd set up in the city and offered him $2 for a half-day of work. Freedom America—for this was the driver's colorful moniker—had readily taken this offer, as it was as much as a full day laboring on the docks as a stevedore.

As soon as they were settled into the bench seat of the cab, Susannah turned to Emmett and surveyed him from head to toe. "You look rather dashing today." She stepped in and rubbed his arm, turning her face up for a kiss. Emmett was dressed in a black mourning suit with a top hat, items, which he admitted, were borrowed from his landlord.

"Thank you." Emmett tipped his hat, as he stepped back uncomfortably. "You are a vision of loveliness."

"*Ahh* wanted to apologize to you." It had been six weeks since she had seen Emmett, their dinner date and attendance at Hamlet interrupted by the drunken men. She'd left the city to avoid ostracism from Francois' children and friends, while Emmett had been quite busy with the recent elections. "*Ahhm* afraid that *ahh* behaved poorly when those Black sailors insulted me."

"There is no apology needed. If anything, I apologize for not being quicker in defending your honor." He shifted his feet awkwardly, not looking at her. He had intended to ask her what she had meant by "losing everything" right before the unhappy incident, but now did not seem to be the time.

"*Ahh* did not mean to yell at you." Susannah simpered. "Perhaps we could spend more time together outside of attending a funeral?"

"I'd like that. Will you be in the city?"

"Yes. Life in the country is unspeakably boring. *Ahhm* about to dry up and blow away if *ahh* stay away another day."

"That'd be a true shame, Mrs. de Villiers," Emmett said with mock horror.

"Maybe we could spend some time in private," she said, her eyes wide and her lips parted ever so slightly.

He blushed, his thoughts a confusing mix of carnal memories, and those same lips drawn back tight and hard as she had snarled at the sailor to "shut his darkie mouth."

It was unlikely that Emmett would ask for her hand today, at a funeral, Susannah thought with a smile, but soon, very soon, they would be wed.

Governor-elect Henry Clay Warmoth cracked his knuckles overhead with a sigh of pleasure. From his office, he could see the Mississippi River as it trundled slowly past his adopted home of New Orleans. Not even Warmoth himself had dreamed that he'd amass such wealth within a few years of resigning from the army, but the connections he'd made serving as the Provost Judge during military occupation had rewarded him tremendously. He'd represented the interests of cotton producers and traders and been paid handsomely for his services, but the insider information he'd become privy to had led to his own fabulously successful investments. And now he was to be Governor of the state. He picked up the newspaper again, its bold headline proclaiming his impressive victory.

New Orleans Daily Bourbon

====================================

The Bourbon is Published Daily (Sunday Excepted) By P.O. Rivard
Terms: Daily $16, Weekly $5; Per Year

====================================

Friday Morning April 24, 1868

====================================

Official Journal of the State of Louisiana

Henry Clay Warmoth Elected Governor!

Election Results—
The officials selected by Gen. Sheridan have confirmed that Henry Clay Warmoth will be the 23rd Governor of our fair state of Louisiana. The Pure Radical ticket headed by the honorable Judge, James G. Taliaferro, and Major Dumas, received 38,046 votes while Warmoth and Major Francis E. Dumas collected 64,941. The Conservative Democrats boycotted the election due to the disenfranchisement of so many ex-Confederate Soldiers, leaving this race between the Radical Republicans, and their offshoot, the Pure Radicals.

Warmoth put the paper down on his desk, his gaze retuning once more to the wide river flowing slowly past. New Orleans was a fantastic place to be young, single, and wealthy. Warmoth certainly relished his lifestyle, but his aspirations wouldn't allow him to rest upon his laurels. The logical next step for an ambitious young man of twenty-five was power, and now he was to be the chief executive of the state of Louisiana. Many of his peers growing up in Fairfield, Illinois, had snickered at and mocked him as he dragged his nose through his father's legal books, but who was laughing now?

He might be a carpetbagger, as the Southern whites liked to label those from the North, but he had a firmer sense of the pulse of New Orleans than any fifth generation native. With the temporary ban of so many white leaders in the area from participation in politics, and the emergence of suffrage for the freedmen, Warmoth had realized that the door was open for a person from away to wrest power from the traditional elite structure.

Warmoth had certainly pulled in the freedmen's ballots, but he had also understood early on that a broader coalition was necessary if he and his party were to maintain any political longevity. To this end, he had courted the ex-Confederates, the Creole elites, and the white men of power like Campbell MacLeod and his ilk. It'd been a gift from heaven when MacLeod had thrown his support behind Warmoth, for the clout he carried seemed to range into every organization of any note in the state.

With this thought, he checked his pocket watch and realized that he should be going, as he was a pallbearer for MacLeod's wife's funeral. What was her name? Izora? He knew that he'd be castigated in the newspapers, especially by Roudanez, the Black editor of the *Tribune*, but it was too late to matter, for the election was confirmed. Those thousands of freedmen votes that he'd garnered would perhaps second-guess their choice at the ballot box when they heard that Warmoth was thick as thieves with the plantation elites represented by Campbell MacLeod.

The service at the St. Louis Cathedral was a ritual Catholic affair, lengthy and full of pomp, and Warmoth found his mind wandering back to the massacre at the Mechanic's Institute. He'd been present at the convention, but had had the presence of mind to appreciate the boiling cauldron outside, and had slipped out a door just minutes before the killing had begun. From the balcony of a friend's apartment he'd watched the violence unfold. He wasn't proud of running and hiding, but he was a survivor, not a martyr. Now, less than two years later, he was soon to be the most powerful man in the state.

As a young, handsome bachelor with money, Warmoth had made quite a stir with the ladies of New Orleans. Now, as a man of utmost influence, he could only imagine the successes he'd find with the fairer sex. He pursued women with the same sly craftiness that he applied to business and politics, but was not above frequenting brothels to fill in the time between conquests. Women were a treasure to be coveted certainly, but he'd yet to find one worth keeping.

After what seemed to be hours, the congregation spilled out for the procession to the St. Louis Cemetery. Eight men in kilts playing the bagpipes led, followed by the clergymen in their sacerdotal robes, and then the long black hearse with the pall bearers on either side. Warmoth was at the rear of the coffin, keeping the slow pace, as the entire cortege shuffled forward. Those come to pay their respects followed along behind, overflowing the street like a flash flood cresting the levees of the Mississippi.

The day was hot for a man not born in the South, even if it was only April, and Warmoth was sweating freely by the time the funeral procession reached the cemetery. As a problem solver himself, he was fascinated with the ingenuity of the burial process in New Orleans. Because of the high-water table here, the original settlers had experienced the unfortunate phenomenon of coffins buried traditionally—underground—rising up and floating away during heavy rains, which were common. Necessity had required the church to grant permission to have above ground crypts, but these took up valuable space in a flourishing and ever-expanding city. The city dwellers were nothing if not inventive, however, and they had come up with an even more innovative way to entomb the dead.

Earlier that morning, the sexton had opened the tomb, a rectangular box rising ten feet into the air with a stone cross on top. This allowed room for three caskets, one on top of the other in three separate cubicles, but as MacLeod's brother and two young children already rested in this tomb, room had had to be made. The sexton had chiseled away the bricks to the top slot, and then swept the sediment of bones and flesh that was once Alistair MacLeod into the opening at the back of the crypt. Somebody with scientific know-how had determined that bodies interred within these brick ovens would completely decompose within a year. Thus, it was decided, the final resting place could be reused a year and a day after the previous occupant, the one-day added, as it was bad luck to have a burial on the anniversary of another.

As soon as Izora MacLeod's coffin was ushered gently into the slot so recently occupied by her brother-in-law, Warmoth began moving towards where Emmett Collins stood with the alluring Susannah de Villiers. He picked his way through a crowd of the most elite men in all of New Orleans, and, from the deference of the muted greetings, was well aware of the prestige MacLeod had bestowed on him in asking for his presence as pallbearer.

"Emmett," Warmoth greeted his friend absently, as his attention was focused elsewhere. "And good afternoon, Mrs. de Villiers."

"Mr. Warmoth." She gave just the slightest curtsy in deference to the solemn occasion. The descending sun was beginning to scatter shadows from the variously shaped crypts across the crowded cemetery, the day slightly cooler already.

"Your radiance casts any gloom from this sad day," Warmoth said, as he brushed his thick mustache on her hand.

Susannah blushed, or appeared to, and pulled her hand back. "Governor," she said tartly, as if in shock at his actions.

"Congratulations on your confirmation, Governor," Emmett said.

Warmoth turned his charisma on Emmett. "I couldn't have done it without you, so, thank you."

"It seems that you and Campbell have become quite tight. Only a month ago I arranged a meeting between the two of you, and today you are one of six carrying the coffin of his wife."

Warmoth studied Emmett's face to see what guile the statement might hide, but was reassured that the young man had spoken his mind without any chicanery, and that his words were merely a compliment. It was for this reason that Warmoth so desired to foster this relationship, for a man without an ulterior motive was an individual to cherish certainly, perhaps even to trust. "I barely knew the woman, but it's certainly a terrible shame," he commented after a moment.

It'd been about six years earlier that Emmett had watched his own mother lowered into the ground. In between these two funerals, he'd seen a great deal of death, but had somehow avoided any formal services other than the mass burials on the battlefield.

"I wanted to speak with you about your future in New Orleans." Warmoth wiped his brow with a handkerchief. "I understand that the Freedman Bureau will be mostly dissolved by the end of the year."

"That is the talk," Emmett concurred. "General Grant is going to turn the problem of the freedmen over to Louisiana now that it has reentered statehood."

"That's a shame. My guess is a few more years, and you'd start to see some real progress, but I well know how hard it is to overcome politics and money."

"That's for sure." Emmett replied. "Too much of one and too little of another."

"Where does that leave you?" Warmoth asked.

Emmett twisted the borrowed top hat in his hands. It was his thought that, by the end of the year, he'd be married to Susannah and thus a plantation owner. The only problem was, he had no knowledge of cotton or business, and he suspected, no desire to participate in either. And of course, there was the suggestion from MacLeod that he enter politics. "I imagine something will come up," he said lamely. Of course, there was that little voice in his head whispering that he wasn't sure he wanted to marry Susannah at all.

"Cicero said that there was no shame in being ignorant of what one did not know," Warmoth said carefully. "However, there is a way I might help you—and you might help me. One of my first priorities as governor will be to push for the creation of a Metropolitan Police force, consisting of Orleans, Jefferson, and St. Bernard parishes. It'll be a modern force, the likes not yet seen in our country. I could use good men that I trust."

"I appreciate the offer," Emmett replied after a thoughtful pause, raising a palm against the sun's glare to look the man in the eyes. "I'll consider it when the time comes."

"I thought that you'd make a fine captain in the cavalry division, what with your experience during the war and your love of horses."

This certainly seemed to be more in line with his own interests, Emmett thought, but would one forego being a plantation owner or a senator to be a policeman? Emmett was glad to have the conversation interrupted by the approach of Campbell MacLeod and Frederick Nash Ogden.

Colonel Frederick Nash Ogden ran his fingers through his bristly red hair that fell in waves down his neck to his shoulders. He'd never seen much call to comb it, and didn't believe that attending a funeral would be the proper time to start. His head was thick, like a block of wood upon a burly body that smoldered with a simmering energy.

His father had moved to New Orleans right after he was born, and then had died when Freddie had been but a lad of three. He had been taken in by one of his uncles, of whom there were three, all successful Louisiana lawyers. Freddie didn't seem to have a calling for further education, responsibility, or much care for anything. When shots were fired at Fort Sumter and the War of Northern Aggression broke out, twenty-six-year-old Frederick quit his cotton clerk job and enlisted.

It was on the battlefields that he found his true calling. He was good at killing and leading men into combat. Unfortunately, the Confederate Army was outmatched in numbers, weapons, and supplies. He'd spent the last year of the war leading a cavalry regiment called the Partisan Rangers in raiding parties in the South. These guerrilla raiders focused on disrupting commerce of the Northern occupation and skirmishing with Union regiments, as well as punishing the uppity Blacks who didn't appear to know their proper place anymore.

I wasn't cut out to be a lawyer like my uncles and cousins, Ogden thought as he twisted his uncomfortable bow tie, and though the Confederacy was outgunned by the damn Yankees, he thought further, the battle for New Orleans is not one that I will squander. I'm done losing.

As far as he was concerned, the War of Northern Aggression had merely entered another stage, the final battle, and he meant to salvage

Southern autonomy if it killed him. He stroked the fashionable beard that hung below his mouth—thin by his lip and growing wider where it hung from his chin in a style called a beaver tail.

Ogden had recently been elected president of the Crescent City Democratic Club, and more clandestinely, joined the Knights of the White Camellia. If there was anything worse than Sambos thinking they were the social equals of whites, it was loud-mouthed northern carpetbaggers coming into his home and telling him how to run his state.

At the conclusion of the entombment, Ogden made his way over to Campbell MacLeod. "My condolences," he said, removing his hat in respect. He thought of his own wife of the past four years, and knew that he wouldn't be able to continue without her.

"Cottonmouth. Damn those snakes." MacLeod shook his head, thinking of the swollen body of his Izora. She'd been at the Lake Cottage preparing it for the summer season when the reptile had surprised her in the bedroom. Her servants didn't find her until it was too late, and by the time MacLeod was notified and arrived, she was dead. There was nothing to do but punish them for their negligence and make arrangements for her funeral. "Come with me, Frederick. It's time to put your quarrel with Warmoth to rest."

"If you mean by blowing his damn head off his shoulders, then I'm all for it," Ogden growled.

MacLeod took him by the arm and guided him through the cemetery. "*Ye* must learn diplomacy. Sometimes *ye* have to let the cottonmouth, I mean carpetbagger, do the work for *ye*."

"Campbell, I'm terribly sorry for your loss." Warmoth was the first to see the approaching men, his voice cautious in the presence of Ogden, whom he deeply disliked.

"She was a good woman, even if she was a *Sassenach*," MacLeod replied, referring to her non-Scottish heritage. Emmett and Susannah added their condolences, before MacLeod pulled Ogden forward and continued, "I believe *ye* know Mrs. Susannah de Villiers, a treasure discovered in Washington, and brought back to our fair city of New Orleans, a new jewel to add sparkle to our society."

* * *

Pinckney Pinchback stood well back among the crypts of the St. Louis Cemetery marveling at the meeting taking place in front of him—the white supremacist, the carpetbagger governor, the social climbing widow, and the unsuspecting lad from New England, all facilitated by the unknown quantity that was Campbell MacLeod, and at his own wife's funeral to boot! Pinchback was not so naïve as to believe that this was an innocuous get-together amongst the most powerful men in New Orleans, and he mentally began planning how and when to elicit the contents of this conversation from Emmett.

The same election confirmations that had raised Warmoth to the position of governor had seen Pinchback defeated in his state senate bid, a shocking result in a ward that was staunchly republican. A Conservative Democrat by the name of Jewell had defeated him by eighty votes, almost certainly the result of some sort of fraud. He knew that many whites like MacLeod considered him and his ambitions with skepticism, while others such as Ogden with outright hatred, but he couldn't change the color of his skin. It had been suggested to him before that he do just that, or pretend so, as his complexion was pale enough to pass as white. But that would be an insult to his mother, and she was the most important person in his life, followed closely by his wife and three children, soon to be four.

Things had been looking up for Blacks politically when General Butler first occupied New Orleans in 1862, but this had changed when the war ended, and the Confederates had returned to dominate the legislature in June of 1865. While freedom was recognized, these southern white men enacted the infamous Black Codes, which required all freedmen to sign yearlong contracts tying them to the land, allowed for their arrest upon the mere accusation of vagrancy, and forbid them the possession of firearms. In response to these stringent laws, the U.S. Congress had passed the Reconstruction Acts, which not only abolished these Black Codes, but also allowed for Black male suffrage.

Nonetheless, qualified candidates such as Pinchback were squeezed out due to the color of their skin, and social inequality was the unofficial law of the land. It had been this way his entire life. True, he'd been born free and given certain privileges due to his mother's relationship with the plantation owner, privileges which most importantly had included an education, but he'd never been able to forget that he was Black. And then when the master died when Pinckney was eleven, they'd had to flee in fear of being re-enslaved. The following year he began working the riverboats, but not a day went by that another employee or passenger didn't remind him quite harshly that he was nothing more than a second-class citizen and always would be.

While General Butler raised a regiment of Black troops during the war, Pinchback became an officer, fighting valiantly for the Union, but then forced out at war's end due to the color of his skin. He'd turned a lucky run gambling into solid investments and become a powerful businessman in New Orleans. Ever present, however, was the realization that he was but one step away from having it all destroyed, the fine home and businesses taken, his neck fitted for a noose over some contrived misdeed. Politics was the obvious next choice if he wanted to make real change in this brutal world, but now he'd been again slapped in the face and reminded of his place in the hierarchy.

Pinchback watched as MacLeod and Ogden disappeared into separate carriages with Black drivers holding the door for them. Even Emmett had a carriage today, his driver, helping Susannah de Villiers into the hansom, also Black. He considered approaching Warmoth, who looked to be walking, but decided against it.

He knew well that the white race would not give him and his fellow Black Americans anything unless they demanded it. Rather, he had to take it. Let the white men have their meetings, establish policy in back rooms and over drinks, and scheme upon how to hold the freedmen down. It did not matter, because he, Pinckney Benton Stewart Pinchback, was going to take his piece of the pie. With that thought, he softly said, "No, I will not accept that. I demand to be recognized as a man."

The Black man with the large top hat sat rigidly on the driver's seat of the carriage. By now, he knew the boss' type. This time was different, though, because the boss was back in the enclosed body, even if the shades were carefully drawn for privacy. It was also earlier than usual, and this made him nervous. After about half-an-hour, he saw what he was looking for. Coming out of the brothel behind them was the lithe figure of a young woman, who was slender and black as the night that now fully enveloped the street. She came spryly down the street, perhaps getting some fresh air before the night's activities, before the onslaught of forced relations with rank strangers crushed down the blossoming of possibility. Right now, she was just a human being enjoying a walk, or looking for some food, or maybe visiting a friend. As she passed, he clucked the horse forward, falling into step with her.

The death of young Black prostitutes—four to date with another four beaten half to death—had been the talk of the Black community in New Orleans for some two years now, but not once had a girl been able to turn down twenty dollars for an hour or two of work. She accepted the blindfold, and he helped her into the back seat, the only difference this time was the presence of the boss in the carriage, who told him to take them to the in-town home.

The boss sat silently staring at the whore. Her eyes were covered with his handkerchief, giving him a chance to examine the merchandise secretly, and this thought made his blood race. She had thick, curly hair, made more pronounced by the blindfold. Her full lower lip trembled a bit with fear, a bit of saliva threatening to drop onto her chin. She was wearing a cheap cotton dress with yellow flowers on the dark material, her calves barely wider than her ankles.

He felt guilty taking her home tonight, but the urge was upon him. As he studied her, his eyes again fell upon her blindfold, and he had an idea that made him smile, the blood coursing through his veins with excitement. It was more daring and involved a higher chance of being caught, but that was part of the game, wasn't it? Besides, what if he *were* caught? She was a whore and he was a man of means. He tapped his cane on the roof, and when the driver stopped the carriage, he leaned his head out and told the darkie to take them down by the levee, behind the old deserted McCann building.

Once they reached the secluded spot, he told the driver to have a walk around and make sure nobody approached, and then he slid the handkerchief down from her eyes, down around her beautiful throat, and told her how pretty she was. And she did excite him tremendously, as always, the racing of the pulse bringing on the familiar revulsion of screwing a Black woman reared, that voice berating him for laying down with what was no more than a farm animal, leaving only one possible conclusion to his tortured mind and body.

The driver watched from the end of the alley. After about twenty minutes he heard a screech, a stifled scream most likely, and then the carriage began to rock back and forth and he turned his back, fighting back the nausea. Not long after, the boss beckoned him back, and as he reached the carriage, the naked and lifeless figure was shoved through the door, followed by a tattered cotton dress with yellow flowers. The boss stepped down after her, with a page torn from a book in his hand, reciting the words from memory, as the night was too dark to be able to read. "After putting him to sleep on her lap, she called for someone to shave off the seven braids of his hair, and so began to subdue him. And his strength left him. Then she called, 'Samson, the Philistines are upon you!' He awoke from his sleep and thought, 'I'll go out as before and shake myself free.' But he did not know that the Lord had left him. Then the Philistines seized him, gouged out his eyes and took him down to Gaza. Binding him with bronze shackles, they set him to grinding grain in the prison." He crumpled up the page and stuffed it into her mouth, before climbing back in for the trip home.

After Emmett dropped Susannah at her home and returned the horse and carriage to the livery up the street from the Marchant's, he paid the driver, Freedom, the two dollars he'd promised, and began to walk home. Yet, restless and worked up from his time with Susannah, conflicting emotions surging through his body, he decided to take a walk. Eventually, he found himself on Rue St. Ann. He could hear the bongos as soon as he turned from Rampart onto the street, and without thinking, pushed open the unlatched gate and entered a world far different than the one he'd just left.

Over a fire there was a large pot containing what smelled to be chicken stew of some sort. Scattered across the yard were Creoles, freed people of color, Indians, and whites—either eating, conversing, or dancing to the rhythm. Seven or eight women, and two men, gently swayed in the flickering firelight. Of course, Emmett remembered, it was Friday night. Manny had told him that this night almost always called for a gathering at the Laveau house to celebrate life. Although he'd seen Madame Laveau many times since the strange events on the bayou, he'd only run into Manny twice, both times chatting for a few minutes about things of little importance.

"Hello, Emmett Collins." Madame Laveau had appeared from nowhere, and now stood at his elbow, surveying the festive yard. "It is good to see you in my home again."

"Madame Laveau," Emmett bowed slightly, greeting the regal woman he'd come to understand was a major power broker not only in the Black community, but also with the French, Spanish, and English of all social classes as well. "I hope you don't mind, but I was walking by, heard the music, the gate was open…"

"You are always welcome here. Have some seafood gumbo." She held out a clay bowl whose tantalizing aroma instantly made Emmett's mouth water. An assortment of strange symbols was tattooed onto her hand, several of them appearing to be snakes.

"Thank you," he replied, realizing suddenly that he was famished. "Who are all these people?"

"They are just people, same as you and I." Madame Laveau smiled reassuringly. "But if you were to force a label upon them, they are the disaffected women and men." She swept her hand to encompass the yard. "They are Choctaws forced off their lands, freed slaves searching for a better life, white women estranged from a society wholly dominated by men, and the Black Creoles who have for years danced the invisible line between enslaved and free. They are all welcome here at my home."

Emmett wondered about his presence, for did it mean that he, too, was alienated from his people—whoever they were, exactly? It certainly seemed possible, as everybody he knew already understood their niche and were busy filling the role that they'd carved for themselves in the world. "And where do you fit in, Madame Laveau?"

"I am a human being, Emmett Collins. Is not everybody one race under God?"

"I see you at the St. Louis Cathedral every Sunday morning."

"Are you asking how I can be a Catholic and a Voodoo at the same time?" When Emmett nodded his assent, she continued, "The Catholic priest tells us of Jesus Christ, a white baby born to a Virgin Mother and God. This view of purity might be relevant and useful to white people, but it does not make much sense for those of us with a darker skin."

"You're saying God comes to people in different guises?"

"Don't you believe that the Almighty knows enough to approach his flock in a manner that they will understand? You met Mister Daniel Blanc at a Voodoo fête, but on another day, he might visit as the Archangel Michael. He is one and the same, and merely adjusts his presence to his audience."

An angular woman with dark hair interrupted their conversation. "Excuse me? Madame?"

"Yes, Sabine?"

"Miss Lulu, she sent me over to tell you Dorinda went out for a walk a few hours back, and never came back." She smiled coyly at Emmett, and he realized with a start that she was a whore who he'd spent a night with some time back.

"I will put out the word to be on the lookout for her. She's the one who sometimes drinks too much?"

"She's been known to drown her sorrows, yes ma'am," Sabine agreed. "Anything you want me to tell Miss Lulu?" The woman stepped away with a lusty look at Emmett. He had, after all, been a gentleman, and most importantly, paid well.

"Tell Lulu to stop by here at the end of the night," Madame Laveau said, and Sabine went out through the gate.

"Is she… I mean what?" Emmett flushed the color of his hair, afraid to give away that he knew she was a whore, and how he knew that.

Madame Laveau looked knowingly at Emmett. "Sabine is a prostitute."

"It sounded like she works for you?" he questioned before he could hold his tongue.

"Over the years I have come across many women of that occupation who have been abused by their clients or beaten by those they work for. I provide a safe house for them to ply their wares." The Voodoo Queen raised her eyebrows. "They pay me for this service in many ways."

"How so?" Emmett blurted, wanting desperately for this conversation to end, but unable to stop himself.

"Information, Emmett, the most priceless commodity known in all of history. All men yearn for sex—yes, even you—and many of these men are powerful politicians, businessmen, even clergy. They all have secrets—confidences that come spilling out when pleasure and intimacy allow their guard to drop. These things are, in turn, shared with me, and I use them as I am able, for the greater good."

Emmett grimaced, his mind racing to his own visitations of houses of pleasure. Whores were sinful creatures of the lowest class, or so he'd thought. Yet he knew many upstanding men who frequented these women of ill repute, and then there was Susannah, who'd sold her body in hard times, and now with wealth and standing, fluttered around with the top of society, indistinguishable from any other high-class lady. Was taking money for copulation really any different than any other occupation? "Ahh," he groaned unknowingly as he wrestled with his thoughts.

Madame Laveau smiled mysteriously. "You do not approve? Is it the woman raising a child by providing a service that all men want that bothers you? Or is it that I provide them a safer environment in which to do this than they would otherwise have? Are we not all God's creatures, as I was saying, whether we see Him as white or Black?"

Emmett tried to order his thoughts in regards to Catholicism, Voodoo, and prostitution, but when he finally made ready to retort, he realized that Madame Laveau had left him, and that his gumbo was growing cold. He moved farther into the shadows, spooning the thick, spicy mixture into his mouth. Perhaps he was one of the disaffected, for he doubted the existence of God. But he had had a spiritual vision with a Voodoo *lwa*. He winced whenever other whites referred to Blacks as Sambos, darkies, smoked Irish, or monkeys. He knew little of the Choctaw Indians present in the yard, but imagined they loved, hated, and bled the same as him. Since he could remember, people had told him that whites were a race superior to black- and brown-skinned people. Even General Chamberlain, who believed Blacks should be free, had laid claim to this white superiority. Now that Emmett had met people such as Pinckney Pinchback and Marie Laveau and Manon, Emmett was beginning to have his doubts, thoughts that, for the first time, went counter to the teachings of General Chamberlain.

"A penny for your thoughts?"

Emmett was pulled back to the expansive courtyard and the party, what was the word Marie the younger had used? *Fête*. Manny stood in front of him, the top of her head now even with his eyes. When had she grown so tall? Not only tall, but also begun to fill out as a woman, and with a quiet confidence in those knowing eyes. "My thoughts are more mixed up than this gumbo," Emmett admitted. "It's going to take a lot more than a penny and a tad bit longer than we have for me to untangle *that* mess."

She touched him lightly on the chest with long, thin fingers that any pianist would envy, her pointer landing first followed one by one in succession until her palm was firmly pressed against his breast. "You should know as well as anybody that time does not exist within Voodoo."

"I'm glad that time has kept me here," he said. He felt light-headed, like his chest, warm under her touch, couldn't expand quite enough to breathe.

"What makes you glad?"

"Helping Black folks out, I guess."

"How so?"

"Creating educational opportunities and social equality," Emmett stumbled over the words that he'd uttered countless times, but in truth, had his doubts about.

"Equality? Do you believe that we are now equal to white people in New Orleans?"

Emmett started slightly at the vehemence of her tone. "The Constitution we just ratified gives Black men the right to vote, establishes a free and integrated public-school system, and guarantees equal access to public accommodations. What more is there?"

"I am not a man, for one. For another, it is just paper, and just as meaningless if no one chooses to enforce it." Manny's eyes were blazing as she spoke, and Emmett realized with a jolt that she was passing from the last moments of childhood to adulthood almost before his eyes, a young woman with robust convictions—and one unafraid to voice them. "Do you really think that white men are going to let us attend school with their children? That they will sit next to us on the trolley, or share a table, or treat us with dignity and respect?"

"I know that there's a long way to go in winning the hearts and minds of Southern whites, but the election of so many Black men should help," Emmett replied, but his mind was asking when she had become so passionate and articulate, as well as tall, and filled-out?

"*Je ne pense pas.*" Manny sighed, the anger seeping out of her, replaced by a hollow fatigue in her voice. "I don't think so," she repeated. "Most Black people have nothing. Whether they are five or fifty, they are lucky to own the clothes on their backs. How will anybody come to think that these homeless, ragged, and hungry individuals are their equals if they lack basic human dignities?"

It was as if she'd been reading his thoughts, and indeed, needed not pay a penny for them. "Forty acres and a mule would've helped," Emmett conceded. "Perhaps Governor Warmoth and the mixed-race legislature will find the money to make a change."

"Madame Laveau does not trust your Governor Warmoth nearly as much as you do." Manny removed her hand. "She says he talks too quickly, and his eyes are shifty."

"He's been nothing but good to me."

"Do you think the representative of the Freedman Bureau is an important ally to have, especially now that Black men have the right to vote?"

Emmett hadn't spoken with very many women in his life, but the few that he had didn't carry forth like this. He couldn't imagine Susannah talking politics, and certainly not in such an aggressive manner. "I suppose we'll have to wait and see."

"Waiting is a luxury for white people, but has been a way of life for

Black people. *Plus ça change…*" she added bitterly. "You know what that means, yes?" He nodded gravely and they fell silent. "I think that perhaps the time for inaction is over." Her eyes glinted as she spoke, suggesting that her vigor had returned.

"What do you plan to do?"

"Only what you have suggested." Manny stepped in closer, so close he could feel the heat of her body, her face turned up to his, her breath warm on his neck.

Emmett stood rigid, and when he spoke, his lips stumbled over the words. "What have I suggested you do?"

"What is the most important thing that Black people can do to improve the quality of their life?" Her lips trembled as she murmured the question.

"Get an education?"

"Yes."

Emmett realized he'd no idea what sort of schooling she'd had, only that she spoke well and that she was in school now. "That's wonderful," he said lamely.

"Tomorrow, I am taking a steamer to Boston where I will be attending a seminary for women. I plan to become a teacher, and then I will return to New Orleans and instruct Black students."

"Tomorrow?" Emmett grasped her arm in alarm. "You leave tomorrow?"

CHAPTER 7

NOVEMBER 2, 1868

New Orleans Daily Bourbon

==

The Bourbon is Published Daily (Sunday Excepted) By P.O. Rivard
Terms: Daily $16, Weekly $5; Per Year

==

Monday, November 2, 1868

==

Official Journal of the State of Louisiana

TO THE COLORED PEOPLE OF NEW ORLEANS!

Tomorrow is the day of the election. You have a right to vote. It is for you to determine whether you can safely attempt to exercise that right.

If you attempt it, let us advise you that only in so attempting should you appear on the streets. If you conclude not to attempt it, do not leave your home.

Emmett lay the newspaper down on his desk. The *New Orleans Daily Bourbon* was the most unbiased newspaper in the city, but with this dire warning, it had cemented the election in favor of the Conservative Democrats, who were the old white-guard of New

Orleans, trying to return the country to the way things were before the War of Northern Aggression. He knew it was meant only as a cautionary warning, but as read, it suggested that staying home was, by far, the best option.

The Crescent City Democrat Club had promised slips of papers at the polling locations ensuring safe passage for those that voted for the conservative Seymour/Blair ticket. It was the thinking that this presidential ticket, if elected, would soon revert Louisiana to home rule and then quickly dispose of all of this equality garbage. The message was clear that the safety of anybody, especially men of color, would be in danger should they not be carrying one of these slips.

The nominee for Vice-President, Francis Preston Blair of Missouri, had been quite clear on his stance towards the Black population, having stumped across the country on a platform proclaiming that the Black population was a semi-barbarous race of fetish worshipers, polygamists, whose men wanted to subject white women to their unbridled lust. The head of the ticket, Horatio Seymour, was more reserved in his criticism of Black rights, crusading instead on the concept that suffrage and equality should be determined at the state level.

Emmett scanned the headlines of *The New Orleans Crescent Fox* to see what lies they were selling today.

SAMBO BEHIND A WOODPILE—

John Smith, Captain of the schooner, *Lucinda,* was wounded when three Sambos ran out from behind a woodpile and attacked him. He was able to fend them off until help arrived. The three Sambos were killed at the scene.

Only way for Negroes to get ahead will be for them to renounce any and all political rights—

Equality is a fine thing in fancy, but there is no such thing as equality in nature, no such thing in this world, and there will be none in the world to come.

Carpetbaggers abuse trust of Negroes—
There is not a shade of difference in the motives of the slaveholder and those of the carpetbagger; only that the carpetbagger puts on the air of a sleek humanitarian... If the Negro knew the true history of his race, he would think the slaveholder altogether more reputable than the carpetbagger.

ARSON AND LOOTING ON DERBIGNY STREET—
A mob of darkies set fire to a house on Derbigny Street on Sunday and then began looting. Good Samaritans at the scene stepped in to prevent the theft, resulting in the death of six Negroes who were, once again, the aggressors.

Emmett had been present at the riot on Derbigny Street, and therefore knew firsthand that this was not the true nature of the events. That evening he'd eaten an early dinner at Pinchback's home, which was a much different experience than his normal solitary meals. Every inch of the house seemed to be taken up by the four children ranging from newborn to six years of age. Pinchback held the baby while the rest of his offspring climbed over and around him with wild abandon, as his wife, Nina, and mother, Eliza, were busy cooking in the kitchen. By the time Emmett left with his belly full, he was as exhausted as he'd been after the day and night spent marching nonstop to reach the battlefield of Gettysburg during the Great War.

He'd no sooner emerged onto the street then he saw flames licking the darkening sky just down the way. As Emmett approached the burning house, he saw a man and woman emerge through the front door carrying a table. Several shots rang out, and they fell just outside the entrance. As the fire began to singe their bodies, a man rushed forward to pull them from the flames. A single rifle shot echoed above the maelstrom of the crackling fire and he fell atop of them.

Emmett had pulled his pistol out of his waistband and pointed it at the shooter, but a crowd of people surged in front of him. Not wishing to hit an innocent bystander, he'd charged through the crowd to see the man fleeing around the corner. He gave chase, angrier than he'd been in quite some time. This man had been shooting people for the offense of helping a man and woman who were burning alive. His anger overcoming his caution, he careened around the corner only to come face-to-face with the perpetrator who stood no more than thirty feet in front of him, a rifle pointed at Emmett's midsection.

"Whatcha want with me?" The man asked.

Emmett's pistol was in his hand, pointing toward the ground. His thoughts flashed through all the possible scenarios. Could he raise it and fire before the man killed him? Should he drop to the ground, roll and fire? Dive back around the corner? Try and talk his way out of it?

The man spit a stream of tobacco juice. "You're that friend of the White Master, ain't ya?"

"Who?"

"Ya think he'll like ya sticking up for a bunch of darkies?"

"I don't know what you're talking about," Emmett replied. He shifted, so that he was sideways to the man, presenting less of a target, his pistol gripped in his right hand, needing to merely raise and fire. "I shot me a darkie back there, and thought I best get out before the law showed up."

"Seems to me ya was chasing me."

Emmett shrugged, the motion allowing the pistol to raise a few inches. "I figured you knew where you were going." He looked left, around the corner. "It looks like the law is heading this way, we best get." As he looked back at the man, he raised his pistol and pulled the trigger, the bullet striking the man in the arm, the man's return fire plowing into the wooden building a few feet from Emmett's head, sending splinters flying into his face. He dove back around the corner, and by the time he dared look, the man was gone. There was a small puddle of blood where he'd stood, but no trace of him.

Emmett walked back to the fire, picking slivers of wood from his face. When the law arrived, they interviewed a host of white men who all told the same story of Black arsonists and looters. When Emmett spoke with the neighbors, however, they told him that the couple who lived there had come home to find the house ablaze and had been shot attempting to save their own possessions. Three other men whom had tried to put out the blaze before the owners arrived had likewise been shredded by bullets.

His thoughts returned to the present and his eye caught the grimy paper he'd found stuck to the front door of his office.

GO BACK NORTH WHILE YOU STILL CAN
YOU CARPETBAGGER – YOUR TIME IS COMING
DO NOT TARRY OR IT WILL BE TOO LATE

He smiled wanly and threw the threat on top of thirty or forty other menacing notes. After the flush of victories in the April elections, in which pro-equality men as well as many Blacks had come into office, Emmett had been certain that a new age had dawned in New Orleans. Manny's warning, however, had often resounded in his ears over the months that had passed since her departure. *Do you really think that white men are going let us attend school with their children? That they will sit next to us on the trolley, or share a table, or treat us with dignity and respect?* Instead of acceptance, the recent constitution had been met with derision. Not only was desegregation not working, Blacks were being verbally and physically assaulted at the slightest provocation and often without any reason whatsoever.

The newly integrated Metropolitan Police patrolled the streets in groups, as alone, they were often attacked and beaten. Again, he heard that cautionary voice. *How will any white person come to think that these homeless, ragged, and hungry individuals are their equals if they lack basic human dignities?* Emmett had to admit feeling superior in the suits he wore as compared to the dirty workmen on the docks or on the plantations. He wished he could provide a helping hand to many of these poor souls teeming the streets of New Orleans, but the Freedman Bureau was closing down, his life was being threatened almost every day, and the opposition to equality appeared indomitable.

The worst was the vicious killer who'd been preying on Black prostitutes and leaving them mangled and dead after raping them. Three women had been found in the last six months with a page of scripture from the biblical Book of Judges stuffed into their mouths.

The page referred to the harlot Delilah who had seduced Samson and stolen his strength by cutting his hair off. The newspapers had termed the man, who beat, raped, and murdered these women, the Black Delilahs of Tremé Killer. The women were all prostitutes in the Black neighborhood of Tremé, hence the name. Emmett wished he could do something about this disturbed and violent lunatic, but his tenure at the Freedman Bureau was winding down, and it was time for him to move on.

Immediately after the election, Emmett planned on asking Susannah de Villiers to marry him. He rationalized that he should see his task as special agent to the Freedman Bureau to completion before he could step into the role of southern white patriarch. These two thoughts so close together made him unconsciously wince. Perhaps it was that Susannah was not the woman he remembered, her anger for being bumped by a Black sailor like a painful stab in his memory, how she'd developed a Southern accent so quickly, and fallen into the role of plantation wife so easily. No matter which way he turned it, Emmett couldn't see himself in the role of plantation master. Maybe they could sell the plantation, as Susannah was bored to death there anyway, and Emmett could run for state senate? He would have to be insane to not marry a beautiful and rich woman, wouldn't he?

There was a knock at the door, and then it was yanked open. Emmett grasped the Colt from his desk and pointed it at a grim Pinckney Pinchback. "Might as well shoot me before some other white man does."

"Good morning, Pinch," Emmett replied, trying to read the flat black eyes of the riverboat gambler turned politician. After Warmoth had been sworn in as governor, he'd immediately set up a commission to investigate voter fraud during the earlier April election, and Pinchback had been named the victor in his senate race. "What bad news do you bring?"

"I had a visitor this morning who found the bodies of three boys on the Carondelet Walk, half submerged in the shallows of the canal. I was wondering if you still have use of that buckboard?"

"I sure do." Emmett stood and pulled his jacket on over his waistcoat. "I don't suppose you want to let the Met handle it?"

"They said they were pretty backed up, might be a while before they could get out there. I figured it'd be best to not let them rot any longer than they have to."

They found the boys about halfway out the canal, dumped in low-lying brush growing with abandon on the side of the little-used waterway. Emmett guessed they were maybe sixteen years old, but it was tough to tell with their swollen and bloated faces. Handkerchiefs were tied around their mouths, whether to choke them or keep them quiet, it was tough to say. Stuck through each handkerchief was a single white flower.

"Looks like a White Camellia job," Emmett said. They both knew well of the underground society dedicated to the promotion of whites and the eradication of Blacks. As a matter of fact, many of the threats Emmett received included some sort of hand drawn version of this flower.

"I believe this one is my neighbor's boy," Pinchback said as they trundled the body up the bank to the waiting wagon. His voice was choked between anguish and rage. "He's a member of the Grant Club. Don't look like he'll be voting tomorrow after all."

"We'll take him home, then."

Pinchback untied the cloth from the boy's face, revealing his genitals, which had been cut off and stuffed into his mouth, the handkerchief tied around his head to keep the severed organ in the toothless aperture. "Son of a bitch."

Frederick Nash Ogden stood at the podium dressed in white trousers with a black jacket, as were the fifty men in front of him. This was a closed meeting of the Crescent City Democratic Club, and only the inner circle members were present at their wigwam on the corner of Jackson and Prytania Streets.

Red spots clotted his pale cheeks as he exhorted his audience with a clear message. "Our directives are very clear, taken directly from the presidential slogan of the Democratic Party. 'This is a white man's country, let white men rule.' This cannot be accomplished if freed slaves and Northern carpetbaggers are allowed to vote. We, who have grown up in a white Louisiana, have lived our lives here, have buried our relatives here—it is up to us to ensure that those who cast a ballot in tomorrow's election are those whose values reflect our own, and not the beliefs of Northerners or beasts not even human."

He paused, surveying the attendees, grunting in satisfaction at the high caliber of men who now paid homage to him, not so long ago the black sheep of his family, the good for nothing, going nowhere, lowly cotton clerk.

"We will not let the Sambos give us white people the short end of the stick again. I hope they come out tomorrow to vote for Grant. That way, we can teach them a lesson. Let them know that the hierarchy has white people sitting on top, and Sambos in the barn with the livestock. I am not going to suggest that you kill any of them, but if it happens? Leave them in the streets as a message to the rest of their kind and to carpetbaggers." Ogden surveyed the cream of New Orleans society. "Our mission is clear. Let's make sure we're on our assigned patrol routes before the sun comes up."

The streets of New Orleans were desolate. Shops were locked up tight. The only movement was roving groups of white Democrats, members of clubs such as Crescent City, the Broom Rangers, and the Democratic Workingman's Club. They mostly carried clubs, but some were armed with rifles and pistols. Emmett and Pinchback approached the polling station as it opened, and surveyed the gauntlet of men they'd have to pass through to vote.

"Well Pinch, it don't look like we're going to be much protection for anybody who wants to vote a Republican ticket," Emmett commented dryly.

"Not once we get killed trying to vote our own selves," Pinchback replied.

"You think we should just sit this one out?"

"As far as I can tell, Collins, you don't really know the meaning of sitting a situation out."

"What's that supposed to mean?"

"It means that everybody down here paying attention has you pegged as an agitator. You're like that William Lloyd Garrison fellow, except you're down here fighting for the freedmen on the front line, and not from safety up in the land of steady habits."

Emmett nodded. "I guess they got me pegged right."

"You just make sure if you live through today you sleep with a pistol under your pillow."

"Fair enough. You ready?"

Pinchback chuckled. "There's only thirty or forty of them." He unbuttoned his jacket to reveal two pistols, one on either hip, butts forward.

Emmett, too, had worn a holstered gun, but also carried a new Springfield Model 1868 Trapdoor rifle. "I don't think I brought enough shells, but I reckon if Grant is going to lose our vote, we might as well take some Seymour votes with us."

"What do you got to live for anyway?"

"I was thinking of getting married."

Pinchback turned his eyes from the Broom Rangers, who were taking their turn guarding the polling station, and stared at Emmett. "You fixin' on hitching yourself to that narrow-faced blonde lady with the plantation?"

"Her face isn't all that narrow," Emmett retorted.

"Any woman who owns three homes is beautiful in my book."

"I might just shoot you myself and save those white folks the trouble."

"Those boys over there hate a carpetbagger worse than a Black. You should probably go get yourself hitched, enjoy the fruits of your commitment, before you come on back here and get yourself killed."

"I wouldn't want to let them down, thinking I'm some sort of freedman lover and all."

"What about that Creole girl?" Pinchback stepped down onto the street, his flat eyes showing just a hint of amusement.

"Who?"

"The one who lives with Marie Laveau."

"Manon? What about her?"

"You told me all about that Voodoo thing a few years back. Seems to me your eyes lit up and your voice got a bit huskier every time you mentioned her. Thought you might cry when you told me she was going up North."

"Maybe you should go…" Emmett began to suggest Pinch do the impossible, but was interrupted by approaching horses from the opposite direction.

"Now, who could that be?" Pinchback squinted into the sun.

"Looks like the law." Emmett replied, happy to avoid a topic that he'd struggled to confine to the distant recesses of his mind. "Maybe while the Metropolitans and Broom Rangers are killing each other we can sneak in and cast our ballot." Down the street, with the rising sun at their backs, came a dozen heavily armed policemen.

"Sounds like a plan, not a very good one, but short of tucking our tails and running, I don't reckon there is much choice." Pinchback stepped off the boardwalk and into the hard-packed dirt street. "I hear six feet of earth makes us all equal."

Emmett thought it a bad time to mention that in New Orleans everybody was buried above ground, and that the crypts were certainly not equal, their competing grandeur denoting wealth and status even after death.

The Broom Rangers were watching the approach of the Metropolitan Police, and almost missed Emmett and Pinchback, but for one man who suddenly shouted, "Where do you think you're going, Sambo?"

"I think he's speaking to you," Emmett whispered aside to Pinchback, as he casually turned his rifle to aim at the man's chest.

"Who are you voting for today?" a man in an elegant suit asked, obviously the leader of this group of well-dressed Democrats.

"None of your damn business," Pinchback replied, patting his vest pocket where his ballot lay.

A growl emerged from the crowd, and as one, they surged toward the man they saw as an 'uppity Negro'. "Hold still," the lieutenant of the Metropolitan Police demanded.

"You've no authority here," elegant suit snarled back. "If you want to avoid a beating, you best leave now."

"We have the authority of Governor Warmoth and the state legislature," the lieutenant replied defiantly, his nerves betraying him as his eyes flickered this way and that.

The Broom Rangers slowly began to spread out, most of them former Confederate officers understanding the importance of flanking the enemy. Emmett fully well understood that violence was only one itchy finger away. Into this powder keg came the thunder of hooves, the impending bloodshed seemingly halted, if only for a moment, as eyes turned to the approaching cavalcade of horsemen led by Frederick Nash Ogden. The steeds came to a shuddering stop, nostrils quivering as they skittered to and fro. "What have we here?"

"This Sambo and his friend think they can cast a vote any way they want," elegant suit blustered with his courage bolstered by the addition of fellow Democrats in the form of the Crescent City Club.

"Senator Pinchback," Ogden corrected him softly. "And Emmett Collins, special agent to the Freedman Bureau for General Howard. I suggest that you let them cast their ballots." It was one thing to kill a freedman or two, but Ogden knew where to draw the line.

Elegant suit started to argue, caught the eyes of Ogden, and thought better of it. He stepped aside and made a grand sweeping gesture, greatly exaggerated, that they should proceed.

"Thank you, Colonel Ogden," Emmett said.

"We must get together soon," Ogden replied. "It is time for you to get on the right side of this debate, before it is too late."

Emmett found himself turning in early that night, exhausted from the turmoil of the months leading up to this dismal election. His thoughts were dark and self-pitying as he lay down on his bed. He'd done all he could, and for what purpose? Certainly not to make a fortune as an adventurer come to milk the cash cow of the South. Everyone hated him. The southern whites thought him a Black-loving agitator at best. Many of the Blacks mistrusted him, too, either convinced by the Democrats that he was using them for his own gain, or from their own experience—any association with Emmett and his Bureau might and often did lead to beatings, whippings, threats, evictions, and murders. How in tarnation was he supposed to know what the right thing was to do and do it?

No, he was resolved. Tomorrow he'd pay Susannah a visit and get down on one knee and ask her hand in marriage. He'd picked a ring of gold months earlier to give to her. Then he would take up his position as plantation owner and hobnob with the inner circle of the Crescent City Democrats. Enough was enough. Pinchback could take care of himself. Marie Laveau would be disappointed in him, but so what? His thoughts turned to Manny, and he wondered if she'd seen snow yet. It was the thought of the young Creole girl getting an education in Boston that caused the ugly knife of self-loathing to twist its way through his gut as he drifted off to sleep…

Emmett looked at the field of snow stretching away in all directions as far as he could see. There was no shrubbery or trees to mar this expanse of pure driven cotton stretching endlessly. He realized there was a man standing next to him, a lithe Black man in a shirt unbuttoned to his waist with suspenders holding up his ragged pants. "You again," Emmett said to Mister Daniel Blanc.

"That would seem to be the case." Daniel pulled his hat from his head, and the black-coiled hair sprang in all directions as if trying to escape. "I have to confess that it's not quite normal for me to be visiting a white man."

"I suppose there must be a reason for it," Emmett replied. A black figure entered the field of snow, cavorting in the virginal powder. It was Manny. Emmett recognized her spirited movement, her lithe body boldly frolicking in snow that slowly turned to flowers, every one different, except for their whiteness. "Is it because of the girl?" he asked, turning to Mister Daniel Blanc, who was no longer there, but had been replaced by Campbell MacLeod.

"She sure is a beauty with those long slender legs and full lips. So dark, like a raincloud sweeping in to nourish the blooms," MacLeod said.

Manny began throwing handfuls of seeds from a basket she carried, flinging them to scatter, some catching the breeze and carrying further, while others slipped through her fingers and dropped at her feet.

"She needs to move to the edges so she doesn't trample all the beautiful camellias." Henry Clay Warmoth now appeared where MacLeod had been.

Black tulips began to grow indiscriminately amongst the white flowers, stretching and reaching for the sun in their enclaves.

"You be careful out there," Marie Laveau called to the girl in the field. "Not so fast!"

A man strode into the meadow, his back broad, and dark-red hair scraggly upon his nape. It was Frederick Ogden. He grabbed Manny's wrist, stopping her from sowing the seeds, an angry exchange appearing to take place, but Emmett couldn't hear it from where his feet were rooted into the ground, unable to aid the girl in any way. One of the black tulips grew taller than the rest and turned into Pinckney Pinchback, his jacket thrown wide, and pistol butts facing forward. Ogden pushed Manny away and pulled a pistol from his waistband as Pinchback drew both guns. The crescendo of sound was thunder-like in the suddenly dark day, blood streaking the flowers, white and Black alike. Manny was running towards Emmett screaming his name…

"Emmett!"

Shadows filled his bedroom. Something hard crashed into his cheek. Hands grasped at his legs and arms. Again, a blow to the head followed by more, a barrage of smashing wallops that never allowed him to escape the daze of half-sleep. He was jerked to the floor, the hardwood smacking his face. He crawled to the door, fighting his way to the parlor entrance, before the weight of a man crushed him flat. His arms were jerked behind him and tied, while a man grasped his hair and repeatedly smacked his head into the floor. He could hear Mrs. Marchant screaming, nonsensical noise that careened from nook to wall to ceiling.

"Shut up, or I will kill your husband," threatened a nasal voice from across the room.

The man pulled Emmett backwards onto his knees, blood streaming from his broken nose and mashed lips. He could see Mr. and Mrs. Marchant in chairs with guns at their heads in a room crowded full of white-clothed figures skulking around in the murky gloom of the witching hour. Emmett wondered truly, what ghouls had come for him on this night.

"Bring him," one of the fiends commanded harshly.

Emmett found himself dragged to the hallway and then the stairs, his arms pinned to his sides, and his legs bumping all the way down. A noose was dropped over his head, and he was dragged across the street to where a lamppost stood lonely in the night. The rope was thrown up over the crossbar that supported the three lanterns that'd been extinguished sometime earlier. He kicked out with his leg and caught one apparition in the groin, and it was then that he realized they were just men, as the scoundrel grunted and cried out in a pathetic tone of outrage.

The moon and stars revealed a group of forty men dressed in sheets with hoods and masks shrouding their faces. The noose jerked tight around his neck, and he was pulled to his feet. With a yell of rage, he rushed several men who held the far end of the rope—and thus his life—and knocked one to the ground. Blinded by blood, arms tied behind him, and with death encircling his neck, Emmett fought these banshees, ultimately to no avail. More hands stepped forward, clutching him tightly, and he was pulled up to his tiptoes.

"You were warned."

"The White Master has ruled."

"Let me be," Emmett gasped, and then the rope cut into his throat as he was pulled into the air. He frantically clawed for a foothold, desperate for the feel of solid ground once again beneath his feet.

Meanwhile, the Knights of the White Camellia watched patiently. That is, until an urgent voice whispered, "Federal Troops are coming." A rustle went through the sheeted bodies and their ranks quickly lost any kind of order. And then they disappeared on the back of a thin breeze. As Emmett dangled with his legs kicking futilely in the air, Mr. Marchant came cautiously out the door, and then dashed to cut him free. Right before the rope was sawed through, a single white camellia fluttered down to the dirt below, and then Emmett crushed it with the weight of his own body.

Emmett was aware of the faint light created by the rising sun as he was helped back up the stairs he'd just been dragged down. It was hard for him to distinguish between dreaming and reality. Was Manny okay? Where was Pinch? The important thing was that he was alive, and his life was about to change. Later today, he was having tea with Susannah at her New Orleans home. He'd ask her to marry him and leave this nonsensical Freedman Bureau behind. He'd shed his image as an agitator, and join the ranks of his fellow white men. Somebody else could pick up the battle flag of equality and carry it forth into combat.

The silence was as thick as the beignets were light at the breakfast table in the Marchant home. A servant had been sent just a few storefronts down to Café du Monde to purchase these fried donuts smothered in powdered sugar and complemented by several flavors of jam. As much as Emmett had protested he was not hungry, the truth was that he was currently finishing his fourth beignet. As he wet his fingers to pick up the last of the powdered sugar from his plate, Emmett finally dared to look up, meeting the distressed faces of his landlords. "I'm sorry that I brought violence into your home."

"We're just happy that you're alive," Mrs. Marchant replied unconvincingly.

"I'll make sure it doesn't happen again." Emmett's words rang hollow in the confines of the dining room, and they all knew that Emmett was choosing hopefulness over truth.

Mr. Marchant cleared his throat, shifted his body, and then rearranged his silverware, before finally speaking. "You must leave."

Emmett didn't care. He'd be married soon. He'd be a rich man. He'd be a respected man.

That afternoon, as he approached Susannah's manor, just the faintest of voices mumbled in the recesses of his mind. *Waiting is a luxury for white people, but has been a way of life for Black people. I think that perhaps the time for inaction is over.* First in a dream, then in a waking dream, this voice, this face, these words spoken at farewell, all were haunting him. He felt pushed and pulled this way and that, last night's near-death experience just underlining the simple fact: whatever he was going to do, he'd better do it fast.

As he settled into a straight-backed chair, one last utterance worked its way through the confused cobwebs of his mind, sneaking past the defenses he'd erected, and whispered in a voice that he didn't recognize, *do you even love her?*

Even though it chafed and itched something terrible, Emmett

had carefully buttoned his white starched shirt all the way to conceal the ragged and raw reminder of the noose around his neck. There was little he could do to cover the bruises and scrapes to his face, or the crookedness of his nose, but when Susannah joined him a few minutes later, she didn't appear to notice.

As soon as they had exchanged the mandatory pleasantries, Emmett blurted out, "There is something we need to talk about."

"Yes," Susannah agreed, looking particularly stunning in a blue dress that bared her long neck. "Yes, we do."

Emmett fingered the ring in his pocket, fumbling over the words in his mind. How difficult could it be to say 'will you marry me'? "The Marchants have asked me to leave by the end of the week," he said instead.

Susannah let that settle in before countering with her own news. "My lawyer tells me that *ahhm* going to lose everything. He says that the judge will be ruling any day in favor of Francois' family. *Ahh* will be thrown out with nothing."

They'd discussed this possibility several times since she'd first told him about it some eight months earlier, but he had doubted it would come to pass. "That's too bad," he said lamely. It was almost a relief that he wouldn't be marrying wealth and prestige.

"I won't be poor again," Susannah said into the silence. "I will not be poor again." The words were clear and almost defiant, with no lazy drawl having dulled their sharp edge, the thought of losing her wealth having chased away, even for a moment, her accent.

Emmett knew that this was his cue to ask the question that would forever bind the two of them together. He pulled his sweaty hand from his pocket, before realizing that Susannah had said something else. "I'm sorry, what did you say?"

"*Ahhm* going to marry Campbell MacLeod."

PART III: LOVE

December 9, 1871–April 16, 1872

CHAPTER 8

December 9, 1871

She stood at the top of the hill with her face flushed from the New England cold, the wet flakes enormous as they landed on her cheeks, only to disappear immediately. Manon had been here for over three years now, and on her very last night here, she was sledding for the first time. Her friend, Leonidas, had borrowed the contraption from a friend. The only direction was down, and this was accomplished in a great whooshing of wind and speed over the icy slope behind her school, in the small town outside of Boston.

"Are you ready?" she called breathlessly over her shoulder.

"As soon as you sit down," Leonidas replied.

She settled herself down, firmly grasping the looped rope in the front. "All set."

"One, two, three!" he counted down as he gave the sled several steps of pushing, before jumping aboard and wrapping his legs up around Manon.

The runners splashed sloppy snowflakes into her delighted face as they careened down the hill, flashing past other revelers out to enjoy this first snow of the year, the hour too late for children but perfect for the young adults who dotted the ridge behind the seminary. Leonidas clutched her tightly about the waist, and Manon raised her arms overhead and screamed in excitement, her motion causing the toboggan to veer sideways and topple over, sending both of them tumbling into the snow.

"Are you okay?" he asked, as he crawled to where she lay convulsing.

"I think I have snow in places it shouldn't be." Manon laughed, her body shaking with the effort.

Leonidas leaned over her and kissed her, his lips surprisingly warm. "You're so beautiful," he said.

"And you are a naughty young man," she replied, pushing him away and rising to her feet.

"Hot cocoa?"

"Where would we go at this time of night?"

"I've some at my house."

"Wouldn't we wake your parents or sisters?"

"They've gone away for the weekend to visit my grandparents."

Thus, Manon found herself huddled in front of a brisk fire with a blanket wrapped around her, sipping hot chocolate all alone with a young man. The two had become friends more than a year earlier, but tonight had been the first time they'd kissed.

"I believe I might be chilled to my very bones," Leonidas said with a shiver. "Do you think I might share that blanket with you?"

She liked the comfort of his body pressed against hers, the flames crackling cheerily, and the sweet drink caressing her throat. *Was this happiness?* She wondered. He took her empty cup and set it on the floor along with his, sliding his arm around her back and pulling her more tightly to his side. His fingers massaged her shoulder and upper arm. Manon turned to him, and immediately found his lips crushing her own, as he wrapped his free arm around the front of her. Manon felt him pushing her down upon her back on the sofa, his hand now pressing her shoulder backward.

Manon gave in and enjoyed the sensation of his lips and his touch. She ground her hips against his as a yearning growled deeply in her bones, a want so intense it made her shiver. And even though she knew he was not the one, no, not her one true love, she let it happen. Afterwards, though she wasn't disappointed exactly, she wondered what all the fuss was about. There had been a series of small peaks of pleasure, and certainly there was the powerful naked intimacy of the act itself. There had also been, remarkably from the lore she had heard, no blood and little pain, maybe due to the briefness of their coupling. Perhaps it was different when you were in love? She wished she could talk to a girlfriend about this, but that would present its own problems. She carefully picked up her clothes and went into the dressing room to get dressed. Leonidas tried to convince her to stay a bit longer, but she had turned the page and was already back in New Orleans in mind, if not body.

She wondered at the feelings that had overtaken her body, and thought of the book by Albert Hayes she'd recently read, in which the author claimed sexual arousal didn't exist in most women, except for those of ill-repute such as prostitutes and nymphomaniacs. What a ridiculous thought, as if she were destined to be a nymphomaniac or a whore.

The wet and wonderful snowflakes had turned into a biting sleet that scratched at her face as she made her way back to her boarding house. Her landlady, Mrs. Hall, chose to not reprimand her for her late arrival and lack of escort. Whether it was due to her many years of model behavior, or because she would be leaving the next day anyway, it was difficult to say. She went immediately up the stairs and into her bedroom, where her steamer trunk, crafted by Madame Laveau's late husband, was packed and ready to go, only waiting the clothes she now wore. Next to it, carefully laid out, was a more appropriate traveling wardrobe.

As Manon peeled off her wet garments, she scoffed at the writings of Doctor Hayes, and wondered, what could a man really know about a woman's mind, emotions, and body? She believed that the poets had a better understanding than the medical profession, such as that man Longfellow. His collection of *Tales of a Wayside Inn* was wonderful, but it was one poem in particular that had stayed with her through the years, that of Lady Wentworth, the gypsy girl called Martha Hilton, turned into a youthful, self-possessed, and beautiful maiden to be married to an unlikely suitor. Not that she wanted some old man to whisk her away into the clouds of paradise, for she had another picked, and just the thought of him caused her to climb naked into bed. The past three years had seen her transformed from a child to a woman in more ways than one. She thought of her very first sexual encounter, but in place of Leonidas appeared the face and body of Emmett Collins, which caused her fingers to trail down her stomach, touching her special place, fluttering, and then kneading, before rubbing more vigorously as she brought herself the pleasure of fantasy in a gasping climax.

And fantasy it was, for she feared, given the horrors she'd been reading about her beloved city, the truth of her destiny was more like that of Evangeline, the Acadian woman in another Longfellow poem, who is separated from her love, and only finds him later in life, as he dies in her arms.

CHAPTER 9

JANUARY 4, 1872

New Orleans Daily Bourbon

==

The Bourbon is Published Daily (Sunday Excepted) By P.O. Rivard
Terms: Daily $16, Weekly $5; Per Year

==

Wednesday January 3, 1868

==

Official Journal of the State of Louisiana

The Fractured Republican Party!

The split of the Republican Party in Louisiana that began last August has been intensified. When Marshall Packard convened the House Legislature in the Custom House and refused supporters of Governor Warmoth attendance, this newspaper thought events had gotten as bad as they could get. Today, at the Gem Saloon, the Custom-House Faction led by Speaker Carter has laid the groundwork to remove Lieutenant Governor Pinchback from his position due to an illegal vote, and then to impeach Governor Warmoth, while replacing him with their own man until the time of the trial. Meanwhile, the Democratic Party sits back and gloats, hoping that this party of carpetbaggers and Negroes tears itself apart, and restores white power to the government of Louisiana.

Black Delilah of Tremé Killer Strikes Again!

The Black Delilah of Tremé Killer has struck again. A young black prostitute from a house of ill repute in Tremé was found in Beauregard Square (still known to the Negro population as Congo Square) two days ago. This is the eleventh body found in this condition, where the woman was taken, beaten almost beyond recognition, raped, and then killed, but the murderer has become more brazen about depositing the body in public spaces and more frequent in his filthy desires. The killer seems to be catering to the shortened nickname being used by the Treme Population, as this is the third victim in a row with a black dot smudged onto their forehead instead of a page of scripture stuffed in their mouth. This time though, a witness saw the murdered girl climb into a carriage, driven by a black man with a tall hat, and also caught a glimpse of a red-haired man inside the carriage. The Metropolitan Police Force has been useless, and begs the question, what if the women were white?

Is New Orleans Under Martial Law?

Federal Troops have been stationed at the Custom House, the Gem Saloon, the Mechanic's Institute, and other key government buildings for the past month. President Grant has declared they are to keep the peace, and will not side with either the Warmoth government or the rival government of Speaker Carter. Some claim that Grant favors the Carter Faction, as President Grant's own brother-in-law, Collector James Casey, is a strong ally. How can a state continue to operate with two rival governments claiming to be legitimate? Perhaps it is time for President Grant and the Federal Troops to step in?

There was a knock on the door, and Emmett set the newspaper down as Police Superintendent Algernon Badger entered the room, flapping a telegram in his hand. "It's official. We have orders to break-up the illegal legislature at the Gem Saloon."

Emmett rose slowly to his feet. His red hair was more tousled than usual, if possible, and his face unshaven. "What does that mean?"

"I want you to take a group of the men and evict them from the premises. Make sure Carter gets the message that he is done."

"And if they resist?"

"Try not to kill anybody."

Thus, an hour later, Emmett was leading about sixty policemen armed with clubs to the Gem Saloon. Going on twenty-four years of age, he had finally fully matured physically, and while not burly, was quite strong, and had been engaged in the business of violence since he was fourteen. They burst through the door and into a swirling melee of bodies—punching, kicking, and bashing.

With casual precision, Emmett waded through the fracas in search of his target, finally spotting Speaker Carter in a corner with two men guarding him, one of them a street tough known as Finnbar, and the other a mean looking Sicilian. Emmett made a beeline to them, first jabbing his club at Finnbar's throat, under the belief that he'd be the tougher of the two men. A meaty forearm knocked it aside, and Emmett barely bobbed his head to avoid the brunt of a sweeping hook, the knuckledusters just brushing his chin. He wheeled on his toes in a full circle, spinning to bring his elbow around into the Irishman's cauliflower ear. He felt, more than heard, the crunch of the cartilage as the man staggered to the side.

The Sicilian stepped forward and thrust a short-tapered blade at his exposed ribs, and Emmett brought the club down hard, knocking the knife from his hand, but in doing so, opening himself to a crushing blow to the forehead from the now-recovered Finnbar. He staggered back with the beefy man closing in, his vision clouded by tears, but his body reacted instinctually, honed by the past ten years into a fighting machine, and a very nasty one at that. He sidestepped and let the momentum of the oversized thug trip over Emmett's leg, sending Finnbar crashing to the floor. Without hesitation, Emmett brought the club in a wide arc overhead, and then down on the back of the man's head with a sickening whop, much like when he used to explode old pumpkins with a stick as a kid. He turned, blinking away the tears, to see the smaller man sidling away as if on some uncertain errand.

Emmett dropped the club on Finnbar's inert form and stepped to the cowering Speaker Carter. He grasped him by the jacket-collar and propelled him towards the door through the havoc, a passageway opening up in the ranks of the fighting men as if by design. He threw the man into the street as others loyal to Carter were jettisoned to join him in the filth of the gutter. Into the wake of this chaos walked Governor Warmoth, who viewed the destruction with satisfaction, nodded to Emmett, and then left for the Mechanic's Institute, so that the legislators still loyal to him could appoint a new speaker.

Later that night, Emmett tipped back a shot of whiskey, and then slammed the glass upon the counter and pushed it at the bartender to be refilled. He'd lost count of how many he'd had. Didn't care. It'd been a long day doing shit work. 1872 had already proven to be a long year, and it was only four days old. This wasn't what he'd signed up for. He'd gone from an important federal official courting a wealthy and beautiful widow, to a single, lonely bachelor busting the heads of thuggish politicians for a living.

I won't be poor again, Susannah had told Emmett. A man could get by if he had nothing, but a woman? There were few choices for a destitute woman, and the idea of returning to the brothel was not on her list.

He'd tried to ask her to marry him, Emmett Collins, but the words wouldn't come out. At the time, he thought it was due to the stinging slap she'd just delivered to his senses. As the days and weeks and months had elapsed, however, he'd begun to, at first just catch glimpses of what and who she was, then to plumb the ugly depths and come out on the other side having tasted the bitterness of a twisted soul. For the plain truth was that he didn't much want to be married to her.

Was it the casual disdain towards her servants? The ease with which she donned—and let fall—the Southern belle act, drawl and all? And he would never forget that sidewalk altercation with the drunken Black sailors. Outside of a few days of amorous congress years earlier, they had little in common. Each of these and all in sum had soured the concept of proposing.

That thought hadn't yet emerged as he'd attended the MacLeod wedding, planning all the while to stop it, disrupt it, and steal her away—and instead doing nothing and sitting quietly through the ceremony. But the past few years on a barstool, with a glass of brown liquor in front of him, had illuminated this undernourished truth that he was not in love with Susannah Shaw de Villiers. He'd woodenly congratulated Mr. and Mrs. Campbell MacLeod, and the next day agreed to join the Metropolitan Police force.

At first, his job had been to protect the peace, which often meant keeping poor freedmen from being beaten or killed by unhappy white men, known as "crackers" for the whips they employed driving teams to and from the city. Over the past few years, his friend, Governor Henry Warmoth, had slowly turned his back on his Black constituents and befriended the wealthy white Southern establishment. This had caused a fracture in the Republican Party that had led to today's violence.

Emmett's reverie was interrupted by the voice of Pinckney Pinchback. "Thought I might find you at this doggery."

"Didn't know you were looking for me," Emmett said more meanly than intended, the whiskey giving his words a hard edge.

"Hello to you as well." Pinchback had used his knowledge of men learned as a riverboat gambler into becoming a skilled politician, first as a Senator and then Speaker and now Lieutenant Governor.

"Sorry, Pinch. Don't mind me."

Pinchback motioned for the bartender to bring him a glass of the good stuff. He'd turned his political success into financial success through meticulous investments, and had recently opened his own factorage on Carondelet Street, *Pinchback and Antoine Commission Merchants*. "Care to take a break from that rotgut and savor a quality bourbon from Kentucky?"

"Wouldn't say no." Emmett offered his glass for a pour from the bottle.

"You hear the Black DOT Killer murdered another one?"

"Yeah, Badger was having a fit about it this morning."

"Is there anything the Met can do, aside from warning the girls?"

"We've increased patrols in Tremé, where most of the girls came from. Other than that, there isn't much to go on, only what one fellow saw a while back, a girl getting into a carriage. Didn't know what kind, but it was fairly large. Nothing about the driver other than his tall hat. Said it was a white man inside with red hair. Doesn't narrow it down much, now, does it?"

Pinchback took a careful sip of his bourbon. "Sure, it does. Not that many men in New Orleans with red hair."

"Just to get people off our back about the whole thing, I might just confess and turn myself in," Emmett retorted hotly.

"I hope it doesn't turn out to be you. You've proven to be quite crucial to my political success." Pinchback raised his glass and tipped it towards Emmett. "That was good work today." He took a slug and set the glass back on the bar.

Emmett ignored the toast, even though he craved the smooth liquid he knew rested within his glass. "Busting up a bunch of politicians from doing their jobs? Not something that people from Maine can be proud of, but perhaps it's a commendable action in the South."

"Perhaps you think that we should just let the opposition party conspire against us? They were trying to remove me as Lieutenant Governor. Don't think for a second that they won't use violence and force whenever they have the upper hand." Pinchback drew a white handkerchief from his vest pocket and carefully touched it to his lips.

"I might as well be an Irish Paddy right off the boats in New York City working for the bosses."

Pinchback replaced the linen in his pocket after folding it carefully. "What part don't you like?"

Several thoughts swirled through Emmett's head, but his tongue finally settled on just one. "I guess if we was busting up a meeting of Ogden and his Crescent City Club, I wouldn't have a problem."

"Right and wrong is not always black and white," Pinchback replied after a moment's reflection.

Emmett took a mouthful of the bourbon, holding it for a few seconds, savoring its smooth taste. It was definitely better than what he'd been drinking, which must have been an extraordinary difference for him to perceive in his present state of drunkenness. "It seems to me that Kellogg and Carter differ from you and Henry in that they want to create more equality for everybody. That seems pretty black and white."

"Real change takes time." Pinchback glared down the counter at a white man giving him an eyeful because he was a Black man sitting at the bar.

"Maybe the reins need to be let out a little bit is all?" Emmett finished his glass and banged it down on the bar. "Hell, maybe it's time to give this nag her head and hold on for the ride."

"I'm going to let you in on something, my friend from Maine." Pinchback leaned toward Emmett, who instinctively tottered closer. "I've always been Black." He returned to an upright position on the stool, his thick forearms resting on the bar, staring forward at the mirror in which he saw a well-dressed Black man and a somewhat grungy drunken white man staring back.

"Perhaps you think I woke up one morning and decided to be Black, or had grown that way overnight. Well, that's not the case. My mother was a slave who fucked her master, and over time, produced me and my brothers and sisters. It got her out of the fields. It gave her and us our freedom. Maybe she even loved the man, I don't know. But she was a Black slave and therefore I was born Black. When I was twelve, the man died and we fled to the north so as not to be thrown back into bondage. All my life I've had to say, 'Yes Sir, I'm sorry mister, I'll get right on that, of course you can have my seat, and I understand you don't want my kind in here.' I've had to look over my shoulder to see who might be coming up to put a blade in me just because of the color of my skin, and I sleep at night with a loaded gun under my pillow, because it might be the night that Ogden and his crew decide it's time to make the 'uppity Negro' who don't know his place disappear forever."

"That's what I'm saying, Pinch." Emmett struggled to hook the words together. "You don't need to be taking it slow. You shouldn't have to fear just because you have black skin."

"And I'm saying that I don't need some white boy coming down from New England and telling me what I need to fear and what I don't." Pinchback matched Emmett's uneven speech with precision, each word articulated and blunt, hard as the man who spoke them. "Opportunity has increased greatly for me over the past ten years, but I agree with Governor Warmoth that if we push too fast that the backlash is going to be harsh. I don't want to see any more Black folk strung up or with their genitals stuffed in their mouths like those boys we fished out of the canal."

"I don't know." Emmett shook his head doggedly. "You can't have it both ways. Henry alienates the Democrats with one hand, and is now shoving the Republicans away with the other."

"Politics is surely no cup of tea," Pinchback agreed. "I'd rather have my back to the wall with three men coming at me with knives than deal with some of these people down at the Mechanic's Institute." He shook his head slightly at some memory that he didn't share. "But I need to know that I, that we, can count on you to watch our backs. The agony is going to get piled higher before it gets better."

"You know I got your back, Pinch," Emmett sighed. "It was just a bad day. Bashed in some mudsill's head just because he was protecting a man who disagrees with my friend, the Governor."

"Word is, you've had a lot of bad days lately." Pinchback continued to stare straight ahead as he judged the impact of his words. "People been saying you've been hitting the grog pretty hard for some time now."

Emmett started to refute this as nonsense, but then shut his mouth. He knew that he was drinking too much, in fact, was able to remember the disdain he felt for men who drank as copiously as he now did nearly every night.

Pinchback waited for an answer, and then judged the silence to be reply enough. "You been over to Madame Laveau's house lately?"

"Not for a bit," Emmett replied.

"That girl is back from the land of steady habits. She was asking about you when I stopped over there today."

Susannah MacLeod found Freedom America in the front hallway speaking in hushed tones with Ben, the butler. "*Ahh'd* like to get some air. Would you be able to accompany me?" She'd been at the White House in New Orleans for the New Year's Ball, and was worried that Campbell would be sending her back to the plantation soon.

"Yes, Missus MacLeod." Freedom retrieved his Micawber top hat, held the door for her, and then took the proffered parasol and opened it. The hat and a black tuxedo were what he was expected to wear every day, now that he worked for Campbell MacLeod. It was a long way from working the docks as a stevedore.

Freedom was careful to shield her from the dangerous sun, wondering at how her skin could be so white.

"Tell me about yourself," she commanded, as they ambled down the side of the street. He'd only taken over as the manservant/driver for her husband the day before, replacing Kitch, who had mysteriously disappeared. She held out hope he would show up, but Campbell seemed pretty certain he was gone for good, and had gone right out and hired a new man. "How did you come by the name Freedom America?"

"When General Butler came into Louisiana, Missus, I walked off my plantation. I found myself living in a Black community in the Bayou, and we struggled day-to-day to eat. There was a nice lady that would bring us food. I wasn't talking much, then, and when she couldn't get my name out of me, she started calling me Freedom. The other part got added later." In truth, he'd escaped the plantation before Butler arrived, and in fact, the woman who brought them food was Marie Laveau, but he didn't think Missus MacLeod needed those details.

"Campbell says you can read and write? Where did you learn about books?"

"My old master let us do some schooling, Missus." This was an outright lie, but he didn't think she needed to know he'd signed up to fight for the Union Army in the *Corps d'Afrique*. When they weren't fighting, General Banks had started a program of educating the Black soldiers. No, he didn't think her new husband would care to know that one whit.

"Do you have family?"

"No, Missus. My folks died before I knew them."

"And you're not married?" Susannah asked.

"I had a wife, once, sort of." Freedom thought of Betty, and the glorious two years with her.

"What happened to her?" Susannah stepped up onto the boardwalk running down Royal Street. She realized that it was right here a few years earlier that she'd had the run-in with those Black sailors.

"She was sold, Missus."

Susannah stopped dead in her tracks, causing the parasol to momentarily leave her face bare to the sunshine. It was easy to forget the reality of slavery. "Did you attempt to find her after gaining your liberty?"

"Mister Collins, he spent most of a year tracking her down."

"Emmett Collins?" Susannah asked sharply.

"Yes, Missus. That's the one. He was an agent for the Freedman Bureau, but more than that, he was a man who truly cared. Not all those people from up North are carpetbaggers, it seems."

"Did he find your wife?"

"In a way. He found a death certificate for her up in Mississippi."

Susannah resumed walking, wondering if perhaps Campbell would let this man be her manservant. Certainly Ben, the butler, could take over the driving duties? Of course, she had Coffey for house things, but Campbell liked a male escorting her about town. The reality was, they weren't together that often, and she needed a driver every bit as much as he did. Ben had been serving Campbell since before his freedom. Perhaps he could add driving duties to his assignments for her husband. With her mind made up to ask Campbell that very night, Susannah went on to ask Freedom more about what he knew of Emmett Collins.

The day after seeing Pinchback, Emmett woke with new enthusiasm.

He filled a tub and bathed, shaved, and combed his hair. He got out his clean uniform, polishing the buttons of his jacket before slipping it on and attaching the belt holding the baton. This was not the heavier, longer club used yesterday, but a shorter, and perhaps more menacing truncheon. Last, he secured his round badge of bronze imprinted with the number "81" in black. He was in Superintendent Badger's office in the police station shortly after sunrise.

"You cleaned yourself up, Captain Collins," Badger stated, his walrus mustache rising and falling in a rippling fashion as he spoke.

Emmett felt his face redden, as he realized the state of disrepair he must have been in if a bit of warm water and a clean uniform would bring instant recognition. He wasn't going to lie to himself, his head was still thick from the night before. The fleeting thought that at the end of the day he might pay a visit to the Laveau house helped clean some of the cobwebs out of the attic. "Yes, sir. Pinch came by and gave me a bit of a kick in the ass last night."

"Suppose I should've done that myself, but you being friendly with the Governor and the Lieutenant Governor puts me in a bit of an awkward situation," Badger replied.

A man stuck his head in the door. "The Governor wants to see you both at his office in the Mechanic's Institute."

A half hour and a brief carriage ride later, Emmett looked around the room and wondered why he'd been included in this gathering. Governor Warmoth, Lieutenant Governor Pinchback, Chief Badger, General Longstreet who was now head of the state militia, Frederick Ogden, and Marie Laveau sat around a long table. No introductions were needed, and the business at hand was immediately delved into.

"Chief Badger," Warmoth began, "can you give us an update on what the Metropolitan Police Department is doing about the, er, incidents involving the prostitutes?"

"Murders," Marie Laveau said quietly.

"Excuse me?" Warmoth looked over at her.

"These are not 'incidents', Governor Warmoth. Young women are being taken off the streets, badly beaten, tortured, raped, and then killed. They are not 'incidents'."

"Prostitutes," Ogden said.

"Young women," Laveau replied.

"Who make a living by pleasuring men for money," Ogden said. "It's not like they're innocents."

Marie Laveau brought the full force of her gaze onto his face, a mirthless smile on her lips. "Do you think less of the men who frequent these establishments, as well as the women who work in them, Mr. Ogden?"

Ogden looked as if he wanted to shrink into his seat. If his wife found out that he visited the brothels on occasion, the love of his life would fly out the door. And if the Crescent City Democrat Club found out it was Black girls with whom he chose to lay? He was very discreet, of course, but this Marie Laveau seemed to know everything that went on in this city, so he wouldn't deem it impossible that she knew his secret.

"Chief Badger?" Warmoth let Ogden off the hook. "What is the Met doing about the Black Delilah of Tremé Killer?"

"Of the eleven confirmed cases, nine of them were abducted after midnight. We have doubled our patrols in Tremé during those hours. We have spread the word that the girls should not walk alone, should not agree to get into a carriage, and in no circumstances should they work outside of the brothels."

"But that's not a reality, is it?" Pinchback said. "There are lots of women who aren't even attached to a brothel plying their wares on the streets."

"I believe the number of murders is closer to thirty," Marie Laveau said.

"What?" Longstreet blurted out involuntarily.

"As the Lieutenant Governor said, there are many young ladies working the streets on their own, and their disappearances often don't get reported, for there is nobody to report it." Marie Laveau looked at each man at the table one by one. "If you remember, the first girls found had been dumped in spots where they might not be found. By my count, this very sick man has taken, beaten, raped, and killed at least thirty young Black women."

"What else do you want us to do?" Badger raised his hands in confusion.

"I believe you have a witness that says the man has red hair?" Marie Laveau looked at Emmett. "That is a start."

"We can't arrest every man with red hair," Badger replied.

"The man is in a fancy carriage with a driver, thus a man of means." Laveau turned her stare onto Ogden. "Or posing as one, perhaps? Are they working together, this Black driver and red-haired mystery man?" The idea that a Black man might work with a white man in such a criminal enterprise had most of the men shaking their heads.

Warmoth broke the silence with a question. "Mr. Ogden, I know that you are pressed for time today, but do you think that you can mobilize the Crescent City Democrats to help out?"

"What is it that you want?" Ogden asked warily.

"Information," Laveau said. "Anything that can be helpful. Have your members ask around."

"You want my people to investigate some dead darkie whores?" Ogden retorted, the blood rushing to his face, again brought up by the knowing look in Marie Laveau's eyes. "I will see what I can do. But now, I must leave for another meeting." He stood up and walked out the door.

"That was uncomfortable," Pinchback said to the closed door.

"We have to include the Democrats in our planning if we have any hopes for success, Pinch," Warmoth said. "If we are stonewalled at every turn, we will never force this…" he paused, looked at Madame Laveau, before finishing, "murderer out into the open."

"Chief Badger, I was hoping you could put together a special detail of men tasked with the sole purpose of hunting down this wretched beast? We," Warmoth looked at Laveau and Pinchback, "thought that Captain Collins could head this up, and in turn, keep all of us informed of any progress."

Badger nodded. "You thinking about ten men?" He looked sideways at Madame Laveau, but didn't say anything. It was the first time he'd had one of his men report directly to the Voodoo Queen of New Orleans, but it seemed perfectly natural, given her stature, connections, and power in both the Black and white communities.

"General Longstreet, I asked you to attend today to see if the militia could provide some support to the Met in Tremé." Warmoth moved the conversation on.

"I can provide twenty men. Maybe Chief Badger and I can get together afterwards and work out how to integrate them into the patrols, cover all the shifts, particularly late at night, it would seem."

"Captain Collins will be tasked to head the patrols in Tremé from now on. Perhaps the three of you can work it out?"

"I will leave you to your planning, gentlemen." Madame Laveau said, her flowing dress with its bright floral pattern rippling around her as she rose to her feet. "Thank you, Governor Warmoth, for treating this seriously. Maybe Captain Collins could stop by my house later to avail me of the plans? I would like to reassure the Black women in New Orleans that their safety and protection are also important."

"It might be late," Emmett said, his head swimming with this latest development.

"I do not sleep very much these days," Madame Laveau said, opening the door. "I will expect you."

Once she was gone, Warmoth sighed in relief. "Whew. I thought Ogden was going to leap over the table and wrap his hands around her throat, but he seemed pretty cowed by her. It was worth inviting him just to see that." He chuckled.

Emmett spent the rest of the day working up the patrols, detailing this one to check in with Ogden and that with Warmoth as events progressed—*if* they progressed, he thought. It wasn't until darkness filled the sky that Emmett was able to report in to Madame Laveau on St. Ann Street. He had an inkling that her request was for more than just an update, and that the return of Manny might have something to do with it. This, he recognized, excited him. He heard the drumming before he reached the gate, and remembered that it was indeed Friday night. He eased into the yard, still dressed in his policeman uniform, suddenly embarrassed that he hadn't been to the house in a few years.

As was customary at the fêtes of the Voodoo Queen, a wide variety of people filled the open space. There were women that he knew to be prostitutes, but luckily recognized none that he'd visited. He was not a frequent customer of the brothels in New Orleans, but had to admit that sometimes the urge grew too strong and the drink coursed too thickly through his veins, causing him to end up at this house or that to relieve his carnal yearnings.

The majority of the crowd was Black women, modestly dressed for the cooler weather, dancing and flitting about, along with a scattering of white women. There were a few men, the Blacks swaying to the rhythm, while the white people seemed to be mostly interested in the more provocative women dancers. And of course, there were a few Indians. Emmett recognized a squaw he knew from the Choctaw tribe, a woman who sometimes supplied him with information that white men couldn't, or wouldn't, share.

Like a queen attending a show, Marie Laveau presided over the festivities from a wicker chair on the veranda of the house. Emmett went up to fill her in on the direction of the investigation, but she waved him off, told him to get some food, and they could talk later. This was fine with Emmett, as he was ravenous, and he found his way to the pot of stew, which he ate standing under the fig tree.

Once the bowl was wiped clean, Emmett's eyes were drawn to Marie the younger, the signature snake curled upon her shoulders, but the woman next to her quickly attracted his attention. It was as if she were part of the earth, her body moved as if by its rotation, her slim form clad in a shimmering dress undulating sinuously, its slow, sensuous motion drawing his eyes like a moth to flame. She had her arms raised over her head, stretching for the heavens, her elbows slightly cocked, her fingers flickering overhead as if reeds in the bayou. She was slightly taller than the women near her, and more lithe, though no stick figure. Her *derrière,* as the Creoles would say, filled the backside of the dress amply, causing Emmett to blush and move his gaze up to her proud shoulders and elongated neck. As she pivoted sideways with the motion of nature, his eyes reached the profile of her face, and a memory of the senses narrowed his focus. The woman gyrated another half step around to coincide with the moon streaking through the light cloud cover to fully illuminate Manny.

She smiled, as if she knew he was watching, even though he was back from the fire by the fig tree. But sure enough, she walked directly through the turbulence to him. "Hello, Emmett," she said quietly, her eyes searching his face.

He stumbled for words. "Manny. Manon. You're back. You've grown up. I mean, your body. You're beautiful."

"Thank you, I think." Her face changed from curious to accusatory. "You told me that you would write."

"I'm sorry about that, but I sure enough tried. I've a half-dozen partially written letters stacked in a book in my room. I couldn't ever get through any of them. Maybe it was because I'd nothing good to say."

"You could have written that I was beautiful. That would have been nice," she teased, enjoying his obvious discomfort.

"Well, I didn't know, I mean, you were just a..." Emmett physically bit his lip to shut himself up.

"You have changed, as well." Manon stepped closer to inspect his face. "Would you call those things on your cheeks sideburns, or did your hair just get away?"

Emmett ignored this barb as he began to collect his wits. "When did you get back?"

"The day before you dragged Speaker Carter from the Mechanic's Institute and deposited him in the street." She smiled wickedly. "It was all the talk."

"Ex-Speaker Carter. His seat has been officially declared vacant and O.H. Brewster has replaced him," Emmett rejoined, with a fiendish grin of his own.

She laughed, her hazel eyes flashing, more blue hue than green or dark in this moonlight. "And this is what you have become in my absence? A street thug doing the dirty work of your political bosses?"

Emmett shrugged. "I'm supposed to be a captain of the cavalry in the Metropolitan Police, but sometimes the distinction between that, and your assessment, becomes blurred. Have you returned to be a teacher?"

"Yes. At the Union Normal School."

"What'd you think of New England?" he asked, having a hard time imagining her anywhere but here.

"I was very lonely at first. My only friend was the woman in whose home I rented a room. She took me in like I was her daughter and filled me with stories of her grandmother, who was known as Mum Bett." Manon smiled as she remembered the kindly woman. "Mum

Bett sued her owner all the way back in 1781 for her freedom, and won, setting a precedent for emancipation of all slaves in Massachusetts."

"She sounds like quite a woman," Emmett acknowledged.

"It was her kindness—and her stories of Mum Bett—that were my inspiration to not give up," Manon admitted.

Emmett had forgotten how much he enjoyed her precise, clipped speech. She appeared to have lost the tinge of a French accent during her stay in New England. "And snow? How did you like snow?"

Manon laughed. "It was very exciting at first. It was so dazzling. Exquisite, really. And then, after a bit, it was just cold and messy." She blushed, remembering the details of her last snowstorm, and the events afterwards.

Sort of like my life, Emmett thought dryly. But things were definitely looking up for the first time in a long while. "And is there a Mr. Manon?"

"You mean, do I have a Mr. Man?" she asked straight-faced.

"You know what I mean. Have you married?" Emmett asked a little more forcefully than he had intended.

"I heard that your widow up and married Campbell MacLeod." Manon switched the emphasis back to Emmett. "I am sorry."

Emmett shrugged. "It was a difficult pill to swallow at first, but then I couldn't remember what it was I liked about her."

Over the past few years, Manon had grown to the realization that most men needed to be told what they liked and what they didn't like. "Your soul was always too good for her. Did you find yourself a new woman?"

"No. I guess I haven't tried all that hard," he replied uncomfortably.

"Why not?"

"I don't know," Emmett mumbled, and then surprised himself with his next words. "Why'd you have to go all the way to Boston to become a teacher?"

"I always knew I was going to become a teacher. As for why Boston, why, I thought you were going to marry that yellow-haired white widow, and I couldn't bear to be around for it." Manon's eyes were stretched into two perfect circles, her pert nose drawn in over quivering lips.

And then Emmett understood. It was Manon. It had always been Manon. Even before he dropped over the wall into Marie Laveau's courtyard, it was Manon. He'd just been too consumed by Susannah de Villiers to fathom the truth. "Why is that?" he asked, stepping slightly forward.

"I think you know the answer to that," Manon replied. "But if I need to spell it out for you, I will. I have loved you since I first found you lying outside my home and laid a damp cloth upon your brow. I do not know why, I just know what is."

"I know," Emmett said. "I'm just sorry it took me so long to see it."

"A great many things have changed," she said.

"I hope not everything." He froze, his insides clenching in regret.

"I am not the same person I was four years ago."

"Neither am I," he said. "But at least I know that I love you, even if it is too late."

"I have told you before, and I will tell you again, Emmett Collins, that time does not run along a fixed line, not in Voodoo, not even in life."

"What do you mean?"

"It is never too late."

He leaned in the remaining inches between them and kissed her, and the long years spent apart melted away as if they'd never occurred. Above them on the veranda, Marie Laveau smiled, and the *lwa* paused to mark this moment, and then the earth resumed its rotation in a dizzying rush that returned the stars to their rightful place in the heavens.

CHAPTER 10

February 12, 1872

"That's a beautiful weapon," Frederick Ogden said with wonder, admiring the massive broadsword over the mantle, its double-edged steel glinting sinisterly in the flickering light of the room, its lobed pommel separating the large handle from the four-foot blade. "Is it a family piece?"

"My ancestor wielded this *claidheamh-mòr* alongside William Wallace at the Battle of Stirling Bridge in the 13th century."

"May I?" Ogden asked in the voice of a boy wanting to borrow his friend's favorite toy.

"Go ahead, but be careful, I keep it sharp—though the smithy curses me for it. Would be a shame to leave a weapon as beautiful as that useless."

Ogden tenderly grasped the blade with his left hand, and the hilt with his right, and lifted it down like a box of eggs. "It's heavy."

"Over six pounds," MacLeod replied. "It's meant for two-handed use."

"One could cleave a man in two with this beast." Ogden carefully lifted the sword back into its resting spot.

"I imagine it could tell a story or two if it could talk," MacLeod agreed. "But come, let's join the others and get to the business at hand."

"I'd love to see what it could do," Ogden said with wonder, finally tearing his gaze from the blade as he followed MacLeod to his seat in the circle of men.

Once they were settled with all eyes on him, MacLeod began the formal session by thanking them for their attendance. "It's not well known that we're meeting," he added, "and I suggest that we keep this secret for a *wee* bit longer."

"As long as it's not too long," Colonel Alcibiades DeBlanc growled. "I didn't start the Knights of the White Camellia so as to wear a hood and robe the rest of my life. Damn things are hot as hell and itchy to boot!"

"Don't *ye* worry, Colonel DeBlanc," MacLeod replied. "The day is coming when New Orleans will resume her position as the jewel of the South. Just a *wee* bit longer, is all I ask."

"I've agreed to hear what you have to say." Colonel DeBlanc nodded his head. "And am willing to keep our common interests quiet for now."

"I'll let Frederick Ogden do the explaining," MacLeod said, resting his hand on the man's shoulder.

Ogden spoke up without rising from his chair. "The Crescent City White League believes that we've a real opportunity for white Southern rule to reclaim the legislature in the upcoming election, and also to place a staunch Democrat in the governor's seat."

"Who did you have in mind?" Colonel DeBlanc asked. He was the de facto ruler of the Acadian population in Louisiana, and thus, controlled thousands of votes.

Ogden turned to the man next to him. "For those of you who don't know, this is Judge John McEnery. He was raised in Monroe, where he still resides, got his law degree from the University of Louisiana, was a Lieutenant Colonel in the War of Northern Aggression. After, he was elected to the state legislature, but never seated."

"I know John well," DeBlanc replied. "And he's a fine man, but a bit soft on the smoked Irishman question, if you ask me."

Ogden broke in before McEnery could reply. "If it was up to me, we'd send all the darkies back to Africa, but sometimes we have to make compromises."

"Some of us need them to work our plantations," MacLeod said. "I think it best we not act rashly, but merely put them back into the subservient role where they belong."

"Sense or no sense, I just get tired of looking at them." Ogden grunted. "But that is the compromise I guess I have to make, which is my point. Colonel McEnery is the smart choice, because he should be able to sway the vote of the more conservative Republicans. Hell, we might even get Warmoth to side with us if the Democrats get too radical on the darkie question."

In the end, all twelve men decided to support the candidacy of John McEnery in the fall election. It was also resolved to try and drive a wedge between the Republicans, and even attempt to lure Henry Clay Warmoth into backing the Democrats. A round of good scotch and fine cigars formalized this pact, the group gabbing until late into the night. Many retired ruing the hour, as all would have to be up and off about their business with the crack of dawn, the next day being a very special one indeed in these parts.

"Happy Mardi Gras, Freedom," Emmett said, as he and Manon ran into the man when they came out of the gate onto St. Ann Street outside of the Laveau household.

Freedom America had the day off because Boss MacLeod, and his wife, Susannah, were attending the parade together. It was Emmett who'd gotten him the job with MacLeod, but it wasn't until recently he discovered there were strings attached, and these strings came in the form of information.

"I barely recognize you, Mister Collins," Freedom said with wonder. Emmett and Manon were clothed in purple cotton robes draped over bright yellow Zouave pantaloons with gold masks hiding their faces. Green handkerchiefs hung below the mask, and white gloves were matched in color by a bowler topper. "Hello, Miss Manon."

"We are carousers of Comus with no color nor gender," Emmett replied.

"You both be bright enough to make a blind man see," Freedom said.

"The Mistick Krewe of the School of Design has designated purple, gold, and green to be the official Mardi Gras colors," Manon said excitedly. "Aren't they great?"

"I guess, sure enough," Freedom said with hesitation. "I heard something that might interest you."

"Do you mind walking with us? We want to be sure to get a seat for the arrival of Rex," Emmett said. "There's a new Mistick Krewe that's been buzzing all week about a king of the carnival." He took Freedom's arm and steered him down the street. "Do you have something to tell me?"

"Boss MacLeod, he had some men out to Rio al Lago last night. I'd gone to bed with my window cracked, and woke up some time later to voices that had that loudness from too much likker. I sure enough recognized the voices. Boss MacLeod and Mister Ogden were sitting on the veranda smoking cigars and still working on that brown juice."

"Go on," Emmett urged, as a group of ghouls jostled into them. Manon wrapped her arm through his so as to not get separated, and her touch made his heart pound with her warmth and closeness.

"Well, one thing stuck out, sure enough. Mister Ogden asks Boss MacLeod why he wasn't running for governor his own self, and you know what Boss MacLeod said?" When neither of them replied, Freedom continued. "Boss said once the Federal troops leave that he'd run for governor and win in such a landslide it would carry him right to the White House. He thinks that '76 would work well enough. He said that it would be best to, to con-soli-date power secretly, and then gradually come out publicly and kick all the carpetbaggers back North and teach us Black folks our proper place."

Emmett nodded. Of course, MacLeod had political aspirations. He had all the money he could ever need. He'd a young bride to flaunt around on his arm, and was able to pay other women to please him as needed, but what he truly wanted was power. They walked another block in silence. "He say anything else?"

"You know that other thing you asked me to keep an ear open for? Any mention of those poor young Black women murdered by that fellow they call the Black DOT?"

Emmett froze. Campbell MacLeod certainly fit the profile of a red-haired man of means. When Emmett had been assigned the special task force investigating the murders, he'd asked Freedom to keep his ears open. "What did you hear?"

"The Boss said that murderer deserved a medal for cleaning the filth off our streets, and that Mister Ogden, he agreed. They both had a good laugh and went back inside."

"Thank you, Freedom. Are you sure you don't want to join us to watch the parade?" It certainly sounded like MacLeod might be harboring some deep racist ideals, but drunken talk of celebrating the killer was a long way from being the killer.

"No thank you, Mister Collins. I got some things to see to, sure enough, but I'm hoping to attend Dan Rice's Circus at Congo Square tomorrow."

"We went last night in Washington Square. They sure know their horses. The riding is outstanding, especially that W. H. Morgan fellow."

"And the dogs. Who would think that you could train a dog to do the things that Professor Davis did? That brown Spaniel bitch, what was her name, Fanny? It was like she was human." Manon sparkled with the memory. "And Pete and Barney, the mules? You will have a great time, Freedom. You must go."

"Ben, the butler for Boss MacLeod, he said there were two boys, six and seven years of age he said, who must be part flying squirrel the way they soar through the air," Freedom said.

"Is Ben still driving for MacLeod?" Emmett had been unhappy when Freedom had moved from driver for MacLeod to personal manservant for Susannah. With their three houses, it was rare for the two of them to be together, thus he had less of an eye on the man's doings.

"Sure is, Mister Collins. Boss MacLeod said ole' Ben could hit a bump in the road that weren't even there, but he ain't found anybody new just yet." Freedom had been rather happy when Missus Susannah had sweet talked her husband into allowing Freedom to become her personal servant, driver, and bodyguard, as the Boss scared him the way he looked at him most times.

"I had to cover my eyes I was so scared for those boys in the circus," Manon said.

"No matter how wonderful these other acts are, Dan Rice is still the master of the ring all by himself," Emmett replied. "He comes out with his dark blue tailcoat, white top hat, and cane, but all you notice are his bug-eyes popping out over those bulging cheekbones. And then he begins to speak with the voice of one of the Sirens, and you find yourself floating along with him until his wit snaps and you tumble all in a heap."

"I sure enough plan on going, Mister Collins. I got my dollar set aside to get a ticket and a bite to eat while there. You two go on now and enjoy your parade." Freedom waved his hand and veered back towards the MacLeod Mansion.

Emmett waved him back and stepped forward to meet him, whispering in his ear, "You keep an ear open, but make sure you watch your back."

"Sure enough, Mister Collins, I'll do what I can."

Emmett had reserved two seats in the stands set up in Lafayette Square across St. Charles Street from City Hall, where a semi-circular platform with immense wings had been set up and decorated to the hilt. The railings were wrapped with evergreens, and a canopy of crimson, ornamented with gold fringe and lace, gave protection from the sun, which was scorching at this time of day, even in February. A collection of flags—French, Russian, Prussian, British, and American—fluttered slightly in the breeze coming off of the Mississippi. Chinese lanterns were strung between the marble pillars of the government office, and an archway of gas jets of various colors illuminated the sky.

"There must be a few thousand people packed into these stands," Manon noted with awe, her eyes trying to take everything in at once. Overhead, a cross with sixty lights filled her vision.

"I think we're the only people in these stands in costume," Emmett replied, uncomfortable in his outlandish get-up amidst a more prim and proper audience.

"So? The beauty is that nobody will know our identity or color, today or tomorrow," Manon whispered back, pressing the green handkerchief covering her mouth against his ear. "We are just two human beings enjoying the parade."

Emmett grasped her hand in his own and squeezed, pulling her closer at the same time. "I'm glad you told me Mardi Gras is French for Fat Tuesday. I haven't had much use for the church since the Great War started, but to know that today, any sin is allowed in the eyes of God, sure is a relief."

"Your time to sin is declining, Mister Collins, as tomorrow we must go to church and begin the forty days of fasting and penance."

"Are you telling me that if I want to enjoy the excesses of Mardi Gras that I also need to adhere to the austerity of Lent?"

Manon gasped. "Look, it is the Grand Duke Alexis." A group of men had emerged onto the stage in front of City Hall, including Governor Warmoth, Mayor Flanders, and various other officials and dignitaries. Easily a foot taller than them all and thus clearly visible was the Grand Duke Alexei Alexandrovich of Russia. His manner was of distracted nonchalance, clearly a man who was used to spending a great deal of time in front of the public. "They say he is six-feet five inches tall and has magnificent dark eyes."

"I don't understand what the height of a man has to do with anything. During the war it just made you an easier target, especially on horseback. Plus, I hear that those eyes you admire so much are a little loose in his head. He almost started a war out west with the Lakota Indians due to his flirtations with an Indian maiden, and rumor has it that his visit to New Orleans may be prompted by none other than the lovely Lydia Thompson in the burlesque show *Bluebeard*."

Manon leaned in and nuzzled Emmett's neck. "What would you know about burlesque shows? And anyway, I like my men your size, Emmett Collins. Why, I could…" she caught herself and drew away. "But tomorrow I must begin to repent, and the less to repent, the better."

Emmett's envy of the towering Russian melted and turned to desire at her touch and implied words, a ravenous craving flushing his body, and it was only with effort that he changed the subject. "That man next to the Grand Duke? The one with the golden hair? That's General George Armstrong Custer; well—I guess he's a Lieutenant Colonel now. He's the finest horseman you'll ever see. If General Chamberlain and the boys from Maine saved the Union Army on the second day of Gettysburg, it was Custer who stopped Stuart from attacking our rear at Cemetery Hill the next day that allowed us final victory."

Manon thought this man also extremely good-looking, but refrained from saying so as the conversation was interrupted by cannon fire. "That must be the start of the parade," she said instead.

The procession had been organized to start at the Henry Clay Statue on Canal Street, before marching the half mile down St. Charles Ave. to pass between the stands where they sat and the stage holding the officials. It wasn't long before Superintendent Badger came into view on horseback with various officers of the Metropolitan Police leading the way. Emmett had been invited to join but had declined in favor of attending the ceremony with Manon. A band marched behind, blaring out the tune, "If I Ever Cease to Love," a choice mocking the Grand Duke in a playful manner, for this was the song Lydia Thompson was famous for in her burlesque show. It was rumored she had sung it for Alexis in a private dinner they shared.

In a house, in a square, in a quadrant
In a street, in a lane, in a road,
Turn to the left, on the right hand
You see there my true love's abode
I go there a courting and cooing
To my love, like a dove
And swearing upon my bended knee
If ever I cease to love
May sheep heads grow on apple trees,
If ever I cease to love
If ever I cease to love
May the Grand Duke Alexis,
Ride a buffalo in Texas,
If ever I cease to love.

Emmett and Manon roared with laughter along with the rest of the crowd at the ad-libbed last lines, the no-holds barred rules of Mardi Gras established. The Lord Chief Marshall came next with eight attendants, and then the man they all awaited, Rex, the new King of Carnival, with a robe, crown, and scepter astride a horse.

What followed was complete bedlam as hundreds of maskers ran and pranced through the street, costumed as kings, peasants, devils, saints, Indians, women of high and low degree, harlequins, birds, beasts, and fish. Emmett squeezed Manon's hand reassuringly as several figures dressed as baboons ran frantically through the throngs acting even more foolish than the others.

"Look." She pointed past the dancing apes, ignoring the hateful behavior she'd had to live with her entire life. A group of Chinese men dressed as heathens carrying signs with such slogans as "Here is the Pack," "May the Best Hand Win," and "This is our Little Game," introduced the next swirling diversion. Thirteen men with wooden rectangular frames that rested upon their shoulders and fell below their knees traipsed in single-file down the center of St. Charles Ave. Each of the frames held an illustration of a playing card, this one a spade, that one a diamond, with all four suits represented. When the King was abreast of the staging, he veered off, and climbed the platform stairs to present the Grand Duke, the Governor, and the Mayor with a souvenir deck of playing cards.

"I hear they're a new Krewe who call themselves 'The Pack.' They sure stand head and shoulders above the rest, and that's saying something," Emmett murmured, awestruck by the creativity of their costumes.

"They are wonderful. What a delightful imagination!" Manon agreed.

The panoply continued unabated as they watched a dizzying array of carriages, carts, milk-wagons, mounted horsemen, and dancing figures, all decorated to the nines.

A wagon passing by with a young Black woman sitting across from a white gentleman struck a chord in Manon, and she turned to Emmett. "Has your special detail come to any result?"

"We have a list of ninety-one men with means and red-hair who live in the greater New Orleans area, but new names keep cropping up. So far, we have managed to speak with only a few of them. But give us time, not that I think it will do us much good. What are they going to do, put up their hands and say, 'you got me'?"

"It seems to be scaring the man into hiding, at least," Manon said. "There hasn't been a Black DOT murder in over a month."

"We've more than doubled the patrols in the Tremé area. Your Godmother sure has a lot of clout, I'll give her that." Emmett thought of the powerful men she'd pulled in to address the problem, and the way she'd made Frederick Ogden squirm in his seat.

"She will say it all stems from having information," Manon replied.

"How does Madame Laveau know so much about everybody and everything in New Orleans?" He slid his arm around the small of her back and pulled her closer to him, if that was possible. "Do Mister Daniel Blanc and the other *lwa* also show her things, like when we saw that man who said he had a dream?"

"Papa Legba first introduced Madame Laveau to *Damballah* when she was but a child. She was at a *fête* hosted by the Reverend John, and was possessed by the supreme Serpent King, and the two have been in a relationship ever since, but he seldom bothers with the problems of man." She nestled into the opened curve of his shoulder and chest with impure thoughts echoing in her brain, her body tingling.

"So how does she know everything? Does she have a crystal ball that shows her the doings of man, as some people claim?"

Manon sighed. "Madame Laveau was a hairdresser in her younger years, and discovered that spending hours pampering wealthy women usually led to a flow of gossip that touched upon every facet of New Orleans society."

"But she doesn't still work as a hairdresser, does she?"

"Not personally, but she currently has nine women in her employment who provide this service for the most elite households in New Orleans. Madame Laveau has made clear to them that no piece of information is too small to share."

"And these society stalwarts talk openly in front of the help?"

"Often times they have been working for these affluent women for years, but yes, they spill everything." Manon took Emmett's bowler from his head and ran her fingers through his hair. "It is a wonder what people will say when their hair is teased, their scalp massaged, and they are made beautiful. It does not hurt that they usually have a champagne glass in hand. Of course, these are some of the most important women in the city, and they don't even see the Black help all around them. They simply don't exist as anything other than inconsequential beings."

"And from these women, you discover things about their husbands as well?"

Manon closed her eyes as she thought of the wiles of females and the duplicity of men. She had been friends with many of these prostitutes before she even knew what a whore was, and had learned much from them. When she opened her eyes mere seconds later, she realized for the first time that the parade was over, the stands had emptied, and although revelry surged upon the streets, they were quite alone upon their bench. "There are, of course, two genders who desire to share information."

"And that is where Madame Laveau's brothel comes in?" Emmett was well aware of the Voodoo Queen's connection to one of New Orleans largest bawdy houses.

"Most men will tell their wives nothing of consequence, while at the same time, share their most intimate thoughts and business dealings with a whore. It's called pillow talk." Manon murmured, thinking of these prostitutes, many of whom she'd known since her first memories—good women who were kind to her, liked to laugh, and were just trying to survive this man's world.

"And does Frederick Ogden frequent Madame Laveau's brothel?"

"He does occasionally," Manon said carefully. "He has a favorite girl, Lily, who he spends time with."

"How about Campbell MacLeod?"

"Mister MacLeod is a regular patron. Usually he sends a coach for Victoria, his favorite, but sometimes visits when his wife is in town."

"And do either Victoria or Lily get beat up?"

Manon pulled herself slightly away. "This, you will have to ask Madame Laveau, or perhaps, Lulu." She thought back to the week when she'd first met Emmett, and Lulu had brought Victoria to Madame Laveau to be treated. She'd been badly beaten on that day, but Manon did not know who had done it.

Emmett marveled at Madame Laveau's network of informers,

maids and footmen and, yes, prostitutes existing in a network throughout the city, in this house and that saloon, in this parlor and that drawing room. It stung that he, too, had been one of those men who had shared his most intimate secretes with a whore, the wound little assuaged by the fact that he had been a boy at the time. "Unbelievable," he muttered.

"What?" she asked.

"Nothing," he replied shaking his head. "It's just that it embarrasses me to be a man when all of our failings are presented in such a manner."

Manon pulled her handkerchief down around her neck and shifted around, pulling Emmett's gently down as well, her lips finding his in an act of forgiveness that turned greedy, their tongues urgently exploring the soft wetness of each other's mouth. She pulled back with a gasp for air before replying in a throaty growl. "Men are no different than women. They want to be powerful and important and desired. They come at it in different ways, but in the end, it is all the same."

The nighttime parade was no less marvelous, as the original Mistick Krewe of Comus paid homage to Homer through depictions of scenes from "The Iliad" and "The Odyssey." Various gods were portrayed—Venus, Mars, and Neptune among them, along with the most noteworthy of mortals, Ulysses, Achilles, Hector, Paris, and Helen to name but a few. The Cyclops was a terrifying one-eyed ogre, and the Sirens beautiful, yet, dangerous creatures with their hair of snakes and voices of golden honey.

CHAPTER 11

APRIL 16, 1872

School was closed for the day as a skunk had gotten into—or more likely been thrown into—the classroom, and the building was airing out, so Manon was able to meet Emmett for a mid-day meal. He'd been on the English side of Canal Street, interviewing a red-haired man who owned a mercantile business, establishing his whereabouts on the nights that Black prostitutes had been killed. This was a fruitless task, as the case of the Black DOT Killer had grown cold, four months having passed since the last murder. As it was, they decided to eat at The White Horse Tavern on Fulton Street.

Emmett arrived first and decided to wait outside for Manon. As he waited, he pondered the continued usefulness of committing so many resources from the local forces of justice to the hunt for the Black DOT killer, who it would seem, had gone to ground. Perhaps it was because of the investigation, or more likely the increased patrols in Tremé, or maybe even the man had moved away. He could be traveling, Emmett mused, but it was the possibility that the man had died that brought a grim satisfaction, even if his identity was never revealed. Emmett grasped the handle of the truncheon at the belt of his uniform as he thought of the man dying, and realized that of all the death he'd ever seen, this might be the only one that would ever bring him enjoyment.

He saw Manon coming down the street, her long legs skimming the boardwalk as she glided past the shops and restaurants lining the sides. He thought, for the thousandth time, how lucky he was that she'd waited for him to get his life together enough to realize the gift that had been presented to him when he had plopped over the fence into the Laveau courtyard some six years earlier. Each day was better than the last.

"Did you have any trouble getting here?" he asked, once she'd reached him.

"You mean finding it?" She gave him a quizzical look. "I grew up in this town, not you, if you remember."

That is not what he meant at all, and she knew it. He sighed and let it pass. He kissed her on the cheek, but she turned to catch his lips with her own. "I missed you," he said, even though they'd seen each other the previous day.

"And I you," she replied. "But let us eat. I am famished."

They sat themselves at a small table in the dining section, which was separated from the bar by a large arched opening. Emmett shared his frustration and unhappiness about his investigation due to the lack of new murders. Manon told of the awful smell emanating from her classroom, and ventured guesses at which pupils might have been responsible, but thought it most probably some boys from the neighboring white school.

Emmett checked his timepiece and realized they'd been there over twenty minutes, and they'd not yet been waited on, even though the man taking orders had passed by several times, and was currently speaking to a couple who'd just come in.

"Excuse me, sir," he said, waving his arm at the server. "We're ready to order."

The man gave him a dark look and turned his back.

"Let us just go somewhere else," Manon said in a low voice.

"He's just a bit grouchy," Emmett replied. "I'll get his attention when he comes by next."

"Let's not make a scene. Remember, this is white New Orleans."

The waiter went to pass by their table again, and Emmett stood up, pulling his truncheon in one fluid motion, and brought it to rest faintly touching the man's Adam's apple. "Excuse me, sir. I said we were ready to order."

The man gulped, but his beady eyes never wavered in their hatred as they glared down a long, hooked nose. "This is the White Horse Tavern. We don't serve any black beasts in here."

Through the red of his rage, Emmett saw the bartender and several kitchen staff approaching. One man held a large butcher's knife, while three others were tapping clubs against their open palms.

"It is against Louisiana law to refuse any person service because of the color of their skin," he said, reining in his anger as best he could.

"Emmett," Manon whispered. "We should just leave."

"Person, the law says, but it does not dictate I have to let animals into my place of business and feed them. There is a trough out back you are welcome to."

Emmett hit him, using the truncheon to rabbit punch his throat, the jab collapsing the man onto the floor, coughing. With his free hand, he swung Manon behind him, as he turned to face the kitchen staff. There were six other patrons in the dining room, all sitting carefully, and four men in the bar who only seemed to have a passing interest in the drama unfolding.

The bartender was a brute of a man, his head totally bald, short sleeves showcasing enormous arms as he caressed the club in his meaty paws, rolling the stick back and forth. "You shouldn't have done that, darkie lover."

"I'm suggesting you go back behind the bar, and we'll leave you be," Emmett said through gritted teeth.

"How do you face yourself each day, traipsing around with a farm animal?" The bartender's brush-like mustache was almost a square upon his face.

Emmett felt his Colt pistol pulled from the holster, and Manon stepped past him with the steel barrel pointed directly at the man. "I see plenty of you white men sniffing around Treme once the sun goes down. Isn't that right? *Sales cochons!* But in the light of day, you dirty pigs don't want anything to do with a Black woman, do you? Maybe you want to punch me around a little? Beat me? Kick me? Does the thought of hitting me excite you, you sick bastard?" She cocked the heavy pistol, holding it with both hands, her hands steady as she took the two steps and pressed the barrel against the man's forehead.

"Manon," Emmett said.

"So do it, mister. Hit me with that damn club. *Espèce de poule mouillée*! Coward, that's what you are!"

"How about we go," Emmett said quietly, touching her elbow.

"Maybe it would be easier if I did not have a weapon? If I could not defend myself? Maybe I should just lie down and play the easy woman for you?" She pulled the trigger, and the hammer clicked on an empty chamber as the man stumbled backwards. Manon allowed Emmett to take the Colt, and the two of them worked their way to the door, never taking their eyes off the bartender and his cronies, who seemed happy enough to see the mixed-race couple leave.

As they were crossing back over Canal Street, Manon looked at Emmett and said, "I know that you always keep an empty chamber for safety's sake, so that it does not go off accidentally and shoot your foot, or somebody else by mistake. But it sure was worth it to see his face. I think he might have pissed himself."

Emmett guffawed, partly from the release of tension and partly because Manon almost never departed from her somewhat ladylike ways.

Freedom America was at MacLeod's White Mansion on Magazine Street in New Orleans when Mister Ogden showed up, the one who always looked like he wanted to stomp Freedom into the ground, and then scrape him off his boots like dog shit. Boss MacLeod had been in uncommon good spirits all afternoon, and Freedom sensed that something was afoot. When the two men had gone into the library, he took the chance of listening outside the door.

Ogden's nasal voice was the first to speak. "It's a go. Douglass is going to be walking from the St. Charles Hotel to the Mechanic's Institute. He told Lieutenant Daniels to be ready to leave the hotel at 6:45."

"Excellent. Your men know what to do?"

"I picked the best of the lot. They'll do what is asked of them." Ogden's voice moved towards the door, and Freedom raised his hand as if prepared to knock in case he opened it. "It sounds like

Pinchback might walk to the lecture with him."

"Even better," MacLeod replied. "That darkie son-of-a bitch has had this coming to him for a long time."

"What about your driver? Can we trust him to keep his mouth shut?"

"I've been needing one I can trust better. He'd make a fine scapegoat. Darkie goes wild and has to be killed, if *ye* know what I mean."

Freedom checked that the Missus was still in her room with the door closed, and then hurried out the door, looking nervously left and right as he descended the spiraling stairs to Magazine Street.

Lieutenant Governor Pinchback pulled forth his pocket-watch and checked the time. The hands indicated it was 6:45, and right on cue, Frederick Douglass descended the stairs to the grandiose lobby of the St. Charles Hotel. The two of them proceeded to the huge arched doorway where four Metropolitan Policemen met them. A pair of officers led the way through the door, past the multitude of white pillars and down the stairs, followed by Douglass and Pinchback. Two policemen followed behind for the half-mile walk to the Mechanic's Institute.

Pinchback looked to his left at the setting sun and judged it would be down by the time the lecture began. There was the normal bustle of activity on Common Street at this time of the evening on a Tuesday. Wagons trundled down the street, while men on horseback weaved their way through the crowded streets, and couples strolled the boardwalk on their way to an early meal. Out front of the billiards hall next door, a clump of men spoke too loudly and whistled at a woman hurrying to her job in the hotel.

As they walked, Pinchback and Douglass resumed their conversation from earlier in the day when they'd taken a boat out on the Mississippi. The two men had butted heads on women's suffrage, with Douglass holding firm in his belief that all people, Black or white, male or female, rich or poor—should be allowed to vote—while Pinchback was equally unyielding in his opinion that politics was too messy for the delicate sensibilities of the fairer sex. It was an argument that Pinchback feared he was losing, as Douglass was extremely eloquent and persuasive in the construction of his view, all the while dismantling the concept of women and men being separate but equal.

When they reached Barrone Street, Pinchback noted warily that there were eight or ten men loitering with no apparent purpose. What really caught his eye, though, was that none of the men made eye contact. They were the sort of white ruffians who would typically hurl some insult, or at least look brazenly at a pair of well-dressed Black men accompanied by the police, but these fellows were keen on pretending they didn't even exist. He thought one of them had nodded at the young lieutenant in charge, but couldn't be sure. What if he had? Perhaps they were just acquaintances.

Even so, as they turned right, Pinchback carefully unbuttoned his suit jacket. He was not wearing the twin-holstered pistols, but still had a Colt shoved down into his waistband, and a small derringer up his sleeve, a throwback to his gambling days. Almost immediately they cut left into the alleyway that led to the back entrance to the Mechanic's Institute. Pinchback risked a look back into the setting sun and realized the loitering men were now following them down the street with purpose to their stride.

Douglass was attempting to summarize his point on suffrage as they started their way down the shaded alley. "So, as you glean from this, women should have every honorable motive to exertion which is enjoyed by man, to the full extent of her capacities and endowments. The case is too plain for argument. Nature has given woman the same powers, and subjected her to the same earth, she breathes the same air, subsists on the same food—physical, moral, mental and spiritual. She has, therefore, an equal right with man, in all efforts to obtain and maintain a perfect existence."

"No offense, Frederick, but would you mind if we continue this conversation at another time?" Pinchback asked.

"What is it?" Douglass became aware of the tension for the first time.

"Get ready to run."

Ben was perplexed. Boss MacLeod had had him pull the Mac-Wagon—the name the boss had given his large carriage—down this small alleyway behind the Mechanic's Institute, and then told him to just wait. Meanwhile, each alcove and window of the alley seemed to host shadowy figures, for he could make out vague movements in the gloom and hear the faint rustle of men stirring. What was going on?

From his perch atop the carriage, Ben looked back to Barrone Street and saw a small group of men turn into the alleyway. He realized the two in front wore the uniform of the Metropolitan Police. He saw the unmistakable figure of Lieutenant Governor Pinchback walking next to a man who must be Frederick Douglass. Ben was hoping to be done tonight in time to go hear him speak, as it was rumored that this Black man was the equal of any white man.

A group of men filled the space behind them as they approached the wagon. The alleyway rustled with the preparation and heightened awareness of the dozens of shadows. The distance closed from a hundred yards with each step, the two policemen picking up speed and lengthening the distance between them and the Black dignitaries. Ben wanted to yell a warning, but what if he was only imagining ghosts? And then the two Metropolitan officers veered to the sides, and he knew it was too late, the trap had been set and was ready to clamp shut. With a sudden clatter of racing hooves, men on horseback came charging around the corner and into the alleyway.

Emmett had been about ready to call it a day when Freedom had rushed into the station. "Mister Collins, I think there is a plan to kill the Honorable Frederick Douglass this very night," he whispered, looking right and left at the bustle of the Metropolitan precinct station. He noticed that many of the men were Black, and that his presence here seemed to draw no undue attention.

"When and where?" Emmett demanded.

"I think it's when they're walking from the St. Charles Hotel to the Mechanic's Building. They said there was policemen involved." Here, Freedom looked again at the officers surrounding them. "They're supposed to leave the hotel at 6:45."

Emmett looked at his timepiece and cursed. He turned and scanned the room. "Lieutenant Johnson!" he waved the man over. "Gather who you can of our cavalry regiment and meet me in the street in five minutes."

It was fifteen minutes before Emmett, at the head of twenty horsemen, skidded to a halt in front of the St. Charles Hotel, only to be told by the front desk clerk that they were too late, that Douglass had left accompanied by Lieutenant Governor Pinchback and guarded by four Metropolitans. The sun had disappeared behind the buildings as they pounded their way up Common Street towards the Mechanic's Institute. There had been no gunshots, nor other signs of attack, so perhaps Freedom was wrong. Maybe, just maybe, Douglass and Pinchback were safely at their destination, and this had been nothing but a false alarm.

Up ahead, Emmett just caught a glimpse of a group of men down the side street turning into an alley. An alley that he knew well led to the back entrance of the Mechanic's Institute, as he'd escaped down that same route six years earlier when chased by a white mob. He yanked the reins to the right and yelled for the others to follow suit, the horses kicking up a cloud of dust that continued in the direction they'd been heading. Emmett held his rifle loosely in his right hand as he steered the horse into the back street, slowing to a trot as they split through the cluster of men at the opening, noting the wagon blocking the far side, the movement in the shadows, and in the middle of it all, Pinchback, Douglass, and four police officers.

Emmett tipped his hat to Pinchback as he walked his horse past them and approached the Western Wagon. Lieutenant Johnson barked orders for the cavalry to surround the official delegation and be alert, an order he didn't have to give twice, as they peered anxiously behind pointed carbines at the nooks, windows, and alleyway openings. Emmett knew that the key to defusing the situation lay within the confines of the wagon ahead, but a piece of him also wanted to taunt the man within.

He dismounted and opened the door of the coach. "Mr. MacLeod! I thought I recognized this wagon. Is everything okay?"

"Everything is fine, Captain Collins," MacLeod managed to say through clenched teeth. "Just having a *wee* bit of a discussion with my associate."

"Ah, yes. Hello, Mr. Ogden. I won't be bothering you then." Emmett stepped down, avoiding looking at Ben, who stood stock-still staring as the Metropolitan Police Cavalry escorted Frederick Douglass and his retinue to the rear entrance of the Mechanic's Institute.

Pinchback insisted on Emmett sitting in the front row with him, and then excused himself to introduce the man of the hour, Frederick Douglass. Emmett gazed around the wide hall where he'd spent a great deal of time over the past six years since arriving in New Orleans. Six years earlier a mob had massacred men for considering Black suffrage at this very location, and now a Black man was orating about self-made men to a mixed audience hanging on his every word. Of course, Douglass had come just a hair from being murdered on this night, but all the same, listening to this man's passion and erudition, it sure seemed like equality was just around the corner, if not here in small measures already.

Pinchback had since finished his introduction of Frederick Douglass to enormous applause and then worked his way back to seat himself next to Emmett. "I'm glad you managed to get off your barstool and save my life this evening," he whispered dryly, settling his wide frame into the too-small chair.

Emmett chuckled. "My backside hasn't seen that barstool for a few months now. I appreciated your words of encouragement, but mostly your news of Manon's return."

Pinchback nodded. "I heard you've been spending time with young Miss Lescaut."

On stage, Douglass' voice boomed. "It is far easier to account for success in others than to explain our own failures. Men are the authors of their own misery or their own condition. The lazy man is the unlucky man, and man of luck of work. Looking into the origin of greatness, it will be found the great man was awake while others slept; economized his time while others were prodigal of theirs; was at work while others were idle."

"How is it that you showed up tonight in the nick of time?" Pinchback asked in a low-pitched voice.

"You're not the only one in town with sources," Emmett replied with a grin.

On stage, Douglass continued. "Neither learning nor knowledge come by praying. Prayer never put out a fire nor saved a ship. When

I was a slave, I prayed lustily three times a day for my freedom, but never obtained it until I prayed with my legs."

Emmett stood and applauded with the others, men and women who appreciated the prayer of action leading to freedom much more than he ever could. "She's made me whole again," Emmett said out the side of his mouth without looking at Pinchback.

"A good woman does have that ability."

"Did *ye* see the smirk on Collins' face?" he demanded of the other men. "He will die for his interference here today, that I promise *ye.* But more so, he will suffer first for his insolence." He leaned out the door so that Ben could hear his orders. "Take us to the Lake House."

Ben was disappointed, as this meant he'd get no chance to hear Frederick Douglass this evening. At the same time, he was relieved to have survived whatever incident had been brewing in the alleyway. It was a half-hour drive, and the cool night air helped to dry the sweat of fear from his skin.

"Put up the team for the night and then wait for further orders in the kitchen," MacLeod told Ben once they'd reached the house on Lake Pontchartrain. He went inside, poured two large tumblers of Talisker, and returned to the veranda to join Ogden, as they waited for the others to arrive. By the time the first of them came, MacLeod and Ogden were both on their second scotch, the brown liquor sliding down their throats smoothly, yet, stoking the fires of their hatred. When the others arrived, they moved into the study.

"As *ye* can see, it is crucial that we win the upcoming elections," MacLeod said to the room in general.

"The hell with those carpetbaggers and Sambos."

"Did you notice that more than half those Metropolitan cavalry were colored?"

"I'll damn well be handing out my own justice before calling that polluted law enforcement agency for any sort of help."

"All to protect some darkie who escaped slavery and learned to read and write."

"Don't forget that our very own Lieutenant Governor is black as dirt."

"I heard he was sending his children to white schools like they was just as good as my boys."

"The other day one of them got on the trolley and sat down next to my wife, and brushed his leg against hers."

"Next thing you know is the carpetbaggers will pass a law allowing them Smoked Irishmen to rape our wives."

It was several hours before MacLeod called for Ben.

"Yes, Boss MacLeod?" Ben hovered in the doorway. He could feel the suffocating tension smeared with liquor and sweat and anger.

"Over here, *loon*." MacLeod waved him over with his cane. "I've a question of *ye*."

Ben picked his way through two of the five men sitting in a semi-circle around MacLeod and stood in the center of the room. His grizzled grey hair was uncovered by his normal top hat, causing him to feel naked and on display more than he already was. "What is it, boss?"

MacLeod stared at him. He'd given Ben his freedom ten years ago when the Beast, Butler, had led his troops into Louisiana, and Lincoln had passed that damned Emancipation Proclamation. Not much had really changed. Hadn't he treated him well? He had a roof over his head. Ate well. Wore fine clothes. Had a bit of change to spend. "Why do *ye* suppose those policemen came down the alleyway tonight?"

"I don't know, boss." Ben shifted nervously, back and forth, his hands fumbling with his trousers.

MacLeod cocked his head sideways. "*Ye* wouldn't have tipped them off, would *ye* have?" He tapped the head of his cane absently on the floor.

"Tipped them off about what?" Ben stammered.

"Don't lie to me." MacLeod stopped the tapping, and looked up at the man he'd known for thirty years.

"I'm sorry, boss, I don't know nothing about nothing."

MacLeod stepped forward, his voice going dangerously low. "Who else could have warned Collins, if not *ye*?"

CHAPTER 12

April 20, 1872

Manon woke before sunrise to begin preparations. Today was the day. Emmett did not yet know that today was the day, but Manon had decided that it was. They'd plans to go on a picnic lunch to a spot that Manon had discovered when gathering herbs with the Choctaw squaws. There was a thin creek that flowed into Lake Pontchartrain that should be bubbling along over the jagged rocks this time of year, creating a gentle backdrop of nature's music as they ate. The running water cascaded down over rocks and pooled next to an open glade surrounded by cypress trees.

As the stove warmed, Manon mixed flour, yeast, salt, and oil, and then set it aside. She put the frying pan on the stovetop and cooked the dozen shrimp, sprinkling various spices on as she cooked them in a liberal amount of butter. After a few minutes, she removed them to cool, and then carefully washed the pan and placed it back over the heat. While it reheated, she mixed the toasted pecans with butter, sugar, milk, and vanilla. She then poured this sticky blend into the large pan, stirring frequently. Once the concoction was syrupy, she removed it from the heat and ladled dollops onto a tin sheet, and left it to cool. Within the hour these pralines would be ready to pack.

She returned to the bread, shaping it into a loaf and putting it in a pan and sliding it into the stove. By now, the shrimp had cooled, and she mixed them with some greens and onions the Choctaw had brought to her the night before. This she scooped into a Mason jar and screwed the lid into the threaded grooves, and filled another jar with a half-dozen raw oysters. She then retrieved a block of ice from the cellar, and carefully placed these two jars and a bottle of white wine against this cooling chunk. The sun had risen in the east when the bread came out, and she carefully wrapped it in a linen towel, placing it in the basket. To this, she added the pralines wrapped in wax paper, a hunk of butter, some jam, two plates, forks, knives, and cups. Now, it was time to primp and preen. She, of course, had to be as delectable as the lunch.

To his credit, Manon noted, when Emmett arrived promptly at 9:00 a.m., he was freshly shaven with a scrubbed look, and wore a neatly pressed suit, complete with bow tie and a watch chain disappearing into the pocket of his waistcoat. It looked as if he'd made some attempt to tame his unruly hair, and he came bearing a bouquet of wildflowers, the most prominent being the irises, deepest purple tinged with yellow, two of her favorite colors.

"These are for you," he said, stepping down lightly from his horse, awkwardly thrusting the flowers at her. "You look beautiful," he added.

"Thank you, they match my tignon." The wrap upon her head was indeed a mix of colored flowers including the purple and yellow iris.

"That sure is some dress," Emmett said appreciatively. Her dress was more functional than elegant, a compromise for a day in the country. Still, she'd made sure the soft, green material displayed her curves fully, lit up her hazel eyes, and made her skin glow like coffee beans in the light of the day.

"You look very nice yourself."

"You sure you don't want to take a buckboard?" Emmett asked nervously, looking first at her dress, then at the picnic basket, and finally at the bag she carried.

"No buckboard will make it to the spot I want to take you today." Manon was comfortable on a horse, even if she had to ride sidesaddle, as she must that day, given her dress. "And I don't intend to take the basket. We can move our lunch to your saddlebags."

Soon, they'd left the city limits behind. Emmett mentioned the bandits who were raiding from Mexico, or so people said, and kept checking the tie that secured his rifle in its scabbard. "I've been thinking about leaving the Metropolitan Police," Emmett said, as Manon veered off the road onto a faint path.

Manon had recognized Emmett's unhappiness in his current situation. She also knew better than to comment, as that would more than likely raise his stubborn nature. "What would you do?"

"I don't know. Maybe raise horses." Emmett rode in silence for several minutes. "How do you like being a teacher?"

"It is frustrating and wonderful all at the same time. Many of the students have been passed along without learning the basics. But for the most part, they are determined to learn and that inspires me." Manon thought of her students, many older than herself, French Creoles, former slaves, men and women who had matured in freedom from bondage, but still felt the heavy yoke of discrimination. "It makes me feel like I am making a difference."

"To make a difference is what brought me to New Orleans in the first place." Emmett spurred his horse up next to Manon as they entered a clearing. "I thought that the Freedman Bureau would be a glorious adventure helping former slaves acclimate. There might have been a little bit of playing the hero in that decision, too."

"Truth and life are usually messier than our ideals." Manon thought about the sewing job she had worked in Boston while getting an education. "But you and your Bureau certainly accomplished many wonderful things. Most of my students come from the schools you created."

"I wish Congress had followed through on their promise of forty acres and a mule."

"And it would have been nice to do just a bit of basking, playing the hero," Manon mocked him.

"That, too." Emmett conceded.

"Well, I admire you." Manon said earnestly. "And if you have my admiration, do you really need any more?" She slapped the reins and urged her horse forward into a canter, and he spurred his mount after her as she flew across the meadow.

The glade was nestled next to a thin stream. The running water cut through rocks, falling about four feet to create a pool that was perhaps ten feet wide and three feet deep at the most. They spread the blanket on the shaded grass, and Manon set out the lunch while Emmett saw to the horses, first leading them to water, and then hobbling them in a dappled spot from which they could still reach lush grass.

"Will you open this and pour us both a glass?" Manon handed Emmett the bottle of wine.

"I guess I thought raising horses might be simpler," Emmett said as he opened the bottle. "It's, well, I feel like I'm just barking at a knot working for the Metropolitan Police." He poured her a glass, and then waited for her to sit before placing it in her hand.

Manon had been secretly wishing that Emmett would leave policing for something that didn't leave her fearful for his life every time he went off to work. If the white southerners had disliked the members of the Freedman Bureau, they had outright despised the progressive nature of the Metropolitan Police, whose officers were about equally split between Black and white. This meant Emmett was open to attack from criminals, yes, but also from otherwise law-abiding citizens who resented—and resisted—any power asserted by one not their own. "That sounds promising," she said. "Horses love you." She pulled an oyster out and handed it to Emmett with a shucking knife. "Here, try one of these."

Emmett made a face. "Shouldn't it be fried?"

Manon laughed at him, a sound not unlike the bubbling creek. "You've never had raw oysters?" She took out another one and reclaimed the knife from Emmett. "You cut it open like this, and then snip it free from the shell, squeeze a little lemon on it, dab it in this sauce, tip your head back, and let it slide into your mouth." She licked her lips savoring the taste. "I find two bites releases the flavor best."

Emmett took the shucking blade back and pried open the shellfish easily enough, but had more trouble freeing the mollusk from its home. He finally succeeded, added the lemon, sauce, and with a grimace let it glide into his mouth. He took two bites, swallowed, and nodded. "Not bad."

"Let me get you another." Manon swiftly shucked an oyster and fed it to Emmett with her long fingers. He then fed her one, and in this fashion, they ate the remaining oysters before moving to the shrimp and greens.

"That was delicious," Emmett said, mopping his plate with a piece of bread. "I could get used to you cooking and feeding me."

Manon took his plate and glass from him and set it by the creek to be washed out later, as she'd other plans for now. She walked slowly back to where Emmett reclined on the blanket, swaying her hips slightly as she'd been instructed by the prostitutes from Marie Laveau's brothel. She'd asked one of the girls in private about sex and seduction several months earlier, and ever since, she'd been getting advice from all of them. Emmett was staring at her as she sashayed her way over, desire taking over his senses even as he tried to suppress his natural instincts. She dropped to her knees next to him, arresting his eyes with her own, the carnality of the moment flushing the air between them. She leaned in and kissed him lightly, her lips brushing his, and then moving to his ear, nibbling slightly, as Emmett gasped.

He turned his head, wrapping a hand behind her neck and roughly kissed her back. She broke apart and nuzzled his neck, her free hand unbuttoning his shirt and running her fingers across his smooth chest before finishing the chore of relieving him of his shirt. Manon leaned her body forward and sideways, bringing their bodies to the ground, where she entwined her leg with his and covered his lips with hers. She pushed him onto his back, keeping her mouth locked upon his, and trailed her fingers again down his chest and rippled torso before sliding her hand into his pants.

Emmett groaned and writhed on the ground, not that he was making any great attempt to get away. She played the game, holding him firmly with her mouth and hand. She was shocked how hard and soft it was all at the same time, bulging in her hand as if with a life of its own. She let him go before his excitement got the best of him, as had been told to her several times, and rolled on top of him. With tantalizing slowness she licked her way down his body until her tongue reached his navel, and then rose to her knees, undid his belt, slipped the buttons through the holes, and pulled his pants down to his ankles, removing one leg at a time until he was naked upon the ground.

Manon stood and pulled her dress overhead, revealing a white chemise with no corset on her top, and pantalets on bottom that revealed her womanhood, the cotton material rising from her calves to a belt. True to the fashion of the day, it left her black pubic hair exposed. She pulled the chemise over her head and watched Emmett's eyes rise from down there to her suddenly released breasts, his jaw slack and mouth agape, breathing heavily. She could feel the breeze through the trees tweaking her nipples, which were already engorged, and she rubbed them gently before undoing the tie to her bottom garment and dropping the material to the ground. She straddled him, feeling the slight piercing pain, and in less than a minute, she felt him convulse underneath her, and she rolled off to the side.

"Wow," he murmured. "Wow."

"I love you, Emmett Collins," Manon replied, twisting onto her elbow and caressing him with her free hand.

Emmett reached his arm around her, grasping her buttocks and squeezing. "I love you, Manon Lescaut."

Manon kissed him. "There are pralines." She crawled over him to the saddlebags, and grasped the sweet pecan treats wrapped in wax paper. With a wicked smile, she wriggled her way back and clambered astride him again, teasing his lips with the delicious desert, before letting him bite off a piece, and then taking a bite herself. They ate three in this way, and it was only when she felt him growing underneath her once again that she sprang up. "Let's go for a swim!"

Emmett looked around nervously for alligators, even though this creek was not their natural habitat and it would've taken an army to stop him from following her naked backside down to the water. It was too shallow for swimming, but Manon pulled Emmett down into the refreshingly cool water, their heads under the cascading flow from the recent rain. They touched and murmured loving comments to each other.

After a bit, Manon took Emmett's hand and led him from the water, grabbing one of the terry cloth towels she had hemmed herself. Emmett took the soft cloth and began to rub her down with it, lightly dabbing her skin, while she undid her hair and let the coiled tresses spring forth around her head in wild abandon. He began with her shoulders, and then pressed himself to her as he skimmed the towel back and forth over her posterior, taking extra time on her rounded bottom, perhaps more than necessary. He then patted her breasts lightly as if afraid he might hurt them, carefully grazing her nipples, and she could feel a tingling down there more intense than she'd ever imagined.

The April sun caressed their deliciously naked bodies in this small slice of paradise, seemingly a planet away from the burdens and cares of everyday life. Emmett pulled Manon to the ground, laying her carefully back upon the blanket, and slid up her body, entering into her with an ease and pleasure she hadn't yet experienced. Their bodies found the rhythm Nature had intended, and a rising crescendo began gripping her body, emanating from down there to her toes and then up through her torso as the trees, sky, sun, and world disappeared, and even the thoughts tumbling through her mind dissipated as she screamed out her pleasure and her body shook and there was only the oneness of them with nothing else in the entire universe.

PART IV: HATRED

December 31, 1872–April 12, 1873

CHAPTER 13

December 31, 1872

Emmett Collins looked around, feeling nothing but love and warmth. A select group had been invited to the Laveau residence on St. Ann Street for the wedding celebration. Emmett and Manon had exchanged vows across the way in the St. Augustine Catholic Church in the Black neighborhood of Tremé earlier that day. Even with the Civil Rights Act of 1866, the Louisiana Statute of 1870, and Madame Laveau's connections to the priests at the white-dominated St. Louis Catholic Church, an interracial couple attempting to get married there invited murderous threats and actions that would have ruined the joyous nuptials of such a day.

St. Augustine's was more accepting, as evidenced by their creed that "All those who know the gifts of God are welcome at His table." Even though Manon was firmly Catholic, she was in agreement with Emmett that she wanted their special day to be something more expansive than the strict Victorian version espoused by the Church, and thus, they were repeating the ceremony structured more upon the ideals of matrimony that they themselves possessed. They'd spent many hours discussing the values they wished in their married life, and settled upon equality, inclusion, independence, integrity, intimacy, and adventure.

The yard to the right side of the house, between the fig and banana trees, had been designated for the band. Pinckney Pinchback had insisted on being in charge of the music for this sacred day, and he'd not disappointed, lining up a variety of musicians for the evening. It seemed that the governor of the state had significant pull, and as a result, the best band in New Orleans, the Thomas Kelly Brass Band, was currently playing a saucy tune called "Shoo-Fly." Scattered across the courtyard was a gathering that included a mix of prominent white citizens, dignified Black Creoles, freedmen and -women of color, as well as members of the Choctaw Nation.

Emmett turned to Marie Laveau who was gently rocking in her chair on the veranda next to him. "Thank you, Madame Laveau."

The gray-haired Voodoo Queen of New Orleans had grown quite frail, but her eyes still sparkled with an inner verve. She reached over and patted Emmett on the knee. "You have brought *anpil kontantman*, or much happiness, to my Manon," she murmured. "It is I who must thank you."

"She is everything," Emmett replied, his mind wandering over the past months as he'd fallen deeper and deeper in love with the older woman's goddaughter. "The *lwa* have smiled kindly upon us."

Madame Laveau chuckled, a thin papery rasp. "Do you truly think that the *lwa* have the time to bother with your happiness?"

"As long as I've known you, people have come to you asking for *gris-gris* to help their love lives, careers, relationships with siblings and parents, their businesses. How can you say the *lwa* can't be bothered?"

"When a woman comes to me and says that her husband no longer loves her and is cheating, I give her *gris-gris* to wear about her neck and tell her to put brick-dust upon her stoop, but there is more to it." Madame Laveau paused to take a drink of water. "Sometimes, I point out that she should bathe daily, or change her clothing, or surprise him with dinner, or drink less alcohol. When a man comes to me and tells me that his boss has it in for him and he fears for his job—I tell him to pray at the altar to the *lwa*, to add oils to his *gris-gris*, but also more than that. I suggest that he go to bed earlier and get to work earlier, that he be more respectful, and that if his efforts prove suitable, the *lwa* will come to his aid."

Emmett laughed out-loud at this wily lady. "Are you saying the *lwa* help those who help themselves?"

"A pot of gumbo does not appear on the dining room table because of a prayer. Nothing happens naturally. Fate, coincidence, serendipity, and synchronicity are not whims of the spirit world, but are the result of the actions you take in your own life."

Emmett looked out over the yard at the motley throng of men and women he'd come to know during his tenure here in New Orleans and realized that it wasn't good or bad luck that had led him to this day of ultimate happiness. "I heard Frederick Douglass say much the same thing, that he prayed three times a day for his freedom, but it wasn't until he prayed with his legs that he was no longer a slave."

Madame Laveau waved her hand at the shindig playing out in front of them and proved she also knew the words of the Honorable Frederick Douglass. "Men are the authors of their own misery or their own condition. The lazy man is the unlucky man, and man of luck of work." She turned and cupped his cheek with her hand. "You, Emmett Collins, were awake while others slept, used your time wisely, and have worked hard for what you believe to be right. For these reasons, the *lwa* have smiled upon you."

Manon skipped sprightly up the three steps to where they sat. "There you are. It is time to eat, and people are insisting we go first." There was a long table running from the front of the house to the fence by St. Ann Street, its top covered with an assortment of food, including baked chickens, jambalaya, gumbo, red beans and rice, light sugared cakes, heavy sweet spirits, rum, champagne, and fancy liquors.

Once they were seated, Emmett tipped his champagne glass to Manon. "To us, Mrs. Collins."

Manon clinked his glass. "To us, Mr. Collins." She suddenly cocked her head. "Shush, the Stackhouse sisters are singing our song."

Emmett was not aware they had a song, but dutifully turned his attention to the three young women who'd taken the stage after Kelly's band.

I stepped on board a railroad car
Beneath the morning sun
I rode the roads till evenin,
And I laid me down again
All strangers there no friends to me
Till a dark girl towards me came

And I fell in love with a Creole girl
By the lakes of Pontchartrain.

I said, "My pretty Creole girl
My money here's no good
But if it weren't for the alligators
I'd sleep out in the wood."
"You're welcome here kind stranger
Our house is very plain
But we never turn a stranger out
From the lakes of Pontchartrain."

She took me into her mammy's house
And treated me quite well
The hair upon her shoulder
In jet-black ringlets fell
To try and paint her beauty
I'm sure 'twould be in vain
So handsome was my Creole girl
By the lakes of Pontchartrain.

I asked her if she'd marry me
And she replied that we wed
The first time we met
Until long after we were dead.
But if it helped to make a vow
In front of family, friends, and God
She would take my ring
And give the priest her solemn nod.

And the Creole lass and the Irish lad
Declared their love
To all they knew
And the Lord above.
That they would face life's tribulations
Through trials thick and thin

A union of two devised
As one from the very first origin.

Emmett leaned over and kissed Manon on the lips. "I didn't know we had a song, but it's a fact that every time I hear that ballad I think of you. I'm also happy that the final two stanzas have changed from heartache to happily ever after."

Manon smiled wickedly back at him. "We make our own ballads in this life. I sat down with Emma Stackhouse and helped her adapt it to better fit us."

"You're a wonderful songwriter, but…" Emmett took a bite of gumbo and fell silent, his thoughts distracted momentarily by the thick flavorful seafood stew. He finally swallowed and continued with his eyes pinned to the table, "I wouldn't exactly give up your teaching job, yet."

She swatted his arm. "Perhaps you could do better?"

"I was just wondering how long after we are dead before our love fades away?"

"Speaking of fading love, I can't believe you put Henry and Pinch at the same table. Is there an evil streak in you I should know about?"

Emmett looked over at his two friends who'd increasingly come to odds with each other over the past year. "I'd love to hear that conversation." At the other table, matters were, indeed, precarious. Warmoth hadn't touched his food, but was on his second whiskey. "I should just shoot you tonight and end this whole mess."

"I'm afraid you wouldn't have much luck with that." Pinchback smiled in his own sardonic fashion and patted his waistband where his Colt resided. "I'm not one of your minions to be pushed and pulled by your every whim. I told you last year when you nominated me to be your Lieutenant Governor, that I'd never become your supplicant tool, and I have stood by that statement every day since."

"Impeaching me on the Senate floor and taking my position as governor is certainly a long way from being a supplicant tool," Warmoth admitted. "But I'm not sure how we got to this impasse."

"Maybe it was when you backed Joseph West for U.S. Senate over me," Pinchback suggested.

"That was only because I needed you here in New Orleans to watch my back."

"You sure it isn't because of the color of my skin?"

"What's that supposed to mean?" Warmoth asked hotly.

"Just that, ever since the last election, you've been moving further away from Black equality and more towards your new friends in whiter circles." Pinchback tipped up his glass of bourbon without taking his eyes off his friend-turned-adversary. "And then last March you locked yourself in with McEnery and the Democrats."

"McEnery is a fine man."

"He's a puppet for Ogden and MacLeod," Pinchback retorted. "And for what? So you get their nomination as senator?"

"That's the pot calling the kettle black," Warmoth countered. "You sold your soul to that group of cutthroats at the Custom House just so you could get their support for Congress."

Pinchback pondered this statement before replying. "They best represent the interests of Black folks in Louisiana, and that is my top priority."

Warmoth laughed, a harsh whiskey guffaw. "Is it true what they say? That your man Kellogg won't shake a Black man's hand unless he's wearing his white glove?"

"It's not a perfect world we live in," Pinchback conceded.

"Well, I'm glad you got a chance to be governor, even if it meant you had to lie and claim I offered you a bribe of $50,000," Warmoth said. This was the major charge that had led to his impeachment and elevation of Pinchback to the position of Governor. "But in a few weeks you'll be replaced by McEnery or Kellogg, and we'll both be banished to the sidelines."

"It was no lie," Pinchback replied. "You did offer me a bribe."

They were interrupted by the sudden appearance of Emmett, who pulled up a chair and sat across from them. "Two relics old before their time. Good to see you getting along. To be perfectly honest, I was a little nervous about this seating arrangement."

"As you should've been," Warmoth said dryly. "But I guess it would be in bad taste to shoot a guest at a friend's wedding."

"And where is the lovely bride?" Pinchback asked. "I must tell her that my wife apologizes for not being able to attend. Our daughter is ill, and she stayed home to attend to her."

"Nothing serious, I trust?" Emmett asked.

"No, just a sore throat and an upset stomach."

"I'm sure you'll get a chance to tell Mrs. Collins." Emmett shook his head. "That still has an odd ring to it. She's out there dancing with Freedom if you want to cut in."

"Maybe later," Pinchback said. "First, we have a wedding gift for you."

"It's right outside the gate," Warmoth added.

Emmett looked to where Manon was swooping to and fro to the music, shrugged his shoulders, and followed his two friends to the street to find a man holding a horse.

"She's a two-year-old," Warmoth said.

"Badger told us you fancy the American Paint breed," Pinchback added.

Emmett walked to the horse and looked her over carefully. She had a white face, except for black rings around her eyes; the white leading down her chest with matching stocking legs and the rest of her was a shiny black, giving her the look of a bandit wearing a tuxedo. He stepped forward and ran his hand along her neck, and then down her muscular rear quarters.

"She has excellent lineage," Warmoth said.

"She runs like the wind," Pinchback added.

Emmett walked around the back, his eyes taking in the graceful lines, before returning to the front of her and taking in her deep blue eyes. He rubbed her pink muzzle and she nipped back playfully. "I will call her Mum Bett," he said.

"Tom here will take her to the stable you use on Rampart Street," Warmoth said.

"We've a separate gift especially for Manon," Pinchback added.

Emmett looked at his two friends with appreciation of all that he possessed in the world. The three of them had been through some difficult times together, didn't always agree with each other, but still maintained a bond of respect. "Thank you."

They returned to the courtyard and the raucous celebration brewing, as a crowd had formed around four couples who were involved in an old plantation dance called a *Cakewalk*. "You're certainly a lucky young man," Pinchback said as he admired the ravishing figure of Manon as she danced with Freedom.

"Thank you," Emmett replied. "Now kindly peel your eyes away from my bride."

Pinchback chuckled and directed his attention to the stage. "That is the Charley Jaeger Silver Cornet Band. They came to cheer me up at my home at one of the more difficult times in my career. I hope they bless your wedding for all of time."

"You've lined up a full slate of musicians. I suppose it's time to see if the Polka lessons were worth anything," Emmett said. "Again, thank you."

At midnight, Emmett and Manon found themselves standing on the bandstand, as Marie Laveau wed them in front of their adopted families and friends. Instead of words such as obey, they exchanged vows they had composed, and bid their undying love and passion for each other not just as man and wife, but also as human beings. At that point, the bongo drumming began, and Marie the Older settled back into her rocking chair, as Marie the Younger took center stage with her Python wrapped around her torso.

Counja, Counja. Counja a-coming now.
Hide your head, it's coming now.
Close your eyes so you won't see it
Boom, boom, it's a-comin' now.
Counja. Counja. Counja is a-comin' now.

A new frenetic energy took over as bodies began to sway and stomp and gyrate. As Emmett held Manon's hand, he thought back to his first Voodoo *fête,* when he'd plunged into the future. There'd been a powerful attraction between them on that night, even though he'd done his best to ignore, to dampen, and to displace this primal instinct. Now, it took every ounce of his being to not ravage her as they pulsated together, their bodies touching, grinding, and bumping as the rhythm of the drums coursed through their veins. His love and lust grew to voracious proportions anchored only by his overwhelming happiness.

It was not until the sun began to light the sky over the rooftop that the last guests gave their congratulations and bid their farewell, and Emmett and his bride went into the room in the house that would be their home until they were able to get a place of their own. They climbed into bed, and for the first time, made love as Mr. and Mrs. Collins.

"Sit down, Freedom," Susannah said. She was fairly bursting with excitement to be on the balcony of the exclusive Pickwick Club for the Mardi Gras parade on this beautiful night of the twenty-fifth of February. "If you're to be my chaperone this evening, you must at least join me."

"I should probably leave the chair open for one of the other women, sure enough, Missus," Freedom replied. The gallery was filled this evening with wives, a few older gentlemen, and a smattering of servants, as the husbands were all involved in the parade as the nucleus of the Mistick Krewe of Comus.

"Nonsense. *Ahh* don't know anybody here. Campbell doesn't like me going out much, and besides, most of the women are old enough to be my mother. Sit. The parade is going to start soon."

Freedom realized this would cross a line that was unacceptable at the Pickwick Club, even if Missus Susannah didn't realize it, and steadfastly refused, standing behind and to the right of her with his hands clasped behind his back. The two of them had spent considerably more time together over the past year, as Campbell MacLeod had given Freedom the role of escorting Susannah as driver, and butler, ever since Ben had disappeared. Boss MacLeod had hired a new driver for himself, a tall and thin Black man with shifty eyes named Cy who Freedom didn't much get along with.

"Look, here it comes," Susannah said pointing excitedly, as the police cleared the streets for the first float. "What does it say?" she asked, trying to see the large gas lit transparency bearing the words of the secret theme of this parade.

"It looks to say, 'Missing Links to Darwin's Origin of Species'," Freedom said proudly, showcasing his increased reading, a skill that had been greatly enhanced by Missus MacLeod's lessons.

"That's the awful man who claims we come from apes," she replied. "*Ahh* wonder what they mean by the 'missing links'?"

Freedom grinned, lost in the moment, the gap of his missing tooth making him look older than he was. "I'd say there is your first missing link," he said, pointing. Behind a transparency that proclaimed "Zoophytes" came a strange sea creature. The larger than life papier-mâché figure had the body of a sponge and the face of a bar drunk, complete with a patched cheek, bruised eye, and cigar hanging from his mouth below a bulbous nose. This strange creature tottered along amongst other plantlike animals of the ocean depths.

Susannah clapped her hands and exclaimed, "It's wonderful." The procession continued with other creatures labeled—coral, mollusks, crustaceans, vertebrata, amphibian, and reptiles in a dizzying whirl of chaos.

"It's quite a spectacle," Freedom murmured.

"Is that…?" Susannah clapped her hand over her mouth in delight. "Is that tobacco grub worm, President Grant?"

Freedom couldn't but help chuckle. "It certainly is." Grant was easily identifiable with his closely trimmed beard, cigar hanging from his mouth, standard wide brimmed hat, and a tax box under his arm.

"Campbell says the man is a blight on our country. If it weren't for him, we could go back to the way things used to be."

"How is that, Missus MacLeod?"

"If the Federal troops just went away, New Orleans could return to the golden age of prosperity."

"It seems that General Emory has been busy keeping the peace," Freedom said carefully.

"Campbell says that Colonel McEnery won the election fair and square, and General Grant took it away from him and gave it to that fellow Kellogg." She fluttered a fan in front of her face. "He says that change is coming."

"I hope that everybody gets a chance to enjoy that," Freedom replied.

"Look!" Susannah leaned forward to the railing in excitement. "That's the problem, according to Campbell. Those sly foxes coming down from the north to steal from us under the guise of reform."

"What are carnivores?" Freedom asked, reading the transparency leading the fox carrying a carpetbag.

"Meat eaters," Susannah replied distractedly. "*Ahh* think that's supposed to be Superintendent Badger." She pointed at a bloodhound dressed as a sleuth with a carpetbag and smoking a pipe, alluding to the woeful features of Badger and the fact that he had come from the North to claim his fortune with nothing but a carpetbag in hand.

"And that must be General Benjamin Butler," Freedom said, as a scroungy hyena carrying a spoon loped into view.

"Why do people call him Spoons?"

"When he first got here, he passed a law against smuggling, and went so far as to prosecute one of New Orleans' finest ladies for carrying a bunch of silver spoons through a checkpoint," Freedom began, but was then struck dumb by a wild scene of monkeys, apes, baboons, orangutans, and gorillas bursting onto the scene—all in the exaggerated blackface of the minstrel show—acting foolishly and providing the parade's answer to the missing link.

Susannah looked over at a grim-faced Freedom, wondering what must be going through his head. It was all just in good fun, she thought, just a friendly poke, as had been the mocking of Grant, Badger, and the others. It was a silent ride back to the White Mansion.

Soon after the wives and their attendants left the Pickwick Club, the men began to arrive, many of them still in costume, others having changed back into their suits, but all jovial and merry at the smashing success of this Mardi Gras. The revelry continued late into the night, with toasts shouted forth every few minutes. The President was castigated, the Federal Army blamed for the state of things, carpetbaggers vilified, and Blacks threatened.

Frederick Nash Ogden spent a good part of the time with his friend, Campbell MacLeod, for once not plotting and scheming, but just enjoying the tremendous success of the day and night. Soon after midnight, though, he began to work his way to the door, for he had a different sort of celebrating in mind. He told nobody he was leaving, because he knew that they would cajole and pressure him into staying, but the urge was upon him, and he felt he was owed a special treat. He did love his wife, but there were certain needs she did not—could not—fulfill.

His driver was outside smoking a cigarette when Ogden emerged from the front door, and the man quickly threw the half-smoked tobacco to the ground and rushed over. He was a tall man, made taller by his hat, and his eyes shifted nervously at having been unprepared for this early exit from the party.

"Get the carriage and pick me up on the corner of Canal and Rampart," Ogden said curtly, walking across the wide street, his cane clicking on the cobbles.

He smiled, the blood coursing through his body with vitality he'd been missing. He tried to be good. He tried to be faithful. He hated that he had a taste for black flesh. Sometimes, however, he couldn't help but give in, and just the thought of what the night held made his pulse quicken and parts of him harden. Tonight, he deserved a treat.

CHAPTER 14

March 4, 1873

The afternoon was gray and still over the mile-long oval racetrack. A hulking grandstand swallowed up the few hundred men and women who had made the trek to the outskirts of uptown as rumors of a horse race swirled through New Orleans. This event had not been announced in the newspapers, but rather had been born in the Gem Saloon of a disagreement between Henry Clay Warmoth and one of the two current governors of Louisiana, William Pitt Kellogg. As insults were traded back and forth, the bartender had suggested they settle the matter of honor by racing horses, instead of the more traditional duel, or the immediate letting of blood that was sure to make a mess of the place after a bar brawl.

Emmett kissed Manon and then vaulted lightly over the wall to the track below. The surface was rough and unkempt as this turf was in the process of being converted into a cemetery by the new owner. This made it the perfect place for an illegal and off-the-record horse race. The ring ran along the top of a ridge that rose above the Basin Canal on one side, and Bayou Metairie on the other, the bayou giving the track and future cemetery its name.

"I haven't run a horse hard other than Mum Bett in quite some time. You sure you want me to jockey for you today?" Emmett asked Warmoth in a joking manner as he ran his hand over the sleek lines of Brutus, his mount for the day. "If it comes down to it I might have to throw the race, you know, with Governor Kellogg being my new boss and all."

"You shouldn't have any problem with that nag of his. I'd worry more about MacLeod's horse, Sawney Bean. He made short work of all the other entrants at the Fairgrounds a few months ago and took home the first place purse," Warmoth replied.

"I hear that young jockey of Pinchback's speaks horse." Emmett eyed the diminutive form of the boy who'd just pulled himself astride his dancing stallion.

"The Black fellow?" Warmoth turned to see the jockey. "Is that Murphy? He's no more than fourteen."

"He weighs the same as a feather and has the strength of a gator is what my sources tell me."

"He doesn't look like much to me," Warmoth sniffed, before turning back to the business at hand. "It's going to be four miles with hurdles," he reiterated what Emmett well knew. "Four laps with four hurdles each lap."

The five prancing horses made their way to the starting line as the owners and trainers moved into the interior paddock, where last minute bets continued to be tossed back and forth. The grandstands across the way once accommodating thousands every race day now looked forlorn and derelict. Recently, a wealthy Baltimore gentleman moved to town and sprinkled money around, thinking that a little green would be enough to gain him membership into the prestigious Metairie Jockey Club. When it didn't, he had bought it and turned it into a graveyard. This was not only a vengeful act on his part, but savvy business, as the business of death in New Orleans was more profitable than gambling on the ponies.

Emmett took one last glance at Manon, who stood at the front railing of the stands with her good friend, Nina Pinchback. The two couples had become rather close over the past year, to the point that Pinch had been upset when he discovered Emmett was riding for Warmoth, who had firmly sided with the Democrats against the more liberal Republicans that Pinchback supported. Louisiana currently had two functioning governments, both claiming legitimacy as they awaited a Federal ruling. Emmett raised his hand in a small wave and steered Brutus to the starting line, where he was positioned between the jockey on MacLeod's horse, Sawney Bean, and Murphy on Pinchback's filly, Sojourner Truth. Brutus was excited for what he knew was to come. Emmett had to rein him in sharply as they approached the starting line, causing the stallion to back-step and toss his head back and forth. Kellogg's rider had the rail and McEnery's horse took the outside position as the starter raised his pistol.

At the crack of the gunshot, Emmett tapped his heels into the ribs of his mount and leaned forward, letting him know it was time and he could now run. Brutus was a descendant of the legendary racehorse, Boston, and was well suited for this contest, which required stamina as well as speed. With a good jump, they immediately moved to the rail. Emmett was bent low with his cheek pressed to the powerful neck of the beast and his knees gripping the rippling torso surging underneath him as they hurtled down the racetrack. He snuck a peek over his shoulder and saw that Murphy had settled Sojourner Truth onto his tail—content to ride second for the time being.

The first hurdle appeared, and the thoroughbred flowed over the barrier like water, and all Emmett had to do was hold on. The hurdles definitely added an extra element of adrenalin to the headlong gallop. Horses, even the smartest, most experienced race horses like these, could take the same jump a hundred times, and on the hundred and first, balk and pull up short, or catch a hoof and go head over heels. In his last race, this had happened to the rider in front of him, the horse flipping over the hurdle, causing steed and rider to go cartwheeling across the ground in a mass of broken bones and lacerated flesh. Emmett had barely avoided the crash, but had seen the broken body of the rider being taken away afterwards, as the screaming horse was put down with a bullet to the head.

He gave a small tweak to the reins, the tug on the bit more a reminder for Brutus to not overdo it, rather than any real call to slow down. At the quarter pole of the first lap, Kellogg's horse made his move and took the lead with a spurt of speed. Emmett was content to let this happen, not wanting to wind Brutus. He knew full well he was the heaviest jockey in the race by far, and it wouldn't do to run the steed to ground too early.

As they flashed past the grandstand, Emmett caught a glimpse of Manon waving her arms and yelling her support. He thought of the past couple months of marital bliss that had been preceded by nearly a year of getting to better know Manon. The fourteen months since Manon had returned from Boston had been the happiest of his life. He'd lived a mostly solitary existence since the age of fourteen, not realizing the barriers of loneliness he'd erected. Each day with Manon was like removing a layer of impediment, until his eyes were able to view the happiness on the other side. Then one day, the barricade was gone, and he entered the Garden of Eden.

With Brutus cruising along on his own, Emmett's mind wandered to his childhood, which generally speaking, had been a hard but pleasant experience until the Great War came along. Since then, it had been a steady dosage of death and suffering, until Manon had sprung into his life and everything changed. New Orleans was a wonderful place to be young and in love, even if they did have to tread carefully in certain areas due to their skin differences. They went to Lake Pontchartrain for wonderfully fresh music in a setting that rarely blinked at their color, roved the countryside for carnal picnic delights, and shared every thought and dream they'd ever had. New Orleans was a place of jubilant music, the best food five cultures could produce, varied entertainment, and beautiful weather. Underlying all this, however, an undercurrent of hatred crackled through the city streets and so many human interactions.

Halfway through the third lap, Sawney Bean made his move, flashing past Emmett on the outside and attempting to take the front-runner. Emmett realized he must follow suit, and gave Brutus his full head as they chased Sawney Bean in passing the Kellogg beast, which had begun to falter. The two horses thundered around the turn with dust kicking in Emmett's face. As the grandstand shimmered past on the right signaling the final lap, Emmett slapped Brutus' rump to let him know it was time to let his years of breeding loose and run on heart and lineage.

At the quarter pole, he pulled even, but at the same time, Sojourner Truth came striding up, her head at Emmett's knee, then neck and neck, and as the three horses strained for the finish line, it was

Sojourner Truth with Murphy astride who eked out the victory by just the tip of her nose, with Brutus in second, and Sawney Bean in third. Emmett felt happy for the young Black jockey and his friend Pinch, even with the bitter sting of defeat that rankled in his heart. He brought Brutus down to a canter, and then a walk as they came back around to the grandstand once again.

"That was a hell of a race." Warmoth was the first to meet him, his face flushed with excitement.

"Sorry to let you down." Emmett slid to the ground, his legs weak underneath him. "We gave it all we had." He handed the reins to a groom, who led Brutus to join the other exhausted beasts in walking the course to cool down after their efforts.

"You were right about Murphy. I'm told that he weighs seventy pounds. That was the difference at the end. Nothing you could do about that."

MacLeod left the side of his jockey and came over to them. "That certainly was a *bonnie* race, Emmett. I thought we had second at least, but *ye* willed that beast over the line just in front of us."

Emmett nodded his head. He'd been attempting to heed the age-old advice of Marie Laveau, and continue cordial relations with Campbell MacLeod. This, however, was becoming harder and harder, as the man began to emerge as one of the leaders of the White League movement, which was the new pro-white organization that no longer felt it necessary to hide. Especially now that the brethren of bigots were beginning to leave their cloaks of secrecy behind to publicly state their spiteful beliefs.

"At least McEnery's nag beat Kellogg's horse," Warmoth said dryly.

"Just like the man himself. Fast out of the gate but no staying power," MacLeod replied. "By tomorrow night Kellogg will be a forgotten name in Louisiana."

"It seems to me that he is firmly established and well in control," Emmett retorted, unable to check his words.

"Grant's commission gives us clear approval as the legitimate government," MacLeod said haughtily.

Warmoth gave him a warning look. "Only the minority report was in favor of our position, Campy."

"The majority report was in favor of a new election under federal supervision," Emmett prodded, wanting to nudge MacLeod more on what might be happening on the following day.

"My people in Congress tell me that Senator Morton, who headed up the investigation, has suggested a course of masterly inactivity," MacLeod replied. "He suggests that the Federal Government wait and see how this plays out. In other words, it is up to us in Louisiana to determine which governor and legislature are legal."

"That would be Kellogg entrenched in the Mechanic's Institute and controlling the Metropolitan Police and the State Militia, one would think," Emmett said softly.

MacLeod glared at him. "It is a decision to be made by the white people who live here in Louisiana, not a mob of carpetbaggers and darkies."

"It looks like a carpetbagger and a darkie won the day today," Emmett replied sarcastically.

"Enjoy your second place trophy, Collins, for tomorrow there will be a different order to the finish, even if there has to be a *wee rammy* to achieve it." MacLeod stalked off with lips pressed together in anger.

"I can only assume a *wee rammy* involves men and fisticuffs at the very least," Warmoth said. "I don't know what good it does to bedevil the man, but you certainly seem to get under his skin." He grinned, showing that even though he was now in league with MacLeod's own political party, there was still a great deal about the man he disagreed with. "You might let Aggie know to be ready for anything tomorrow," he added cryptically before walking off.

Emmett went to congratulate Pinchback and his jockey, Murphy, just as Manon and Nina came skipping across the track. "What a race!" Manon said animatedly.

She hugged him fiercely and he kissed her before turning to the young jockey. "I thought we were going to get the victory, and then you came up on the outside like your horse was fresh as a daisy. Congratulations."

"Thank you, sir. Sojourner sure can run, and that's the truth."

"Ha." Pinchback slapped Emmett on the back. "I was mad at you for riding for Warmoth, but then I found this young man, and my ire turned to pity."

"It would've been more fair if you rode your own horse," Emmett rejoined.

Pinchback now slapped his own belly. "I wouldn't make any beast carry me four miles at a gallop."

"I'd say we're closer in weight than me and Murphy." Emmett shook his head. "At least the new governors finished behind you former governors and the uncrowned king of New Orleans."

"You know that Governor Kellogg is the legitimate head of state," Pinchback remonstrated with Emmett.

"I only know that I agree with his politics." Emmett grabbed the other man's arm and whispered in his ear. "Rumor has it there is something planned for tomorrow."

"It has been brewing for some time now. I'll be seeing the Chief later if you want me to give him a warning."

"Let him know that MacLeod and Warmoth both hinted at some sort of coup, and that I'll meet him in his office at sunrise to discuss strategy."

"My horse wins the race, and I get to be your errand boy?" Pinchback cast his famous sardonic look at Emmett. "I guess I'll just have to fit it into my busy schedule."

"I would've guessed you'd have more time on your hands now that your Senate seat has been put on hold," Emmett said with a straight face.

"You were just hoping I'd go to the capital so you could win a horse race."

"Speaking of horse races," Nina Pinchback broke in. "I won $5 from your wife, so we can do without the salary of a senator."

"I suppose she suggested you get the money from me?"

Manon slapped his arm. "Of course not. I paid her already. I took the money from your pocket this morning."

"I guess dinner is on the Pinchbacks, then," Emmett said. "And I feel a powerful hunger coming on."

"Sorry," Pinckney Pinchback replied. "Nina has to get home to the children before my mother strangles one of the boys, and I have some business to attend to, including running errands for you."

"Sounds about right. Seeing as we lost the race, and are broke and friendless—we might as well just go home and eat some stale bread."

They walked together to their buckboards before parting ways. "It's not my fault that I lost the money to Nina," Manon moaned with a false snivel once they began the short trek back to St. Ann Street in the wagon.

"What would your students say if they knew you were gambling your money away?" Emmett chided her good-naturedly.

"I thought it was a sure bet you would come in last place," Manon replied, "but I still had to bet on my man. I think they would understand."

"Last place?" Emmett leaned over and squeezed her thigh firmly, causing her to squirm and giggle. "I would have won if that slender waif of a boy had eaten more than a grape in the past forty-eight hours. Or if Warmoth had let me ride my own horse. Mum Bett would've rose to the challenge."

As the gray sky turned black, they quickly hurried the three miles to home. Emmett dropped Manon at the gate so she could make them some chicken sandwiches. He then brought the buckboard and horse to the stable, taking a minute to visit Mum Bett and feed her an apple, before walking the short distance home.

They'd just begun eating when Marie Laveau shuffled into the room. She pulled up a chair and silently eyed Emmett before speaking. "I heard you lost at the racetrack today to a boy who still speaks in the voice of a girl?"

Emmett grimaced, all the while wondering at the speed with which Madame Laveau gathered information. He'd come straight here from the secret affair, yet she was already fully aware, and probably knew more details than he did. "Manon says it's because the two of you are feeding me too well."

"At least your *défaite* today was not at the hands of Campbell MacLeod."

Emmett set his sandwich carefully down on the plate. He knew that Madame Laveau was not one much for idle chatter. "It could've gone either way. Today I beat his horse by a nose."

"I have a girl who visits with Mr. MacLeod."

Emmett searched his memory for her name. *Was it Victoria?* "And what does the Scottish devil tell her?"

"He says the time is coming, and soon that the carpetbagger scum will be kicked out of Louisiana. And then the Blacks will know their place at the feet of their master." Madame Laveau had known many evil men in her seventy-two years of life, but still she shuddered thinking of MacLeod. "He says that all the foreigners will have to go, the Irish, the Sicilians, and the Federal Army can then be employed in preventing Mexican bandits from crossing the border instead of protecting the false Republican Party."

"How about the Scots?" Emmett asked.

"He is the devil," Manon whispered, afraid to be heard even in the confines of her own home.

"Madame Laveau, I need to ask you a question," Emmett said.

"He beats her," she replied, somehow knowing the question not yet asked.

"What does Victoria look like?"

"*C'est une jeune femme à savourer!* She is young and nubile, with legs like a filly and a neck like a swan. And black as night."

"How do you know he beats her?"

"Lulu brought her here a few years back, and she was in a bad way. I had a talk with him and said never again. Since then? I see her with a bruise on her face, maybe a bit of blackening to her eye, perhaps walking stiffly? She won't admit it, but I know."

"Why does she continue to see him?"

"I would guess he pays her well to allow him to do what he does," Madame Laveau said, her eyes troubled. "He must be stopped." She stood and walked to the doorway on her way to the veranda—where she would often sit late into the night—before stopping and turning once again. "I have seen things that no person should see, and certainly no living being should have to live through. It is not too late. He must be stopped."

Emmett stared at the empty doorway, lost in thought. Over the past few months the Black Delilahs of Tremé Killer had reemerged, murdering three girls in as many months, their horribly mutilated bodies left in public spaces like some dreadful warning of impending Armageddon. Instead of scripture stuffed in their mouths, these girls had a black dot smudged on their foreheads, the killer embracing the nickname the public had bestowed upon him. Emmett had wrapped up the task force as a futile effort, and returned to his cavalry unit, just before the first young woman in the latest trio had been found in Jackson Square. He had since put the detail back together and again increased patrols in Tremé, but victims two and three of the year had followed, suggesting that the killer's appetites were accelerating. He had focused his efforts upon red-haired men of means who had been away, but of the two he'd turned up, both had solid alibis.

MacLeod liked to sleep with young Black woman, and had a history, perhaps an ongoing disposition to beat them, but obviously he had not killed Victoria. There was a difference between the Black DOT Killer and a man who liked rough sex. He must talk to Victoria, and perhaps see if Freedom could snoop around a bit and discover any incriminating evidence against the man.

With their appetites satisfied, Emmett and Manon cleaned up and retired early from the long day. In the bedroom, they discerned that they were not completely sated and hungered yet for each other's touch, and craved an intimacy that could not be dampened by the evil of others. For a brief period, they were able to forget the hatred of man and dwell in the delicacy of love, before tumbling into mixed dreams of love and hate.

As the sun came up in New Orleans, Emmett found himself in a second-story office overlooking Lafayette Square, drinking a cup of coffee with two of his most trusted officers. As the morning progressed, Corporal Thomas and Emmett slipped out into the still quiet streets for a box of beignets. It was just as they bit into the first deep fried nugget of sweetened dough that the first group of men trickled into the square across the street, soon followed by a swarm of boisterous multitudes, all white.

"I thought we were supposed to be focused on catching the Black Dot Killer," Corporal Thomas said, looking out the window.

Emmett pointed towards where Campbell MacLeod was huddled

in discussion with Frederick Ogden. "As a matter of fact, MacLeod has moved up the list to become our prime suspect."

"I wasn't aware we had a list, but that's good to know."

At 9:00 a.m., MacLeod took the makeshift stage and addressed the gathering. "The election results were clear. Governor McEnery was chosen to lead the state of Louisiana. The legislature forced to meet at the Odd Fellows Homes is the legitimate governing body of our state." The crowd of hundreds interrupted his speech with yells and whistles and threats to Kellogg and his followers. "The Federal Commission has suggested that Governor Warmoth remain in office while another election takes place, but the Republicans refuse to let the people of Louisiana decide their own fate."

"Give us back what is ours! Give us back what is ours! Give us back what is ours!" the swelling throng chanted.

"The white people of Louisiana demand justice," MacLeod thundered from his pulpit. "William Pitt Kellogg must be held accountable for his crimes against the state."

"Run him out, run him out, run him out," the hysterical mob, now pumped up to a hysterical frenzy, screamed.

"Carpetbaggers from the North are controlling your lives. They want to sit in their lace-curtained parlors and dictate what is best for *ye* while counting the money they steal from your dinner tables. Louisiana should determine its own fate. We have rights as a state."

"States' rights! States' rights! States' rights!"

"Without property, without money, without education—the darkies oppose the good white people of Louisiana. Social equality is a curse imposed by foreigners upon our state. We must destroy a forced and unfair and unnatural social equality."

"No more equality! No more equality! No more equality!"

"The only thing in the way of white Louisiana reclaiming what is ours and making our state great again is the Metropolitan Police. Today—today!—we change that!" MacLeod roared holding his thumbs high in the air. As the crowd went wild, he swiveled to his right. "I turn the podium over to General Frederick Nash Ogden."

Ogden made his way onto the weathered boards. "The time is now for us to reclaim our heritage and restore our very culture. The

Northerners want to tell us how to share while the Sambo buck's only desire is to rape our women."

Emmett's first lieutenant turned from the opened window. "I guess we wouldn't be very welcome down there, now would we?" The man was Black, as was roughly half the force.

"I don't know who they hate more," Emmett replied. "You Black folks or us carpetbaggers from the North."

"From the sounds of it, their hatred includes all of us wearing this here badge," Corporal Thomas replied, pulling his star and crescent from its hiding spot in his pocket. "Even us white men born and raised right here in New Orleans."

Emmett held up a finger as Ogden proceeded to give directions on the planned uprising. They listened as the military leader of white New Orleans broadcast an attack that wasn't in the slightest bit secretive. The White League was leaving its previously covert presence behind, coming out into the open as it judged public opinion was on its side.

"Sounds like St. Peter Street will be the target," Emmett said, moving towards the door. "This is where we part ways. Lieutenant Johnson will inform Chief Badger, Corporal Thomas will warn the central precinct, and I will meet you both with the cavalry on the corner of Canal and Chartres."

An hour later, Emmett led his company down Chartres Street towards Jackson Square, which was across from the arsenal and the Cabildo building and was to be the point of attack. Corporal Thomas had returned with the news that the central station was well prepared, and Lieutenant Johnson arrived with Chief Badger and another 125 men armed with Winchesters, and a twelve-pound Napoleon cannon in tow.

A gunshot rang out, and Emmett looked up to see a man on a third floor balcony with a rifle. He whipped his pistol up and snapped a shot at the man who hurriedly retreated inside. Emmett waved for four men to enter the building and flush out the assailant. A bullet kicked up dirt in front of Emmett's horse from another window, and immediately a fusillade of gunfire shattered the window in return. A man jumped out of a doorway and discharged his weapon, killing a horse to Emmett's left, and he spurred his mount forward knocking the man to the ground.

In this fashion, they crept down the street as they cleared the way for Badger's foot police and the twelve-pound Napoleon.

They came to a gun shop from which a barrage of fire filled the air with flying lead. It appeared that the rebels had raided the store for its weapons and now turned these same arms against the approaching cavalry. Emmett saw one man go down as he led a charge with guns blazing. The plate glass window exploded in tiny slivers of flying shrapnel, and Emmett jumped his horse through the opening with two pistols blasting as the men within beat a hasty retreat out the back of the building.

The St. Louis Cathedral bell began to ring the noon hour as they approached Jackson Square. The last gong was drowned out as the weapons of hundreds of members of the White League erupted, sweeping several cavalrymen from their saddles. In a remarkably short time, they had taken up position in this central park of New Orleans' old city. Emmett ordered his men to take cover and allow the foot police through, who brought with them a barricade they hastily erected at the mouth of the street. A cheer could be heard resounding from the police station on the left, evidence that the men inside had held their ground and were heartened by the arrival of reinforcements.

After an hour of largely ineffective tit for tat gunfire, Badger gathered Emmett and several other captains to confer. "What do you think, Collins? How do we get them hotheads out of there without getting slaughtered?"

"Give them a few shots of the Napoleon, and I will lead my cavalry through them like a knife through butter. Then you can mop up with the foot soldiers," Emmett replied with hot eyes, the adrenalin of battle coursing through him. This was certainly better than beating up legislators and arresting drunks. It was nice to have the enemy out in the open for once, instead of searching for some mysterious murderer.

"You don't think that Colonel Emory and the Federal Troops will be, let's just say, dismayed by so much bloodshed? It seems to me that this day could force Grant's hand to call for a re-election and put Warmoth back in charge for the time being." Badger was as much friends with the former governor as Emmett. It was Warmoth, after all, who had hired Badger as Chief of the Metropolitans. That being said, neither of them was happy at his alliance with McEnery and the White League.

Even open warfare was constrained by politics was the message Emmett heard, but he bit his tongue. "What do you suggest, sir?"

"I thought that we might fire an empty shot with just black powder, and give them some time to think about that, and then follow it up with grapeshot over their heads. Once they hear that whistling metal and lead singing in the air above them, they'll realize how precarious their position is." Badger wiped his brow. "They are, after all, our fellow citizens."

Emmett bowed his head, the blood thirst that battle brought softening ever so slightly. "Of course, Chief," he said. "But if that doesn't work, I will drive them into the Mississippi."

They fired two black powder cannonades to let Ogden know they possessed heavy artillery, and followed it up with the grapeshot as planned. As they were preparing to attack, several Federal officers from the Jackson Barracks came down St. Peter Street with a white flag. Badger and Emmett rode out to meet them, and from the other side came Ogden, who approached with a limp, and blood staining his boot.

"Colonel Emory is on his way with troops to end this melee," the Lieutenant stated as soon as they were all gathered. "His orders are for you to cease and disperse, Mister Ogden."

"We are only claiming what is ours. And it is *General* Ogden," the bristly redheaded-barrel of a man replied.

Emmett snorted. The man had been a colonel in the war, so any title of general was certainly self-anointed.

The Lieutenant looked around. "It appears that if you stay, the day is already lost before Colonel Emory can get here… General Ogden. Whatever the case, it's clear that you are the aggressor, and our orders are to keep the peace. The Metropolitan Police have every right to blow you to hell with artillery. Just a warning: if anybody is detained, it will be you and your men."

"What will be, will be." Ogden turned to go.

"Colonel?" Emmett caught the man's attention. "We'll give you one hour to decide."

Ogden turned to mark Emmett with his eyes. "Your day is coming, carpetbagger. The army will not always be here to protect you. You and that Sambo whore of yours."

Emmett urged his mount forward as he reached for the pistol at his belt, but Badger jostled in front of him. For a long moment, Emmett contemplated drawing his weapon and killing the man, and would have but for Badger's hasty action. With a dismissive shrug, Ogden turned and walked back into Jackson Square.

In exactly one hour the barricades were pulled aside, and Emmett and his company of forty cavalrymen thundered down Chartres Street. As they turned catty-corner to the right and into Jackson Square, a roar went up from the policemen in the Cabildo building. Emmett was yards ahead of the others, his eyes searching for Ogden with his saber in hand, as a bullet would not satisfy his hunger appropriately, but the square was devoid of any life, even the birds having left, scared off by the day's commotion. Emmett cursed as he pulled his men up. He ordered them to search the grounds and apprehend anybody found, but he well knew that the enemy had flown the coop.

The rest of the day was spent mopping up the insurrection around the city. The Democrats had managed to capture one precinct station, and this was retaken and arrests were made, known outspoken enemies of the Republicans. It was a weary Emmett who reported in to Chief Badger at the end of the night that the city was firmly under their control.

"Good work, Collins," a fatigued Badger replied. "I'm sorry I stopped you earlier."

"We were under a truce flag," Emmett said tightly. "I let my emotions get the best of me."

"All the same, it has consumed my thoughts ever since. I wonder if perhaps it would've been better to let you kill him."

"That wouldn't have been the honorable action."

Badger sighed and tapped his fingers on the desk. "Perhaps not, but what he said was right," he muttered, and then quickly clarified, "Not about your lovely wife, Collins, but about the fact that the army will not always be here. Right now, we have the upper hand, and right is on our side, perhaps why the Federal troops bother to back our actions, but..." he trailed off with a note of despair.

"We are few, and they grow in number," Emmett finished for him. "While the Republican Party bickers, the Democrats consolidate around their hatred of interlopers and fervent desire to prevent equality."

"I think that's how Henry sees it," Badger said, referring to Warmoth. "When the army leaves, we can't just be a party of misplaced Northerners and freed Blacks. We need to gain the sympathy of the more moderate Democrats, or we will eventually be squashed underfoot like so many palmetto bugs."

"Are you suggesting that we follow him into the camp of McEnery? That we throw our hats in with the likes of MacLeod and Ogden?" Emmett retorted angrily.

"Not at all," Badger replied soothingly. "I think Henry played his cards prematurely and lost. It seems to me that, in this case, any compromise, any change, these are only reached through strength. When the Republican Party stands tall in New Orleans, the less conservative Democrats will come to the bargaining table. But then we must be ready for real compromise. Too fast of a social and political change leads to a reaction that is swift and repressive."

"Maybe you're right." Emmett rose to go to the door.

"But you haven't heard the good news yet," Badger said softly, just loud enough to cause Emmett to pause. "Governor Kellogg has given us the go-ahead to disband the rival McEnery legislature. Meet me back here at eleven tomorrow morning so that we can begin the process of enacting real change in Louisiana."

Manon had spent the day waiting tensely on the gallery for updates on the day's fighting, knowing that her man was at its epicenter, but she eventually relaxed and allowed herself to slip inside to get something to eat. The gunfire had become more sporadic over the past few hours, ever since the crescendo from the direction of Jackson Square around noontime. Madame Laveau had left her a plate of rice and red beans, on which she liberally sprinkled Tabasco sauce, a wonderful new concoction produced by a gentleman down on Avery Island. She poured herself a cup of water, warm, but it would do its job of quelling the fire of the red pepper and vinegar sauce.

She dreaded receiving the message that Emmett was in the hospital fighting for his life, and the very thought of him injured in one of a thousand horrible ways made her cringe. Anything would be better than the alternative, of sliding his casket into a tomb at the St. Louis Cemetery. She'd gone so far as to wonder whether or not he'd be allowed into the Laveau burial chamber, or would he have to be cremated, the resulting ash and bones to be swept into a common burial chamber with countless strangers? Either way, Manon had taken to staying up waiting on the veranda for Emmett to return after days of violence like today.

Three light taps on the door startled Manon, and she carefully laid down her fork wondering if is it was but a figment of her imagination. Two candles flickered, nestled into their lavender hurricane globes with brass holders, shimmering off of the silver breadbox and illuminating the merciful painting of Jesus. The mahogany Louis Philippe clock showed the hour to be ten, way past a social visit. But again, the gentle knock came, if yet more insistent this time, tap-tap-*TAP*. Perhaps it was a Choctaw Squaw asking for a bit of milk for her infant, or a drunken man desperate for a love potion, but in her heart she feared the worst.

A window in the kitchen allowed Manon to peer out at a solitary figure standing on the gallery, indistinguishable in a hooded cloak. What odious business brought this shadowy apparition to her doorstep on a night when she feared the death of her husband? Was this Baron Samedi come to collect on the unfathomable coupling of the Irish lad and Creole lass? With a trembling hand, Manon opened the door just a crack, and then with a deep breath, threw it wide.

"Mrs. Collins?"

"Yes?" Manon looked down to be sure she had indeed thrown red dust on the threshold this day to protect against evil spirits.

The angel of death raised her hands and pushed the cowl back to reveal a very human female figure with copious blonde hair. "*Ahhm* Susannah MacLeod. *Ahh* wondered if *ahh* might have a word with you?"

Manon stared at the woman more surprised than if she'd been Baron Samedi come to collect the night's grisly bounty. "I cannot imagine what we might have to say to each other," she said.

"Please," Susannah pleaded. "Just a few moments of your time."

"Say your piece and be gone from my home," Manon replied.

Susannah shuffled her feet. "Could we move from the light of the doorway? Maybe sit in the rockers over there in the shadows?"

"Does your husband know you are here?"

"No," Susannah replied, shaking her head. "He'd be most perturbed to find out." There was a silent plea in her voice as she nervously looked over her shoulder to the street.

"How did you get here?" Manon asked with suspicion edging her words.

"Freedom brought me. Freedom America. *Ahh* believe you know him?"

"Where is Freedom?"

"He's around the corner with the coach. *Ahh* was worried about it being spotted out front of your place," Susannah replied. "He wanted to escort me, but we couldn't very well leave the team on the side of the street at this hour."

"In this neighborhood," Manon finished for her.

"*Ahh* will admit *ahh* don't usually frequent this part of town," Susannah conceded.

"Nobody's going to harm you at our home," Manon countered.

"*Ahhm* not worried about your neighbors."

"We will sit in the rocking chairs," Manon said, relenting. "After you."

Susannah settled herself daintily on the edge of chair, and then slid carefully backwards. It wasn't often that she could sit without a large bustle to contend with.

"What brings you here tonight, Mrs. MacLeod?"

Susannah inhaled deeply. "Yesterday, Campbell came home very angry. He told me that he was going to murder my previous suitor, but first, he was going to kill his cheeky Black… slut, and make him watch her slow death before dispatching him to the grave."

"Your husband is not a very nice man."

Susannah stared sharply at Manon, and then laughed deep from her lungs. "No," she gasped, "he's not a very nice man at all," and then she was crying.

Manon went inside and returned with a handkerchief.

Susannah took the cloth and dabbed at her face, fighting to gain control as heaving gulps wracked her body. "Emmett is one of the few men to ever treat me with respect. *Ahh* just thought you should know so you both might be prepared."

"He is a good man."

"It was a different time. A different place." Susannah sighed. "Do you think that it's easier to be a whore than a Southern lady?" she asked.

Manon stared impassively at this woman who'd been her adversary in love, and was now her enemy in politics and race. "I think it is difficult to be a woman, no matter what or where you are."

"He never really loved me," Susannah said quietly.

"Who?"

"Emmett, of course."

"I know that. He was a boy driven by boyish needs." Manon looked to the gate to make sure her man hadn't arrived home. "In many ways he is yet a boy, but in other ways, wise beyond his years."

"Does he love you?" Susannah asked.

"Yes," Manon replied simply.

Susannah nodded, but then blurted out, "*Ahhm* with child."

Manon studied her face for a sign of emotion, good or bad. "Children are a blessing," she said.

"Yes, of course," Susannah replied. "*Ahh've* never known love. Married three times, and been with countless men, and never once had a man love me. Emmett was the closest *ahh* ever came, mostly because he treated me well."

"Your husband does not love you?"

"*Ahhm* just the latest of his purchases, and not even one of the most liked," Susannah admitted.

"You will love and be loved by your child," Manon said.

"Yes. *Ahh* believe you are right." Susannah stood up, pulling the cowl back over her head. "*Ahh* should be going."

"I think that would be best," Manon said.

Susannah walked to and down the stairs and was halfway to the gate when she paused and turned back. "*Ahhm* glad Emmett found you," she said, and then continued on her way.

CHAPTER 15

April 12, 1873

It was a beautiful spring evening to end an absolutely wonderful day, and thus, Manon smiled as she walked arm in arm with her husband from Henry Warmoth's lake cottage in the direction of the streetcar stop. They'd come out early this morning and spent the day sailing, wading, eating, and listening to music. Nina and Pinckney Pinchback had stopped by for a midday meal with their children in tow, the four toddlers sparking thoughts of motherhood in Manon as she watched them splash about in the water, wrestle, and just plain enjoy every simple thing available to them. Manon felt a flush of emotion languidly navigate her body as she thought about reading a book with little Nina, just seven years of age, while the boys were off fishing with the men.

The girl had carefully gotten the book out of her bag and was intently staring at the words, which were too advanced for her to understand. That didn't stop her from trying. It was a book Manon knew well, called *What Katy Did*, and thus it had opened a door of connection between the two of them. Nina's mother had been reading the novel to her at night, and they were about three-quarters of the way through. Little Nina said excitedly to Manon, "I want to do the same things when I grow up that Katy does. I want to paint famous pictures, and save people from dying, and go on crusades on a white stallion." Manon had refrained from telling her in the end, after an injury, Katy does none of these things, but merely takes over the running of the family's household. Instead, she told the girl that no matter what, she should never give up her dreams.

"What do you think about children?" Manon asked Emmett as they walked.

"I think children are grand," Emmett replied. "I particularly liked Bismarck, who has the same wry sense of humor as his dad."

Manon was silent, hoping Emmett would make the next jump on his own, but when it was not forthcoming, and the New Orleans railroad depot was, she continued, "What do you think about us having children?"

Emmett stopped short. "Are you telling me something?"

"No," she replied. "It was just a thought."

"Of course I want loads of little moppets running around," Emmett said enthusiastically. "Little lasses that look like you… and lads with my strong chin," he added, posing to showcase his profile.

"I am not so sure how strong your chin is," Manon replied gravely. "But, perhaps we will get lucky."

"Yes," Emmett agreed. "Maybe they'll all look like you. I'd love to have seven or eight beauties running around the house."

"Little Nina was absolutely adorable. I have never really spent any time with her before today." She tugged his arm to begin walking again. "Here comes the train car."

"But," Emmett said carefully, "I'm not so sure now is the best time."

Manon released his arm and stared at the approaching trolley, the "bobtail" streetcar pulled by a single mule. She wondered if it was difficult for the beast to haul all those people back and forth every day. "I am not saying we have to get started immediately," she replied. "But for curiosity's sake, why do you say now is a bad time?"

Emmett thought of MacLeod and Ogden's attempted coup the previous month, and the verbal onslaught that he faced every day as part of the hated Metropolitan Police. As well, the mysterious Black DOT Killer weighed upon his thoughts every single day. He was becoming increasingly concerned about his ability to protect his young wife from the rising tide of the White League, much less with her pregnant, or with a baby, although the thought of a tiny little version of Manon made him smile. "It's only that you just started teaching. Would you give that up to stay home?"

The streetcar made the wide turn and pulled up in front of the depot. Several people got off, and Manon and Emmett waited for them to disembark. The car would be half-full, as there was a crowd of seven or eight boisterous men, two women, and another couple to board ahead of them. As Emmett went to hand his two nickels to the driver, he was met with a hostile look.

"We're full."

Emmett looked over the man's shoulder to see that there were, indeed, many empty seats. "It looks to me that we might find a seat."

"This is not, and will never be a star car." Prior to 1867, Blacks were only allowed on cars with a large black star on it, which were rare and often overcrowded, while whites could board any car they wanted.

"Star cars have been illegal for six years," Emmett retorted.

"No Sambo has boarded my car ever, so I reckon that makes you wrong." The man slapped the reins and the mule strained against his harness and the streetcar began to move forward. Emmett stepped between the man and mule and grasped the reins to stop it.

"I'm a Metropolitan Officer, and I demand you let us on."

Manon tugged on his arm. "Let us just get the next one. It should be along soon enough."

"Listen to the Sambo wench and take your hands off the reins," the driver practically spat out, and then added disdainfully, "Officer."

"What's the hold-up?" One of the men aboard the streetcar stepped out, followed by several others.

"This man wants to stain my streetcar with his dirty tart," the driver said. "And I won't have it."

Emmett felt his anger rising. It was something ancient within him, a growing fury that threatened to explode, to lead to the berserk. The insults to his wife, to his love, to his Manon—this he could not abide. He realized that eight or nine men had poured forth from the streetcar, all wearing the same black bowler upon their heads, several with suspenders, one with a jacket and vest, but more importantly, all with pistols poking haphazardly from their waistbands.

Emmett realized they were yelling at him to let the hinny go, and Manon was pleading with him to let go, and then a man with such spotty facial hair it reminded Emmett of the underbrush in a swamp, grabbed his wife and jerked her out of the way, just as the man in the jacket grabbed Emmett's arm.

In the rush of chaos about to ensue, Emmett tucked away all emotion in one corner of his brain, the day growing still and quiet as it always did before a fight. He struck down hard on the wrist of the man grasping at him, and followed this with an uppercut to the bottom side of the man's chin, and immediately a crushing blow to the cheek of the already teetering well-dressed bloke. Over the now prone figure, Emmett drew his pistol and pointed it at the others just as swamp face curled his arm around Manon's neck and produced an Arkansas toothpick, the slender blade flowing to a tip pressed against her neck. As Emmett stared down the barrel of his revolver, several of the others produced their weapons, held in shaking hands directed at him.

"What's going on here?" This from a man who had stepped out of an elegant Landau that had stopped in the street. He wore a high silk hat and a Prince Albert coat with a white vest, which matched the color of his pointed beard and short hair.

"None of your business," the man with the knife said over his shoulder.

"It's Colonel Swenson," a second man with a better view whispered.

"Is that you, Jonathan?" Colonel Swenson asked, making way for two younger men to step out of the carriage flanking him. "The Jonathan that works in Mr. Perkins' store?"

"Yes, sir."

"Tell me, what seems to be the problem?"

"This man was holding up the streetcar, Colonel. We was just wanting to get down to Bourbon Street and he had ahold of the reins and wouldn't let go."

"Is that right?" Colonel Swenson asked. "What do you have to say for yourself?" He turned to Emmett with a direct gaze that was gentle and chilly at the same time.

"My wife and I were on our way home, and this man," Emmett nodded at the driver, "refused us service due to the color of her skin."

Colonel Swenson shifted his gaze to Manon and her assailant who still held a knife pressed to her neck. His eyebrow might have ticked up slightly, but he seemed otherwise unruffled by the tenseness in the air. "Are you in the habit of attacking women?" he asked the man softly.

The man turned red, his arm dropping from her throat as he stepped back. Manon hurried to Emmett's side. Emmett realized the driver of the carriage was casually pointing a shotgun at the group of men and slowly lowered his own pistol. He in no way wanted to provoke gunfire now that Manon stood next to him.

"May I suggest a solution?" Colonel Swenson again spoke in a soothing voice. "Perhaps I could offer the gentleman and his wife a ride with us?" He half-turned and swept his arm to his carriage. "And you men will proceed along on your streetcar?"

The Landau was a tight fit for the five of them. It was opened up so as to enjoy the cool evening, and had two bench seats, facing each other. "Emmett Collins. And this is my wife, Manon. Thank you for your help, Colonel." The three men had wedged themselves in the row facing them.

"Pleased to meet you. My name is Svante and these are my sons, Eric and Albin." They were about Emmett's age, perhaps a shade younger. "You don't speak like a native Southerner, Emmett. Where do you hail from?"

"I was born in Maine, Colonel."

"Much like my native Sweden, in climate anyway," Swenson observed. "And what brings you to New Orleans?"

"I was an aide to General Chamberlain during the war, and he got me a job working for General Howard down here in the Freedman Bureau. After that was done, I just stuck."

The driver clucked his tongue and slapped the reins and the carriage proceeded down Canal. "Well, I guess I best come clean then. People down here have taken to calling me Colonel, but it holds no real water. Before the war, back in Texas, Sam Houston gave me the title as I had raised a regiment to keep the peace. When the war began, I had to flee to Mexico because of my pro-union beliefs. I came back here to New Orleans after to open a mercantile store. Somehow, the title has stuck, much like you in New Orleans."

"I'm sure glad those men paid you the respect of a Colonel, sure enough," Emmett replied. "Do you still own a store here in town?"

"I sold that years ago," Swenson replied. "I started up a bank in New York City, but my daughter, little Greta lives here, and I own a sugar plantation out on the North Bend. And what is it that you do now, Emmett?"

"I'm a captain in the cavalry regiment of the Metropolitan Police."

"Mm. Interesting. I was just talking with my boys about starting up a cattle ranch back in Texas. I own a significant chunk of land in northwest Texas, right under the panhandle. We were just discussing putting together a *remuda*. I would love to hear your insight, being a cavalryman, but first, tell my driver where you live."

Emmett gave the address on St. Ann and they proceeded to talk horses, which had become quite a passion of Emmett's over the years. He suggested a stallion of Spanish blood, as the short and limber Andalusian stallion, when mated with the Spanish mustangs that ran wild in Texas, were well suited for herding cattle. He prattled on, and before he knew it, they were pulling up outside of the Laveau house.

"I didn't get a chance to ask about you, Mrs. Collins. Before you disembark, tell me something about yourself?" Swenson had been intrigued by the intelligent eyes and regal bearing of this young Creole woman, and was curious to hear her story.

Manon looked deep into his eyes. "I have a dream, Mr. Swenson, that someday, somewhere, I might be judged by my character, and not for the color of my skin, nor for my gender."

Swenson's eyes widened, and then he nodded. "I believe there is a place for everybody," he replied.

"Why'd you leave New Orleans and go to New York?" she asked, as she climbed down from the carriage.

"Too many of the local people hate an old scalawag." Swenson shrugged his shoulders. "I thought with the end of the war I could come back and live my life, but the people in Austin made it quite clear they held a grudge, and it was much the same when I tried to resettle here. I believe the local white population hates a white Republican worse than a person of your color, but I do admire your fortitude. As it turns out, my bank up north has done quite well, and now I have too much money to be treated poorly, so I'm able to visit. I spend most of my winters here now."

"Well, thank you again, sir," Emmett said, turning to go with Manon at his side.

"Let me give you the address of my sugar plantation and my home up north," Swenson said, scribbling on a piece of paper. "When putting up with local hatred like today becomes too much, perhaps you could help out in Texas with our horses. I'm told that out in Indian Territory, they care more about your character than your color."

Two days later, Emmett was on a steamer as it chugged its way up the Red River at a steady twelve miles an hour. On either side were cotton plantations stretching a few miles before butting up against low hills that were overgrown with long-needle pines. From his days at the Freedman Bureau, he knew that little had changed for the Black laborers on these fiefdoms in rural Louisiana. If anything, their lives had become more difficult, as the pay they received was barely enough with which to eat, the owners controlling the local stores, and thus the prices. One option was to leave and go to New Orleans where an overflowing workforce jockeyed for the few unskilled jobs available, but even that was fraught with danger, as those that spoke of leaving the plantations were often threatened with violence to keep them bonded to the land.

The morning before, the day after the run-in on the streetcar, Emmett had been attending the morning service at the St. Louis Cathedral, the sermon always delivered by the Reverend Father Chocarse, a Dominican, when a hand on his shoulder was followed by a whisper in his ear, and he was hustled out of the church. Normally, Emmett would have been at St. Augustine's for Sunday service, but as it was Easter, Marie Laveau had insisted Manon and he attend with her. She was probably fuming that he had disappeared so early in the service, but he really had little choice in the matter, even if he wasn't sorry to be relieved of the tediousness that he found the church doctrine to be.

The untimely summons was from Governor Kellogg, a "request" to report immediately to his office in the Mechanic's Institute. Once there, he found the Governor, Chief Badger, and two other men who were introduced to him as Judge Register and Representative Ward. Once they were all seated in the spacious room with the window thrown open for air, Governor Kellogg cleared his throat and got right to the point.

"There've been rumors of an escalation of violence in Colfax over in Grant Parish. Three days ago I sent two officers to investigate, but they never returned. It appears we cannot wait for their report." He nodded at the two newcomers. "We've just learned that animosity is one itchy finger away from a snapping point. Will—Representative Ward—will fill you in on what you need to know."

"As I'm sure you're aware, this past election was fiercely contested in the rural parishes." Representative Ward awkwardly smoothed the rumpled suit he'd donned when he arrived in New Orleans, having gone abruptly from soldier to politician. "Colfax is the seat of Grant Parish, and R.C. here," he nodded at Judge Register, "was fairly elected to his position, but the Democratic Party refuses to recognize him."

Emmett nodded. It was a common enough experience in the rural areas for Republicans to be elected with the support of the local Black population, but the Democrats, with white support, usually had the upper hand in organization and weapons, if not numbers. Might, and not ballots, was increasingly determining election results. "I'm sorry, but where is Colfax in regards to New Orleans?" Emmett faintly remembered the name of the town as a friend had been murdered there a couple years back, a fellow he'd known from when he worked for the Freedman Bureau.

"It's about 220 miles northwest," Ward replied, and noticing Emmett's pursed lips, added, "But it's reachable by steamship traveling up the Mississippi and then branching onto the Red River."

"We were forced to break into the courthouse early one morning to gain possession," Judge Register interjected. "The Sheriff deputized ten men with shotguns to hold our position. On the first of April, the Democrats with an army of poor white crackers tried to drive us from our commission, but we managed to withstand their assault."

Emmett digested this, sensing that what was so lightly passed over had probably been an all-out, guns blazing confrontation. "What's the population of Grant Parish? I mean, what is the breakdown between… Blacks and whites?"

"Pretty equal." Kellogg declared, knowing that this parish had been gerrymandered by Warmoth to keep it in Republican hands. "I believe the Black population has a slight edge in numbers."

"Tell him about the murder," Badger urged Judge Register.

"Eight days ago, one of the deputies who had initially taken possession of the courthouse was killed in front of his wife and child. He was repairing a fence no more than two-dozen steps from his front door when a posse of white riders came sweeping into the yard. They shot him full of lead, terrorized the wife and children, and rode off whooping that they were going to finish the job."

"So I called out the militia, and along with them we got about a total of 150 men holed up in the courthouse, protecting the lives of another 200 women and children who came to town for protection." Ward coughed vigorously, his face ashen, suggesting a bout with consumption. "C. C. Boyle—he's the white feller who claims to be Sheriff—has been going around the countryside claiming that the Black folks in the parish plan to kill all the white men and rape their women, which is right enough a lie, but that don't matter, for every white man within a hundred miles is coming to crucify the whole mess of us."

And that was that. Yesterday's Easter plans flung to the winds, hell to leather to muster, arm, and outfit the crew. So, here Emmett was, with his cavalry unit of thirty-two men, chugging up the river on a steamer. Sometime in the middle of the night they had had to disembark and clamber onto another paddleboat as they transferred from the Mississippi to the Red River. A thin tendril of smoke curled into the sky around the next bend, indicating they were close to their destination. He turned from the railing and the murky water to pass the word along for the men to saddle up.

The dock was eerily vacant as the steamer tied up. Emmett was the first down the gangplank, leading Mum Bett cautiously down the decline. Once everybody was on solid ground, Emmett hoisted himself into his saddle as an example for the others to follow. His Lieutenant looked to him for further orders, and Emmett merely nodded in the direction of the smoke. Although they could only see wisps of smoldering ash rising to the sky, Emmett knew they were not from a cooking fire, but from a burnt out building. The cavalry was too late.

As Emmett led his mounted men down the dusty street, each man with his carbine crosswise over the saddle, he was again struck at the apparent desolation of the place. A few Black women and children were shuffling here and there in apparent confusion. As they approached the blackened square in the middle of the small country town, they came upon the first dead body, a Black man pinned to the ground with a bayonet, his face and body cut and bloody. Somewhere in the distance, a woman began to scream, not in pain or terror, but in anguish.

There were thirty or forty dead men lined up in two rows a couple of hundred yards from the fire. Interspersed around them were more victims sprawled grotesquely where they'd fallen, some trampled, some tortured, and all very, very dead. No matter how shallowly he breathed, Emmett couldn't escape the sickly sweet, very distinct smell of burning flesh. He saw several of his men cover their faces with handkerchiefs, and he followed suit, but it didn't much help.

The scene of carnage and death reminded him of his first battlefield, back when he had been just fourteen, riding next to Colonel Chamberlain. They had been given orders to make certain the Confederates had indeed retreated from the field, and their still-raw regiment of the 20th Maine had picked their way through the bodies on either side of Antietam Creek. It wasn't until later that Emmett learned there had been over 20,000 casualties in that single day of fighting.

"Lieutenant, make sure the area is secure, post pickets, and then create details to see if there are any survivors."

"What about the bodies, sir?" Almost all of the bodies were adult Black men, but there were some white men as well.

"We'll give their kin a chance to come and claim them before we bury those that aren't claimed." Emmett looked up at the blazing Louisiana sun and knew they couldn't wait too long. Hopefully, the women and children were still close-by, and alive.

Bodies were found down by the river and out towards the Smith Quarters where many of the Blacks had lived before emancipation.

This brutal massacre hadn't been limited to those in and around the courthouse, but had stretched to include any Black people in the near-vicinity. Ward and Register had filled him in on the history of the town a bit at their Easter meeting. The largest plantation owner in the area had founded Colfax, as was the case with most rural towns. He'd been a real bastard, Ward claimed, but his son was just the opposite. After the war, Willie Calhoun had given the freed slaves the homes they lived in, supplied them with good jobs, and even created a school for the children. This may have been due to the fact that he'd fallen in love with a Black woman who he now lived with as his common-law-wife. Emmett couldn't but help wonder if it was this olive-branch offer of equality that had caused such a vicious backlash from the local white population to a race of people who no longer understood their place in the hierarchy.

Emmett directed his men to create travois in the Choctaw fashion to pull the bodies into town behind their horses. The basic design of two poles with a blanket stretched between them was more dignified than merely dragging the men by a rope. They were depositing these dead men with the other thirty-seven clustered corpses, when that of a middle-aged Black man gave a rattling gasp that suggested life. The doctor was hurriedly fetched as they pulled the breathing man from among the other bodies.

"Water," the man croaked. His head and face were encrusted with blood.

Emmett crouched down next to the man with his canteen and tipped the cooling contents gently to his parched lips. "Slow," he said, as the man choked on the first tiny sip.

Emmett left the man to the doctor's ministrations and checked on the pickets. He gave orders to set up camp upriver from the killing ground to ensure the water was fresh—and upwind from the remaining unburied corpses rotting in the heat.

It was only later that Emmett sat across a table from the sole adult male survivor in a deserted house they'd taken as their command post. The man still wore the sooty and bloody cotton pants and shirt from earlier, but his face had been mostly cleaned of blood, and a bandage was wrapped around his skull.

"Can you tell me what happened?" Emmett asked gently.

"They done shot us down like dogs," the man muttered bitterly.

"How about we start at the beginning?" Emmett looked around the parlor, taking note of the intricate china and the fancy longcase clock. He wondered if the white man who owned this house would be coming to reclaim it soon. "What is your name?"

"Levi. Levi Nelson."

"Tell me, Levi, what happened after Mister Ward and Judge Register left Colfax?"

A cloud of anguish passed over the man's face, his eyes growing blacker, if that was possible. He rubbed the bandage on his head and cleared his throat. "Cap'n Allen, he done had us dig a trench 'round the cou'thouse. We dug a hole 'bout two feet deep and might've should've worked a little fasta 'cause they done come at us 'fore we been finished."

"Who came at you?" Emmett asked, pushing the canteen closer to the man.

"I fixin' it was Mister's Boyle and Hadnot. They had about twice as many men as us." Levi tipped the water container to his mouth and drank.

"How many men did you have defending the courthouse?"

"'Bout one-fifty."

Emmett closed his eyes, thinking about the fact that this man was the lone survivor among so many. "Go on."

"They been carried them fancy new rifles that the army has and all we had was some Enfields and shotguns." He cleared his throat as he thought back to the events of the previous day. "It was just afta the middle of the day. I been saw that Boyle ridin' 'round town yellin' at the women-folk that we'd done left them and callin' us sons-of-bitches and tellin' them to get out and they wouldn't get hurt."

"And then they attacked you?"

"They done came at us straight on, but we turned them back. We been feelin' good 'bout that little skirmish then, but a-sudden we was takin' cannon fire from the levee on the Red. En-fil-AY-did fire, Cap'n Allen said. Swept right through the side of us like a turkey shoot it was. Well, it didn't take long for it to be ever' man for hisself. I run into the cou'thouse with a bunch of others. When we turned to look..." Levi drifted off with a look as distant and haunted as if he'd seen his own ghost.

Emmett gave the man a few moments. He knew that the provocateurs of this slaughter were long gone by now. Levi appeared to be the only surviving fighter, leaving Emmett little to do but try to untangle the events of the previous day and finish burying the dead.

"What did you see?"

"Them that done fled was runned down by men on horseback and knocked to the ground and beaten and stabbed and shot. Course some were already drunk and hollerin', draggin' the women off into the bushes, dancin' around the burning houses. Them that was wounded was pinned to the ground with bayonets so no one could escape until they was ready to torture them. It done went on for nigh an hour before the mens started driftin' back to where we was in the cou'thouse."

Emmett had seen the handiwork of these isolated killings. Mens' faces beaten to a pulp so that their own families wouldn't even recognize them. Bodies shredded with so many bullets that the insides had been sliced away, leaving the skeleton exposed. "What happened then?"

"We done waved a white flag out the door. That man Hadnot and another rode up and Cap'n Allen he went out to meet them. All a-sudden several shots rung out and that man Hadnot went down, but it ain't come from us, that bullet there, it came from the white folks tryin' to shoot Cap'n Allen and done missed."

"Are you sure about that?" Emmett leaned towards the man, realizing for the first time he had gray tufts of hair poking out from his bandaged head.

"We'd all done laid down our weapons. There weren't no more than forty of us left and we was ready to give in. No, sir—that man done been shot by one of his own."

Emmett sighed. He knew there wasn't a court in the land, this land anyway, that would believe that, or any of this for that matter. "Go on."

"They done yell at us to come out, but I warn't fixin' to be no kind of corpse and nuf'n they said was gonna get any of us to move. Then they done sent old Epeius towards us with a bamboo fishing pole swaddled in burning cotton. They must of done captured him and made him do it and no one inside could not shoot him, not old Epeius, and before we knew it, the roof was afire. Not much we could do but come out with our arms held high all a-yellin' we done give up. Abraham and a few others said no to that path and stayed inside and we could hear them a-hollerin' and screamin'."

"Is that when you were shot in the head?"

"No, sir. They done beat us 'round not a little bit, but then tied our hands and tethered us to a pole. By then, all the mens started fixin' to celebrate their victory and more and more bottles of likker came out. After a bit, I could hear thems arguin'. That Mister Cruikshank, he was fixin' to kill us all, but Sheriff Boyle stood up for us and said we should stand trial."

At the mention of liquor, Emmett thought to pull his flask from pocket and offer it to Levi, who took it and drank greedily, his eyes closing and sighing before capping the flat container and returning it.

"But the more them white mens drink, the more of them done wanted us dead. A bit after dark, that Sheriff Boyle, he threw up his arms and done walked off. A few other mens followed him and soon enough I heard horses racing off over yonder."

Emmett closed his eyes, knowing what was coming, but mentally giving a positive check mark next to the name of Boyle if the day of reckoning ever came, for in a difficult time he'd at least tried to impose justice, even if he had failed.

"It might could have been no more than a quarter of an hour that the mens done came over to us with that hard look in their eyes and the stink on theirs breath from all that rotgut likker. They done told us they was fixin' to lock us up in the sugar shack and lined us up by two's hobbled to each other and we done started walkin' with a fence of white folks on horses on either side. We hadn't taken more than five or six half steps when a sound like popcorn on a skillet went off. Pop. Pop. Pop. Pop. Pop. That's done all I remember."

New Orleans Crescent Fox

==

The Fox is Published Daily (Sunday Excepted)
By S. H. Hannity
Terms: Daily $16, Weekly $5; Per Year

==

Wednesday Morning April 30, 1873

==

Official Journal of the State of Louisiana

The Colfax Troubles—

The radical newspapers of the North and here in New Orleans would lead you to believe that somehow the respectable white people of Colfax are responsible for the recent violence in Grant Parish.

It is a known fact that the duly elected officials were of the McEnery Party in Grant Parish and that a mob of uppity Negroes ran amok creating a disturbance that needed to be addressed. This core of Negro men led by William Ward and J. C. Register stirred up a hornet's nest by parading around town threatening white families, breaking into homes and expelling good citizens, and even went so far as to desecrate the deceased son of Judge Rutland by dumping him from his coffin into the yard!

With little recourse, Sheriff Boyle called out the militia to quell the riot. Given every opportunity to surrender, these Negro interlopers refused. The radicals would have you believe it was a massacre on par with Fort Pillow, which General Forrest proved was a falsity. In reality, when the Negros shot and killed Representative Hadnot under a flag of truce, the die was indeed cast.

It is a universal rule of law that when beleaguered troops invite conference, and shoot down the ambassadors sent, they forfeit all clemency. This was the way with Julius Caesar and most certainly will be the way with the Indian Chief who recently slayed General Canby.

> The Negroes stupidly brought this upon themselves. We hope this lesson will teach them the folly of appealing to arms for the redress of fancied wrongs or the vindication of imaginary political rights. They ought to know that a war of races means the extermination of the black race.

Emmett set the newspaper down. "I can't say I'm surprised." He was sitting in a private box at the New Orleans Fairgrounds with Warmoth, Pinchback, and Badger.

"'The Blacks stupidly brought this upon themselves'," Pinchback muttered as his broad forehead creased in fury. "'The vindication of imaginary political rights'?"

Warmoth clucked his tongue in sympathy as the horses came out for the final race, once again pitting their steeds against one another, this time in the more typical one-mile sprint. "It's what I've been trying to say all along. We have to proceed slowly. I came to that conclusion during the Riot of '66."

"Massacre. That was a slaughter of innocents just like this was," Pinchback said bitterly.

"That only emphasizes my point, Pinch. The local white people for the most part are not ready to be represented, to be policed, to be judged—by Black men."

"Damn it, man, it's been eight years and things have only gotten worse."

The starter's pistol shot interrupted them as the horses lurched into motion with powerful thrusts of their hindquarters propelling them forward, a cloud of dust behind. From the start it was a three-way race between Warmoth's mount, Brutus, Pinchback's filly, Sojourner Truth, and MacLeod's horse, Sawney Bean. The four men stood, urging them on, the ten-knot breeze strong in their faces. At the end, Sawney Bean passed Sojourner Truth and appeared secure of the victory before a burst from Brutus in the final half-furlong pulled out the triumph for the Warmoth gelding.

"I hope it was worth it," Pinchback said, handing the man $100 in greenbacks.

Warmoth chuckled. "Every cent of it."

To Emmett's perplexed look, Badger whispered to him. "Henry doubled the pay and stole Murphy from Pinch."

So that was how, Emmett thought, nodding in understanding, Brutus had stolen the race at the very end, Murphy being the seventy-pound Black jockey who had beaten Emmett the previous month.

"I'm not saying it's right, Pinch." Warmoth tucked the money into his billfold. "But there's been slavery here in America for over 200 years, and it might take a few more years than eight for white men to accept Blacks as their equal."

"I realize the problem of social equality. That I can see. But I can't comprehend the slaughter of 150 men. That, I cannot understand."

"Humans are perhaps the meanest animals on the planet," Badger said quietly, his manner as calm as his bloodhound eyes. "You get a pack of humans together sensing weakness, and it might as well be feeding time in a gator pond."

"People are angry." Warmoth puffed on his cigar. "Most of the white folks around here are poor, especially out in the countryside. Very few people have recovered from the war—a war by the way, which took away their rights, property, and dignity."

"Most of the *white people* are poor?" Pinchback asked in a rising voice that was much higher than his normal deep tone. "You got Black families starving to death, running around half-naked on the streets for want of a set of clothes! What about them?"

"And I tell you that if they had the upper hand," Warmoth retorted, "they'd treat the whites no different than the whites are currently treating them. We don't live in a world that believes in charity. People in the South believe that you make your own way and don't ask for help. And if you can't handle that, go back to one of those fancy northeastern cities like Algernon came from. I have made my peace with the South."

"That would be fine if everybody started on the same playing field," Emmett interjected.

"What's that mean?" Warmoth eyed him over a ring of smoke.

Emmett chose his words carefully. "It means that you had a lot of advantages as a boy with your father being the Justice of Peace. Badger here was put through Milton Academy. Hell, Pinch was the apple of his rich father's eye until he died. How is an uneducated Black man with nothing supposed to make good?"

"How is an uneducated white man with nothing supposed to make good?" Warmoth turned the question. "Because most of the people are uneducated and have nothing. The best they can do is shove others down, so they feel a sense of superiority."

"There was another Black whore found dead yesterday," Badger said. "I'm thinking the Black DOT Killer is a white man trying to prove he's better than Blacks, especially those that sell their bodies."

"You think the killer is trying to scare Black folks into remembering their place—and keeping to it?" Warmoth asked.

"I think it's some twisted lunatic who deserves a special place in hell," Pinchback said angrily. "But from the Samson and Delilah passage, it seems that this particular man has a taste for Black whores, but feels that they in turn are stripping his power away because of his weakness for them."

"What about the investigation?" Warmoth turned to Emmett. "Any progress?"

"Not to make excuses, but I keep getting pulled off it," Emmett said. "Last month I was putting down an armed insurrection here in the city, and last week I was burying massacred Black people by 'law-abiding white men' 200 miles away up in Colfax."

Badger looked at him. "Go ahead, tell them what you think, anyway."

"I don't have any proof," Emmett said carefully. "It's just a theory."

"A damn good theory if you ask me," Badger replied.

"Let's hear it," Warmoth pressed.

"Well, we have a second witness that saw the last victim right before she was found dead, getting into a carriage with a tall Black driver with a top hat. This supports the idea that it is the mysterious red-haired man, a man of means, with a deep hatred or anger towards Black women." Emmett paused, collecting his thoughts. "Campbell MacLeod frequents a prostitute in Tremé who fits the description of most of the victims, thus far."

"Lots of men visit with Black whores," Warmoth protested.

"Do they beat them?" Emmett asked. "Madame Laveau told me

that MacLeod had beaten this girl, Victoria, extremely badly. She suspected he continued to do so even after she warned him off, though in a more controlled fashion that wouldn't leave marks. And so I had a chat with her right before I headed out to Colfax."

"Go on," Pinchback urged, his eyes flat and hard.

"It took a bit of prodding, but once the dam broke, the water didn't stop flowing for some time. Her body could be a street map of New Orleans, there are so many bruises running up, down, and across her. She showed me her back and arms. Even with her dark skin, you can see the bruises. She says he avoids her face after Madame Laveau's warning. But apparently he can only get an erection if he beats her, and does so methodically until he's ready and then takes her. Calls her all sorts of filthy names. She says that once he is able to enter her, the rest of the transaction is over in less than a minute."

"Why the hell does she keep seeing him?" Warmoth asked, waving his cigar.

"He told her he'd kill her if she ever said anything, but I suspect it's the money as well. He gives her an extra twenty dollars each time, more if he gets carried away and injures her beyond the normal."

"I'd say that's a pretty good suspect, right there," Pinchback said.

"There's a difference between beating a whore and killing her," Badger noted.

"What are your intentions from here on out?" Warmoth asked.

"We have to tread carefully," Emmett said. "We got close to the killer a year ago, and he went to ground, or at least disposed of the bodies more carefully. We do check with the brothels, but they don't always know when a girl is missing—or if she's just run off with a 'friend' or some such." Emmett let the others process this thought he'd had recently. "As for MacLeod, he is wealthy, powerful, and has a growing army at his disposal, so we best have solid proof before accusing him, and perhaps the backing of the army."

"How do you plan on getting that proof?"

"Short of catching him in the act—or as near to as possible—I'm not sure we can do more than watch and wait. I've got four men on him working in shifts, watching his movements," Emmett replied.

They digested that thought in silence. After a bit, music began to drift up to them from the stage in the paddock. Emmett pointed as he asked, "Is that the band you hired for my wedding, Pinch?"

Pinchback nodded. "Sure enough. Charley Jaeger's Silver Cornet Band. Good group of boys."

A commotion from the entrance to their booth suggested the ladies had returned. Manon rushed up behind Emmett, kissing him on the cheek, followed by Liza Badger, Nina Pinchback, Pinch's mother, Eliza, and Warmoth's date, Sally Durand.

This sudden intrusion of the women into such serious talk made Emmett reflect further. Perhaps the issue of race was difficult in New Orleans at times, but it in no way matched what was happening in the countryside. Just last week he'd been burying bodies burnt and desecrated just because of the color of their skin, and now here he was enjoying the fair in a mixed company of Black and white, with no confrontations, other than a few stares and muttered comments.

"Oh, the fair is wonderful." Manon said, glowing with enthusiasm. "We went into the brick house, and the art was marvelous. One painting was by a gentleman named Fitzgerald that had thirty figures that represented flowers. They were clothed but their faces were so dreamlike they could only exist in some fairy tale."

Emmett stood and kissed her in turn. "I'm glad that you enjoyed it. We went to walk around and it was such a crowd we just came back here to watch the races."

"There was a contraption called the Victor Scale, and all the women were climbing onto it to be weighed." She pulled a certificate from her chatelaine, the front-flapped purse hanging from her waist belt, and unfolded the paper to show him. "It says I weigh 128 pounds."

"Oh, that I know from the other day when I tried to pick you up." Emmett grinned as she swatted his arm.

"The hot cornbread on the fairway was fabulous. It had the most delicious taste."

"Did you bring me a piece?" he asked with wide eyes.

She ignored him, leaning forward with a whisper. "Of course everybody wanted to watch the bloke with the Singer Sewing Machine for hours. Everybody was oohing and aahhing and I couldn't have cared less."

"Who will darn my socks?" Emmett chided her good-naturedly. "At least you could have brought me a piece of cornbread."

"I made you chicken stew just last night," Manon replied. "I don't see *you* in the kitchen all that much. Seems to me you must have learned something being a bachelor for all those years."

"I was in the army, remember? After, I learned how to open a can or eat at the boarding house is what I learned," Emmett replied. "Should I be getting ready to leave?"

"Before the winners of the lottery are announced? I think not."

As if on cue, the organizers of the fair began setting up the drawing for the lottery. The top prize was $1,000, but there were many smaller items such as a stove, a sewing machine, and lesser dollar amounts. They announced the five winners of a thousand dollars each as Manon and the others peered intently at their tickets. None of them had triumphed, and so, with a toss of her head, she declared herself now ready to leave.

They made their goodbyes to the others and exited the private viewing boxes. Manon was going on about the wonderful things she'd seen today, especially in the brick building containing the art, and in a small lull, Emmett admitted that the cricket match had entirely puzzled him in regards to rules and scoring. It would seem that most of the grandstand had chosen this time to leave, and it was like a logjam during the spring of his youth in Bangor, as they fought their way down the hallway to the stairs.

At the bottom of the steps they happened into Campbell MacLeod and Frederick Ogden in a group of seven or eight local businessmen. The bustling crowd of people escaping the grandstand shoved Manon into MacLeod, who instinctively wrapped his arm around her to keep from stumbling. It was hard to tell if he recognized her or if his actions were purely instinctual when thrust together with a beautiful woman. One hand slid down to cup her buttock while he pulled her tight with the other, the leer on his face proclaiming to the world that his raised position in life allowed him to grope her if he so desired.

Without thinking, Manon brought her open palm up hard into the bottom of his chin, slamming his jaw shut and erasing the predatory hunger in his eyes. At the same time she shoved with her other hand

and sent him stumbling back into his associates who kept him from falling. Manon was flushed with anger, but a voice long drilled into her sent a warning piercing through her outrage. *What are you doing? You can't strike a wealthy white man!*

MacLeod righted himself and spit a thin stream of blood to the side, flecks of it dotting his chin. "*Ye* bitch," he said in a low and hard tone of barely contained rage. "I'll show *ye* how darkies used to be treated, and I bet you'll like it." He stepped forward, raising his arm with the intention of striking her back, but was interrupted by Emmett stepping between them.

"That's my wife you're referring to."

"Collins. Of course. I thought I recognized the lass."

"And if you apologize, we can all go on about our business."

MacLeod lowered his arm cautiously. "She struck me."

"You're lucky she hit you before I could react." Emmett stared at the man. His face was impassive. "If you ever paw my wife like that again, I *will* kill you."

"I believe the little darkie lass rather liked it," MacLeod retorted.

Seasoned fighter that he was, Emmett drove the blow not at the chin of the man, but rather to a space about two feet behind MacLeod's jaw, so that his fist carried through the punch and crumpled the man into a heap on the ground.

Ogden stooped to assuage the damage. "You knocked him plum out. I think you might have busted his jaw."

"He's lucky to be alive," Emmett said with the sangfroid fighting always created within him. He had been agitated and extremely nervous, terrified, even, in his first few battles of the Great War. By the time of the Gettysburg conflict, however, Emmett had learned how to internalize his fears and slow everything down around him, allowing him the time he needed to react to danger. "Tell him that when he comes to." He took Manon's elbow to guide her away.

"He's an old man," Ogden replied bitterly. "Old enough to be your grandfather."

Emmett paused, subtly moving Manon away from him and to a side. "Perhaps you would be a more suitable opponent?"

"Your day will come, carpetbagger."

"Why not today?"

Ogden shrugged. "I'm not much for crowds. When I deal with you, I'll make sure there'll be nobody around to stop me from stomping your face."

"You better bring some of your henchmen and come in the middle of the night wearing sheets then." Emmett wondered if Ogden had been present a few years back when he'd almost been lynched.

"Times are changing," Ogden replied. "Disguises and cover of night are no longer necessary, as the Federal Troops tire of protecting the usurpers of Southern white power. When I come for you, it will be in the middle of the day. Of that you can be certain." He turned and stalked off followed by the others, including an unsteady Campbell MacLeod, supported on either side, as the crowd parted like the Red Sea in front of them.

PART V: REDEMPTION

SEPTEMBER 13, 1874–SEPTEMBER 19, 1874

CHAPTER 16

SEPTEMBER 13, 1874

Emmett tipped back in his chair. There was a sheaf of papers on the desk in front of him, but his thoughts were far from what they contained. He knew that the White League had grown in strength over the past year, and that Frederick Ogden was training men in military maneuvers with the intent of taking over and leading New Orleans. The reports on the desk detailed the growing predicament facing the Metropolitan police and the state militia, a crisis that would, he judged, most likely come to a head in the next few days. He also knew that Campbell MacLeod was pulling the strings, and was the real leader of the White League. What filled Emmett's thoughts at the moment was whether or not the man's brutality rose to the level exhibited by the Black DOT Killer.

There had been five murders in the past year that fit the method utilized by the Black DOT Killer. Men had been watching MacLeod during that period, and he'd always been in either his lake house or the White Mansion. Of course, there was the chance he'd slipped out, as the prostitutes were always taken, beaten, raped, and killed in the hours between midnight and dawn. But Emmett had to face the possibility that perhaps MacLeod was not the killer. If not, then who? They would have to return to the beginning and start the entire investigation anew.

Was there any real evidence against the man, or was Emmett hoping it was MacLeod for his own satisfaction and the safety of

Manon? There had as yet been no repercussions following Manon and Emmett's very public physical shaming of the man, but Emmett knew MacLeod had not forgotten. To be slapped by a Black woman, and in public? No, he would not forget that, not for a single minute of a single day. Emmett sincerely hoped to produce evidence against this man, so that he could arrest him, lock him away, watch him swing from the gallows, and thus be released from the looming doom that MacLeod promised. As it was, they had been talking of leaving New Orleans, but it wasn't in Emmett to tuck his tail and run, especially after having endured so much through the years.

Corporal Thomas coming through the open door, dressed in rough work clothes, interrupted Emmett's reverie. He'd been watching MacLeod at his lake house, and was the reason Emmett was still at the station at almost midnight. To Emmett's searching look, Thomas merely shook his head in a negative. "He's been at his house all afternoon meeting with a steady stream of men. Ogden was there for quite some time, as were various other leaders of the White League, but the lights went out about an hour ago, and it's been quiet since."

"Who's with Lieutenant Johnson out there now?"

"Andrews."

"How about MacLeod's driver?"

"He left with Ogden and another man at about ten o'clock. I'm thinking he was bringing them into town and then will be returning for the night."

"What do you think?" Emmett stood up, thinking it was time to get home to his wife. "Should we drop it?"

Corporal Thomas shrugged his shoulders. "The man is mean, immoral, vengeful, and twisted, but I can't say that he is the Black DOT Killer."

"Okay, then. Get some sleep," Emmett steered Thomas out the door and onto the street. "Tomorrow we will pull off of MacLeod and start from scratch." The two men parted ways to walk their separate directions.

Instead of going home, Emmett walked down towards the river, wanting the fresh air to clear the cobwebs from his head. He turned onto Front Street, thinking he'd walk to Canal and up to Rampart, circling his way home to St. Ann, when Campbell MacLeod came out of a saloon. Emmett shook his head, thinking that the cobwebs had become delusions, but that was the unmistakable balding scalp and reddish-yellow hair clinging to the sides of his head, as well as his wide body and rolling walk. He was going in the same direction as Emmett, so Emmett just kept walking, following the man across Canal Street in the direction of the White Mansion on Magazine Street.

He must have snuck out, then. It was possible that he'd left the lake house right after Corporal Thomas, but there was no Lieutenant Johnson following him. Thomas had said men were coming and going all day. It would not have been hard to slip in with a group and leave the lake house behind. Why would he do that? He must have known he was being watched, Emmett guessed, and had something to hide.

MacLeod went into his house, which remained dark inside, and Emmett wondered if the man had gone straight to bed. Then he realized there was a faint glow from one window.

Emmett was stumped. What should he do? Go back to the station and send a message to Lieutenant Johnson that he was watching the wrong house? But he couldn't leave—the man unwatched was certainly up to something, whether it was White League business or something far more sinister, only time would tell. Just thirty minutes earlier, Emmett had decided the man was innocent of the murders, and now he was certain he was not. Or was that just wishful thinking?

It was in the middle of this pother that Emmett became aware of a carriage pulling up. It was MacLeod's regular driver, a man called Cy, but instead of holding the door for Ogden or another crony, this slender Black man with the tall hat was helping a young Black lass from the carriage. Emmett was well aware that MacLeod had developed a relationship with a new whore after Victoria had disappeared, helped by Madame Laveau and Emmett, to flee, going to live with a sister in Mobile. This was not the new prostitute who MacLeod overpaid for the privilege of beating, but she was of similar age, size, and features.

Emmett slunk around the corner to avoid Cy's prying eyes, sure as well that the eyes of another were peering out the windows to see the package being delivered. MacLeod seemed to require the services of Rhonda, the new whore, about once a week, usually here at the White Mansion. But this was not Rhonda, and in the past year, there had never been any other girl than her.

Deeply troubled and his suspicions aroused anew, Emmett crossed over through two backyards to end up at the back of the White Mansion. He was past the point of going for reinforcements. The moment was now to finally pin the man down, and Emmett did not plan on letting this opportunity slip by. The back door was locked, so he stood on the railing, and pulled himself up to the second floor veranda. This door opened, and he carefully eased through. The room he was in was dark, but he could see a faint light outlining the door across the way, and he picked his way cautiously across the shadowy room to press his ear to this doorway.

"*Ye* filthy bitch."

Everything in Emmett wanted to shove open the door and confront the man, but so far MacLeod was not revealing himself as a killer, only a man who mistreated prostitutes. For Emmett, this was crime enough, but, while he knew that to arrest him for this might be embarrassing to the man, any judge in the city would quickly toss out the charges.

"Call me master."

"Yes, master."

"You've been a bad little slave, haven't *ye*?"

"Yes, master. I'm sorry."

"*Ye* have one chance to make amends, or I'm going to have to hurt *ye*."

"Yes, master."

Emmett turned the knob and cracked the door. MacLeod was in a chair with his back to him, and he could see the girl on her knees in front of him. So far, she was not a victim, but merely fulfilling a service. Suddenly, MacLeod grabbed the woman on both sides of her head, pushing her backwards, and then kicked her viciously in the face, knocking her to the floor.

"You're just like all the others." He stood up and stripped off his pants, and then his shirt, so he stood naked with his back to Emmett.

He took two steps forward to where the woman lay cowering on the floor and kicked her again. "*Ye* want to take away my power?"

"No, master. I'm sorry, master. Let me try again."

"*Ye* had your chance. Now we do it my way." He grabbed her by the hair and lifted her up, and with his other hand grasped her breast and twisted. "I trusted *ye*, Delilah, and now *ye* are trying to use your powers of seduction to take my power from me." He punched her in the face and she tumbled back to the floor. "*Ye* work for the Philistines, don't *ye*? They sent *ye* to spy on me and find my weakness so that they can capture me, didn't they?" He stepped forward and kicked her in the side. "But, I'm on to *ye*. *Ye* cannot use your feminine wiles on me, because I will take my pleasure, and not be granted them by some harlot."

"Please, God, no," the whore whimpered.

"No sense praying to God. God has sent me to root out your filth and exterminate *ye* from this earth," MacLeod raged, reaching down and tearing her dress from her body. "*Ye* who try to tempt me into sin will be punished by death."

Emmett stepped through the door. "That's enough," he said quietly.

MacLeod turned towards him, wearing nothing but socks, his flaccid body gleaming pink in the faint light. "Collins."

"I'm taking you in, MacLeod."

"*Ye* can't arrest me," MacLeod replied. "I am the White Master and *yer* a lowly Negro-loving do-gooder carpetbagger."

"You are a sick man, is what you are."

"Cy!" MacLeod yelled. "We have an intruder."

Emmett pulled his pistol from the holster. "Put your clothes back on." The woman, her nose bleeding copiously, moaned and crawled away from MacLeod.

The door to the left burst open and the tall Black driver named Cy came through it holding a club, which immediately crashed down onto Emmett's arm, the gun skittering across the floor. Without the Colt, and his right arm gone limp from the blow, Emmett instinctively drove his left fist up under the man's chin. He then tried to step around him, but Cy wrapped his long arms around Emmett in a bear hug and squeezed like a vise. The room began to spin as Emmett fought for air, and, with no other choice, he let his legs collapse and fell to the floor, breaking the hold.

Emmett rolled to escape, but Cy grabbed him by the neck, and began to knock his head against the floor. He tried to gouge the man in the eye, but found his hand slapped away. He felt himself growing weaker, and in desperation grabbed Cy's genitals and twisted. The demonic Black man howled in pain, momentarily releasing his hold, and Emmett tried to crawl away from him, only to find his leg entrapped and the man again looming over him, pummeling him with hands the size of dinner plates.

Emmett became aware of something under his shoulder, and his good arm found the handle of his Colt .45. As the world began to darken around him, he lifted the weapon up, shaking, and shot the man in the face, his features dissolving in a shower of blood and bone. He pushed the limp body off of him, and dragged himself into the chair at the table. MacLeod was gone, the prostitute cowering in the corner. Cy was quite dead.

The next day at noon, MacLeod led a mounted posse down Canal Street. Surrounding the Henry Clay statue was a huge crowd of white men, many having already turned to drink at this early hour. The mood was a mix between surly, angry, and jubilant. As they moved towards the statue of the 'Great Compromiser' in the wide center of the street, men shifted grudgingly out of their way, until they looked up to see Campbell MacLeod, the Great White Master, as he had come to be called. The poor whites, it seemed, missed the system of slavery, and all that it embodied. The ideal of a master presiding over all was a central tenet of the plantation society, an ideal unmet since the end of the War of Northern Aggression. Campbell MacLeod had filled that void. Men scuttled out of the way then, calling ahead for the throng to part ways and let him through.

When MacLeod reached the center, a man in a light-colored business suit came striding in from the French Quarter side with several other gentlemen in tow. When he sighted MacLeod, he veered off and approached him.

"I have delivered the ultimatum to Governor Kellogg." R. H. Marr had been selected to be the spokesman for the newly formed White League.

"The man is no governor," MacLeod replied curtly. "I am about to visit Governor Penn, the one and true governor of the state of Louisiana."

"Sorry, sir," Marr stammered. He'd been hand-picked by the Great White Master to defend the nine men brought to trial for the Colfax Massacre, and his able defense had won him esteem, but he knew how fragile MacLeod's allegiance was. "Kellogg has refused to abdicate."

MacLeod nodded. "*Ye* know what to do." He turned his horse and urged his mount around the monument.

Before MacLeod and his posse had traveled the short distance to Camp Street, the voice of R. H. Marr bellowed from the second-floor galley of the Crescent City Billiards Hall. "The carpetbagger Kellogg has refused our offer of clemency. Go home and get your guns. The time to fight for our way of life is here. Redemption is near. Soon we will return to the white way. Be back here by two—fully-armed and ready to wage war."

The three short blocks between Canal and Poydras Streets were barren of life, except for the White League's armed regiments, who, over the last few days, had flooded the city with pamphlets warning people to stay home unless they wanted to aid in the destruction of carpetbagger tyranny. Blocking their way down Poydras Street was an overturned streetcar, mattresses, bales of cotton, and various pieces of furniture.

MacLeod nodded to Captain Phillips as they picked their way around the barricade, noting with satisfaction that similar obstructions blocked each cross-street left and right as far as he could see. This was the American Quarter, whereas the forces of the Metropolitan Police loyal to Kellogg were holed up in the French Quarter on the other side of Canal Street, which was once again the battle line between the Democrats and the Republicans. On the right was Lafayette Square, and on the left was the Kurscheedt & Bienvenu hardware store, now the temporary command post of "General" Frederick Ogden.

"Wait for me here," MacLeod said to his entourage. He dismounted and entered the store that had a little bit of everything, the normal clutter exaggerated as the center had been cleared for several large desks, tables, and an assortment of chairs filled by several men. "General." He nodded to Ogden, before turning to Penn. "*Ye* will be assuming the role of governor?"

Davidson Bradford Penn met his level stare. "Yes. McEnery has decided to visit friends in Vicksburg."

MacLeod shook his head, thinking back to the night a few years ago when he'd introduced and vouched for the man. At every previous moment of potential danger, he had disappeared on one pretext or another. "*Ye* are prepared to take office?"

"I am."

"Good. Any word on the Federal troops stationed in Mississippi?"

Penn touched the shoulder of the man next to him. "Do you know Major Burke? He's a member of my staff, but more importantly for this discussion, he's in charge of all of the railroads in this area."

"And?"

"I can assure you that it will take them a great while to reach here by train," Burke said with a straight face. "Delays are imminent and impending."

"Excellent." MacLeod smiled for the first time in two days.

"We've cut all telegraph wires between depots and leaving the city," Ogden interjected. "Word of our uprising should not get out for several days at best."

"It's more that we are merely redeeming what is ours to begin with," MacLeod growled, storm clouds returning to his face.

"Of course, sir," Ogden stammered.

"I know something of your ideas, Ogden, but what's the larger plan? How will we take back the reins of power?"

"Within the hour, there will be thousands of white Democrats fully armed and assembled at the Henry Clay statue." Ogden replied. "It's my belief that Longstreet and Badger will believe this to be the enemy to be dealt with. When they move to disperse the crowd, we will hit them with twenty-six companies totaling 1,500 organized militiamen."

MacLeod nodded approvingly. "The main attack will come along the levee and up Canal Street?"

"Yes, sir."

"It seems impossible that they can hold against such overwhelming odds. They will be like a worm under our boot heels."

"Yes, sir."

"Do not rest until it is done, then. Remember, there will be no security, no peace, and no prosperity for Louisiana until the government of the state is restored to the hands of the honest, intelligent, and tax-paying masses; until the superiority of the Caucasian over the African in all affairs is acknowledged and established."

At the same time the White League was planning their strategy, Emmett was sitting in the Cabildo building preparing for the impending attack. Governor Kellogg, Chief Badger, and General Longstreet sat with him at a table with a map of New Orleans stretched in front of them. He'd told Badger that MacLeod was the Black DOT Killer, explaining the bruises on his face, but now did not seem the time to spread the news. After they put down the impending insurrection, then he would arrest the disgusting lout, once his mob was defeated. Across the street was Jackson Square, where just a year earlier, they'd overcome a putsch by the Democrats led by the same man, Frederick Nash Ogden. This time, reports had it, the man had gathered a much larger and well-armed force for his rebellion.

"I've tried to contact General Emory in Holly Springs, but it appears that the telegraph wires have been cut." Kellogg shared the bad news to start the meeting.

"We're also out of contact with all of our other police stations," Badger acknowledged.

"How can we know what's going on? What are we going to do?" Kellogg was near to panic.

"I'm told that there's a rally taking place at the Clay statue on Canal," Badger said in his most soothing voice, circling the spot on the map.

"What do you believe their objective is?" Kellogg's face was pale and his right eye was twitching with nervous tension.

"They will first target supplies of munitions," Longstreet replied. "Over the past week we've seized several loads of weapons intended for the White League, most noticeably on the steamer, *Mississippi*, just two days ago."

Emmett looked at the ruffled, slightly rotund, and bushy-bearded former top general of the Confederacy. Eleven years ago this man had been directing troops against him on Little Round Top at Gettysburg, and now they fought side-by-side.

"I'd concur that weapons will be their first objective." Badger appeared especially mournful this morning, having gotten little sleep, his already recessed eyes dark with fatigue. "And the largest cache of munitions is right here."

"How many men do we have?" Kellogg asked, his voice rising in pitch.

"We have a thousand well-armed and trained police and militia," Longstreet replied. "More than a match for a crowd of street rabble."

"You will remain in the Cabildo?"

"And allow them to run roughshod over the city?" Badger shook his head.

"What do you suggest?"

"We will leave a force of 500 men here to defend the Cabildo and the Capitol, while taking the other 500 to disperse the crowd," Longstreet said.

Kellogg leaned forward to the map. "You can escort me to the Custom House, then."The Custom House was on the French Quarter side of Canal Street, and was a Federal building that the opposition would most likely avoid to prevent offending President Grant in this struggle for power in New Orleans.

Badger tapped the map with his finger. "I believe it'd be a moral boost for the men if you held office here."

Kellogg shook his head. "It's important that I align myself with the Federal Government as the legitimate Governor of Louisiana."

Emmett shuffled his feet. He missed Warmoth's leadership as governor. He wasn't sure that he agreed with the middle-of-the-road politics his friend had moved towards, but the man wasn't afraid to be at the center of the scuffle.

"We will advance down Old Levee and Peters." Longstreet had no use for politicians and cared little what the man did. "Governor Kellogg will accompany me to the Custom House, and then my force will fall in behind Chief Badger, who will disperse the rabble. I would suggest leading with the cavalry regiment." He looked over at Emmett. "And then moving in with infantry."

Thus, Emmett astride Mum Bett, the American Paint mare that Pinchback and Warmoth had given him as a wedding gift, found himself in the vanguard of the most elite members of the Metropolitan Police. As they reached Canal Street, he looked up to the right where they caught their first glimpse of a seething mass of humanity whose tumultuous cacophony had been building to a crescendo as they advanced. In addition to his unit of thirty mounted police, an additional seventy had been added from other units and the militia. He formed them into two battle lines facing away from the Mississippi River, with three lines of infantry behind.

On the other side of the Custom House, the militia under General Longstreet emerged to provide support for their advance. Emmett gave the sign to proceed, and the cavalry began to walk their mounts up the street. He was leading a hundred men into a horde of 5,000, but they had superior organization and were better armed, and had the support of another 400 following up behind. He was certain that the mob, once duly confronted and taking its first casualties, would disperse in the face of his disciplined units.

The mob grew quiet as Emmett led the Metropolitans up the wide street, but did not budge as they stood shoulder to shoulder watching the approaching police. A shot rang out from the roof of the Pickwick Club, and the sergeant next to Emmett toppled from his horse with half of his skull missing. Other scattered shots rang out from the City Hotel on the opposite side, and Emmett hesitated, for he didn't have the manpower to search out and eliminate these snipers. The only option was to advance into the enemy so that the snipers didn't have clear targets.

Emmett was about to give the order to attack the group of unruly and armed citizens, but at that moment, a breathless courier arrived on foot with news that enemy militia were flanking General Longstreet's position, and he was to fall back in support. They moved back down Canal taking sniper fire from both sides, as the throng surged forward behind them like a rising river after a heavy rain.

As Emmett's cavalry retreated, organized militia came down Magazine, Toulas, and Commerce Streets from the American Quarter. Emmett saw the unmistakable robust figure and matted red hair of Colonel Ogden on Tchoupitoulas Street, and snapped a shot with his Winchester. He must have hit the man's horse, for both fell to the ground, and with regret, Emmett saw the man clamber back to his feet. He thought about galloping his horse over to finish the job, the image of the man threatening Manon the previous year fresh in his mind, but he knew his job was to control the men under his command.

At the bottom of the street, Chief Badger was setting up artillery at the Iron Building, the old water works facility, facing the levee on the Mississippi River. Emmett had his cavalry dismount and kneel at the Custom House, facing the mass of humanity sliding down towards them as well as the side street of New Levee from the American quarter. The battery by the Iron Building began belching shot from the two Napoleons, and then the harsh sound of the Gatling gun began its steady rat-a-tat-tat.

Putting his Lieutenant in charge, Emmett reported in to Badger. From this vantage, he could see men scurrying from cotton bale to cotton bale on the levee. Companies were massing on the side streets of Fulton and Front and by the Pontchartrain Railroad Depot. Badger held his right arm crookedly where a bullet had smashed the bone, and his hand was bleeding profusely from another cartridge that had passed clean through. Snipers filled the windows on the American Quarter side of the street. By the time Emmett reached Badger, there were only four men left standing in the battery, the rest having been picked off.

And then came the Rebel scream, a sound Emmett had not heard since near the end of the Great War. Meant to raise the courage of those attacking and instill fear in those awaiting that attack, the noise was enough to raise the dead from St. Louis Cemetery and drive them to exact some horrible revenge. Around the levee flowed a seething mass of humanity, the men running full-speed, intent upon their prey up the street. A heavy fire erupted from the side streets, the lead raking Emmett's already thinned company.

"Hold your position," Badger yelled.

At that moment, the gathering from the Henry Clay Statue fired their motley array of weapons and then came spewing down Canal in a flood. Emmett began to move the fifty yards back to his regiment, but had gone no more than two steps when he saw Badger's leg crumple from yet a third bullet, and as the Chief slid to the ground, his body shook with a fourth impact. At this blow, the Metropolitans broke and fled in the face of the enemy. The shattered survivors streaked in full-scale panic onto Welles Street and towards the safety of the Cabildo in the French Quarter.

Emmett turned back to check on his friend, turning him face up, blood covering his arm, his leg, and his body. A man with the gray shirt of the Confederacy swung his rifle at Emmett's head, forcing him to duck. Emmett shot him under the chin with his Winchester, and dropping the rifle, pulled his pistol out, and shot another man charging at him. He realized that he was the last Republican on the street and made the difficult decision to leave Badger for dead. With his head held low, he churned his way towards safety as the waves of humanity converged upon him from three directions. Bullets blazed about him and even tugged at his uniform, but he managed to gain access to Welles Street without falling. Behind him, he heard cheering as the White League celebrated their victory.

The reserve troops were stationed at the old St. Louis Hotel, temporarily functioning as the State House, and at the police station located in the arsenal at the Cabildo. Emmett made his way to this second venue, a block further into the French Quarter, where he found twelve men from his regiment with another 200 police and militia. The ranking officer was sedated on the floor, having been shot through the stomach, and Emmett was forced to take charge.

The thick stone walls of the Cabildo would be difficult to storm, a strength that he repeated to the men in order to calm their frayed nerves. He then set up a sentry system of two hours on followed by four hours off. They broke out the cache of Winchesters so that each watch post had five extra rifles assigned. And then they waited. This was always the hardest part for him, this waiting. He'd rather be charging headlong into enemy artillery than twiddling his thumbs wondering what was happening out there, but there was no chance of convincing any of the exhausted and demoralized men into leaving the safety of their castle.

Companies of organized White Leaguers moved through the streets around them, the sounds of men smashing windows to pilfer stores discernible in the otherwise quiet dusk, but there was no move to attack the holed up remnants of the Metropolitan Police. It was twelve hours after the onset of the battle, at 3 a.m., that a small group of men approached under a white flag of truce. Emmett went out to meet with them. He was told that New Orleans had fallen and the White League was in possession of every other police station and arsenal in the city. General Ogden, as the White League had taken to calling him, had taken the city, but was willing to allow them amnesty if they laid down their weapons and returned to their homes before dawn.

Emmett brought this offer to the men and told them he wouldn't blame anybody for leaving. He then went into the office to let them decide their own fate. An hour later, when he came out, everybody was gone except for the dozen remaining members of his regiment.

"That's it, then," he said, and shook each one of their hands.

Emmett tucked his two pistols under his jacket, and in that darkest hour before the sun started its ascent, they split up to return home. Emmett turned up St. Ann Street, coming to a blockade of a White League company who parted in front of him, true to their word, and allowed him to continue on through. Several of the men nodded, giving him respect for having fought valiantly.

As he approached his home with Manon under the roof of the Voodoo Queen of New Orleans, each step heavier than the last, his thoughts turned to the grim reality of the day. Even if the Federal Troops showed up to expel the White League from the reins of government, the writing was on the wall. Kellogg had proven himself a coward. Badger was more than likely dead. The Metropolitan Police as a vital, functioning police force was completely shattered.

Rumor held that Longstreet had been wounded. The White League controlled the state outside of New Orleans and now had flexed their strength in the city, proving they were the true power brokers.

Worst of all, it was not just a shift in political ideology. The central tenet holding this new White League political entity together was its hatred of carpetbaggers and people of color. There was no place left in this once-hopeful land, now returned to its bad, old ways, for a marriage between a carpetbagger and a Black Creole. They would have to leave New Orleans.

CHAPTER 17

September 18, 1874

Manon leaned forward and touched her forehead to the only available space on the white altar in the front room of the Laveau household. On either side, statues of St. Peter and St. Marron flanked her, while a variety of candles flickered in the drafty room. Charms, beads, perfumes, potions, and a wide variety of herbs scattered their way across the surface, almost burying several dolls that emerged from the chaos like the dead trying to climb out of their tombs. Chamois bags of *gris-gris* that had never been delivered or picked up were sprinkled throughout the organized chaos.

"What is it, my child?"

The voice startled Manon, but she didn't open her eyes or move other than the initial involuntary twitch. "I can't seem to see my way, Madame Laveau," she replied.

"Life's journey is certainly a twisting path. It is often hard to see what is around the next bend, thus you must be ready for anything."

"I fear that past events may be clouding my vision."

"You should not feel guilty about what happened up in the land of steady habits," Madame Laveau said.

Manon stood, opened her eyes, and turned to face the woman who'd raised her like one of her own daughters. "How do you know about that?"

Madame Laveau smiled with her eyes and perhaps a slight twinkle in the lines at the corners of her mouth. She did not reply.

"I liked it. I was lonely. He was nice to me," Manon whispered.

"And what is it that you are sorry for?"

"I should have saved myself for Emmett."

"There was no Emmett at the time," Madame Laveau said gently. "There is no reason to feel guilty."

"I have not told Emmett that it happened."

"That is your decision. You have no requirement to tell him everything that happened in your past." Madame Laveau sat down in the high-backed over-sized chair across from the altar. "But I believe that it is best to do so."

"I went to St. Augustine today to confess this, and also that of the sin of lying with a man before I married him, but I was too scared to speak the words."

"There is nobody to be scared of but thine own self."

"What do you mean?"

"The Catholic Church serves many useful purposes, but when it comes right down to it, God is just another white man telling you who you are and how you should act and how you should feel."

Manon blinked. "You go to church every Sunday. Every day I see you praying at this altar. Why, if you don't believe?"

"I pray to find strength within myself. The only divine spirit is the one that resides within each of us. We can call it God, or *Bondye*, or even Papa Legba, but they are only symbols of our soul."

"I am the divine spirit?"

"Of course you are."

"And heaven and hell?"

Madame Laveau smiled. "Be true to thine own self."

"I have heard Emmett say those words. Are you suggesting that my own truth will lead me down the correct path?"

"He is a thoughtful young man with a kind soul. You have chosen well with that one."

"He believes we need to leave New Orleans." Manon turned to look at her own image in the mirror.

"What do you see?"

"What do you mean?"

"In the mirror. What do you see?"

Manon stared intently, trying to understand the underlying meaning of the question. "I see me."

"You see your only master. There is no plantation owner with a whip. There is no white man called God that dictates your actions, nor a Black man called *Bondye*. No man is your master, not even your husband."

"But I should honor him."

"You honor him by being true to thine own self." Madame Laveau rose carefully from her chair, and leaning on her cane, walked closer. She placed her palm on Manon's forehead—its coolness bringing peace. "You must first understand your essence before you can comprehend how that fits into the puzzle of life."

"How do I do that?"

"You must be honest in your own mind. When I was younger, I believed in this world created by men. I bowed my head to God, *Bondye*, and *Damballah*. I married a man who I consented to be my master and me his subject. And then I realized I was God, *Bondye*, and *Damballah*. My first husband didn't understand this and I had to send him away, and in this way consummated my own essence."

"Are you saying there can be no bonds, whether in religion or marriage?"

"Of course there are elements that bind us in this world. The love between a man and woman is certainly a powerful and tasty dish, but only if it is based upon equality."

"Equality, yes, but separate strengths certainly."

Madame Laveau returned to her seat, perching herself gingerly on the high wooden chair. "Perhaps you believe that a woman cannot pull the trigger of a gun? Or that our minds are not made for deeper thoughts like politics? I might not be able to vote, but I will tell you right now that not much happens in New Orleans without my opinion being heard, weighed, and considered."

Manon nodded. She knew full well the political and social clout of Madame Laveau. "When you married for a second time, did you not promise to obey your husband?"

"Christophe understood that I was my own person, not just a woman or a wife, but a being, and in this way we honored each other for many years before his death."

"I do not remember him as anything more than a gentle shadow in my youth, but I understood you found happiness together." Manon regretted not having known him, but had heard much about their grand love affair. "Do you think we must leave New Orleans?"

"Last year you made an enemy of the man who is now the most powerful force in the state of Louisiana. Do not misunderstand me—I believe you striking Campbell MacLeod was the right thing to do. But we live in a world where Black women don't strike white men. To stay is to invite danger upon yourself, but danger lurks in every corner of this earth."

"It is not just myself I fear for," Manon murmured.

"Bringing another life into this maelstrom is an integral piece of your decision," Madame Laveau concurred.

Manon nodded. Of course her godmother, the Voodoo Queen of New Orleans, knew that she was pregnant, even though she and Emmett were keeping it secret.

"The girl you brought to my house the other night is in a safe place." Pinchback settled back in his chair. He'd met Emmett here at the Phoenix House for a midday meal, and was now on his second bourbon. "But, I'm not sure her words will hold up in a court of law. It would help if you stayed around to provide your version."

Emmett took a careful sip of his still nearly full first bourbon. "We haven't made the decision easily, but our mind is made up. We plan to leave within the week."

"I didn't take you for the running type," Pinchback said, the words coming out more harshly than he intended.

Emmett shrugged. "MacLeod will never go to trial. Who is going to arrest him?"

"You are probably right," Pinchback said. "It just irks me to see him strutting around town, and now to know that he is the Black DOT Killer, and we can't touch him?"

"I don't know what else can be done."

"Politics is like the ocean," Pinchback responded. "You wake up tomorrow and the tide will have turned."

"I agree."

Pinchback looked at him and understood all of the unsaid words. "It certainly looks like the Democrats have grasped the upper hand for the foreseeable future."

"MacLeod and his anointed prince, Frederick Nash Ogden, now control Louisiana. They are the only law in the rural parishes already. When Grant pulls the army out, as he is wont to do soon, New Orleans will follow suit."

"Even now, Kellogg is no more than a puppet." General Emory and the Federal Troops had arrived in the city two days earlier, which also happened to have been two days too late, and restored Kellogg to his position of governor and reinstated the Republican legislature, but it was now abundantly clear that this government was nothing but a sham.

"My sources tell me that MacLeod will run for governor in '76." Emmett thought of Freedom, and knew he must get word to him to leave MacLeod and escape while he still could.

"And he will win," Pinchback said quietly.

Emmett bowed his head. There was little keeping him here. He'd miss a few men, such as Pinchback. Even though he disagreed with his most recent politics, he'd regret leaving the gregarious Warmoth behind. He'd also become quite close to Badger, who lay clinging to life in the hospital. He knew that Manon would be deeply saddened to leave her godmother, Marie Laveau, behind, as well as various other assorted friends. But, the one thing that lingered in the back of his mind, the one thing he worried over late at night, was what felt to be unfinished business with MacLeod. He couldn't get past the notion that he was abandoning a task uniquely his own, but the means to fulfill the undertaking and jail the beast eluded him.

"And where is it that you'll be able to go and leave all this mess behind?" Pinchback waved his cigar in a sweeping gesture encompassing all of the city and state.

"We've narrowed it down to two places." The conversation had begun the morning Emmett walked into the Laveau home four days earlier just as the sun was coming up. With his face blackened from firing his rifle, his shirt rent with bullet holes, and a mixture of his own blood and others spattered upon him—Emmett had sat down heavily at the kitchen table across from Manon and told her that he believed it was time to leave. "Either Texas or France."

Pinchback laughed. "Well, that couldn't be two more opposite ends of the spectrum. What, pray tell, is your criteria?"

"We don't particularly want to leave the United States," Emmett replied thoughtfully. "And I've been told that out in northwest Texas, they care more about your character than the color of your skin."

"That sure would be refreshing," Pinchback concurred. "What do you propose doing out there?"

"We've got some money set aside, and I was hoping to go into breeding horses. I met a man recently who is opening up ranches down below the panhandle who suggested they'd be happy for me to outfit a remuda for them. I could do real well with a stallion and a brood of mares. We'd file for a homestead and grow some crops and raise our child without the fear he was going to be lynched due to his hue."

"That sounds like a dream," Pinchback grudgingly admitted. "Where does France come into play?"

"We're trying to weigh the force of the changing winds." Emmett looked out the window of the Phoenix at the dusty street outside. "Will the Redeemers be content to take back New Orleans and Louisiana? Will they stop at the Mason-Dixon Line? Will Washington be caught up in the shifting times sending the entire country back to antebellum years?"

"Hell, I don't think they much care out on the frontier of Texas what Congress says and does."

"I'd like to be able to sleep at night not fearing that MacLeod's henchmen were going to come for Manon. I know that sick and twisted man desires his revenge for her slapping him."

"I guess France might be outside of his reach," Pinchback agreed.

"Times are changing. We need to be ready for what the modern world has to offer. France is much more accepting of mixed couples, Manon speaks the lingo, and I could learn."

"And you leave in a week? When do you decide whether you go west or east?"

Emmett smiled. He was embarrassed to share the decision-making process with his sophisticated friend. "We hope to get input from Mister Daniel Blanc."

Pinchback whistled softly. "I never got caught up in that Voodoo, but it's certainly not something I'd dismiss. I've heard too many stories to be skeptical. How do you plan on contacting this spirit?"

"There is a *fête* on St. Ann Street tonight. Marie the younger is the master of ceremonies, but Marie the elder will be present in her seat on the porch. Mister Daniel Blanc has given me insight once before, and I'm hoping that he'll guide me a second time in my journey."

Pinchback stood up, his cigar still in hand. "I must get back to work trying to piece together a legislature that has been cowed by recent events, and all the while, try to protect my constituents, none of whom are spirits. There's a rumor that a Black mob might try to overrun the police station in Tremé. I can't say I blame them, but the public outrage would be disastrous."

"I'll let you know my decision before we leave." Emmett rose and shook the hand of the man who had become his best friend in New Orleans.

"Give my best to Algernon. Tell him I'll try to visit tomorrow." Pinchback left unsaid the concern that the police chief might not live to see the next day.

As Emmett emerged onto the street, he paused and looked around the city he'd come to love, and then began to walk resolutely to the Charity Hospital where Chief Badger currently resided. He'd have to leave the French Quarter and cross Canal Street into the American District, a thought that didn't bring him much comfort, but it was only a block from the Custom House, where Federal Troops had established a stronghold in the middle of the two warring factions.

There were rumors that several of the wounded men by the Iron House had been finished off with a bullet to the head, but not Badger. Out of respect for the courage displayed by this titan of New Orleans, a young White League captain had ordered his men to gather a mattress that had been used as part of a blockade, and on this they'd carried the fallen chief to the hospital just a block away.

Activity had resumed in New Orleans with the restoration of order. Shopkeepers were out boarding up shattered windows and sweeping the boardwalk, while others with buckets of water and soap were scrubbing blood from the wood. Emmett marveled at the tenacity of the human spirit. The horrors of yesterday were brushed aside with the dawning of a new day, and the knowledge that nothing could change the past. At the same time, it was incredibly difficult to escape the past and to change the future, much less the present.

With a deep breath, Emmett walked past the Custom House and crossed over Canal Street. As he entered Tchoupitoulas Street in the American Quarter, Emmett remembered that it was at this spot that he'd taken a shot at Frederick Ogden just four days earlier, missing him but striking his horse, causing them both to tumble to the ground. He wondered if events would've been different if he'd killed the general of the White League Army at that critical juncture, much as having Badger and Longstreet both wounded early on had doomed the Metropolitan forces to defeat.

As if his thoughts raised true life forms from the apparitions of his imagination, Frederick Ogden and Campbell MacLeod came trotting up the street on horseback with the usual posse of aides, bodyguards, assistants, and friends. MacLeod raised his hand, and the group of eighteen to twenty men reined in, forming a loose semicircle around Emmett. He carefully unbuttoned his jacket, knowing if a confrontation were to take place, he'd most certainly die, but could hope to at least take MacLeod, and maybe Ogden, with him.

"Emmett, my boy, what brings *ye* across Canal Street?" MacLeod was magnanimous, his recent victory oozing from every pore.

"I thought I might pay a visit to Superintendent Badger."

MacLeod clucked his tongue. "I feel terrible for the man. That was a real *rammy* the other day."

"I'm guessing that this was told to you, as you were tucked safely away, sending others to do your dirty work." Emmett just couldn't help it, no matter how much he told himself to keep his trap shut and go about his business, there was something about the smug demeanor of the Scottish plantation owner that nettled him. "You're better fitted for taking, beating, raping, and killing women, aren't you?"

"I heard *ye* were spreading lies around about me," MacLeod said. "I couldn't figure it out, but then it came to me. Emmett Collins likes Black whores. Hell, he even married one. You're trying to pin the Black DOT Killings on me to cover your own hide."

Emmett gaped at him. "Me? You're a liar, MacLeod. But worse, you're a sick, twisted man. And a coward."

Ogden stepped his horse forward. "Personally, I had a front row seat to the Metropolitans breaking and running like chickens when a fox enters the henhouse."

"And I'm sorry that I missed and killed your horse instead of you," Emmett retorted. "Next time I'll take better aim."

Ogden blanched, and then regained his composure. "You missed your chance, Collins. Perhaps I'll give you another one when I visit you and your Sambo whore with a rope."

Emmett pulled his pistol from his waist and pointed the barrel at Ogden's head. "And I warned you about your language and your threats." The move caught them unaware and empty-handed. Several mens' hands began to creep towards their gun belts or saddle scabbards. Only one man carried his rifle in a shoulder sling, a position from which he could employ the weapon with far greater speed than any of the others. "Tell your boys to take their hands off their guns or they will be searching for your limited brains all the way down the street."

"*Ye* were always more headstrong than smart, Collins," MacLeod said angrily. "Can't you see what's happening here? Redemption. After nearly fifteen years of fighting, Louisiana is returning to white Southern rule. Your opposition merely signs your death warrant."

"I'll die knowing no more girls are going to be hurt by you," Emmett said grimly.

MacLeod waved his arm up the street. "*Ye* all get along. I want to have a word in private with the Irish lad." When nobody moved to go, his face flushed. "Go now. Wait for me at the corner."

Like chastised children kicked from a candy store, they began to move off then. Emmett couldn't but help be interested in what MacLeod had to say that demanded privacy. "What is it, then?" Inside, he was tussling with whether or not he should take the opportunity to kill this man. He knew that he would be torn apart by MacLeod's posse, but it was the thought of killing an unarmed man that held him back.

"I believe *ye* misunderstand me, Emmett. I don't hate Black people. I don't hate the Sicilians or the Mexicans. They are no different than the bulk of the poor white people. Poor white, Black, brown, or whatever color, are meant—no, *demand* to be ruled by men of superior breeding, culture, and education. All of the great civilizations have flourished in this way. Greece, Rome, France, Great Britain, just to name a few—their societies prospered, their wealth burgeoned due to the leadership of the few elite members of society."

"That is the intention of our democracy," Emmett agreed. "To elect the very brightest and ablest amongst us to govern." And judges and juries and executioners to ensure men were not wrongly imprisoned or killed. It was not for Emmett to play the part of deciding guilt and executing punishment at the same time, but if he didn't, MacLeod was going to get away with all those gruesome murders, and most likely continue his brutal and savage avocation.

"But the founding fathers never intended for poor, ignorant, and unsophisticated men to be able to cast a vote. Thomas Jefferson believed that an educated citizenry is a vital requisite for our survival as a free people." MacLeod dismounted and stepped closer to Emmett to avoid being overheard by pedestrians walking past. "And 400,000 freedmen certainly constitute an uneducated mass of voters."

"And you would disenfranchise the freedmen of Louisiana due to the institution of slavery having deprived them of means, an education, wealth, everything that gives a man dignity?"

"Poverty has stripped the potential for political intellectual capacity for most men in this country. How can *ye* expect a man with a third grade education to make an enlightened decision on whom to elect to represent him? They need to be told how to vote. They needed to be guided in their choices."

"That is democracy as I know it," Emmett said, a question in his voice. "Men with a higher degree of understanding in how government works sharing their beliefs to the constituents, hoping that the majority will agree with their judgment on the issues of the state."

"But it has become too complicated and the average uneducated man wallows in confusion as he listens to all of the competing claims," MacLeod spoke urgently, wanting to be understood. At one point, he'd seen his younger self in the eyes of Emmett, but now all he saw was disgust. "Before the War of Northern Aggression, everybody fit into their niche. The plantation owners were the most educated and cultured men. They acted as paternal figures for the majority of the white population. The poor white crackers were content they were not at the bottom of the social ladder, and the darkies had no choice but to obey. That way, we were able to keep the status quo."

For the first time, Emmett began to realize what all the fuss was about. "You mean to say if we lump all the poor people, Black and white, together, they will begin to look around for a target to lash out at?"

"Exactly!" MacLeod exclaimed, excited to have his point understood. "If a constant rift is not kept between the crackers and the newly freed darkies, they might realize the scale is tilted against them."

"Would it be so bad? Perhaps you have enough to share."

"That would be the end of civilization as we know it. What happened in France when the peasants rose up against the aristocracy? Beheadings, chaos, looting, destruction, and the end of the Catholic Church in that country."

"Until Napoleon Bonaparte came along to restore order," Emmett mused, and then with dawning realization, added, "You think you're Napoleon!"

MacLeod was oblivious to the horror in Emmett's voice. "*Ye* might say that is my role. It's a different time and a different place, but the events are remarkably similar. The War of Northern Aggression was really no more than a revolution that freed the slaves and gave them a false sense of equality, much like the peasants of France in 1789. *Ye* carpetbaggers have run the gamut of the assembly, the reign of terror, and the directory. The time is now ripe for an emperor to rise from the ashes of the havoc *ye* have sown."

"And to accomplish that, you have to pit the poor whites against the recently freed slaves? So that they leave you out of the mud, regarding you instead as some paternal figure to all the people of Louisiana while they hate upon each other." Emmett, now that his tenure here was coming to an end, finally began to understand the politics of the opposition.

"Not just Louisiana, my boy. I will unite the south and then the entire United States in my dream of restoring the plantation class, and in turn, our country to its former glory." MacLeod's eyes were shining with the vision of grandeur in his mind. "But I will need loyal people around me in my rise to the top. I know that we've had our differences, but I want *ye* to consider joining my efforts at redemption."

"You want me to forget that I know you are the Black DOT Killer?"

MacLeod waved his arm dismissively. "That doesn't matter. I am the White Master. I am the Boss. I am Samson. I am Napoleon. I am everything to everybody. Nobody will believe *ye*, and if they do, it won't matter."

"You will pay for your crimes," Emmett said, but he could hear the hollow echo to the words.

"*Ye* know better than that. The Governor is a coward and will not deign to come after me. Your man Badger is on his deathbed, as is Longstreet. The Met and the militia are in shambles. Who is going to make me pay? I am the most powerful man in Louisiana. I am your master."

Emmett stared at MacLeod with loathing. He felt dirty, now that he'd been exposed to the man's innermost twisted core. "You've been to the crossroads and sold your soul," he muttered under his breath, feeling sick and faint at the evil in front of him. The beating, raping, and killing of some fifty women was only a minor detail in the horror that MacLeod wanted to propagate upon the United States of America, all to fulfill his perverted vision.

MacLeod stepped closer; his puffy-red face no more than an inch from Emmett's, his tongue rolling over his thick lips. "What's that?"

"If I could be assured of preventing your ascension to power, I would gladly lay my own neck under the descending guillotine," Emmett replied in a voice foreign to his own ears, as if the *lwa* were possessing him. "But you need not worry about me. Manon and I are leaving Louisiana for parts yet unknown."

"Leaving?" MacLeod asked in a shocked tone. "*Ye* can't leave until our business is concluded here."

"I have no further business with you, unless it is watching you piss and shit yourself and slowly strangle as you twist from the gallows." Emmett replied. He then turned on his heel and walked away.

MacLeod watched him march off, astonished and dismayed at the rebuff. He had no intention of taking Emmett into his inner circle, but only wanted to bait him before destroying him and that whore of his. He touched his jaw where the harlot had struck him—Campbell MacLeod, in a crowd of people, in front of his own disciples—and vowed silently to have his revenge before the happy couple made their escape. He imagined his hands striking her face, ripping her clothes from her body, twisting and kicking, and the helpless screams and pleading for mercy. After beating her, he would cut off the hand that had struck him, and have his way with the whore while she bled. Just the thought of it stirred his manhood. Revenge and satisfaction were coming soon. And when Collins came after him, as he most certainly would, MacLeod would lay a trap and capture him—and *his* death would be even slower.

Manon was waiting for Emmett in the front lobby of the Charity Hospital, having already gathered directions to Badger's room. She went to kiss him, and paused at the blackness in his eyes. "What is it?"

"I just had a chance encounter with Campbell MacLeod."

"Was it similar to the last time… we collided?" Manon asked.

"If possible, I feel more violated than you were, and was not able to salvage any satisfaction from the encounter as you did," Emmett replied darkly. "I quite believe he has made a pact with Baron Samedi."

"If he has made a covenant with the *lwa* of the dead, all he has accomplished is the creation of his own casket. Baron Samedi is quite the trickster, and despises those that take themselves too seriously."

"I believe MacLeod would fit that description. He as much claimed to be the second coming of Napoleon Bonaparte."

"Hmmm. I do not know my history as well as I should. Was Napoleon a twisted and sadistic pig?" When Emmett didn't answer, Manon continued, "Let us go visit Algernon. It sounds like Baron Samedi must have a twist in store for the man who believes he is the reincarnation of Emperor Bonaparte."

Badger had garnered himself his own room due to his stature, a slight improvement on the overflowing and dirty common rooms with crowded single beds, now filled by the injured from the recent street battle. The man had propped himself up in bed, his gray face mottled with the red of fever.

Lizzy Badger, his wife, rose as Emmett and Manon came in, stopping them just within the doorway. "Thank you for coming," she said, allowing each of them to kiss her on the cheek.

"How is he?" Emmett asked.

"The doctor says he will die if they don't amputate his leg," Lizzy whispered. "But he refuses to let them take it."

"Many men who lost a leg in the Great War have led fruitful lives," he said, covering the shudder the thought had provoked.

"Talk to him. His children need him. I need him," she pleaded, and as tears cascaded from her eyes, she excused herself and stepped past them into the hall.

"Algernon." Emmett touched the man's arm to gain his attention.

The police superintendent blinked and brought his eyes into focus. "Emmett."

"I'm glad to see you alive. I watched you go down at the Iron House and was certain you were dead," Emmett said guiltily.

"I might as well be dead," Badger croaked. "They want to take my leg. Why do they want my leg?" he asked confusedly.

"To save your life," Emmett said gently.

"What good is a man with one leg? Those damn White Leaguers have crippled me. They have beaten me."

What could be said to that? Emmett wondered. The man was right. The White League had indeed won. Badger was left the shell of a man. Emmett was running away. Warmoth had traded sides.

"A living man with one leg can be a wonderful father and husband," Manon said, stepping forward.

Badger turned his head towards her, blinking again as he tried to refocus. "Hello, Manon," he said.

"You men always think it courageous to die for your principles, when the hardest thing to do is just to live life as it comes," she said hotly, feeling little sympathy for the man who was willing to abandon his family. "Lizzy needs you. Sidney needs a father. Do you want your baby growing up never knowing you?"

Badger ran his tongue over his upper lip. It felt like sandpaper on a raw wound. "Perhaps you're right."

Manon nodded. "You know I am right." She took a damp cloth and laid it on his brow tenderly.

"What's happening out there?" Badger asked tiredly. "Nobody seems to know anything."

Emmett went on to update him on the situation in New Orleans with the reinstitution of the Kellogg government, glossing over that it was no more than a sham, and that everyone knew who was really pulling the strings in Louisiana now.

Badger gave Emmett a note to be delivered to the White League captain who had ordered his broken body to be carried to the hospital over the objections of several of his men.

Manon let it slip that they were planning on leaving Louisiana when she promised to check in with Lizzy before they departed, news that Badger took in with a grim nod, not surprised at their decision.

As they left, Badger asked that they send the doctor in.

CHAPTER 18

SEPTEMBER 18, 1874

Later that night, near to the witching hour, Emmett found himself on the veranda of the home on St. Ann Street speaking with Marie Laveau. The yard was filled with twice as many attendees as the normal Friday night *fête.* Marie the younger had moved her altar from the house for this special occasion, including all of the items that littered the top—the salt, brown sugar, iron filings, arrowroot, spices, pieces of High John the Conqueror root, sweet basil, camphor leaves, and bottles of Red Drink. This shrine flanked the fire, and in the center of the courtyard she had spread a white sheet edged with burning candles, upon which she shook and shimmied, while the dancers surrounding her gyrated madly to the steady bongo drums beating from all sides.

"I'm sorry to be taking your goddaughter from you," Emmett said.

Madame Laveau rocked steadily in her chair. "You are doing the right thing. There is no place for either of you in New Orleans any longer. Certainly not as a married couple with child."

"Once we get settled, we can send for you." Emmett knew this was a futile offer, but he felt obligated to try.

Madame Laveau snorted. "I turned seventy-three last week," she replied. "I was born a French *sitwayen*, but when I was two years of age, Thomas Jefferson bought me and everybody else in Louisiana, making me an American citizen. I have never left New Orleans. I have attended services in the St. Louis Cathedral ever since I can remember. I was but a child when Colonel Jackson along with several units of color defeated the British in 1815. I danced for years around the corner in Congo Square. I remember when the courts decided that Blacks from Africa could not be *sitwayens*. I was here for the arrival of General Butler who gave freedom and entitlement to all of my enslaved brothers and sisters. It is here that I was born, have lived, and will die. And after death, I will be interred in St. Louis Cemetery."

"It's just that I feel… guilty. It's difficult times for anybody in New Orleans, especially if you are of color or from away."

Madame Laveau chuckled—a raspy tinkle that suggested her mind was livelier than her body. "I may have grown too old to get around, but I am still paid visits every day—the politicians, plantation owners, officers of the police and militia, both Democrats and Republican alike. There is not a soul in this city who would dare raise their hand against me. I am the Queen."

Emmett nodded. "Do you think that we are wrong to leave?"

"Christophe Glapion was the only love of my life. At the time I met him, he was white and therefore we could not marry or live together. For me, he changed his color by claiming to be a quadroon, and we were able to live many happy years together. Although you have legally married Manon, the ostracization you will face will be much worse than anything I had to experience. You deserve the happiness that I enjoyed."

"It's not in me to run away," Emmett said, watching his wife sway to the rhythm.

"Life changes. You have a wife and are expecting a child," Madame Laveau said, following his gaze. "Leave Campbell MacLeod to me. Once everything settles down a bit, I will make sure he gets his due."

"How?"

"I have told Rhonda that he is the Black DOT Killer, and she has agreed to slip something in his wine next time she visits with him. Now that Cy is no longer there to watch his back? He will disappear into the Bayou and nobody will be any the wiser."

Emmett kissed the woman on the forehead as a silent thank you for her support, and slipped down the few steps into the organized bedlam below. It eased his mind to know that Madame Laveau had plans for MacLeod. He had overlooked her as one who might help stop this violent killer, and he sensed that was part of her power, how easy it was for the powerful and arrogant to underestimate and overlook this frail and elderly Black lady.

Marie the younger was singing in a deep voice, "*Sauté crapeau, to chieu brûler, prend courage, li va repousser.*" This was a common song at the Friday night *fête*, and thus, it was a bit of Creole that Emmett understood. "Jump, bullfrog, your tail will burn, take courage, it will grow again." It had taken him quite some time to be convinced this was the actual translation.

The followers all yelled back in unison, "*Dansé Calinda, Bou-doum! Bou-doum! Dansé Calinda, Bou-doum! Bou-doum*!"

The *Calinda* had developed into a very risqué dance, and the revelers began to shake and shimmy even more suggestively than before, mimicking sex, the sinewy black and white limbs and torsos writhing in ecstasy as their bellies, bottoms, and breasts convulsed orgasmically. *Bou-doum* had originated as a saying when a Creole child fell down, but now caused all to throw themselves to the ground and twist and contort their bodies.

Emmett waited for the bodies to again rise before approaching Manon from the rear and wrapping his arms around her, letting her movement be his own. Marie the younger pointed at the two of them and began to sing another love song, this time in English. "In our shack, we will eat fritters, my dear baby, you know I love you, you sing like the birds in the woods. For your beauty, I would walk in front of a cannon, for your beauty, I would walk in front of a cannon. In our shack, we will eat fritters, my dear baby, you know I love you; so often you have confided your sorrows to me—sometimes I said no, sometimes I said yes, then I felt so sorry, that I asked you come in my shack to eat fritters, to eat fritters..."

And then the bongo drums began to increase in intensity. Manon turned around, wrapping her arms around Emmett's neck and staring into his eyes as she ground her pelvis into his midsection provocatively. His arousal rose, the blood coursing faster through his veins as if keeping up with the hurrying beat of the drums. Everything around began to fade to nothing, and then Emmett looked into Manon's eyes, and was yanked into that dark tunnel where he'd been once before, with creatures rustling out of sight, and hissing noises piercing the sound of rushing wind. There was a light in the distance, and as he got closer, he realized Manon was next to him, and on the far side was Mister Daniel Blanc.

They exited from the tunnel through a bush and were on the Mall, as the locals in Washington, D.C., called it. Emmett remembered when he'd first marched past this grassy area with the 20th Maine back in 1862 when he was fourteen years old. They'd turned and crossed in front of the White House, and he'd seen Abraham Lincoln standing and watching them pass. The somber and silent resolve of this president had moved something in Emmett even then, and it was the empathy emanating from the man that he carried forward with him, through the war, past the assassination of Lincoln, on to New Orleans, and would continue to bear as he moved into the future.

There was a huge crowd filling the space. All faces were turned to the Capitol building, in front of which had gathered politicians, dignitaries, and men of merit. Emmett realized that all of the men present wore the derbies and top hats of the day upon their heads, meaning that this trip was certainly not too distant into the future. Nobody seemed to notice their strange presence here, as Emmett was dressed for a *fête* and not a formal occasion, while his companions were the only woman within sight and a Voodoo *lwa*.

Mister Daniel Blanc led them effortlessly forward through the throng. The left-side wing of the Capitol building appeared to be their destination. Colossal American flags hung down from the gallery upon which about a hundred people were perched. Emmett realized that each had a white handkerchief in their left breast pocket, as did most everybody in the crowd around him.

A thin man with a very black beard, offset by streaks of gray mixed with brown upon his head, was standing at the podium. Emmett was only aware that there had been absolutely no sound until, as if flipped by a switch, a tumultuous uproar erupted around him.

"And now, I would like to present the twentieth president of these here United States of America, Campbell MacLeod."

President MacLeod stood up and strode over to the podium with his mincing steps, where he shook the man's hand. "Thank you, General Forrest." He shuffled some papers, looked out over the Mall, and began to speak.

"We, the citizens of America, are now joined in a great national effort to rebuild our country after the horrors of the War of Northern Aggression, and the even more devastating period of Reconstruction. Together, we will determine the course of America and the world for years to come. We will face challenges. We will confront hardships. But we will get the job done.

"For too long, a small group in our nation's Capitol has held our people hostage, while us white people have borne the cost. The citizens of our nation have had to pay the expense of keeping a standing army within our own country, while Mexican bandits run roughshod over the border.

"Our hard-earned dollars have been spent on the livelihood of an inferior race of people living amongst us who have neither the ability nor the desire to contribute to society.

"From this day forward, a new vision will govern our land. From this moment on, it's going to be white America first. Every decision will be made to benefit white American workers and families."

The crowd erupted in cheers, and more than one hat was tossed in the air. Emmett found Manon's hand and squeezed it supportively. The white crowd, almost all men, was delirious with happiness.

"We will unite America once again, and to do this, it is essential that we make a change. The darkies were never meant to be here, and thus, we must send them back to Africa, and will not stop until every black blemish upon our great country has been removed."

The crowd went wild screaming in ecstasy.

"The time of Republican misrule is over. Now arrives the time of action. Do not let anyone tell *ye* it cannot be done. We will not fail. Our country will thrive and prosper again. A new national pride will again unite us.

"So to all white Americans, from north and south, west and east, hear my promise: *Ye* will never be ignored again.

"Together, we will make America strong again. We will make

America white again. Thank you, God Bless *Ye*, and God Bless America."

As the crowd went wild cheering, the earth opened up underneath Emmett and Manon, and they went hurtling through space and time until the ground stopped their fall, and they were on their hands and knees in the courtyard of their home being helped to their feet by many clutching hands.

It was hours later, when they finally lay down in their bed, that Manon broached the yet unspoken thought. "We have to leave the country. Our decision is made for us. We must go to France."

Emmett didn't reply, other than expelling a breath of air from his lungs.

Manon waited for more, and when nothing further came, she rolled up on an elbow so that she could see his face. "What?"

"It's only..." Emmett trailed off.

"You don't like to run away," Manon finished for him.

"Campbell MacLeod is going to be elected president in six years. He'll be the face and brains of our country. How can we flee and let that happen? Especially when we now know that his plan is to drive out every person of color?"

Manon contemplated this. "Leave him to Madame Laveau."

"We saw with our own eyes the monster giving his inauguration speech. He plans on casting out over four million people due to the shade of their skin. Those are the lucky ones, for I am positive many will die in the process. And what is to prevent some other system of enslavement from being introduced? Especially in those places and states where it is more than just a fresh memory, and with the worst kind of yearning nostalgia, at that."

"It is impossible to know what the future holds," Manon whispered.

"But we saw it as plain as day," Emmett argued in frustration.

"Voodoo teaches that time is not linear, but floats through the present, past, and future. As well, there are many potential paths from one instant to another. What we witnessed at the Capitol building was not what *will* happen, but what *may* happen."

Emmett didn't reply, but he felt his deepest fears had been validated. A sadistic murderer with a hatred of Black people was going to be elevated to the highest office in the land, and he, Emmett, was going to run away? He was going to leave the fate of the country in the hands of a seventy-three-year-old lady?

As if knowing his thoughts, Manon straddled him, pulling her nightshirt over her head to reveal her naked body. She took Emmett's hand and placed it on her belly, and then leaned down to kiss him languidly on the mouth. They made gentle love. Long after Manon had fallen asleep, Emmett whispered into her tangled hair, "I know we have to leave, my love. I know we must go to France. But I feel that I will leave a part of my soul here when we do."

CHAPTER 19

SEPTEMBER 19, 1874

Emmett woke after just a few hours' sleep, and carefully eased himself from the intertwined limbs of his wife and love. He grabbed his clothes and boots, and dressed in the hallway so as to not awake her. The house was quiet at this time but for Marie Laveau, who was in the kitchen with coffee made. She handed him a cup and motioned for him to sit.

"Do you ever sleep?" Emmett marveled at the stamina of the old woman who had still been on the veranda when he passed by her earlier this morning on his way to bed.

"I am afraid that Baron Samedi will come for me when I close my eyes," she replied with a crease of a smile. "So I try to get my rest in short snatches before he can make the journey to collect me."

"Mister Daniel Blanc showed us a terrifying vision last night," Emmett said.

"Tell me what you saw."

Emmett told her about MacLeod becoming President, and of the plan to ship all of the Black people back to Africa, and the misgivings he had about leaving.

"I told you I would take care of him," Madame Laveau said. "Do not worry about the vision. The future is only a series of endless possibilities. We cannot change the past, but what is yet to come? That which has not happened is merely a blank book, to be written in as we can, though not always as we wish."

Emmett finished the cup of the hot liquid, and then slipped out of the courtyard, still littered with those who'd been too exhausted for the trip home. He passed through the gate, and went down to the wharf by Jackson Square. It was the third ticket agent that supplied him with what he needed.

The General Trans Atlantic Company's agent sold him two steerage tickets on the Steamship *Ville de Paris*, leaving in two days' time, bound for Brest, France, in the northwest corner of the country and less than four hundred miles from Paris, an overnight train ride. Due to availability at this late date, he obtained the fare for $15 off the standard $35 price.

He was in line at Café du Monde when Henry Clay Warmoth came through the door. Spotting Emmett, the former governor made a beeline for him. "I was just about to put out the word that I needed to see you. What's this about you leaving New Orleans?"

Emmett knew that the man didn't believe in Voodoo, and hence, the vision from the previous evening would merely be discounted as malarkey. "Hello, Henry. You're also on my list of people to visit."

"Is it true? Are you going to Texas like that damn Pinchback said?"

"We've decided upon France." Emmett thought of the threat the previous day from MacLeod, and decided to keep the exact destination a bit more under wraps.

"France? What the hell is in France?" His mustache bounced upon his upper lip in apparent consternation.

"People who are less likely to judge a person's worth—or that of their wife and children, for that matter—by the color of their skin," Emmett retorted.

Warmoth started to reply to that, thought better of it, and then began again. "I could help you become a rich man if you let me."

Emmett shook his head. "No. Thank you."

Warmoth chuckled. "You've always been too honest for your own good." He then turned serious and looked Emmett in the eye. "It's probably best you leave. I heard MacLeod has been talking of getting even with Manon after what happened at the race track."

A shiver ran down Emmett's spine. What did they say caused that? When somebody walked across your grave? For the first time this old wives' tale made sense to Emmett, but it was not his grave, but Manon's that somebody was treading upon. This seemed to suggest that they wouldn't be buried in the aboveground crypts of New Orleans, he thought. He reached the front of the line and ordered a dozen beignets. He was going to miss these square treats covered in powdered sugar once they were gone, but people said France had wonderful bakeries. The clerk placed them carefully in one of the new flat-bottomed paper bags for him.

"What is your business with MacLeod?" Emmett turned to his friend. "How can you stand shoulder to shoulder with a swine of his caliber?" He thought back eight years to the charity dinner, at which MacLeod had first introduced Emmett and Henry.

"Is it true that he's the Black DOT Killer?" Warmoth asked quietly. "Are you that certain?"

"Henry," Emmett began. "I saw it plain as day. He didn't know I was there and he bragged about it to a whore even as he beat her half to death. When I went to stop him, his driver jumped me, and he managed to get away. That was the day before the White League claimed the city as theirs."

"I knew he was evil, but I had no idea..." Warmoth trailed off.

"Even without knowing he was the Black DOT Killer, I don't understand how you could have joined forces with him. He is immoral."

"Who was I to support? Kellogg? The man's a coward, who moreover was, and is, Grant's puppet. Once Pinch threw in with that crowd, there was no viable candidate. Besides, I knew that McEnery was pliable, and hoped to shape him, not realizing at the time who is really pulling the strings." The words came slowly and painfully, as if Warmoth was realizing the grave error of his ways even as he spoke. It was not like him to admit being wrong, and this was certainly as close as he'd ever come.

"You know that he intends to be the President of the United States," Emmett said carefully. "He plans on running for governor in '76, and using that as a stepping stone for the 1880 election."

"Perhaps, then, my friend, I will join you in France." Warmoth smiled and held out his hand.

Manon woke to find Emmett gone. With a yawn, she slipped from bed, pulling the cotton nightshirt over her body, the bottom hanging to her ankles. The house had an empty feel to it, but there was coffee in the kitchen. She would be sad to leave this home behind. It had been difficult to go away to college in Boston, but she'd known she was coming back. This upcoming journey had a more permanent aura about it, and she felt the sadness dripping within her being. She placed her hand over her belly, wondering if the child would be a boy or girl. It did not matter, for they would be safe.

Her thoughts were interrupted by a sudden cry from the veranda in the unmistakable voice of Madame Laveau, followed by the crash of a falling body. Before Manon could react, the door burst open and filled with men of seedy demeanor. She attempted to run back into the interior of the house, but a hand grasped her shoulder, and she was slammed into the wall, crumpling to the floor with the wind knocked out of her. A knee was planted squarely in her back, her hands tied, her mouth gagged, and she was dragged to an enclosed wagon and deposited within.

There were two older men with unkind eyes across from her. The thinner of the two leered at her with a greedy look, his tongue running over his lips between spitting tobacco juice out the opening in the door. The other was a thickset man with a bowler on his head and a carefully groomed mustache who sat with a pistol aimed at her, even though she was tied tight. Neither one of them uttered a word, but she could hear the riders outside keeping a constant chatter, through which she came to understand that they worked for MacLeod, and that she was being taken to Rio al Lago. Manon tried futilely to come up with a plan of escape. The best strategy appeared to be to make ready for any opportunity that might present itself.

Freedom flicked the reins of the two-horse team to urge them up the hill. They were almost to Rio al Lago. Susannah had come to him mid-morning with a request to go to the plantation home nestled between the river and lake, as the gossip had swirled around New Orleans with malicious lips that her husband was the Black DOT Killer. At Rio al Lago, there would be more privacy and fewer people stopping by as if spontaneously but with unasked questions burning in their eyes. Could it be true? Freedom wondered.

Over the past eighteen months, a forbidden friendship with the lady of the house had blossomed, a bond based initially upon his hunger for learning, and her boredom as she was increasingly ignored by her husband and shunned by others of high society as one lacking the proper lineage. Susannah had given birth to a baby boy a year ago, and since then, Campbell's absences had become longer and his patience for her had worn thin. It had been Freedom who had pitched in to lend a hand with young Duke, although only when Boss MacLeod was not around, of course.

The four-hour trip to Rio al Lago had been filled mainly with discussion on the book, *A Tale of Two Cities*. While Freedom's reading ability had improved greatly—he was able to understand the words of the novel, but comprehending it without the knowledge of 18th century English life and mores was an entirely different matter. He was just flabbergasted by the actions of one of the men in the novel, a problem he often had with the works of fiction he read, because men and women were always doing noble things on the written pages, and that didn't seem to jive with his own understanding of the world.

"So, you're telling me that this here man, Carton, gave his own life so the husband of the woman he loved could live?"

"Carton respects the fact that Lucie has chosen Charles Darnay to be her husband, and recognizes that she is happy with him. Partially because he is aware of his own moral deficiencies, but also because of Darnay's sterling character." Susannah held an oriental parasol to shield her fair skin from the sun as the buggy trundled over the rutted path. "It is the noblest form of love possible."

"To me, it sounds like he gave up instead of trying to win her hand." Freedom was well aware of her closeness on the bench seat just scant inches from him.

Susannah sighed in exasperation. "If you truly love somebody, you put their happiness in front of your own satisfaction." She winced as she said this, because this was only true in novels. In real life, you spurned those you loved for the stability of money and status, at least, she thought, it always seemed to her that she had had no other choice.

"I think I understand," Freedom said, adjusting the soft felt hat on his head to shield his eyes from the glare. "Because his love is so strong, it causes the happiness of Lucie to be more important than anything else, even life itself."

"Yes. The only way he can secure her joy of life is to take her husband's place on the gallows. He has nothing else to offer, and thus gives all he has for her."

"Secure?" Freedom asked. "I take it that's a good thing?"

"Guarantee. Make sure of."

"It sounds pretty far-fetched to me." Freedom turned with a grin. "I'm not sure I ever met a real person yet ready to give up their life for a feeling about someone else."

"No? What was the Great War about, then? Wasn't it about a feeling, and the notion that slavery was incompatible with the laws of nature and inherently wrong?" As she spoke, part of her acknowledged that her doubts about her husband and his hate-mongering beliefs—beliefs making him for no good reason superior over Freedom and his ilk—that those doubts, once an occasional quiet whisper, had become an ever-rising tide she could no longer ignore.

Freedom thought of the countless men who had given up their lives to emancipate an entire race of men, women, and children they didn't even know in most cases. Perhaps there was something more important than self-preservation and narcissism. "I'll have to think on that."

They came up to Rio al Lago, the plantation on the Mississippi River, and swung around to the rear of the country manor. Freedom had to drive past the horse stable, the forge, and the workers' small shacks to drop Susannah off at the back of the plantation home. Boss MacLeod's other carriage was there, waiting to be put away. Four men sat idly in chairs on the veranda. This was not good news. Freedom had been certain Boss MacLeod would have stayed in the city, basking in his recent victory.

"Is Mister MacLeod here?" Susannah asked, stepping down from the carriage seat, knowing that it would be a problem if these men told Campbell she'd been riding up front with Freedom.

"Sure is, Missus MacLeod," replied the thickset man with a bowler on his head. "But you don't want to be bothering him right now."

"Why is that, Alvin?" Susannah sensed disobedience from the man, an insolence that had been growing recently amongst the associates of her husband.

"He's taking care of some business, Missus," the thin man said, spitting tobacco juice over the railing.

The notion of climbing back into the carriage and having Freedom drive them back to the house on Lake Pontchartrain fluttered through Susannah's mind, but she was too proud to slink away like one of Campbell's flunkies in front of these men. She swept up the stairs and past them, going straight to her bedroom, which was on the opposite side of the house of Campbell's, as was his study.

Freedom went about putting the horses in the barn, rubbing them down after the long ride, and getting them some grain. He counted twelve horses still stained by sweat, suggesting there were at least ten men here, as two manned the Mac-Wagon. The thin man, whom Freedom knew was named John, came into the barn with several other men, and silently watched him.

"Saw you sitting up there with Missus Susannah," John said.

"Wasn't nothing to it," Freedom replied. "She wanted to get a bit of fresh air. Said it was too stuffy in back."

"Looked like the two of you was pretty cozy. I'm betting the White Master will want a word with you, once he takes care of the Voodoo whore."

Freedom froze, but then went back to rubbing out the chafed spots from the harness. He wished they hadn't come here, but maybe he'd been meant to? "He got that good-for-nothing goddaughter of Marie Laveau in there?" he asked thickly.

"That's the one," John spit a stream of tobacco onto the Buckskin Freedom was brushing. "Then I reckon he'll want a word with you. Don't you be going anywheres."

Freedom figured if he took the Morgan and made a run for it, nobody would catch him. That bay was the fastest horse on the place, and Freedom knew how to ride. He could get to New Orleans in two hours if he hustled, and warn Mister Collins they had his wife. In his heart, he knew it would be too late. He'd heard, same as everybody else, how Manon had slapped Boss MacLeod at the Fairgrounds, and then Mister Collins had knocked the man out. No, if he went for help, Miss Manon was as good as dead—or worse, if the boss was really that wretched killer of Black girls.

Freedom took his pocketknife out and went about prying off a shoe from each of the horses in the barn. Then he put halters on the bay and the roan, the team he'd driven here, and put bridles for them in a feedbag. They were far from fresh, but to take any other horse would invite curiosity from the rabble. As he walked them from the house, one of the men asked where he thought he was going, and Freedom gestured to the grassy area a few hundred yards south of the house. Once there, he hobbled the two animals, and left the bag with the reins on the ground next to them. They would have to make their escape without saddles.

Hidden from the back of the house, Freedom skirted around the living oaks, and made his way to the front. He eased through the door and up the stairs, stepping carefully to avoid the creaky spots he well knew. He peeked into the open study door and saw Boss MacLeod sitting by himself at his desk, drinking a scotch. It was such a serene scene that Freedom began to doubt his information and fears. Slowly he worked his way to the man's bedroom and cracked the door. Against the far wall was Boss MacLeod's canopy bed, the bedposts of dark walnut rising to the cross-rails, with just a bit of white material wrapped around. At the end of the bed was Manon Lescaut, her arms in a Y shape above her head, bound to the corners of the bedposts, as were her legs at the bottom. She was gagged, but Freedom was glad to see, otherwise unharmed and still clothed.

With a quick glance down the hallway, Freedom stole into the room, his hands shaking as he took out his pocketknife. If he were caught, he would be dead. But if he didn't act, Emmett's wife would surely die—and just as likely his own death would follow soon after.

With any luck, they could make their way out front and to the two hobbled horses before anybody knew they were gone. With enough of a lead, they might just make it to New Orleans, especially with the horses in pursuit coming up lame. Manon was staring at him with wide eyes, but she held still so he could free her. The blade had trouble sawing through the thick rope, and Freedom had only managed to cut one arm free when he sensed evil behind him.

"That there is my special treat," MacLeod said.

Freedom was torn between turning and facing the man, and trying to cut Manon's other arm free. He was saved this decision by a gunshot and a tremendous blow to his back that threw him into Manon, before he slid to the floor, his legs rubbery under him. He wrapped his arms around her waist, trying to not fall all the way to the floor, but a hand grabbed his hair from behind, and he was pulled over backwards.

"This is the problem with giving *ye* people your freedom," MacLeod roared. He kicked Freedom in the side, and then the head. "Give an inch, and then *ye* want my wife. *Ye* don't know your damn place." He picked his foot up and stomped down, the spurs on his boots slashing Freedom's face. This brought him within range of Manon's free hand, and she raked his face with her nails. He bellowed in pain, turning to punch her in the face. He then went back to kicking and yelling at the inert form of Freedom on the floor.

"Campbell, what are you doing?" Susannah screamed, standing in the doorway, trying to understand the picture of her husband kicking one man to death while a Black woman stood tied to the end of his bed. "Stop it. Stop it!"

MacLeod laughed hysterically, as he walked toward her with a dangerous wildness to his eyes. "Ah, the whoring wife, come to find Freedom." He laughed maniacally at his poor joke, grabbing her by the throat and flinging her to the floor where she landed in a puddle of Freedom's blood. She tried to crawl away, but he caught her leg and smashed her face into the wood floor. And then he was tearing at her dress, taking her from behind, all the while chanting filthy language, the like she'd never heard from him.

It was over in mere seconds, and then he was lifting Susannah by the hair. "Go to your room, and stay there," he said. He turned back to Manon, a calmness coming over his features, as he looked at her still dazed eyes from the blow he'd struck her. "I believe I will burn *ye*."

CHAPTER 20

September 19th, 1874

As Emmett made his way to the St. Ann home, his pace quickened as the chill returned to his bones. A black cloud was going across the sun, and what had been a warm day suddenly felt brisk from the wind off the river.

Marie Laveau met him at the gate. There was an angry blue lump on her forehead, and her eyes flashed with an anger Emmett had never witnessed.

"They came for her right after you left."

Emmett stared at the odd-shaped knot bursting from the skin below her *tignon*. "Who?" It was not clear whether he meant came for who, or who came, but he had the sinking feeling that he knew the answer to both questions.

"There were seven men and they took Manon with them," Madame Laveau replied harshly. "They struck me and left me senseless on the floor. As they left, several guests went to intervene and they shot them."

"Who were these men?" Emmett demanded with fear contesting his anger.

"It was MacLeod's men."

"Are you sure?"

Madame Laveau nodded. "I just got back from talking to my girls. Indiana told me she spent the night with a man dropping gold pieces who was bragging about being on a mission for the White Master to teach some uppity Black girl her place. He said they'd come to town to fetch her back."

"I hear that is what they are calling MacLeod now."

He would need his rifle, field glasses, and plenty of ammunition. It took him no more than a minute to gather these things, and soon after was saddling Mum Bett at the stable just down Rampart Street.

As he left the city limits, he broke into a canter, the mare stretching her long legs out as they loped towards the plantation of Rio al Lago. At some point, he looked next to him, and realized that Mister Daniel Blanc was keeping pace with him upon a black steed that was breathing fire, whose hooves hovered just above the ground.

"There are seventeen of them," the *lwa* said in words that melted into Emmett's mind.

Emmett looked away, and then back, and the *lwa* was no longer there.

Marie Laveau closed her eyes to think, and when she opened them, the kitchen was filled with people. She looked around in wonder at the silent faces that merely awaited instructions, as if sent here by the *lwa* to assist her in her time of need. But it was more than that, she well understood, for the *lwa* aided those that helped themselves. Surrounding her were the souls she'd devoted her entire life to helping.

They were women and men from all walks of life. In her kitchen were Choctaw squaws, prostitutes, hairdressers, gamblers, homeless, deformed, crippled, and albinos. There was a deacon from the St. Louis Cathedral standing next to a prominent Voodoo conjurer, and behind them was an illiterate slave beside the wife of the plantation owner who used to own him. Orphans she had taken in and raised as her own now stood before her as doctors, teachers, and lawyers.

"My children are in danger," Marie said in the voice of *Damballah*, the Great Serpent King, the *lwa* of peace and harmony, and ruler of the intellect, the mind, and the keeper of cosmic balance. "I need the presence of Pinckney Benton Stuart Pinchback, and any members of the cavalry regiment of Emmett Collins brought here at once."

The underprivileged and privileged, as well as all in between, filtered out the door as one and went to do the bidding of the Voodoo Queen, not because of her stature, but because of her compassion.

Emmett trained the field glasses on Campbell MacLeod's plantation home. He was on a small bluff east of the collection of buildings about a half-mile away, but Manon was clearly visible tied to the whipping post in the back of the house. There appeared to be several men loitering nearby, but they were partially obscured by one of the several live oaks ringing Rio al Lago.

"If you wait two hours and come at the house from the west, you will have the sun at your back and in their eyes," Mister Daniel Blanc spoke quietly in his ear.

"I can't wait that long," Emmett replied.

"You have time."

"Did they beat her? Did they…?"

"Not yet."

Emmett couldn't quite make out the features of his wife as she stood tied to the post, but he could imagine her scared and angry eyes burning forth from a battered face. Two men walked up to her and dropped something at her feet. "What is that? What are they doing?"

Mister Daniel Blanc was now lying on his back upon the flat stone, his eyes closed with a twig in his mouth. "They are piling wood and brush around her."

"What for?" Emmett asked, stupidly.

"They plan to burn her, of course."

Emmett turned on his heel and strode to his horse.

"Not for a few more hours. You have time."

"I have time? My wife is tied to a post in her nightshirt, and men are preparing to burn her, and you say I have time?" Emmett paused long enough to face the *lwa,* and realized he was talking to his horse.

"Trust me, Emmett Collins. You must wait two hours and come from the west with the sun at your back."

A little after five, Emmett walked Mum Bett from the west. He still wore the jacket and waistcoat from earlier in the day, and a bowler pulled down tightly over his head. When he was about five hundred yards away, what little cover there was ended abruptly in short grass. He stopped here to push back his coat to reveal the double-holstered pistols at his hips. He reached down to check the tapered Bowie knife in his right boot before pulling the Winchester from the saddle scabbard. There were seventeen of them, after all.

Emmett's mind briefly sifted through the memories of Manon, beginning with the young girl who had nursed him after the Mechanic's Institute massacre, and then had been his guide into the Bayou for his first Voodoo *fête*. His reminiscences raced ahead six years to Manon returning from Boston as a grown woman, and the abrupt realization that she was the one he loved, had loved since forever. He smiled as the memories of their courtship flitted through his mind, leading minute by minute to the first time they made love by the stream. He thought of his vows to love and protect her for all time, and the idyllic life they had carved out on St. Ann Street.

With a deep breath, Emmett touched his heels into the flanks of Mum Bett, and they burst from the arroyo towards the enemy, and the love of his life. It brought back memories of the war, except he'd always been one of thousands then, and now, was alone. When he was two hundred yards out, the pounding hooves registered with the men outdoors, and they looked up directly into the sun. As they shielded their eyes, Emmett drew a bead on the man closest to Manon and pulled the trigger. The man staggered back a step and tottered before crumpling to the ground.

Emmett knew that hitting a target at this distance from a running horse was nothing but luck, and perhaps the guiding hand of Mister Daniel Blanc. Whatever the case, the math was now sixteen left. He'd already ejected the spent cartridge and levered a new one from the magazine into the chamber in the split second these thoughts flickered through his consciousness, and he snapped a shot at the next man over. It was a clean miss as men ran for cover, spilled from the house, and dropped to the ground.

As he pulled the trigger for a third time, he sensed the whiz of a bullet past his face. At Gettysburg, he'd been one of the members of the 20th Maine regiment who'd become heroes coming off Little Round Top in a sweeping wheel charge into the teeth of the Confederate Army. This action had so surprised the enemy that they were unable to surrender or run away fast enough. Emmett hoped the shock value of this improbable assault would have similar results, but he had his doubts. Nonetheless, he furiously worked the lever of the Winchester, and sprayed shots at every available target. A bullet grazed his shoulder with a stinging sensation as he dropped a man running across the yard. He risked a look at Manon and realized her mouth was open like she was yelling, but he could hear nothing.

He reached the back of the house and sprang from the saddle, letting Mum Bett run off, blood streaking her neck. He dropped the rifle and drew both pistols. He was now in the middle of a ring of men who risked hitting each other if they missed. From the side of the main house, Freedom America emerged with a rifle, diverting the attention of the men momentarily. Emmett felt the impact of a bullet in his leg, just above the knee, the blow sweeping him from his feet. From a prone position he shot a man in the face and another in the midsection.

He risked a look at Freedom, who was walking into the middle of the fracas like a preacher on his way to church, except in this instance he was mowing down men with bullets. Emmett saw Campbell MacLeod step from the house behind Freedom with a shotgun, and he rolled over to bring his Colt .45 to bear, pulling the trigger three times, but his haste caused the bullets to miss their mark. From his hip, MacLeod pulled the wide double-trigger, and the buckshot tore gaping holes in Freedom's back.

Emmett cursed inwardly, steadied his hand, and took the shot again, but the pistol clicked on an empty chamber. He had in mind revenge for Freedom, but also the hope that killing MacLeod might save Manon's life, even if Emmett was killed. With the White Master dead, would his henchmen actually burn a woman? As he brought the other .45 to bear, he felt the concussion of a bullet to his skull and everything went black.

Emmett found himself sitting at a round table in the middle of a crossroad. The roads stretched away in hard packed dirt towards the four cardinal directions as far as he could see. He surmised he was on the south side of the table, as the sun appeared to be setting to the left, a fiery red ball descending over the horizon. The darkening sky was streaked with black formless clouds making for a surreal scene, with the only light being the red glare from the almost-gone sun.

He had four playing cards in front of him, one down, and three up. Showing, he had a three, an eight, and a nine of hearts. Across from him was Mister Daniel Blanc. He also had four cards in front of him, but they were all face down. His face was impassive as he stared back at Emmett, giving nothing away as to his intentions.

Emmett shifted his eyes to the right, where an old man with a wrinkled black face sat, a wide-brimmed straw hat upon his head, and a pipe in his mouth, a thin wisp of smoke rising from the barrel. His hat was half black, while his eyes matched the other side that was red. The rooster on his shoulder, perhaps confused by the setting sun, broke the silence with a piercing cock-a-doodle. These clues led to the conclusion that this must be Papa Legba, the guardian of the crossroads, the lwa *between the human and spirit world. His cards were also face down in front of him.*

To his left, with the setting sun at his back, was the lwa *Baron Samedi, for it could be nobody but. His face was a gleaming skull with empty sockets covered by dark glasses, and cotton plugs into the holes where his nose should have been. A tall top hat was perched jauntily upon his shiny-white pate, and a black tail tuxedo snugly fit his slender form. In his lipless teeth was clutched a fat cigar, and a half-full rum bottle sat on the table in front of him. It was Baron Samedi to whom Emmett knew he must give his attention, for the* lwa *of the dead also had just one card down, and three others showing.*

"Your bet," Baron Samedi said in his nasally voice.

Emmett peeked at his hole card, which was a five of hearts. He looked at Samedi's up cards to see a jack, ten, and nine, all spades. What were they playing for? He wondered as the sun crept ever lower on the horizon.

"Pass," he said after a bit of consideration.

Baron Samedi stared at him from the amber reflective lenses. "I win, I bury you right over there," he said, pointing to a freshly dug hole in the southeast quadrant.

Emmett nodded. Now he knew the stakes. He realized the bet was supposed to be for his life, but he changed it. "I win, Manon lives."

Baron Samedi flinched slightly. He had designs on that little filly himself. No matter, then. He tossed a card up in front of Emmett. Queen of hearts. Emmett realized there wasn't the slightest rift of breeze. Without looking, the king of the dead threw a card in front of himself. Ace of spades.

"Your friend Pinchback is coming to save you. There will be an ambush, and he will join us if I win." Baron Samedi took off his glasses and stared at Emmett with his soulless sockets.

And suddenly, Emmett knew he was bluffing. A distant voice in his head that sounded faintly of Marie Laveau told him the man had a diamond as his down card. He nodded. He also understood that if he gambled his own life, the trickster of the dead would pull a fast one upon him.

"Campbell MacLeod."

"What about this MacLeod?" Baron Samedi asked in surprise.

"I win, you take him, and you leave Manon unharmed."

Baron Samedi chuckled and took up his copper mug of rum and swilled it down, tiny rivulets streaming back out from the corners of his mouth. He tipped over his down card, showing a king of diamonds. Emmett flipped his own down card, filling out his flush, and victorious, looked up to realize he was sitting alone.

Had he been left at this crossroads to die? He was not ready for that. Had Samedi accepted his last bet or folded? Emmett rose to his feet and walked around the table and began to walk north. There was just a sliver of sun showing to the west to give a glint of color to his way. Then he heard Manon calling his name from somewhere ahead, and he broke into a run as the world darkened around him once again.

Emmett stirred as the boot toe dug into his side. He opened an eye, but couldn't see anything. There was something crusty upon his face. Again, he heard Manon yelling his name. He realized that he must have arms and hands, and from a long way away, he twitched his fingers. With a supreme effort, he dragged his right arm up across his body, and wiped at his face. He could smell the rank, coppery stink of his own blood, and a lot of it.

"Come on Collins, wake up, we can't wait for *ye* forever, and I do so want *ye* to see this," came MacLeod's braying voice. With the blood cleared from his vision, Emmett looked up to see the looming figure above him holding a shotgun aimed at his head, while a boot dug into his ribs.

"Emmett, I love you." The voice of Manon swept the last cobwebs from his brain. He tilted his head in the direction of his wife. She was still tied to the whipping post, and several men were piling more wood and brush around her.

"Ah, there *ye* are, Collins. I wouldn't want *ye* to miss the burning of the black Delilah," MacLeod said nastily. He touched his thinning red hair. "The harlot thinks she can tempt me with her vulgar sex and then sell me out to the Philistines? I will burn her to ash and tear this country to pieces before I will allow that," he was now shouting, spittle dotting the red splotches on his face.

"Let her go," Emmett croaked. "That was the bet."

"What bet are *ye* talking, you fucking loon?" MacLeod crashed the butt of his shotgun down into Emmett's ribs. "I am talking about saving the human race from extinction through sexual temptation of black whores and *ye* are mumbling about some bet?"

Emmett looked around the area, noting with satisfaction a number of MacLeod's posse in a pile, waiting to be loaded onto a wagon and taken to be buried. He grimaced as he saw the mangled body of Freedom America lying where he'd fallen. But was he yet alive? It seemed that his body had stirred, a motion so subtle Emmett couldn't be sure he'd actually witnessed it.

A boot cracked into his ribs. "I asked *ye*, what bet are *ye* talking about?" MacLeod's voice was beginning to crack, his tone turned to a shriek, his emotions and anger so high that the words came whistling out of his mouth like a boiling teapot.

Emmett counted seven men who appeared healthy, while another two were breathing, but slumped upon the back veranda. He risked a glance at Manon, tied to the post, and saw Lucy, the cook, behind her, working frantically at the ropes that bound her.

"Aw, the hell with *ye*. It's time for a good old-fashioned witch fry. Light the fire," MacLeod cackled, his excitement causing him to sway back and forth, almost like he was doing a jig.

The unmistakable square head of Frederick Ogden turned towards MacLeod. "It's not right burning a person alive."

"She's not human," MacLeod replied harshly. "We will cook her like a fucking cow and eat her when we're done."

Ogden stared impassively at MacLeod. He'd heard the rumors, same as everybody else, that the man was the Black DOT killer, but had chosen to avoid thinking on whether it was true or not. If it was, it impinged on Ogden's own designs on redeeming the south. But now, here he was, being ordered to burn a woman alive, and something about that just did not sit right with him.

"Set the fire." MacLeod was now aiming the shotgun at Ogden. "She is a fucking harlot and temptress trying to steal the power of white men. We must erase her from existence before it is too late."

Ogden looked over at the darkie goddaughter of the Voodoo Queen as he wondered if MacLeod had reloaded the gun or not. The girl was human, even if an inferior being, she was flesh and blood, and he believed she even had a soul. But MacLeod held the shotgun level, even if it shook slightly, and Ogden, finally cowed, turned back, and motioned a man to light the rag tied to the end of a stick doused in whale oil.

MacLeod laughed a horrible, high-pitched shriek of pure joy. "Prepare to burn, Delilah, you whore!" With his free hand he began rubbing the front of his pants with a mad twist of sexual ecstasy.

And then Emmett saw her. While all eyes were on the drama unfolding around Manon, Susannah Shaw de Villiers was walking up behind MacLeod. She carried a long, gleaming blade crosswise to her body. Emmett risked a look back at the man lighting the torch to see that he now had it blazing away, and had only a step to take and set the dry brush ablaze around Manon.

As Susannah swiveled and brought the blade over her head in a sweeping motion, she screamed in a warrior's fury that would have put even the most full-throated Rebel to shame, and then brought the ancestral sword of Campbell MacLeod in a downward arc powered by weight and gravity and pent-up savagery released. He turned to look at her, his eyes widening in disbelief and then terror as the steel cleaved into his neck at an angle between collarbone and chin, coming to rest only after his head was mostly severed. Blood spewed out of his mouth, the splatter from the neck showering Emmett in red, and then his head toppled to the side, hanging by a flap of skin, and the Great White Master fell to his knees, and then forward onto his face, dead in the dirt.

For what seemed forever but was surely only a handful of moments, all of nature froze in place at this unexpected turn of events. Frederick Ogden broke the silence as he backed away from Susannah, slow, nervous steps betraying animal fear. Emmett began to crawl towards Manon, but a man kicked him in the side and knocked him to his back. As he struggled to get back to his knees, his eyes were drawn to the field hands' quarters, the former slave homes—and from these scattered buildings men and women carrying various weapons were emerging as phantom-like apparitions.

"Boss?" one of Ogden's henchmen asked nervously.

"What is it?"

"Look."

Susannah stood motionless, hands at her sides, eyes vacant. Ogden turned from her, his eyes hesitating as he mentally counted the numbers. There were approximately thirty Black men and women, standing in a semi-circle around them, brandishing a motley collection of machetes, sickles, cane knives, and pitchforks. "Shoot them. Kill them all. We will blame the massacre on Mexican bandits."

"We got Injuns," a man said nervously, pointing in the direction Emmett had come from. About a dozen Choctaws, painted for war, sat astride horses. Several had rifles, and the rest had bows drawn back and notched with arrows. Emmett again began to crawl towards Manon, but was again kicked in the side.

A gunshot rang out, and the man who had kicked Emmett fell to his knees, and then toppled face-first into the dirt. All eyes swung to Manon, who stood with a smoking pistol in her hand. Apparently, Lucy had been successful freeing her, as well as arming her. The weapon, held in two hands, was now pointed at Ogden.

"I wouldn't have burned you," Ogden said.

The pistol was rock-steady in Manon's hand. "You get out of here now."

Ogden's gaze swept around the Black field hands and the Choctaws. "This is not your fight," he called in a raspy voice.

The Blacks and Indians merely stared back.

"Go on, now. Get."

A man, shimmering in the dense air, came around the corner of the house. His kinked hair sprouted wild upon his head, and he wore the old cotton shirt of a slave. Slung crosswise on his hips was a pair of six-shooters.

Ogden glared at Manon, and then over at the workers' quarters, and then the live oak from behind which the Choctaws had emerged, his face beet-red from anger and frustration. And then they all heard it, the pounding of horses' hooves on hard ground, coming from the direction of the New Orleans road.

"Oh, the hell with it. Let's go." Ogden moved towards the barn where their horses were tethered. "Bring Bruce and Scott," he said, waving his arm at the two injured men on the veranda.

Manon took the few steps to where Emmett lay huddled on the ground and dropped down, pulling his head into her lap as the clatter of horses leaving mixed with the approach of others. The Black field workers and Choctaws had disappeared as if they'd never existed, and Manon wondered if she'd seen what she'd seen.

Pinchback led a posse of about forty men thundering into the yard. Twelve of the shattered remnants of Emmett's cavalry unit had shown up at the Laveau house, but an additional twenty-five assorted citizens, having heard that Emmett was in trouble, accompanied them as well.

"You look terrible," Pinchback said, looking down at the huddled form of Emmett, curled into the lap of Manon. He motioned for the doctor to set down his rifle and pick up his black medicine bag.

"Thanks, Pinch," Emmett replied, whether sarcastically at the comment, or genuinely for showing up in the nick of time, it was hard to say.

Pinchback looked up, his eyes finding Susannah de Villiers standing in her green dress streaked and marred by dark stains. In front of her, with his head askew, lay Campbell MacLeod in an ever-widening pool of blood. As if awakening from a deep sleep, she shook her head, and stumbled forward to a man lying face down. She rolled the man over to reveal Freedom's battered face. Susannah sat down cross-legged and cradled his head in her lap, stroking his short-thick hair with her fingers. Freedom was no longer with the living.

Pinchback eyed the pile of dead men, and judged there must be about ten of them. He stood for a minute, contemplating the strategy. It wasn't much different than politics in New Orleans, this picking up the pieces and striving for the best outcome, all the while making compromises. A scapegoat was needed. Somebody to take the blame was a prerequisite for any solution to a mess.

"Can everybody hear me?" Pinchback looked around to the posse and those they had saved. "Good. Here is what transpired here, today. Mexican bandits attacked Rio al Lago. A terrific battle was fought, and MacLeod and the others were killed, but luckily, this cavalry regiment out on patrol, came along and drove the outlaws off. We buried MacLeod and his men over there." He pointed to a clearing off to the side. "Everybody got it?"

He approached the lady of the house. "Mrs. de Villiers? I'm going to have some men take you to your home in New Orleans. They'll help you with anything you need."

Susannah looked up as the shadows began to lengthen. She brushed a lock of curls from her face with a bloody hand, but didn't seem to notice. "I want him brought there as well."

Pinchback gave his best smile. "We'll have Mr. MacLeod brought there as well."

She snorted and laughed the bitterest of laughs. "Not that twisted bastard. Bury him with the others, or better yet, drag him off into the brush and let the animals at him." She looked down at the dead man in her lap. "Please arrange for Freedom to come with me."

"Of course," Pinchback replied. "I'll send someone to make arrangements for his burial as well once we're back in the city."

"Thank you."

He then went over to Emmett and Manon. "Who rode off when we arrived?"

The doctor had managed to swathe Emmett's head in a bandage to cover the glancing wound of a bullet, and was busy attending to his leg.

"It was Ogden and some of his cronies," Manon said with hatred.

"Good." Pinchback rubbed his hands together. "He will not want his name associated with whatever was going on here. He will never refute the story I have concocted, but he will seek revenge."

"We are leaving for France as soon as we are able," Manon said.

Pinchback nodded. "Yes. Emmett told me. I'm going to have you brought to Warmoth's plantation until you're healthy enough to leave. That's the only place you'll be safe, now that the White League is in control of Louisiana."

"Texas," Emmett grunted through gritted teeth.

"What's that?" Manon leaned her ear closer to her husband.

"We'll be going to Texas," Emmett said, and then gasped as the doctor pulled the bullet free. "Now that MacLeod is dead."

Pinchback gave the orders, and soon men were digging graves, harnessing teams, and preparing to continue on. He walked to the other side of the live oak, and lit a cigar. In the darkness, illuminated by a streak of moonlight, he thought he saw a man with wild hair, watching, two guns crisscrossed across his waist, also smoking a cigar. He felt no threat, and raised his hand in greeting or parting, he was not sure which, only that some recognition was required.

Pinchback thought about redemption. MacLeod and Ogden called themselves redeemers—men trying to return life to the way it had been before the war. In that, they had been partially successful. The Great War, or War of Northern Aggression, as the Southerners liked to call it, had ended the system of slavery. What would be barely noted in the annals of history was this second war fought for equality, a war that had, for the time being anyway, been lost. Ogden would continue on, claiming victory, claiming redemption of the old ways.

In many ways, Freedom America had also redeemed himself, for he'd finally fought back. Born in slavery, he had escaped, and eventually been freed by the Great War, but had always played the subservient role to the white master. Although he'd died today, here at Rio al Lago, he'd finally taken a stand for what he knew to be right, and in this way, had achieved his own kind of freedom, redeemed if only in a valiant death.

It was no secret that Susannah de Villiers had married Campbell MacLeod for security, not realizing at the time that she was, in turn, bartering away her happiness. It had required cleaving her husband in two, but she too, had gained redemption. She'd misplaced her soul for a brief period of time, but in the end, she had regained it—and with it, her respect.

And of course, Emmett and Manon were the real redeemers, overcoming hatred with love. They had proven that character trumped money, and that belief in good, and love for each other would be the ultimate victor. They might be forced to leave New Orleans, but they were together, having forged bonds wrought deep in anguish and suffering—and love, and would always have each other, and the dignity of standing for what was right.

As Pinchback silently smoked his cigar, he realized that redemption had been realized by both vanquisher and vanquished on this September day. This one skirmish was much like the Battle of New Orleans in 1815, when Colonel Jackson defeated the British almost four weeks after the war had ended. One could argue the battle was pointless, while others would cling to it as a shining shred of hope in an otherwise dismal time. The notion of white superiority had not been extinguished, but on this day, it had certainly been challenged.

He would go home and raise a toast to Emmett, Manon, Susannah, and especially to Freedom. And then, tomorrow, he would rise and go back to work, because equality was a never-ending battle.

ABOUT THE AUTHOR

Over the years, **Matthew Langdon** (aka Matt) **Cost** has owned a video store, a mystery bookstore, and a gym. He has also taught history and coached just about every sport imaginable.

This is the third historical novel by Cost. *Joshua Chamberlain and the Civil War: At Every Hazard* was published in 2015, in which Emmett Collins grows into manhood during the Civil War. Emmett returns in this work, *Love in a Time of Hate*. *I am Cuba: Fidel Castro and the Cuban Revolution* was published by Encircle Publications in 2020.

Encircle Publications has also published Cost's Mainely Mystery series including *Mainely Power*, *Mainely Fear*, and *Mainely Money*, as well as the Clay Wolfe / Port Essex Mysteries, beginning with *Wolfe Trap*. *Mind Trap* will be published in December of 2021, and *Mouse Trap* in the spring of 2022.

Cost lives in Brunswick, Maine, with his wife, Harper. There are four grown children: Brittany, Pearson, Miranda, and Ryan. A chocolate Lab and a basset hound round out the mix. He now spends his days at the computer, writing.

If you enjoyed reading this book,
please consider writing your honest review
and sharing it with other readers.

Many of our Authors are happy to participate in
Book Club and Reader Group discussions.
For more information, contact us at info@encirclepub.com.

Thank you,
Encircle Publications

For news about more exciting new fiction, join us at:
Facebook: www.facebook.com/encirclepub

Twitter: twitter.com/encirclepub

Instagram: www.instagram.com/encirclepublications

Sign up for Encircle Publications newsletter and specials:
eepurl.com/cs8taP